MORE
THAN
THIS

MORE
THAN
THIS

SHANNYN
SCHROEDER

Kensington
KENSINGTON PUBLISHING CORP.
www.kensingtonbooks.com

KENSINGTON BOOKS are published by

Kensington Publishing Corp.
119 West 40th Street
New York, NY 10018

All Kensington titles, imprints, and distributed lines are available at special quantity discounts for bulk purchases for sales promotion, premiums, fund-raising, educational, or institutional use.

Special book excerpts or customized printings can also be created to fit specific needs. For details, write or phone the office of the Kensington Special Sales Manager: Kensington Publishing Corp., 119 West 40th Street, New York, NY 10018. Attn. Special Sales Department. Phone: 1-800-221-2647.

Kensington and the K logo Reg. U.S. Pat. & TM Off.

First Electronic Edition: January 2013
eISBN-13: 978-1-60183-007-4
eISBN-10: 1-60183-007-6

First Print Edition: January 2013
ISBN-13: 978-1-60183-147-7
ISBN-10: 1-60183-147-1

Printed in the United States of America

To Shorty—
Dream big

Acknowledgments

I've believed in this book for a long time, but I've had a lot of help getting it here. First, all of my friends at Chicago-North RWA helped me become a better writer. They are brilliant women, and I've learned so much from them. Next, I need to thank my critique partner, Paly Kari, who always tells me when a character is doing something stupid and who will help me plot because I hate it. My agent, Fran Black, loved my story enough to take me on as a client and helped me improve it before going out on submission. And finally, to my editor, Peter Senftleben, a huge thank you for helping me make this the best story possible. Your notes and suggestions were dead-on, and not once did you make me cringe over revisions.

CHAPTER 1

Only girls' night out could save this craptastic day, a heck of a way to spend her thirty-first birthday. Quinn pushed through the door to O'Leary's Pub and allowed the surrounding dark wood to soothe her. She needed to banish the images of the glazed expressions of her colleagues at the end of the workshop she'd presented. A night with the girls would lighten her mood. But Quinn was early and the others hadn't yet arrived.

Customers' chatter washed over her, relaxing her, as she moved through the crowd. The noise offered welcomed anonymity.

She'd spent months preparing for the presentation, but being exhausted from her ex-husband's late-night visit hadn't helped her enthusiasm. Nick was still messing up her life. Two minutes into the workshop, she realized she would've been better off spending the time in the classroom with her hormonal students.

Her gaze scanned the room to find a source of comfort: Ryan O'Leary. Behind the bar, his lithe body slid past the other bartender. Perpetually mussed black hair swung across his forehead, barely concealing the dark slashes of eyebrows. Ryan reached out to grab an empty mug. He joked with patrons while he pulled the beer. His sleeves were pushed up, revealing toned, muscular forearms, the kind any woman would want circling her body.

Ryan was a living stereotype: the overly friendly bartender who joked too much and listened to any tale of woe a person told.

The thing was, she liked him anyway.

Using the brass rail below the bar, she boosted herself onto a stool.

The other bartender, who looked enough like Ryan that they had to be brothers, headed in her direction. Quinn saw Ryan tap his shoulder and overheard him say, "I got this."

A moment later, Ryan appeared in front of her. His intense blue eyes crinkled with his smile, putting her at ease.

It was also the same grin he threw at every female in a fifty-foot radius. But she enjoyed it, even if it wasn't just for her.

He placed a napkin in front of her and asked, "How's my favorite English teacher today?"

Something about the way he asked made her answer honestly. Even in the middle of serving drinks, her response seemed to matter. She sighed. "I've been better. How are you?"

"Busy, which is good. Teenagers giving you a hard time?"

"No, it's always the adults who are the problem. Give me a roomful of teens over adults any day." She understood how to talk to the kids, and it didn't matter if they liked her as a person.

"What can I get you to make your day better?"

"Frozen strawberry margarita." Misery over her failed lecture swamped her. She began to think not even Ryan's warm smile would break her funk. She'd been counting on the success of the presentation to give her a boost with Principal Carlson to get the Honors English position next year. Dwelling over Nick's news made her day worse. Of all people to be blessed with a baby! He didn't even want to be a parent.

Someday she'd celebrate pregnancy. Unlike Nick.

Someday.

Someday had become her mantra for years. Someday had already taken too long. She had no baby, no husband, and she hadn't fought for a job she really wanted. *God, I'm such a wimp.* She wasn't going to wait for someday anymore. Thoughts of babies took over her brain.

Ryan returned with her drink. Over his shoulder she caught sight of a cow with an O'LEARY'S PUB sign hanging from its neck and a photo of a burning building stood behind it, an image from the Great Chicago Fire. She'd never noticed it before.

"What?"

The question startled her. She hadn't realized Ryan was still there, watching her. "Nothing. I love the cow. Are you related to the infamous Mrs. O'Leary?"

He chuckled. "No, both my parents are off-the-boat Irish. My dad thought it was funny to let people think that."

Quinn looked over her shoulder toward the door.

"Waiting for someone, or did you just come in to see me?" Ryan teased.

She turned back to him. Her toes curled painfully in her too-tight navy pumps. How this man managed to put her at ease one minute and make her feel nervous the next baffled her. "I'm meeting my sister and our friend."

"It's good to see you here on a day other than a Friday. I was beginning to think you only came in because the other teachers made you."

It wasn't far from the truth. A friend from school had convinced her to at least put in the effort to socialize with colleagues. It wasn't that she didn't like the other teachers or didn't want to be friendly; she didn't know what to do with herself in social situations. Her sister, Indy, had inherited Quinn's share of the social butterfly genes.

Strangely, over the past eight months, O'Leary's had become a comfortable place for her. She appreciated the friendly atmosphere. Ryan's flirting made it enjoyable. "I like it here. Your bar makes people want to hang out. And guys don't crawl all over women trying to get their attention."

He leaned closer and she caught a whiff of his cologne, woodsy with a hint of spice—or maybe it was just him—and she almost moved in to sniff. She had expected him to smell like alcohol, but he didn't. He'd never been so near before, and the scent distracted her. She recovered in time to hear him add, "If you ditched the stuffy suit, more of these guys would hit on you."

Heat crawled up her neck. "What's wrong with my suit?"

The navy pleated skirt and matching blazer was her best business suit. Granted, she only wore it for presentations or parent–teacher conferences, but it was the most professional-looking one she had.

"It's not sexy."

She shook her head. *First, the man sucks me in with a gorgeous smile and great smell; then he insults me.* "I'm not looking to get picked up."

"Sure you are. Everyone is."

She sipped her drink to cool her throat. Self-consciousness made her straighten her pleats. His gaze bore into her, but she couldn't meet his eyes. "Thanks, but no thanks. My ex worked in a bar, and I swore I'd never make that mistake again."

"One ex-boyfriend screws up, so every man in a bar has to pay?" He looked at her skeptically, as if her point was ridiculous.

She'd learned plenty from her three years of marriage to Nick. As a bartender, he'd spent his nights surrounded by flirtatious women. Nick would tell her, "Hard to ignore women throwing themselves at you." Like most men, he didn't know how to stop at flirting.

"Ex-husband," she shot back, realizing her tone implied his critical look earlier had been dead-on. "Most guys who are looking for a woman in a bar are not serious about anything. There might be a few who are nice guys, but I'm willing to risk missing out on those to save myself the grief of dealing with all the rest."

He stepped back and leaned against the register. "Don't you ever wonder if you're missing out on Mr. Right by shutting down a proven method for meeting people?"

"Who says I'm looking for Mr. Right?"

He tilted his head and raised his eyebrows in disbelief. Okay, he had her there. She was always hoping for Mr. Right. Unfortunately, he didn't seem to be looking for her.

"I don't think a guy picking up women in a bar is looking for a woman like me."

His grin was slow and slick and spread smoothly across his face. "Think you're that special?"

Despite the embarrassment gnawing at her—she was not a braggart—she flashed him a grin of her own. She briefly tried to remember her reasons for not spending more time talking with him. "I know I am."

"You know, I like you. Can I buy you dinner?"

She felt a blush heat her cheeks, and she fought ducking her head to hide it. "I told you I'm meeting friends."

He looked at the ceiling and tightened his lips before speaking again. "I didn't mean now. I meant some other time, at some other place."

"I don't think so," she said quickly; then she saw Kate winding through the crowd. "My friend's here. I'll see you later."

She eased off the stool and signaled to Kate. She couldn't believe Ryan had actually asked her out. He flirted with just about every woman he saw. She wondered how many he asked out on an average night.

She and Kate gravitated to a semicircular, high-backed booth. Kate looked as tired as Quinn felt. Did Kate ever sleep? Having three small kids had taken its toll on Kate's once-elegant appearance. But even in old jeans and a sweatshirt, Kate exuded a confidence Quinn didn't possess.

"Thanks for driving in. I appreciate it. I wasn't sure what time I'd get out of my meeting and I really needed a girls' night tonight."

"Of course I'd drive in," Kate said while pulling her into a quick hug. "Happy birthday. I don't think I've ever been here before. It's a nice change. Part of me misses coming this far into the city."

"I like it."

"Hi, guys," Indy said as she reached the booth. "I haven't been here in forever."

"You're on time. That's a first." Quinn slid toward the center, placing herself between her sister and Kate.

"Happy birthday, cranky-pants." As Indy sat, the waitress arrived to take their drink order. "I was in the area showing a house. You couldn't have picked a better spot."

As they placed their order, Quinn scanned Indy's appearance. Everything chic, from suit to hair and makeup. After her assessment, she asked Indy, "Know what I was just thinking about?"

Indy shook her head and waited.

"My Someday List."

Indy's nose crinkled and her coral-colored lips spread into a wide smile. "Really? You still have it?"

"No, but I was thinking about what a failure it was."

Kate interrupted, "What's a Someday List?"

Quinn answered, "It's a list Indy and I started as kids of the things

we wanted to do someday, when we were older and could do whatever we wanted."

"Like what?"

"I don't remember everything. Most of it was typical stuff. Go to
Europe, fall in love, get married, buy a house, have kids." The last
thought sank in her stomach.

Indy laughed. "I remember thinking your list was boring. I had
things like skydiving, snorkeling, and having sex in public on my
list."

"You've accomplished all that and then some, haven't you?"
Quinn said, both admiring and envying Indy's adventurous attitude.

"You know it." Indy took a long sip of her drink. "What made you
think of the Someday List?"

Quinn sighed. "Nick came by last night."

"Looking for a birthday bang, huh? Was he worth it?"

Kate quickly touched her hand. "Please say you're not thinking of
getting back together with him."

"God, no."

"Uh-oh. Vulture at eleven o'clock."

Kate's warning had Quinn and Indy looking up, but the height of
the booth blocked the view.

"At least he's cute. Rock, paper, scissors?"

Quinn groaned. She always lost this childhood game. "Can't we
flip a coin?"

Indy responded with, "One, two, three, shoot."

True to form, Quinn lost. Damn. She hated to be the one to turn a
guy down. Her toes tapped inside her pumps as anxiety itched at her.
She stared at her hands and practiced her response silently.

"Hi, ladies. Enjoying your evening?"

Without looking up, Quinn began, "Sorry. We're not . . ."

Her eyes wandered up the length of faded jeans and a well-worn
rugby shirt, and found his gaze already locked on her. Relief swallowed the anxiety as she smiled up at Ryan. "Oh, hi, it's you."

"Hi." The killer grin bore into her.

Her hands twisted in her lap while she tried to figure out if he'd
overheard their conversation.

"Colin?" Indy asked as she studied his face.

Ryan's shoulders stiffened. "No, Ryan."

"Oh my God. It is you." She placed a flat palm on her chest. "Indy. I worked here about eight years ago."

His brow crinkled as he focused on Indy's face. "Yeah, I remember now. You used to sing while you worked."

"It's been too long. How's your dad? I'd love to see him." Indy's voice rose in excitement.

Just when I thought my day couldn't get worse. Indy bounced from the booth and wrapped her arms around Ryan in a quick hug, peppering him with questions Quinn could no longer hear. Her heart pounded in her ears. Her stomach plummeted.

Not Ryan. He was hers.

Well, not hers, hers, but this was her place. This was where she came to drink. Her friendship with Ryan, however slight, was hers, not something Indy had handed her. Quinn's chest tightened and her nails dug into her palms. In one swoop, Indy would take him from her. She could never compete with her sister. His flirtations, however ridiculous, would stop.

And she would miss them.

"Did you have a problem?" he asked, leaning his arm on the back of the booth.

Quinn's attention snapped back. She schooled her face to hide her embarrassing childish emotions. "No, we're fine, thanks."

"Sure? When I asked about your evening, you started to say you're not . . ."

Heat crawled back up Quinn's neck. "I was going to say we're not looking . . . for a man. I thought you were some guy hitting on us."

"All of you beautiful ladies can't possibly be taken."

Indy ran her finger around the rim of her glass. "Well, Kate's married and I'm involved, but Quinn's—"

"Not looking." She poked her toe at Indy's shin.

Ryan's denim-blue eyes focused on hers as if she sat alone at the table. She prayed he wouldn't ask her out again in front of Kate and Indy. That would be mortifying.

"If you need anything, please let me know. Enjoy yourselves." He nodded to them and left.

Quinn watched him move to the next table before turning to Kate. "You could've warned me."

"Who is he? He didn't stop at other tables. He made a beeline for us. I'd say he aimed for you after he caught your reflection in the mirror." Kate pointed at the mirror hanging on the wall across from them.

"I think you're right, Kate. Looks like Quinn's got an admirer." Indy inched closer, waiting for some juicy gossip. "What's the deal?"

"There is no deal. I come in here on Fridays after work. Ryan and I occasionally talk."

Kate reached out and put her hand on Quinn's arm, warm and firm, the diamonds of her wedding band glittering. "Honey, that man is not looking to talk. Mark has only one thing on his mind when he gives me that look."

"If he's interested, why not give him a chance?" Indy asked, leaning out from the booth to check out Ryan's ass. "He hasn't changed much since I worked here. His dad ran the place with Ryan's brother Colin. They're both yummy."

Quinn should've known. How could she possibly keep track of all the places Indy had worked? If she crossed all of them off her list of places to go, there would be few left. Indy'd had more jobs than most. She always bounced around looking for something better, more exciting.

Indy nudged Quinn. "Why not go out with Ryan? He's obviously into you."

"He's pushy and overly friendly and he's too cute." *He gets under my skin, and you had him first.*

Indy snickered. "Oh, yeah, that's a reason to not like a guy. Charm. A total deal breaker."

Quinn couldn't control the eye roll. "I don't think he's interested in me in particular. He's *too* smooth. It's like he can have any woman he wants and he knows it."

"So can Brad Pitt. Doesn't make him any less attractive." Indy took a long drink.

"He's a player. I've already gone that route. He's no better than Nick." Comparing Ryan with her ex-husband hit a bull's-eye. Nick had sucked her in easily with his charm, and he had been a mistake. Voicing it out loud made her feelings more real, a more acceptable reason for avoiding Ryan's advances. Why was she scrambling to find a valid reason?

"You have to admit Nick was fun. I bet Ryan would be too." Indy wagged her eyebrows as if Quinn didn't understand.

Quinn huffed.

Kate interrupted. "Anyway, back to Nick. Why did he come to your house?"

"He pretended to want to wish me a happy birthday. Brought me roses, which he should know I hate. He really came by to tell me he got someone pregnant and he didn't know what to do."

Indy said, "Figures. It was only a matter of time. Anyone we know?"

"I didn't ask." She twirled her glass in front of her. The strawberry slush was nearly melted. "That's what got me thinking. I've been sitting around waiting for life to happen. It's time for a change. I want a baby."

Indy shook her head. "I'm not following. You want a baby because Nick's having one?"

"No. I want a baby because I've always wanted a baby. I'm just tired of waiting for it. Nick's visit was a wake-up call for me. He's moved on with life, and I'm running on a treadmill. I need to do something different."

"How the hell do you get from 'I need to do something different' to 'I want a baby'?"

Indy looked angry and Quinn couldn't figure out why. "I've always wanted a baby. I'm ready to have one. I'm not going to wait anymore."

"So you just decided to get pregnant?"

Quinn rolled her eyes. "Have you ever known me to just decide to do anything? I've been researching options. I want this."

Kate had been suspiciously quiet. Quinn had been counting on her support.

"It's really hard, Quinn. I'm married and it's hard. I couldn't imagine doing it all alone. You're picturing the fun times. There's a lot more to it. Babies don't fit into a tidy, organized path."

Shit. This wasn't going the way she'd thought. "I know that. I'm not stupid. I can handle the unexpected."

Indy choked and almost spewed her drink across the table. After dabbing a napkin against her mouth, she said, "Who are you kidding?

You are the queen of orderly plans. You don't do anything outside your comfort zone."

"I'm going to work on that." Quinn waited and slowly said, "Yeah, summer is coming and I'll have more free time than I'll know what to do with. I'm going to use that to figure things out."

"You're not teaching?" Indy asked.

"Remember, I told you I refused to teach summer school because Carlson passed me over for the Honors teaching position. He wouldn't even take my application." She'd been questioning her rash decision ever since. Maybe it was petty and juvenile, but it had felt good to not be a team player for a minute.

Indy shook her head. Her long blond hair slipped over her shoulder and down the front of her jacket. "I know what you said, but I didn't think you'd actually follow through. If you have the summer off, I think you need to expand your horizons."

"Okay . . ." A familiar knot settled in her stomach. Indy with a plan always made her nervous.

"You need to move outside your comfort zone."

Kate's eyes lit. "That's a great idea."

She pulled a notebook out of her purse. "Okay. Let's start. This will be fun. Let's make a list. What's first?"

Quinn stared into her drink.

"I say we start with my list," Indy said.

Kate looked at Indy with wide eyes, like a mother telling a child she didn't need a cookie. "You don't need a list."

"I mean Quinn should do the items on my list. Those'll break you out of your rut."

Quinn's face warmed at the thought. She couldn't do Indy's list. Especially sex in public. Right now she didn't even have anyone to have sex with in private.

They sat in silence for a few moments. Quinn added, "It would be fun to take a cake decorating class. It's something I've wanted to try."

"Oh, yeah, more classes. Really thinking outside the box. Haven't you done enough school?" Indy's sarcasm hung around Quinn and threatened to ruin the mood.

Kate wrote down the suggestion. Her sleek, dark ponytail bobbed as she took notes. "Leave her alone, Indy. It's her list. I'd kill to be able to have time to do anything fun and unusual. What else? How many things are we looking for?"

"I don't know. How many do you think I can get done in a summer?" Quinn looked at the other two women, hoping for inspiration and getting none. "Maybe we can think about it and make the list next week."

Indy's eyes lit. "Good idea. I'll put a call out to women I know and get some ideas." She immediately pulled out her phone and began texting.

"Thanks, I think. So we'll make my entire list next week. Let's meet at my house," Quinn offered.

"In the meantime," Kate interjected, "what are you going to do?"

Indy's eyes narrowed. "You need to date."

"Sure, go straight for the easy stuff." Quinn's sarcasm was lost on Indy. Her stomach flipped. Dating had not been very fruitful over the last five years.

"How's this . . . I'll take public sex off the list if you promise to go on at least five dates over the next two weeks."

Quinn's jaw dropped. Of course Indy would name the one thing that would freak her out. Where would she find five men to go out with her? "How am I supposed to do that?"

"Not my problem." Indy winked. "Try the Internet."

Kate smiled and joked, "Issuing a challenge like that is kind of low."

Quinn stared at her sister. Finding five dates would never be difficult for Indy, but for her it was a challenge of huge proportions.

"Look, you said you're in a rut. This'll pull you out. Consider me your tow truck." Indy usually got her own way, and without her Quinn would've missed out on a lot of fun. Indy was right. She needed to get back into dating.

"Fine. You win."

Ryan stood at the opposite end of the bar from Quinn's booth. Watching in the mirror, he saw a new side of Quinn. She was relaxed. When she'd first come into the bar with a crowd of teachers, she'd hung back from the group, ordered one drink, gulped it down, and left. It was like she had to make an appearance and she did the bare minimum. Now, she'd invited other friends here.

He couldn't believe he'd almost been busted eavesdropping on her conversation. And, of course, it had to happen right when they got to a good part. He wanted to know if she got laid for her birthday. Judging by the way she looked when she came in, she hadn't been given a birthday orgasm. He almost wanted to offer to change that, but knew she'd shoot him down.

A slight tap on his arm had him turning to look at his younger brother, who was supposed to be stocking alcohol.

"Who's the gorgeous blonde?"

"Who?"

Michael hitched his chin up toward the mirror. "The one you've been staring at."

"Oh. That's Indy, but I was looking at her sister. Short dark hair."

Michael looked at all three women. "She's not your usual type."

"I know." The concept rubbed at him like a wool sweater.

"Hey, man." Michael bumped his arm. "I wanted to thank you for the hours here. I really need the extra cash."

Squeezing in an extra bartender minimized someone else's hours, but he found a spot for Michael. "Are you going to tell me what you need the money for?"

"No."

Ryan studied his brother. "Are you in some kind of trouble?"

"Not at all. Don't worry."

Easier said than done.

Ryan turned back and looked at the mirror. In the reflection he saw Quinn open her mouth with laughter. He wished he were close enough to hear the sound. She tucked her short sway of dark hair behind her ears, revealing her soft features. Her golden brown eyes found his in the mirror and he smiled.

Just then, perfume wafted up to his nose and Moira wrapped her arms around him, planting a kiss on his cheek.

"What's that for?" he asked.

"That's to say thank you for fixing my broken window. My landlord's an ass."

"No problem. It's what brothers are for."

Over the top of Moira's head, he glanced back at Quinn. The corners of her lips turned down. He enjoyed a challenge every now and then. Quinn definitely presented a challenge.

CHAPTER 2

Quinn stood outside her loft, wishing that she'd been smart enough
to meet this guy at the restaurant, if that's what you could call it. It
had barely been a step up from fast food. Now he stood in front of
her, still talking about himself, when all she wanted to do was curl up
on the couch with a good book. This is what she got for picking a guy
based on his online profile. Next time she'd make sure she had at
least a phone conversation before making a date.

Jeff suddenly stopped his rambling and asked, "So, I think we really
hit it off tonight, right?"

She stared blankly at him. Lying had never come easy to her. "I
had a pretty good time."

He stroked her arm, and she locked her knees to stop herself from
pulling away. He wasn't a bad guy. He didn't give her the creeps. Jeff
was even kind of good-looking: tall with dark hair and brown eyes, a
little on the skinny side. But something turned her completely off.

When his hand stopped stroking her arm and his fingers interlocked with hers, the sweatiness of his palm was apparent. Eww.
How was she supposed to disengage without seeming like a bitch?

"I'd like to see you again."

"Maybe. Why don't you send me an e-mail and we can set something up?"

"Can I have your number?"

She shifted slightly to the left, nearer to the door. "I don't like to give out my number to too many people. This was just our first date and all."

"But definitely not our last." He leaned in to kiss her.

She saw it coming, thought she'd get a little peck on the cheek, but his mouth crashed into hers. When she didn't immediately open her lips, his tongue poked and prodded. It was slimy and gross. When she tried to step back, he pulled her closer. The quick move startled her and in her shock, she inadvertently opened her mouth.

That was one hell of a mistake. He jabbed his tongue so far into her mouth, it was like he wanted to inspect her molars. And he was a sloppy kisser too. Saliva everywhere.

Her stomach started to churn just as he pulled away. "How about we take this upstairs?"

Not in this lifetime. "I don't sleep with guys on the first date."

"There's a lot of territory between a kiss at the door and sleeping together." He waggled his eyebrows at her.

Like she wanted to dry-hump that? "No, thanks. I should be getting in. It's late and I have work tomorrow."

"Oh, okay." He really sounded disappointed. "Maybe we can get together this weekend."

She slid toward the door, hoping he'd get the hint and not try to swoop in for another kiss. "I'll be pretty busy this weekend. End of the school year stuff. But send me an e-mail. Good night."

She didn't wait for him to respond. She practically ran for the door. After scrubbing her mouth twice and then throwing her toothbrush in the trash, she called Indy. She plopped on the couch and put her feet up on the table. While Indy's phone rang, she stared at the green nail polish on her toes. What a waste of a perfectly good pedicure.

When Indy finally answered, she laid right into her. "You and your stupid idea."

"What'd I do now?"

Quinn sighed. "You told me I needed to date. I can't date. There's something genetically wrong with me."

"There's nothing wrong with you." She paused. "Well, there's nothing genetically wrong with you."

"You're funny. How do you do this? How do you go out and meet guys and have them be normal?"

"Honey, it's all about numbers. That's why I said five guys in two weeks. Within those five, you might find one halfway decent guy. The other four will be comprised of weirdos, sickos, and losers."

"Is that supposed to make me feel better?" She tried to figure out what category Jeff fell into.

"Sure. If you keep at it, you'll find someone. Then you can give up on this silly idea of being a single mother."

Quinn picked at the loose threads on her favorite burgundy throw pillow. "It's not a silly idea. I would be a good mom. Finding a husband hasn't worked out for me."

"You haven't tried finding a husband. You gave up after Nick, and we both know it."

Indy was right, as usual, when it came to men and dating.

"Cheer up. I have a growing list of ideas for how you can spend your summer. It's gonna be a blast."

Somehow, Quinn didn't think she'd agree. They said their good-byes and hung up. Quinn went back to the information she'd been culling from the Internet. All of her choices for becoming a mom sat in this one blue folder. Over the course of the last few days, she'd been adding information, and the file was growing quickly.

She wasn't being silly. She was thirty-one and had no prospects for a husband. Millions of women were single mothers. She knew she could provide a good life for a child. Her biological clock wasn't just ticking, it was like a bomb ready to detonate. She didn't want to leave her future to fate. She could control what happened in her life.

In the meantime, she'd play Indy's game and do things outside her comfort zone to prove to her and anyone else that she was ready for this challenge.

Quinn waited for Indy and Kate. They were supposed to meet at her house to make her summer list, but Indy had insisted they go back to O'Leary's. While sitting in the same circular booth they'd shared last week, she tried to rid her mind of all of the images from her last date. She hated that Indy talked her into joining the stupid dating sites.

Running a finger down the side of her glass, playing with the condensation, she sighed. The cool droplets trickled down and she stopped them with the pad of her finger. Her patience grew thin. She could understand Kate being late. *She* had kids and had to drive in from the suburbs. Indy picked the time and place, though.

It was like her sigh acted as a cue for Ryan. He was suddenly standing in front of her, pulling a chair from a nearby table. Turning the chair around, he straddled it. "Hi."

The intensity in his eyes belied the friendly smile.

She had a hard time holding his gaze. Every time she did, the rest of her surroundings faded. "Hi."

He crossed his arms over the back of the chair and leaned forward. "You look lonely."

She fidgeted with her glass. "I'm alone. That doesn't make me lonely."

His voice lowered a fraction. "True, but you look sad. Want to talk?"

The sigh heaved from her chest. "I'm not sad. Not lonely. I'm irritated because Indy wanted to meet here and she's late. Like always."

The smile widened. "If she's always late, why does it bother you?"

"Because it does." She couldn't keep the exasperation from her voice. "Why are you here?"

"I'm the owner, remember?"

She inhaled deeply. "You know what I mean. Why are you sitting with me?"

"I'm visiting with a friend."

The eye roll made her feel fifteen again, but she didn't care. "You don't want to be my friend."

"Sure I want to be your friend. Unless you'll let me take you out on a date and kiss you senseless."

"I already turned you down."

"Then I'll settle for being a friend until you see what a catch I am."

Her eyes wandered to his lips and she briefly imagined the kiss he could offer. "If you're such a catch, you can have any woman. You don't need to chase me."

"It's not a chase, but a challenge."

His words sounded like a promise he intended to fulfill. Her blood warmed and her heart bumped heavily against her ribs. He was all wrong for her, but every time he got close, her body didn't seem to care. Why did he keep flirting with her?

A throat cleared next to them and they both straightened. Kate stood beside the booth. "Hi. Am I interrupting?"

Ryan stood. "Not at all. I was just leaving." He extended his hand. "Good to see you again . . ."

"Kate," she supplied, taking his hand.

Ryan returned the chair to its proper table and disappeared from Quinn's sight.

Kate sat next to her. "Earth to Quinn."

"Huh?"

"What was that?"

"I'm not sure." Confusion coated her senses. During her brief conversation with Ryan, she'd felt encased in a bubble where everything else ceased to exist. It was disconcerting, to say the least. She scooted around the curve of the table to let Kate have a seat.

Kate's eyes filled with worry. "Are you okay?"

Quinn shook her head clear. "Yeah, I'm fine. What do you want to drink?" She waved the waitress over. "I think we should go ahead and order dinner now. Indy can order when she finally gets here."

The waitress strode up to the table and Indy breezed into the booth, out of breath, sandwiching Quinn between herself and Kate. "Sorry I'm late," she mumbled, and turned her attention to the waitress. "Hi, Jenna. I'd like a big-ass martini, dirty. I need to celebrate."

"Do you want to order dinner now?" Quinn asked, trying not to let her irritation show.

"Sure." Indy perused the laminated menu while Quinn and Kate placed their orders. "I'll have a salad. Add grilled chicken. No dressing, just lemon slices, please."

Jenna left to put in their order and Indy turned to Quinn. "I really am sorry for being late. I had a huge call at work. A new client wants me to find him a home. He's looking to spend big—like a million big."

Quinn choked on her pop. "A million? How does anyone have that kind of money to spend in this market?"

"I don't know. But you can understand why I spent extra time talking to him."

"Congratulations." At least Indy had a legitimate reason for being late.

"Exciting," Kate added.

"Hold the congrats until I actually make the sale." Indy sipped the martini Jenna deposited in front of her. She dug through her giant purse and produced a sheet of paper. "On to tonight's festivities."

"What's that?" Quinn asked as Indy slid the paper over. A list of thirty sloppily numbered ideas stared at her.

"I polled every woman I could find and they generated a list of things to do on your summer off. I know you've already done a couple, so you can mark them off. Let's see what's left."

Quinn pulled out a pen and carefully marked the items she'd already done. "I've only done seven. Pretty sad, huh?"

Kate offered a sympathetic smile. Indy reached across and grabbed at the page. "More than I thought. I bet you're cheating. Let me see." She snatched it away before Quinn could stop her.

While Indy scanned the list, Quinn said to Kate, "I'm really excited. There are things on the list that sound like a lot of fun."

Indy interrupted. "Wait. When have you ever gone skinny-dipping?"

"Do you have to yell?" Quinn leaned closer. "The summer I was sixteen. Miller's Pond."

Indy smirked. "I don't think it counts if you were alone in a secluded area."

Quinn sneered at her sister. "I wasn't alone. I was with Toby Miller."

"Toby? Eww."

"Oh, shut up." Nothing had happened between her and Toby. He spent the entire summer complaining that Indy should've been dating him instead of his older brother.

Indy looked up from reading. "You've never had a summer romance?"

Quinn raised her eyebrows and she could see Indy scanning memories of summers past.

"Not even as a teenager?" Indy asked.

"I've never had a boyfriend over the summer. Ever. Every relationship I've had started and ended without hitting summer. Except Nick."

"How sad. I never realized."

"That's because you were too busy with your own romances." Indy had had a new boyfriend every summer as a teenager. Quinn remembered being horribly jealous and had hated being born the Ugly Duckling in Indy's shadow. She hoped she didn't still sound jealous.

"Well, then, it has to be on the list," Kate said.

Quinn winced. She didn't want to admit to her pathetic attempts at dating this past week. "Give me the list back so I can decide what I want to do."

Indy's grip tightened on the page and she scooted farther to the edge of the booth. "Uh-uh. I think if we're gonna help you, we should get to pick the things from the list for you."

Quinn made another quick attempt to grab it. "Give it back, Indy."

"We all know, without looking, you'll choose the safest, most pedestrian items possible. The point here is to live a little. Move over here, Kate."

Quinn turned to see an evil grin on Kate's face.

"Speaking as someone who no longer has an identity beyond Kyra's mom or Mark's wife, I want you to step outside your safety zone. It'll be worth it. It'll be good practice." Kate stood and slid to the opposite side of the booth next to Indy.

Indy smoothed the crumpled page, and Kate pulled a small notebook and pen from her purse.

Quinn felt herself beginning to sulk.

Indy flashed a wicked smile. "Trust us. I'm your tow truck."

"I'm going to the bathroom." In the hallway outside the washroom, Quinn dawdled, looking at the various photos and newspaper article replicas about the Great Chicago Fire plastered on the walls. The dim light made it difficult to see, so she stepped closer to the wall.

A door opened less than a foot to her right and a man stepped out. The warm glow of light poured into the dark hall. He was backlit, and Quinn couldn't see his features, but she had no doubt it was Ryan. His gaze landed on her and she sucked in a breath of surprise.

"Quinn. Looking for me?" He pulled the door shut behind him.

"No." She shook her head and waited for her eyes to readjust to the dark.

"Why are you lurking in the hall?"

"I'm not lurking. I'm keeping myself busy while Kate and Indy plan my summer."

"Indy's here?"

Quinn didn't need to see the smile; she heard it in his voice. The familiarity of her sister's name on his tongue didn't surprise her. The prick of jealousy poked her chest and she crossed her arms. *That's why Indy insisted we meet here.*

As if oblivious to her mood, Ryan put his arm around her shoulder and walked back into the bar. "Let's see what's on the agenda for the summer."

She felt the warmth of his hand on her shoulder and their bodies collided as they returned to her table. Her failed attempt to block the enticing smell of his cologne irritated her. She barely stopped herself from stomping back to the table. *I will not make a scene. I said I wouldn't date him, but he could've had the decency not to flirt with me when he's interested in Indy.*

Quinn slid out from under Ryan's touch and into the booth opposite Indy. Upon Quinn's arrival with Ryan, Indy pushed past Kate and hopped from the booth. She threw her arms around Ryan's neck and planted an exaggerated, smacking kiss. *At least she has the courtesy to keep it on the cheek.*

"That's a hell of a welcome. Can you teach your sister to do that?" His hands rested comfortably at Indy's waist.

She laughed and Quinn's face reddened. "That's to thank you for referring your friend to me."

Indy sat back down and tugged at Kate's sleeve to pull her closer. "Quinn, scoot down so Ryan can sit."

Quinn narrowed her eyes at Indy. "Why don't you move over?"

Ryan stepped closer, towering over Quinn. "I'd like to sit here."

"I'm sure," she mumbled, but slid closer to Kate and the middle of the semicircular booth.

"Don't be rude to Ryan. He sent the millionaire my way," Indy said.

Quinn's eyes widened and her mouth slipped open.

"I'm glad Griff called. He's been busy and I wasn't sure how fast he'd get around to it." Ryan inched toward Quinn but looked at Indy.

"When you said you had a friend looking for a house, I thought you meant a North Side bungalow, not a North Shore mansion." Her gaze remained locked on Ryan's.

"If I told you, you wouldn't have believed me. Even if you did, it would totally ruin this moment." He turned to look at Quinn and smiled.

She snapped her jaw shut. The jealousy still simmered in her chest, but now with a bit of confusion stirred in.

"I still owe you a big thank you," Indy continued. "When I make the sale, I want to take you out."

Ryan smiled. "Don't thank me yet. You haven't met Griff."

"I don't care if he's purple with green spots and wants a house to match. I'll make it happen."

"I don't doubt it. Quinn said you're planning her summer. Anything interesting?"

Quinn forced her voice to work. "I'm sure there's plenty."

Indy nodded and her mouth spread into a wide grin. "I asked every woman I could find to name something all women should experience. We're deciding what Quinn should do."

Ryan returned his attention to Quinn. "Why are they choosing for you?"

"Indy wants to choose for me because I'm too pedestrian." She sneered at the last word. "Because I'm not reckless with everything I do in my life, Indy thinks I don't know how to have fun or adventure."

"Is she right?"

Heat flushed her cheeks. *Of course he thinks I'm boring. Compared to Indy, I am.* She frowned and her muscles twitched in anger. She'd had enough.

Being told she's boring on top of having to witness their flirtation was too much. She grabbed her purse and nudged at Ryan. "Let me out." When he didn't move, she hissed, "Please."

He rose and she pushed past him, heading for the door. On her way out, her shoulder collided with two other people, but she couldn't even mumble an apology. She shoved the door open and gulped in air. She felt so flustered she couldn't think, much less speak. Why did she care what he thought of her?

She moved away from the door and leaned her back against the cold, rough brick of the building. Men hit on Indy all the time. It had never bothered her before. This one shouldn't either, and probably wouldn't if he hadn't spent the last eight months flirting with her. As she calmed down, the door swung open and Ryan appeared in front of her. She didn't straighten but crossed her arms over her stomach.

"Are you okay?" he asked, stepping closer.

"I'm fine."

"I wasn't trying to piss you off. It was only a question." His soothing voice skimmed across her skin like cool satin on a summer night, but it did nothing to chill the warming of her blood.

Why was he here? Why didn't Kate come out to check on her?

"Why don't you go back in and plan an adventure with Indy?"

He chuckled, low and quiet, without humor. "You think I want your sister?"

She kept her gaze trained on the fold of her arms, afraid of what she might find in his eyes. "Why wouldn't you?" she asked quietly.

Ryan stepped so close the hairs on her arms bristled and her heart thumped. His voice was little more than a whisper. "She's not my type."

"Indy is every man's type." She'd hoped for sarcasm, but her tone was resigned. Quinn raised her eyes but needed to tilt her head up to meet Ryan's.

He laid his left palm flat against the brick beside her head and looked down at her, first at her lips, then into her eyes. His intent was there, and she licked her lower lip in reaction.

Oh, God. Don't kiss me. She sucked in a quick, shallow breath.

His blue eyes darkened a fraction and he lowered his head.

Quinn's arms dropped to her sides. *Push him away, you idiot.* Instead, she tilted her face upward a bit more, her scalp scraping against the brick.

Ryan's lips touched hers, moist and soft. Her lips parted as they connected. His tongue glided along the interior edge, teasing hers to come out and play. Their tongues tangled, smooth and slick. Every nerve in Quinn's body purred like a well-tuned engine.

The traffic and bar noise surrounding them disappeared. As Ryan leaned closer, his body heat battled the cool night air against her exposed skin. The woodsy scent of his cologne mixed with passion and overwhelmed the smell of food and alcohol floating from the bar. There was nothing but him.

Blood roared in her ears as she became acutely aware of every subtle shift of his body.

Quietly, he pulled away, trailing his fingers down the side of her throat, past her throbbing rabbit-pulse, to her collarbone. Her skin puckered at his touch.

She opened her eyes and blinked to focus. *Is he talking?* She inhaled deeply, sucking in his scent.

He took a half step away from her. "Too pedestrian, my ass. Your dinner's on the table." Without further comment, he strode back into the bar.

What the hell was that? Quinn took a few more breaths and allowed the sights and sounds of her surroundings to return to normal. He'd said he wanted to kiss her senseless, and he'd succeeded. That was the kind of kiss she'd been waiting for. Maybe a date with Ryan wouldn't be such a bad thing. For kisses like that, she could overlook a lot.

Quinn reentered the bar and crashed into Kate.

"Hey. Are you okay? Ryan went out to find you, but we didn't see him come back in."

"I'm fine." Quinn looped her arm through Kate's and propelled them both toward the booth.

Once Kate sat, Quinn scanned the bar and found Ryan. He stood at the edge of the hall with a buxom blonde, whose girlish grin began as flirtatious and moved toward seductive as she licked her lips and ran her hand down Ryan's arm. Last week a redhead, this week a blonde. She should've known.

Quinn sat quickly, silently berating herself for her moment of insanity. This was the reason she needed to avoid good-looking, charming men. How embarrassed she would've been had she asked Ryan out. She could still taste him on her lips, and he was already moving on.

"Everything okay?" Indy asked tentatively.

The tension Quinn held eased. "Don't worry about it. Let's eat and you can show me the list of how you think I'm spending my summer."

"Here." Kate handed her a sheet from her notebook. "The list is totally doable and you can get part of it done before summer starts, giving you extra time to find your romance. Complete these eight, then you've done half the list Indy and company developed. A respectable percentage."

Quinn stared at the scrawled list. "Did you intentionally choose things to freak me out?"

Indy laughed. "We picked the most fun things. You'll notice there's no public sex. Be glad Kate wouldn't let me add skydiving."

"How am I supposed to do this?"

"Don't worry, we'll help. It'll be fun." Kate patted her shoulder. "I'm looking forward to it."

Quinn scanned down the list. Dread rose immediately, but her nerves were still humming and the excitement of a challenge won. If she'd created the list herself, she wouldn't have challenged herself this much. Indy knew how to push her, that was for sure.

1. Play hooky.
2. Sing karaoke in a crowded bar.
3. Ride a motorcycle.
4. Indulge at an expensive restaurant.
5. Take a vacation alone.
6. Pose nude for a photographer or artist.
7. Have a fabulous summer romance.
8. Have a night of multiorgasmic, mind-blowing sex.

The bubbly blonde giggled as she caressed Ryan's bicep. For the life of him he couldn't focus on a damn thing she said. All his concentration was trained on slowing blood flow to his dick. Kissing Quinn had done more to him than expected. If she had stopped him, he could've walked away. If she had given him a prudish, puckered-up kiss, he would've taken the hint. He'd just wanted a brief taste, but once he started, he wanted more. When was the last time a kiss stirred him up like that? Ever?

The woman in front of him—Kristi?—continued to chat. He looked at her bright blue eyes and knew he could walk out with her and get laid. No strings. No effort.

But he didn't want to.

What the hell was wrong with him? He had a good-looking woman in front of him giving him every go-ahead signal possible, and he wasn't interested. In fact, the thought caused his dick to wilt a little.

He stared over Kristi's shoulder to the front door. Had Quinn come back? She wouldn't leave Kate and Indy. As much as he wanted to, he couldn't go back to their table. What would he say? Quinn had made her position on dating him clear. At least for now.

"Are you listening?" Kristi asked.

Ryan looked down at Kristi's narrowed eyes. "Sorry. I got distracted by something at the bar."

"Well, I guess if it's work and not some other woman distracting you . . ."

His cell phone rang and he reached into his pocket to retrieve it. Moira. Thank God. "Hey, Kristi, I need to take this in my office. I'll catch you later."

She looked stunned. "Oh, okay."

Ryan turned toward his office, unusually grateful for a familial interruption. "Hi, Moira. What do you need?"

"Who says I need anything?"

"Cut the shit. You only call while I'm at work when you want something." She figured he'd be distracted and she'd be able to convince him of anything. He'd been aware of her tactics for years.

"Fine. There's this huge charity fund-raiser thing next month I want to go to."

"So?"

"I need an invite."

"I don't even know what you're talking about, so I'm sure I don't have an invitation."

"I bet Griffin does."

"No." It was one thing for his family to bug him for favors. He had no intention of using his friend.

"Ryan, this is a huge society event. Anyone who's anyone will be there. Only select reporters have been invited so they can control the kind of coverage they get. This could be my big break. If I can write an exclusive insider's view, I might be able to get a byline in the *Trib* or *Times*. I'm tired of slugging through with this paper."

"I can't help you." He felt bad. Moira worked hard, but there wasn't much room for advancement at her current job.

"Please. Just ask Griffin. He probably has an invitation he's not even using. You know how he hates those things."

Ryan sighed. "You're sure this isn't some pay-five-thousand-for-your-dinner kind of fund-raiser?"

"I'm sure."

Who was he kidding? Even if it were, Ryan would come up with the money to give to Griffin to cover his sister's entrance. "I'll ask him, but I'm not promising anything."

"Thanks. You're the best."

By the time he hung up with Moira, his body had returned to normal. He sat at his desk and thought about Quinn. He didn't look for relationships. His last attempt taught him that until his family could function without constant mediation by him, a relationship couldn't work. It couldn't stand the strain and demands of the O'Learys. They had to come first; they only had each other.

Quinn pulled something from him he didn't even know existed— a desire for something more.

Shuffling papers on the desk, he realized he had nothing he needed to do tonight. He should go back to his other bar, Twilight, and check on things there. He couldn't make himself do it, though. It would be like admitting he couldn't face Quinn. Not that he was rushing back to the bar to kiss her again either.

A knock sounded on the door.

His manager, Mary, didn't enter but stuck her head around the corner, and said, "Sorry to interrupt, but there's a guy here who says he needs to talk to you."

"Who is it and what does he want?"

"He wouldn't say, but—"

"Then he can wait. I'll be out in a little bit."

"Will do." She exited, closing the door behind her.

He leaned back in the leather chair and began to consider Quinn.

Another knock. He didn't need someone bugging him right now. He crossed the room to the door. He swung it open, expecting to see Mary again.

The face staring back at him, though, was nearly identical to his own. Colin.

Ryan stood, dumbfounded, staring into the dark blue eyes of his older brother. They hadn't seen each other in years. *Not since Dad's funeral. What the hell is he doing here now?*

Colin opened his arms wide. "Is that how you welcome family? Come here." He pulled Ryan into a bear hug.

Ryan eased back and studied Colin. He'd filled out some, but he looked well. "Have you been to see Mom yet?"

Colin shoved his hands into the pockets of his faded jeans. "No, I hoped you could help with that. I don't think I can face the wrath of Eileen O'Leary without reinforcements."

"Ah, shit. That's a hell of a thing to lay on me. She'll be ticked at me now, too, since you came here first." Ryan blew out a breath. Their mother would be hurt he came to Ryan first, but she'd gush all over Colin for days. Part of her blamed Ryan for Colin running out. Somehow she could never see Colin for who he was. "Come on. Let's get this over with."

Colin threw an arm over Ryan's shoulder. "Thanks. I knew I could count on you. Tell me what's been going on. Any family gossip I need to catch up on before I walk into the house?"

As they headed out to Ryan's car, Ryan's brain scanned everything that had happened to their family since Colin disappeared. He knew Colin called their mother, but he had no idea what she'd told Colin and what she hadn't. He decided to keep it light and let the rest of the family tell him whatever they wanted.

CHAPTER 3

Ryan pulled up in front of his mom's house and glanced at the clock. If he was lucky, the house would be empty. He could install the garbage disposal he'd promised and get back to work. The job itself shouldn't take too long. His goal was to get back to O'Leary's early enough to see Quinn. It was Friday and she'd be coming in with the other teachers, like clockwork.

He looked down the block. Of course luck wasn't on his side; Moira's car was there, which meant both Mom and Moira were inside.

He grabbed the box containing the disposal and his bag of tools, and raced up the front steps. Moira had the door open before he could use his key.

"I'm glad you're here. Mom has been talking about this damn disposal for days."

"I know. Who do you think gets the call before you?" He walked through his childhood home, noting the smell of dinner in the air. In the kitchen, he bent to kiss his mom on the cheek. "Hi, Mom. I told you I'd be here today. I'm just running a little late."

"Oh, I wasn't worried. I told you I'd call a serviceman."

"And I told you I'd take care of it." He eased over to the sink and set down his tools. Opening the cabinet, he saw that nothing had been removed. Probably for years. He unloaded two containers of dish soap, boxes of plastic bags, trash bags, four pairs of bright yellow rubber gloves, and some crap he couldn't even identify. Then he scrubbed sticky scum from the bottom so he wouldn't lay in it. Ten precious minutes later, the cabinet was empty and he could get to work.

The room quieted as soon as he pulled out his tools. Maybe it was his lucky day. The old disposal came out without a problem. As he unboxed the new one, Moira came into the room.

"Guess who I saw yesterday?"

Great. Not only was she not keeping Mom busy, she expected him to gossip.

When he didn't respond, she continued, "Colleen Miller. You remember her, right? Her brother is best friends with Rory Reardan."

Ryan grunted and hoped she'd get to the point.

"Rory is cousins with Norah, who just happens to be friends with Margaret, Cassie's sister."

While Moira rambled, he'd managed to get the new disposal in place. At the mention of Cassie's name, he paused. Moira stopped.

"Well, aren't you going to ask?"

"What?"

"What's going on with Cassie?"

"Why bother? I figure you're in here bugging me because whatever it is, you're dying to tell it. I'm going to have to listen whether I want to or not." He tightened the nuts in place and siliconed against leaks.

"She's getting married."

"Huh?" His voice echoed beneath the sink.

"Cassie is getting married."

The words sank in and he waited to feel a reaction. Nothing.

"Well?"

He didn't have to crawl out to know she was bouncing on her toes, looking for something.

"You have to say something. I have to send something back through the grapevine."

He pulled out of the cabinet and said, "Congratulations?"

"I know you're not still hung up on her. But what if she thinks you are? I have to be able to tell Colleen something that will get back to Cassie. As it is, it looks like you've been pining away for her. I couldn't mention a girlfriend because you don't tell us anything."

I don't tell you anything because you're like a damn tabloid. Thoughts of Quinn entered his head, which was why he was in a hurry to finish his job. The last thing he needed was Moira catching wind of his interest in Quinn. "I have no girlfriend. Tell Cassie I wish her well."

"She never was right for you."

Not wanting to hear her tirade, he turned on the faucet and flipped the switch of the disposal. The noise effectively drowned out Moira. When he was sure it was operating right, he flipped the switch again. Machine and woman stopped at the same time. How he'd wished for a switch like that growing up.

Before Moira could rev herself up for round two, their mother walked in.

"Stew's almost done. Go wash up, Ryan."

He packed his tools back in his bag. "Sorry, I can't stay, Mom. I have to get to the bar. Mary needs to get off early."

"Always off to work. You're worse than your father. Colin could help."

"Colin probably needs time to settle in." Ryan tried not to let his disgust show to his mother. Colin had never made his life easier. He kissed her on the cheek again. "I'll see you Sunday for dinner."

Moira followed him through the house. "Hey, Ry, one more thing."

He turned.

"Have you talked to Griffin about the benefit?"

"Yeah, he didn't know offhand if he had a ticket. He doesn't keep track of that shit. He'll call you if he has the invite."

A slow smile spread across her face. "Thanks, Ry. You're the best. I don't know why Cassie thought she could do better than you."

He shrugged. "Maybe having all the O'Learys poking their noses into her business constantly was a bit much."

"We're family. That's what family does. You just need to find someone who wants a big family. I have friends," she added with wide eyes.

"No, thanks. I'll see you Sunday. Are you bringing a date?"

She snorted. "Are you kidding? After the grilling the last guy got, I don't think I'll bring anyone home until I've already eloped."

"Can't do that. It'd break Mom's heart. See you later."

He rushed back to his car. He'd have barely enough time to shower and change before going to the bar. He thought briefly about Cassie. He really was happy for her. She didn't mesh well with his family. Hopefully she found someone who could make her the center of his universe.

By the time he walked into the bar, he figured he'd missed Quinn. He hadn't counted on her sticking around after the majority of the teachers left. If she kept hanging out without the horde of teachers, she must like something about the place. He banked on it being him. Especially after their kiss. He should probably say something about the kiss, but what? *I want to do it again?*

He strolled over to the bar where she was sitting on a stool. He stepped next to her, her soft scent grabbing him, and whispered in her ear, "Can't get enough of me, can you?"

She jumped a little and then smirked. "I have a date."

"Really? That's two dates in one week. Both of them here." Was she trying to send him a signal?

"Your bar is conveniently located. I don't want any guy I meet on the Internet to know where I live. I learned my lesson there."

So she wasn't actively pushing other men in his face. "Is this one as bad as the last?"

"Who says my last date was bad?"

Her face remained calm, almost to the point of being unreadable, but her eyes gave her away. He leaned his elbows on the bar. "I watched the date. You couldn't wait to get rid of the loser."

She wrinkled her nose. "He wasn't as bad as the one I didn't bring here."

"Internet dating is a bad idea. Everyone lies about who and what they are. You can't believe anything."

"In case you haven't noticed, I'm not really good at meeting people. I can get to know them a little online. I hoped it would make me less awkward in person."

"Awkward isn't a word I'd use to describe you."

"I don't think I want to know how you'd describe me."

Sexy, sweet, intriguing. No, she probably didn't want to hear that description. At least not from him.

A man walked up on the other side of Quinn and tapped her shoulder. "Excuse me, are you Quinn?"

"Yes."

Ryan left them to their introductions, but he already knew the date would end badly. One look at this guy and Ryan could tell he'd been drinking. He watched Quinn and her date from across the room. He knew Quinn was a smart woman. How could she not see this ass was a waste of her time?

It was time for him to leave for Twilight, and he'd only come in to see Quinn, but he wanted to watch this play out.

As he mingled with his usual customers, Ryan kept an eye on Quinn. Intelligence she had in abundance; people smarts, not so much. He didn't need a degree in psychology to see that.

She shifted uncomfortably several times and kept tucking her hair behind her left ear. The guy was on his third whiskey and she had yet to ask for a drink. Quinn rose and carried her purse toward the bathroom. Ryan hoped she had enough sense to end the date. When five minutes passed and she hadn't returned, Ryan went to find her.

In the shadowed hall outside his office and the bathrooms, Quinn stood quietly watching her table.

"What are you doing?" Ryan asked.

"I'm waiting."

"For what?"

"For the loser to get the hint I'm not coming back." Her dark hair barely skimmed her chin and it swayed with every slight movement of her head.

A quiet chuckle stuck in his throat. "Tell him to get lost."

"It would be more trouble than it's worth. He'll get the hint."

"What if he comes looking for you?"

Her eyebrows drew together. "Do you have a back door I can use?"

"He's that bad, huh? I'll tell him to leave." He took a step forward, intent on making sure she never felt afraid in his bar.

Her smooth fingers wrapped around his forearm. "Please don't. He'll cause a scene and I'd never be able to show my face in here again."

His skin warmed beneath her touch. He closed the small distance between them. "Why are you putting yourself through this?"

Her light brown eyes widened, and even in the dark hall her sincerity was plain. "Because I promised Indy I would go on at least five dates within the next two weeks. I need to step outside my comfort zone."

She tugged her hand away and crossed her arms. Her eyes darted, as if keeping contact was a battle. Her voice lowered a fraction. "You don't know how hard it is to find a normal date."

"What makes you think that?" He pushed his palm against the wall next to her head and caught the soft, powdery scent of her perfume. Did it make him an ass that while she talked about dating other men, his thoughts focused on kissing her again?

She shifted and tucked her hair behind her ear. When she looked up again, her face had returned to the usual polite, impassive front. "Come on. I'm in here often enough to see you with all kinds of women. I'm not judging you, but you can't compare picking the flavor of the week to dating."

He didn't address her comments. She was right—he liked women who required nothing from him but a good time. It wasn't a concept she'd understand. She'd definitely require more. He hadn't attempted anything more serious since Cassie. "So what's your plan? Cast a wide net and see what you catch?"

She shrugged. "Indy said it's all about numbers. I spent a bunch of money to join the stupid dating site. They guarantee I'll meet someone special. It's in my best interest to keep trying. Besides, I try to weed out the worst of the bunch."

His burst of laughter made her jump, so he placed a hand on her shoulder. "Sweetheart, if you think you're weeding out the bad ones, your radar is broken."

Her lips pulled back, but it wasn't quite a smile. "I was born without radar."

She eased away from him to peer around the corner. Her date was still there, gulping another whiskey.

Ryan felt sorry for her. The men she chose weren't right for her. He didn't even know her well and he knew her choices sucked. Helping her didn't make sense; he'd get nothing out of it, except for the chance to see her smile. It might be his best chance to show her he wasn't all bad. Then maybe she'd give him a chance. "It's lucky for you my radar is overdeveloped."

"How does that make me lucky?"

He leaned close to her ear and inhaled her scent again. The feminine fragrance shot into his system and warmed his blood. "Because I'm the best wingman you'll find."

"Wingman?"

Ryan sighed. Had the woman spent years in a closet? "Keep meeting your dates here. I'll let you know which ones are losers."

Her mouth hung open slightly, like she had questions to ask, but she said nothing.

He poked her shoulder and pointed to the back exit. "There's your escape."

Tension left the set of her shoulders. "Thanks for listening and the quiet escape. I owe you one."

"Go out to dinner with me." *Where the hell did that come from?* She wasn't ready to take him seriously yet. He'd agreed to be her friend. She wouldn't be swayed easily.

Her nervous laughter was a relief. She nudged him with her elbow. "Thanks, but I think we've already covered that. I'm not looking to be this week's flavor. Going out with you would be a colossal mistake."

The thought of tasting her made him hard. He walked her to the door. He hadn't thought in terms of a relationship in a long time, but hearing her call the possibility a mistake irritated him. How could she know what he wanted if he wasn't even sure? "You're probably right. It couldn't hurt to ask."

After she exited through the back, Ryan walked to the bar and told both the bartender and waitress to cut off Quinn's date. He knew the man would look for more liquor once Ryan told him Quinn had left.

Ryan walked to the table and looked into the blood-red eyes of the date. Gritting his teeth, he managed, "Excuse me, sir."

"What'ya want?"

Ryan inhaled and reminded himself he didn't need another bar fight. Irritation battled courtesy. "I wanted to let you know your date left."

The man heaved a deep sigh. "Bitch."

Ryan stiffened and his hands flinched, but he remained silent.

"They're all bitches, ain't they? Can't even get a decent night out, much less get one to spread her legs."

Ryan couldn't believe Quinn thought this had even the remote possibility of being a good date. No one was that good an actor, not even online. Ryan leaned down, closer to the drunk. "Be careful how you speak about people. That woman happens to be a friend of mine. Maybe if you weren't a drunk, slurring and slobbering all over yourself, she wouldn't have felt the need to duck out of here."

The drunk scrambled to his feet but plopped back on his ass.

Ryan straightened again. "I'll call you a cab. You're not fit to drive." He waited until the man's gaze met his. "Don't bother contacting Quinn again. She's not interested."

The following week dragged. Students were restless with spring fever, and Quinn found she had as much trouble focusing as the kids. She felt burned out and couldn't wait for summer, but her list nagged her every day. She had gotten nothing done and hadn't even put forth much effort.

Except for the stupid dating sites.

That made tonight a two- or three-drink night, so she dropped her car off at home and had her colleague and friend Brian drive her to the bar.

It was still too early for the regular after-work crowds to be in a bar. Quinn found herself fussing with her hair as she scanned the room looking for Ryan. She didn't know what had gotten into her. She barely knew him. *But she did know the man could kiss.*

Brian nudged her over to the bar to order. "Hey, Jenna. I'll have a beer. And Quinn will have—what froufrou concoction will it be today?"

Quinn rolled her eyes at him and focused her attention on the bartender. "Let's make it a Long Island iced tea."

Brian reached down from his six-foot-three frame to touch her shoulder. "Do you know what's in that?"

"Yes, I'm not driving. I'll be fine."

Jenna nodded and began to mix and pour. As if she could read Quinn's mind, she said, "He's not in right now."

"Huh?"

"Ryan. He's not here." She pushed a tall glass in front of Quinn.

"I wasn't looking for him."

"Sorry. You looked like you were." She swiped the bills Brian laid on the bar and turned to the next teacher.

How sad that Jenna lumped her into the group of women Ryan talked to any given night. Every time she saw him, he was engaged in conversation with a different woman. Did they all stand at the bar searching for him?

Quinn sat at the table, staring at her pocket calendar while she sipped on her drink. Only two weeks left of school. If she was going to play hooky, she'd have to do it soon. But she had to prep the kids for finals. *Why did Indy even put this on here? I get plenty of time off.*

Brian slid into the seat across from her. "What's going on? I hear Shari Ackerman's going to teach summer school in your spot."

Quinn shook her head. "Do you think she can handle it?"

"What's to handle? It's three hours a day with a captive audience."

"I've taught that class for the last seven years. Those are not the bright, engaged students she's used to teaching." Quinn swallowed the bitterness of being passed over for the position Shari got. Quinn really wanted to teach the Honors classes.

"Everyone's got to start somewhere. Me, I'm going to start at the bar and work my way toward a game of darts."

Brian walked off and before she had the chance to refocus on her calendar, Ryan took Brian's seat. "Good evening, Ms. Adams. Enjoying your night here at O'Leary's?"

"Jenna said you weren't here." She sat back and crossed her arms against her chest.

"You came in looking for me?" He leaned forward at the table.

"No." Her eyes widened. "She *assumed* I was looking for you and offered the information." She reached out and turned her glass in circles, avoiding his eyes.

"What's up? Haven't seen you in a while."

"It's only been a week."

"I've gotten used to you stopping by more often."

"I've been working. The end of the year is a busy time." This was the third time she'd seen him since the kiss, and he'd said nothing.

"What's this?" He tapped her calendar.

I guess we're still ignoring the kiss. "I'm trying to choose the best day to play hooky."

Ryan's laughter rose above the noise of the milling crowd. "You need more help than I thought. Sweetheart, a hooky day isn't something you plan. You just do it. You don't think about work. The day is supposed to be fun."

Quinn groaned and thumped her head on the table. "I can't do that."

"Didn't you ever cut class?"

Quinn raised her head. "No. Perfect attendance all four years. Eight if you count college."

His crinkly-eyed smile returned. "Oddly, I'm not surprised by that fact. If you're not comfortable with it, why are you doing it?"

"Remember the list Indy and Kate created for me last week?" *You know, the night you kissed me senseless one minute and moved on to a bimbo the next?*

He nodded and she continued, "The first item on the list is to play hooky."

"Playing hooky should not be stressful. Everyone does it. Lighten up. Pick a day and have fun. Your students will survive without you. Most of them have played hooky and can appreciate it."

She slammed her calendar shut. "Okay. Monday it is, then."

He shook his head again. "Not quite spur of the moment."

"Hey, I'm a work in progress."

Ryan hung up his phone. It had been his third call from his mother. She wanted to verify he was coming to family dinner. Colin's home—time for a big celebration. It didn't matter that Colin hadn't accomplished anything over the last three years. Coming home was achievement enough. He rolled his shoulders to ease the tension.

He left his office and stood in the hallway facing a decent-sized crowd, early for a Friday night. He took two steps into the bar and saw Quinn still sitting at the same table. He'd figured she would've left by now. She never had more than one drink with the other teachers. She only stayed late when she had a date. A tall blond man bent over and kissed her head. Ryan's stomach clenched with the realization that she wasn't pulling away.

Had she actually found a decent date?

He relaxed moments later when he took the time to recognize the man—he posed no threat.

Ryan watched Quinn after the man left. She drummed her fingers on the table and sipped more alcohol. She pulled her phone from her pocket and opened and closed it. A frown creased her face. No one joined her. She spoke to no one.

He took it as an invitation and sat across from her again. "The guy who left. You do know he's gay, right?"

"Huh? You mean Brian?" A giggle escaped. "Yes, he's a friend from work."

"Just making sure your gaydar isn't as broken as your asshole radar."

She straightened in her chair. "I think it's time for me to go."

Ryan reached out to grab her hand. "Don't take offense. I'm being a good wingman. It would ruin my reputation if I let you date a gay guy."

Quinn leaned back in her chair. Her head tilted to one side. He saw the unfocused glaze in her eyes. *She's drunk.* "How's the dating going?"

A crooked smile etched her face. "Dating sucks. All the Internet sites that promise you'll find someone special run at the sight of me. I give up."

"What are you talking about?"

She shook her head with a sigh. "I haven't been having any luck with the dating site I signed up for. You've seen them. I don't think I'm asking for too much. A guy with a job, at least average intelligence, and he has to be able to kiss. I can overlook a lot of things if a guy can lean in with a kiss to make me forget where I am. I don't have it in me to work with a guy on his kissing."

Ryan snickered. "The guys you go out with can't kiss?"

"One guy was like a lizard. He kept jabbing his tongue in and out." She flicked her tongue out repeatedly.

Instead of laughing at how ridiculous she looked, Ryan had the urge to pull her close and give her a non-lizard kiss. Her tongue flicking made him imagine where else she might use it. He stared at her mouth, not hearing what she said.

He blinked and refocused. "What'd you say?"

She barreled on, unfazed. "So I tried to sign up with a different site. They wouldn't even have me. I tortured myself honestly answering their tedious questionnaire, only to have them tell me I'm unmatchable." She paused and gulped the last of her drink. "What the hell does that mean anyway? Am I unlovable because they can't figure out with whom to pair me?"

"I told you you're looking in the wrong places. Real men don't troll the Internet to find dates. We're visual creatures. We like to see the product upfront."

"Thanks for the information. I'll take it under advisement. Brian told me I'd find someone when I least expect it. With any luck, when he shows up, he'll know how to kiss. Until then, maybe I need a break from dating." She tugged her jacket off the back of the chair.

He quickly stood and blocked her from getting up. "You're not driving, are you?"

"No, Officer Friendly. I'm not stupid. I came with Brian. I'll call a cab, since it's obvious my sister isn't coming." She pushed her chair from the table.

Ryan held out a hand to help her up. "How much did you drink?"

Her hand was cool and smooth in his and he didn't want to let go.

"Three of those. I think it was only three." She jammed one arm into her jacket and fumbled to find the other side.

He reached around and helped get her other arm through. "I'll give you a ride home."

Tugging on the collar of her jacket to close it put him too close to her body. His thoughts wandered to being alone with her. He pulled back to keep a clear head.

"No, thanks. I hardly know you. And I'm pretty buzzed. What if you turn out to be a creep?"

"I would never take advantage of a woman who has had too much to drink. *Ever.*" His sharp tone had her head snapping up from fumbling with the buttons on her jacket. He smoothed his tone. "You know me well enough. Better than these guys you've been meeting."

He tugged her sleeve. "Come on. It'll give us a chance to get to know each other. I'm a better wingman for friends than acquaintances."

She flipped open her phone and dialed. After a moment, she spoke quietly. "Hey, call me in twenty to make sure I got home okay. Yeah. Bye."

When she closed the phone, Ryan handed her a glass of water. "Drink this before we go. It'll help."

Quinn gulped it quickly. "Leave it to the barman to know all the tricks."

He grabbed her elbow and guided her through the maze of patrons. Right now, he had a golden opportunity to be alone with Quinn.

Ryan shepherded her to his SUV in the parking lot. It was a vehicle he used for bar business more than anything. If she puked, he'd rather it happened in the SUV than his personal car. Although she walked with her head held high, Quinn wobbled. He continued his hold on her arm to make sure she didn't fall.

"Where do you live?" he asked.

"You know those industrial buildings on Laramie they turned into lofts a few years ago? I live on the fifth floor."

He opened the passenger door and helped her slide in. Trendy neighborhood. Not a far trip at all. He'd be there within ten minutes. He'd hoped to have more time to get to know her. Maybe he could get her to agree to a date while she was drunk. A little underhanded, but he'd take it.

"Tell me about yourself," he prompted.

"What do you wanna know?"

Her usual prim and proper voice had slipped into the realm of easygoing. It was a side of her he'd like to see more. "Anything. Were you born here in the city? Have you lived here your whole life? Do you have family other than the sister who blew you off tonight?"

"Slow down on the darn questions, would ya? My brain can't move fast with so much liquor swirling around." She inhaled deeply. "I was born in southern Illinois. I moved here with Indy for college. She's my only sister. My dad still lives down south, so we don't see each other often."

They rode silently for the next few blocks. Ryan thought she dozed off, but then she spoke again. "How long did you go out with Indy?"

Surprise made him swerve the car. "Indy? Indy and I didn't date."

"Oh." She became quiet again until the wrinkles of confusion on her face smoothed. "It's your turn. Tell me about you."

"I've been in Chicago my whole life. I come from a big family. Six kids including me. My father died a few years ago."

"Sorry. My mom died when I was seventeen. It sucks."

She straightened in her seat as the car stopped. Quinn fumbled for the handle and flung the door open. "Thanks for the ride."

"Wait. Let me walk you up."

"I'll be fine." She swung her legs out and pushed against the door frame to stand.

Ryan stood beside her before she stepped away to close the door. "I want to make sure you get in safely. Then I promise I'll leave you."

"Trying to be chivalrous to trick me into dating you? Won't work."

She allowed him to take her keys from her hand and help her to the door.

"What will work? One date and if we're not compatible, I'll leave you alone."

"I told you I don't date guys I meet at a bar, especially the ones who work there." She pointed to the elevator that looked like the original from the building's warehouse days.

"What have you got to lose? You said the Internet dating thing wasn't working." A rumble and thunk echoed in the empty hall as the elevator arrived.

"If I waste my time with you, I might miss the guy I'm supposed to meet. The one who can kiss me and make me forget where I am." She stepped in ahead of him.

Was she implying his kiss didn't cut it? Not possible. Instead of being angry at the accusation, he viewed it more as a dare. "I bet I can make you forget where you are."

She pushed the button for the fifth floor and turned to face him. "You could, but then you'd be too busy with whatever other woman is within a hundred yards. I think I'll keep looking."

"Maybe I'm just casting a wide net like you are." She didn't respond and he paused for a moment. Maybe she was implying he wasn't what she was looking for. Thinking back, every date he'd seen arrived in a suit. The last time he'd worn a suit was to his father's funeral. "How can you find anyone if you don't date? You said you were giving up. Taking yourself out of the game prevents a guy from kissing you, doesn't it?"

She smiled. "You have me there. I'll think on it when I'm sober and get back to you."

She leaned against the wall as the elevator climbed floors. He held back the urge to pull her to lean into him. She still looked sad. Her pouty lips begged to be kissed. At the fifth floor, the elevator gave a little shudder before the doors slid open. Ryan continued to hold Quinn's elbow as she led the way to her door. There were only two lofts on the floor. He jabbed the key into the locks and swung the door open.

He waited, half hoping she would invite him in. She said nothing as she tossed the keys on a side table beside the door and hung her jacket on a hook. Her phone rang in her pocket. She fished it out and held up a finger to tell him to wait.

"Yeah, I'm fine. I made it home safe and sound. I even got an escort to my door." She barked out a laugh. "Not gonna happen. Talk to you tomorrow."

She clicked the phone shut and turned her attention to him. "Thanks for bringing me home. I appreciate it."

"You could repay me by letting me take you out on a date."

"Sorry. I have a list to work on. Getting involved with you would be too complicated." She pulled at the door to signal he should leave.

"But we could be friends, though, right?"

She nodded her head and smiled. "Sure."

It was her version of a brush-off, but he'd take what he could. "We can get together as friends for a cup of coffee."

"Maybe. I'm going to bed now. Thanks again." She began to close the door, but he stopped it with his palm flat on the cool metal.

"Drink at least one more glass of water before bed. It will help counteract the dehydration of the alcohol. The hangover might not be so bad." His hand slid away from the door. "Bye."

"Bye. Thanks."

He waited in the hall until he heard the snick and chunk of her locks being thrown. Ryan walked back toward the elevator but spied a door leading to the stairwell. He had no desire to ride in the rattling death trap again. As he bounded down the flights of stairs, his mind raced. He wanted a date with Quinn Adams, and she would take careful planning.

CHAPTER 4

Quinn woke the following morning, early as usual, but felt sluggish. A slight throb ached over her eyes. She hadn't slept much, but when she did, dreams plagued her. Images of Ryan had taken over her night.

In the steam of the shower, she tried to convince herself it was the alcohol that wreaked havoc on her subconscious. Or was it the id? Either way, the sexy dreams filled her head. Her verbal diarrhea with Ryan hadn't helped her anxiety level. She always talked too much when she drank.

As she pulled on a tank top and shorts, she wondered at the thought of being an old maid. At what point would she become a spinster? The depressing thoughts grabbed her before she could push them away. Growing old alone frightened her.

She knew what she needed, a temporary fix. Comfort Cookies— deep, dark, double-chocolate-chip cookies.

Quinn yanked her hair into a small, high ponytail and entered her kitchen. Here, she could rid herself of the thoughts of men. She didn't need them while she baked. Baking was a hobby, a solitary art, and she could focus on the measuring, the mixing, not Ryan.

She pulled the ingredients she kept at the ready in the pantry. For her, these cookies were comfort food. She used to make them with her mom. And they made their way onto everyone's list of favorites too.

Quinn pulled out the different types of chocolate, bittersweet and unsweetened baker's chocolate, and chopped the blocks into smaller pieces before dumping them into the double boiler. The radio played as soft background noise. Between the smell of melting chocolate and the music, trying to push Ryan from her thoughts should have been easy.

But it wasn't.

He'd been a total gentleman last night. Not that he hadn't been in the past, but she'd expected him to try something, even if it was just to get her to agree to a date. But he didn't push it. He was just being nice.

While the chocolate began to melt, she cracked eggs into a bowl and began the task of mixing them with sugar. Sometimes she'd use her stand mixer, but today she wanted to mix by hand. It would take longer, and it utilized every muscle in her hand and arm. For her it was therapy. The rhythm of the whisk scraping the side of the bowl combined with the beat of the music. Her mind relaxed and let the sounds take her back to childhood.

The ringing door buzzer startled her. Who would come to her house on a Saturday morning? She had few visitors regardless of time or day. She turned the flame lower on the chocolate so it wouldn't scorch and pressed the call box. "Yes?"

"Good morning, Quinn. It's Ryan. Can I come up?"

She rubbed the back of her hand over her cheek. Why was he here? She never should've let him drive her home. "Why?"

"You said we could have coffee. I brought the coffee to you."

The end of the night blurred a bit, but she knew she hadn't made a date. She sighed, knowing he wouldn't disappear if she ignored him. She buzzed him up.

Quinn waited nervously at her door for the elevator when the stairwell door flung open. She jumped and turned to see Ryan holding two paper cups. She crossed her arms over her chest to steady herself as the desire to bolt into her loft surged in her chest. She masked her face as well as she knew how. "Hi. I don't remember making a date, most definitely not for today."

"I didn't say we made a date for today. You said maybe we could have coffee sometime. I figured you might need coffee, so I stopped by before going to work. How are you feeling?"

The tone of his voice always seemed like he had a joke he was dying to tell, and as it coasted over her, she felt the tense muscles in her shoulders relax.

He stood two short feet away, deep blue eyes smiling down at her. He smelled good. His aftershave mixed with the aroma of chocolate and caffeine. It was intoxicating. Then it hit her. This man was like her Comfort Cookies, without the calories. Way too good to be true.

"I'm fine."

"Is now a bad time?"

"Uh, no. I just started baking cookies." She was torn. Invite him in or ask him to leave? She glanced over her shoulder, knowing she needed to mix the chocolate. "Come on in."

She kicked the door wider and walked back to the kitchen.

"No hangover?"

She couldn't help but smirk. "No, someone suggested I drink lots of water before going to bed. It helped tremendously. I woke up with only a slight headache." His visit doubly surprised her now because of the reason. He wanted to check on her?

She kept her back to him as she tried to sort out this new information. She was beginning to see Ryan in a new light. He was a nice guy in addition to being charming. This could be her downfall. She turned the flame back up on the chocolate and gave it a stir.

"Here." Ryan reached from behind her and pushed a cup at her. His voice was hesitant, and if Quinn didn't think it impossible, a little nervous. "I didn't know how you take coffee, or if you even drink it. I took a chance on a light, sweet mocha. It smells like you like chocolate, so I think I did good."

Quinn accepted the cup and inhaled deeply. She leaned the spoon on the edge of the pan. "You can never go wrong with chocolate." She took a small sip, allowing the caffeine to hit her system. As the warm, chocolatey coffee slid across her tongue, thick and rich, she closed her eyes and let a small moan of ecstasy escape her throat.

Ryan laughed quietly and her eyes popped open.

"Thank you. This is really good."

"Sounds like it." He looked around the mess on her counters. "Can I help?"

"Huh?"

"Making cookies. Can I help?"

Could he? The only person she'd ever baked with besides her mother was Indy. And Indy usually just ate the raw dough. She'd always enjoyed the solitary nature of it, but here was Ryan asking to be included in this personal process. Behind him, her list glared at her.

Step out of your comfort zone.

"Sure." She handed him a spoon. "Stir the chocolate until it's a smooth pool of yumminess."

"Sounds easy enough."

"It's not difficult, but if you don't pay attention, the chocolate will burn." Quinn turned back and mixed flour, baking powder, and a pinch of salt in a separate bowl. She tried to ignore his presence without being rude.

"Do you bake a lot?"

"I don't know if I'd say a lot, but I like to bake. It's relaxing, especially when I have stuff to think about."

"What else do you do for fun?"

She remained quiet for a minute. What did she do for fun? "I like to read."

But even that wasn't always for fun. More often than not, she read something related to teaching. "I like to watch reality TV."

"Like *Survivor*?"

"No, more like *The Bachelor.*"

He huffed out a sound of disgust. "That is not reality."

"I know that. But for the most part, it's regular people. They just spend an inordinate amount of time doing stupid crap. It's fun to watch and doesn't require anything from me." She turned to check on the chocolate. "How's the chocolate?"

"Looks melted to me." He scooped the spoon through the lake of chocolate and lifted it to show the smooth drizzle. "Now what?"

She turned off the flame. "Dump the chocolate into the egg mixture I already made."

He grasped the handle of the top pot of the double boiler and poured the chocolate over the batter.

After the chocolate was incorporated with the eggs and butter, she added the dry ingredients slowly. When it was all mixed, she said, "Now we fold it together with the chocolate chips so it stays kind of fluffy. We don't want to beat it."

One eyebrow shot high on his forehead and she knew she lost

him. Dumping chocolate he understood, folding it was a different matter. "Like this."

She used her spatula and gently folded the chocolate in.

"I can handle that." He reached for the spatula and his hand brushed hers.

The charge between them startled her. He stood so close she thought for sure he was going to kiss her again. She stepped quickly to the side to let him access the bowl.

She stood on tiptoe and pulled down her stoneware cookie sheets. The stone was smooth and shiny from years of use. They were heavy, but they gave her perfect cookies every time.

"All mixed. Now what?"

Ryan looked like a kid baking for the first time. He displayed his excitement on his face. Most guys would be bored or would only care about the finished product. Ryan was enjoying the process.

Rather than take over, she handed him the cookie scoop. "Scoop the dough and plop it on the pan. Leave space between the cookies. You should get a dozen per pan."

He played with the scoop for a minute, squeezing the handle to get an understanding of how it worked. "Like scooping ice cream."

"Yep." She eased onto a stool and watched him drop dough on the pans. It was weird teaching Ryan to bake Comfort Cookies. She'd always imagined that the first person she'd teach would be her own child.

"Have you decided what you're doing on Monday?"

His question brought her back to the kitchen, away from her thoughts. "Monday?"

"You're playing hooky, right?"

"Oh, that. I have no idea what I'm going to do."

He finished filling the two pans and she slid them into the preheated oven. After setting the timer, she returned to her stool. What was she supposed to talk about now?

"I bet my sister Moira would love these cookies. She loves everything chocolate, and there appears to be about a hundred kind in these."

Within minutes, the inviting smell of chocolate filled her kitchen. "You're more than welcome to take some with you. You can tell her that you made them yourself." She dipped a finger into the remaining batter. "A good cookie always starts with good dough. This is Indy's favorite part." She licked her finger. "Sometimes we don't even get a second batch in the oven. We just lick the bowl clean." Dipping her finger in again, she felt his eyes on her. "Try some. It won't hurt you."

His hand snaked out and grabbed her wrist. He guided her finger to his lips and licked the batter off. Jolts of pleasure ran up her arm and her eyes widened.

He did *not* just do that.

She yanked her hand away. "Wh-What are you doing?"

He shrugged with one of his careless smiles. "Trying the cookie dough. I didn't think you'd want my grubby hands in the bowl."

The innocent look on his face baffled her. Did he really not mean anything by that? He made no other move. He'd been nothing more than friendly the entire time he'd been there. Maybe she was reading more into his actions.

His phone chirped. He pulled it out and checked the screen. His brows furrowed and his lips tightened.

"Problem?"

"A text from my sister. I'm being summoned to my mom's house."

"You don't look too happy about it." Other than mentioning his sister earlier, he hadn't done much talking about himself. She wondered if he was hiding something. He said he had a big family, but that didn't mean he liked them.

"It's not that. They're changing plans again, that's all. I have to juggle some stuff." He tucked his phone back into his pocket. "Unfortunately, that means I have to head out now."

Disappointment hit her quickly before she swiped it away. "Can't you wait for the cookies? They'll be ready any minute."

"I better not. Save some for me." He headed to the door and she followed.

"Thanks again for the coffee," she said.

"I told you I knew how to be friends. Thanks for letting me hang out with you. Talk to you soon."

She stared after him as he moved through the stairwell door. He made a hasty departure. She smiled at the kindness of his visit. There was definitely more to Ryan O'Leary than she'd thought.

In the kitchen, the timer went off, and she removed the cookies from the oven and set them out to cool.

Quinn sipped at the last of the decadent brew Ryan had brought. The essays in her bag needed to be graded, but she ignored them. She thought long and hard about her life. By now, she was supposed to have what Kate had: a house, a husband, and kids. Her first marriage had been a joke, and she couldn't even find an adequate date. But she still wanted children.

Eyeing the list tacked to her refrigerator above the artwork created by Kate's kids, Quinn thought of the possibility of starting a family. As soon as school let out, she'd seriously start making plans. Adoption, in vitro, artificial insemination . . . There was a lot to consider, but if she could handle the list Indy made, she could conquer anything.

Sunday afternoon, Ryan sat at his desk, sucking down his third cup of coffee. The numbers on the spreadsheet in front of him blurred. The family dinner usually held on Sundays had turned into a whole-day affair on Saturday to give Colin a proper welcome home. Of all the things to pull him away from Quinn, he didn't think Colin had been worth it.

He didn't believe Colin had reappeared out of some sense of family. He wanted something, but Ryan couldn't figure out what. As much as he'd wanted to press the issue last night, their mother had been too happy to have Colin home.

Colin's appearance made his mother happy, but Ryan couldn't handle the gushing and fussing. He couldn't wait to escape the family dinner. Claiming bar business, he'd thought he could get away. Colin following him to O'Leary's last night had not been part of the plan. He'd successfully avoided Colin for the two weeks he'd been home. He knew it had been too good to last. His brother closed the place drinking with friends he hadn't seen in years.

Ryan couldn't wipe the image from his mind. It was like being stuck in a time warp. Part of him had expected their dad to walk in and yell at Colin. Ryan drank last night to forget the grief Colin had caused Dad. Ryan was still paying for it.

His office door opened and Ryan lifted his eyes expecting to see Mary. Instead, Eileen O'Leary stood in front of him. "Hi, Mom. What're you doing here?"

"I need to talk to you."

Shit. He didn't need any more on his plate. His mother sat in the chair in front of his desk.

"You need to give Colin a chance." As usual, his mother offered no preamble or small talk; she got straight to the point.

"To do what? Fuck up everyone's lives instead of just his?"

"Watch your mouth. He's your brother."

Ryan inhaled through his nose and reined in his anger. Lashing out at his mother would solve nothing. "He's the one who left."

"He's back. And he's staying. He's moved back home."

Figures. Colin always took a free ride. Ryan looked at his mother. She sat straight in the visitor's chair, hands folded in her lap, and ice in her eyes. She wasn't about to let this go.

"What do you expect from me?"

"He needs help finding his way. He thought going out on his own would make it happen. He's as lost now as he ever was."

Ryan shook his head. Colin wasn't lost; he was lazy.

"He's not like you, Ryan. You were always driven to succeed. Picked what you wanted and fought for it. Colin has a harder time figuring out what he wants."

"Did he tell you all this?"

"He didn't need to."

Ryan huffed and rolled his eyes. Eileen slapped a hand on his desk. "I know my boy. Just as I know you want to make him pay for not being here."

It amazed him how quickly the brogue blasted from her lips whenever she was angry. He'd lived with it his whole life, but never got used to it. The Irish brogue was a beautiful lilt in the mouths of his cousins, but from his own mother, it was venom-filled.

He had no choice but to give her what she asked. "I'll try, Mom. That's all I can promise."

She stood. "He's family, Ryan. Your brother. You have to do more than try. Your father would want you to make it right. He'd expect no less."

She left as quietly as she came. Good old Mom. She didn't care if it was a low blow to pull out the guilt card. Irish Catholics were masters.

* * *

Monday morning, six-fifteen, and Quinn lay wide-awake. Her stomach churned. She held her phone in her hand and hit speed dial.

"What?" Indy answered groggily.

"I did it. I called in sick. Now what?"

"Go back to sleep. I'll call you at a decent hour." She hung up.

"Great. Her brilliant idea and she won't talk to me." Quinn tossed the phone on her nightstand and rolled over.

Three hours later, her phone rang. She reached for it and stopped. What if it was school? Would she have to pretend to be sick? Could she? She blew her bangs off her forehead and crumpled the dust rag in her hand.

Her heart thumped nervously as she waited for the machine to answer.

Indy's voice called, "Hey, Quinn. It's me. Are you there?"

Quinn picked up the line. "I'm here."

"Too bad. You're supposed to be out having fun. What are you doing?"

She tossed the rag on the table. "Spring cleaning I put off."

"Oh, God. You are such a sad case. You do *not* take a sick day to clean. You need to go *do* something."

"Like what?"

"Look, I have a couple of showings scheduled for this morning and a closing this afternoon. Keep yourself busy, with fun, and we'll do something together later. Don't you have any other friends to hang out with?"

"They're all at work. Where I should be. I called Kate, but Kyra's sick. The only people I know with flexible jobs are you and Nick."

"Do *not* call Nick."

"I didn't say I'd call him." But the thought had crossed her mind. Her ex was always good for having fun.

"My clients are coming. Find something fun to do. I'll call you soon."

Quinn turned back to her bookshelf. She'd finish what she started and then find something fun.

Ryan stood outside Quinn's loft. He reminded himself they were hanging out as friends. She wasn't ready to accept anything else from him, regardless of how hot their kiss was or the continued chemistry they shared. He rang the bell, but she didn't answer. He rang again.

"Hello?" she questioned hesitantly.

"Hey, Quinn. It's Ryan."

She didn't respond, but the buzzer sounded, allowing him entrance. He eyed the elevator and chose the stairs.

Her door was open, and Quinn wasn't standing in the doorway. It was an improvement over his last visit. Country music floated quietly from the kitchen. Quinn stood on a step stool wiping down the binding of each book on the shelf before setting it aside.

This is worse than I thought.

Without looking at him, Quinn asked, "Why are you here?"

"Indy called me—"

"That's what I figured. You can leave. I'm fine."

She scrubbed furiously at the shelf, ponytail on her head bobbing in rhythm. The cotton pants hung loosely on her legs but contoured to the shape of her behind. The baggy T-shirt did nothing for him. Her feet, however, with red-painted toes were incredibly sexy.

He'd told Indy he'd leave if Quinn told him to. He'd lied. "Why don't you go shower and change, and we'll get out of here?"

"I don't need your pity date."

"It's not pity. And it's not a date. We're a couple of friends playing hooky and spending the day together." He leaned against the arm of the couch. As often as he fixed things for his family, he could help her too.

Quinn turned and looked at him suspiciously, but stepped off the stool. Dust rag balled in her hand, she crossed her arms. "Thank you for the ride home Friday night and the coffee Saturday. It was really nice of you, but I don't think we can be friends."

"Why?"

"Because you kissed me."

"We don't have to stop being friends because we kissed." He straightened and stepped closer.

Her eyes met his. "*You* kissed me. I don't know how to do the friends with benefits thing."

He barely stopped his laugh. She would bolt if he laughed. "That doesn't surprise me. But I said nothing about benefits. Just friends." He extended his hand to shake.

Quinn took his hand tentatively. Hers trembled. For a woman who kept cool and reserved, the slight motion hinted at something, but he couldn't put his finger on it.

Ryan rocked back on his heels. "You can't cross this off your list if you spend the day cleaning."

"You sound like Indy." She blew her bangs up and out of her eyes.

"It's a good thing you have me. Go change."

She measured him and sank her teeth into her bottom lip. White teeth against pink flesh stirred his blood.

"Where are we going?"

"It's a surprise." He hadn't yet figured out what fun they could have with their clothes on.

"That doesn't work for me."

"Too bad." He sat on the couch and propped his right ankle on his left knee.

"Then I'm not going." She recrossed her arms.

"I'll drag you out of here looking like that, lemon furniture polish scent and all. It's your choice."

"You can't drag me."

He leaned forward and cocked an eyebrow. "Wanna bet?"

"You wouldn't dare."

Her challenge made him want to go all caveman and throw her over his shoulder just to prove he could. "I would." He rose from the couch and she stumbled back.

"Fine. I'm going upstairs."

"I'll be waiting."

She stomped up the stairs and closed a door. Ryan took the time to do what he hadn't done on Saturday—explore Quinn's loft. The main floor was basically a wide-open space with the ceiling at the second floor. Windows lined one wall, bookshelves another. She had more books in piles in various places in the room. A desk tucked in the corner near the stairs held her laptop.

He wandered into the kitchen and stopped in front of the refrigerator. A neatly typed list stared at him. It drew his attention amidst the colorful artwork. The first item was "Play hooky." He read through the rest.

Blood rushed southward as he got to the bottom of the list. The passion of the kiss they'd shared closed over him. The sudden realization that she'd seek another man to accomplish these tasks hit him. Like ice water dumped on his head, Ryan's warm thoughts were doused.

Indy knew about this. Hell, she created it, yet she sent me over here anyway.

Ryan left the kitchen and returned to his place on the couch. Reading the list invaded Quinn's privacy. He probably shouldn't have read it. He'd come here today as a friend, but he'd use all the ammunition he could get his hands on.

Quinn's bounding down the metal steps caught his attention. The sight of her pushed aside all thoughts of friendship. A bright blue Cubs T-shirt was tucked into the waistband of tight jeans. The teacher had become the girl next door. She had her damp hair tucked behind her ears. His gaze wandered to her feet. Unfortunately, she wore black canvas sneakers.

"Ready?" she asked.

"Whenever you are."

"Are you going to tell me where we're going?"

"Maybe." He opened his arms for her to lead the way. As she walked by, he caught the scent of her perfume. It wasn't the same soft scent he'd smelled before. It was darker and more enticing. Remaining friends without benefits might be more difficult than anticipated.

Quinn paused before heading to the door and pushed a plastic container of cookies at him. "Before we go, I have something for you. Here."

"What's this?"

"Cookies from Saturday. You told me to save you some."

He took one of the cookies and sank his teeth in. Her breath locked in her chest, waiting for his reaction.

A groan sounded from deep in his throat. "These are amazing. How do you keep from eating them all at once?"

Ignoring the pleasurable sound and what it did to her insides, she answered, "Self-control. Everything in moderation."

"I'm not good at either of those," he said, biting into a second cookie. His look said he was referring to more than eating cookies. He returned the lid to the container. "I better leave these here or I'll eat them all."

Quinn walked to the elevator and pressed the button. Being alone with Ryan made her nervous. Friends or not, they'd shared a memorable kiss. Every time she looked at his face, she thought of his mouth on hers. She reminded herself he probably kissed a different woman every night.

"We could take the stairs," Ryan said.

"Are you claustrophobic?" The elevator dinged and Quinn stepped in.

"No. I don't trust this particular elevator. It's so old it might collapse at any moment."

"I take it all the time. It's fine." She pressed one and the elevator lurched. As they rattled past the third floor, she added, "It only gets stuck on three a couple of times a month."

"Are you serious?"

Quinn laughed. "Unfortunately, yes. But it doesn't last long."

They exited the elevator and the building. Quinn looked up and down the street for Ryan's SUV. "Are you driving or am I?"

"Neither. We'll walk; take the bus if we need to."

"To where?"

"Today, we're tourists." He paused. "I know, you've lived here for years and you know everything the city has to offer."

He laid his hand on the small of her back to guide her down the street. It didn't make her flinch or cringe. She didn't even want to step away. His warmth crept pleasantly up her spine, and she hated that she enjoyed it.

He continued, "But when was the last time you looked at the city? Really looked."

When had she? Ten, twelve years ago when she moved here? She'd always thought she'd re-explore with her husband and kids. Day trips into the city from their quiet suburban home. How had she lost so many years?

"See?" Ryan broke her thoughts. "You don't even remember, do you? The city is always changing, evolving. Every time I do this, I discover something new."

She stopped. She slid her sunglasses off her face. "Do you pretend to be a tourist often?"

"Not often. I used to once a year. It's been a few since I did it last."

He too seemed lost in thought for a moment. She wondered if he had regrets as well. "So where did you get the idea to play tourist?"

"My dad. I think he came up with it as a way for us to hang out together. When I was a teenager, we'd do it three or four times a year. I got to play hooky to hang out."

"Sounds like fun." She heard the pleasure in his voice and part of her envied the relationship he'd had with his father.

"What about you?" he asked over the rumble of a bus and the traffic they encountered as they arrived at the busy intersection.

She wrinkled her nose at the black exhaust. "What about me?"

"What fun stuff did you do with your dad? Or mom?"

"We were never the kind of family who did stuff together." She paused. "But one of my favorite childhood memories was when my dad took me to Wrigley Field."

Ryan's hand closed gently over her elbow as they crossed another street, dodging cabs. Quinn enjoyed the warmth of his touch. His sunglasses obscured his eyes, and she wanted to see the shade of blue they'd be out here in the sun.

"Tell me about Wrigley."

"It was spur of the moment, which made it extra special because Dad planned everything. The Cubs were having a phenomenal season. Ryne Sandberg played second. Rick Sutcliffe with his walrus mustache pitched. And Mark Grace played first base. I had a crush on him."

"You remember the players?"

"Not all of them, but I watched a lot of baseball that year. Everyone thought they'd go to the World Series." It was long before the drinking started. Mom was still alive, keeping Dad happy. It felt like a lifetime ago.

Ryan snickered.

"What?"

"I've never been much of a baseball fan, but everyone knows the Cubs won't ever go to the World Series."

"Nonbeliever." She took a deep breath and felt the sun warm her face. "My dad was sure they'd go all the way. He wanted to be part of it. So we drove up here and went to the game. I'd hoped it was going to be a night game since it was so new back then. Unfortunately, those tickets were harder to get."

They walked in silence for the next block. She didn't know why she'd shared one of her most treasured memories with Ryan. She rarely spoke of her childhood. So much of it was overshadowed by the mess her family had become.

"Where do you want to go?"

She shrugged. "You're the expert. You pick."

"You're probably a museum girl. So let's do something different. Have you been to the bean?"

"The bean?"

"The big silver sculpture thing shaped like a bean."

"You mean Cloud Gate. No, I haven't been there. I've seen pictures of it."

"Let's start there. It's a beautiful day."

Her phone rang. She stopped to dig through her purse. When she produced the phone, Ryan grabbed it. "Hey."

He opened the phone. "Hi, Indy. Yes, we're fine. She won't have access to her phone until later. Uh-huh. You too." He closed the phone and slid it into his back pocket.

"Give me my phone."

"No."

"What do you mean, no? What if school calls?" The thought sent nervous flutters through her stomach.

"That's why you can't have it. Today is about having fun. If you let your job interrupt, it won't be fun."

"If I'm worried about missing a call, I won't have fun either."

"Don't worry. I didn't turn it off. Think of me as your personal screener." That grin again. The one that promised fun.

Quinn huffed but continued walking. Taking a day off required a lot of effort. Looking at Ryan, though, she decided there were worse people to spend a day with.

When they got to Cloud Gate, quite a few people were milling around. As she skirted the edges of the small crowd to get closer to the hunk of metal, Ryan brushed past her to hurry her along. She touched the cool metal and Ryan put his face close and stuck his tongue out. His reflection, distorted in the curved metal, made her smile.

"Come on. Make a face."

"I don't think so."

"Fine. Go spin in a circle under it. I've heard it's like being drunk."

"You're crazy."

"Maybe, but it'll be fun." He tugged her under the arch and they spun.

He was right. It was fun. She laughed so hard at her dizziness, her sides ached.

CHAPTER 5

After wandering around the bean, they walked through the gardens and made their way over to Crown Fountain. Quinn's face lit up when she saw the fountain spouting water over the backdrop of faces.

"Wow. I've never seen this either. How cool." The faces on the backdrop changed and shifted. Quinn walked closer. She giggled as a little girl, maybe four years old, scurried past and ran under the flowing water.

The girl squealed in delight. Quinn's head tilted back and she laughed loud. The sound was exactly what Ryan had been waiting to hear. Without thinking, he grabbed her hand and pulled Quinn under the stream of water. Her shriek was every bit as loud as the girl's.

"I can't believe you just did that." She pushed her wet hair off her forehead and narrowed her eyes at his dry body. He'd managed to swing her under the water while keeping himself out of it.

"I thought you'd like it." His eyes wandered down the front of her shirt, which was half wet. Her nipples protruded from the shirt, and he realized the water was colder than he thought it'd be.

She had a sudden gleam in her eye and he knew she wanted revenge. He backed away from the fountain. She didn't have the strength to pull him, but he didn't want to be tackled either. Her footsteps were slow and deliberate as she stalked him.

"Come on now, Quinn. You don't want to do this."

"Oh, yes, I do."

He grinned, hoping to distract her. "Let's make a deal."

"For what?"

"What do you want?"

"A dry shirt."

He considered his options. "You got it." He whipped his shirt off and held it out.

Her mouth gaped. "You're nuts. What am I supposed to do with that?"

"Put it on."

"Then your shirt will be as wet as mine. And you'll still be walking around . . ."

Her voice trailed off as she studied him. She didn't hide her appraisal of him and he didn't hide his smirk. "We'll find a place for you to change."

Hours later, they'd finished their walk through Millennium Park, consumed a completely unsatisfying lunch from a hot dog vendor on the street, and toured around Buckingham Fountain. After waiting for Quinn to put on her now-dry Cubs shirt, Ryan had a thought. "Let's go to Wrigley Field."

"Why?"

"Why not? We can walk over to Clark and hop the bus. We'll be there in no time."

"We don't know if there's a game. Even if there is, the chances of getting tickets are slim."

"So what? Let's go." He tugged her hand to turn her toward Clark. Her hand was smooth and he interlocked his fingers with hers. Her fingers stiffened momentarily, but she didn't pull away. His thumb rubbed the back of her hand. The tension melted. She was warming to his touch.

The afternoon bus was empty and they both slid into the graffiti-ridden, orange plastic molded seats. Quinn sat next to the window and he stretched his arm along the seat behind her head. He leaned over to make a remark about something outside, all of which disappeared like smoke when he smelled her hair. It wasn't flowery and overpowering, but slightly fruity and sweet. He wanted to bury his face in it. Instead, he allowed his fingers to brush over the silky strands.

Her back stiffened at the touch. She shifted to turn to him.

"Sorry. I couldn't help myself."

She smiled at the apology. "You said you had self-control issues."

"If I didn't have those issues, you wouldn't be having fun today." He straightened a bit. "You are having fun, right?"

"Are you kidding? This is the most fun I've had in years."

He released the breath he'd held. She was so reserved, he'd half-expected a polite, "I'm having a nice day." There was something sweet in her that she tried to hide, so he wasn't quite sure how to read her.

"We're almost at our stop." He stood and pulled the cord to signal they were getting off.

Quinn stood and the bus jolted to a stop. She pushed into him and he grabbed her hips to steady her. She shook her head. "Sorry. I'm out of practice. I haven't taken the CTA since college."

"No problem." Except his hands didn't want to leave her curvy hips. They longed to stay and explore.

"Hey, you gettin' off?"

Ryan turned to the driver. "Yeah, have a good day."

Quinn stepped off behind him, seemingly oblivious to his desire. They crossed the street and found all the ticket windows closed. No game.

"Well, it was worth a shot." He shrugged. "What do you want to do now?"

Quinn looked at her watch. He placed his hand on her wrist. "For today, time is irrelevant."

She tilted her head. "Don't you have a business to run?"

"I'm so good, it runs itself." Her raised eyebrows made him continue. "I have a great manager who can handle everything without me." As if to defy him, his cell phone rang. He pulled it from his back pocket. Moira, whom he'd already ignored twice. "I need to take this."

He left Quinn staring at the stadium while he answered. "Hi, Moira. What do you want?"

"Mom wants to know if you've talked to Colin."

"We all had dinner together on Saturday. We spoke." He shoved his hand into his pocket. Quinn stood three feet away, arms crossed.

"Not stupid reminiscent crap."

"I talked to him. I didn't throw him out of the house."

"Like Mom would let you." She sighed into the phone. "Look, I'm calling because it's breaking her heart to watch the two of you. You used to be so close."

That was before.

"Come by next weekend. We'll try dinner again."

"I'll stop by, but I don't know if I'll stay for dinner." He closed his phone and realized he just offered to give up yet another weekend for his family. He turned back to Quinn. "Where were we?"

"I was saying you've adequately fulfilled your babysitting duties. We can go home. I don't expect you to give up your whole day." She tapped the face of her watch.

He covered the watch again and then slid his hand from her wrist to her palm. She looked at their interlocked fingers like it was the first time she noticed his touch. "I've enjoyed spending my day with you. I gave up a day in my stuffy office shuffling paperwork."

"I've had fun too. Thank you."

He pulled her arm to bring her closer. "If you want to thank me, let me take you out to dinner. For a real meal, not a hot dog on a corner." He saw the debate behind her narrowed eyes.

"Fine. You win."

"Good. We'll go back to your place so you can change and then we'll drive to my place. I'll make reservations on the way." They began walking to the bus stop.

"Tonight? You want to go out now?"

"Sure, why not?"

"We spent the whole day together. I'd think you'd need a break from me."

"Then you'd have time to change your mind. Do you have any preference for dinner?"

"No."

Her phone bleeped in his pocket. He pulled it out. A text message from Nick. Indy had warned him about the ex.

She released his hand and held out hers for the phone. "Who is it?"

"Nick." Ryan tucked it back in his pocket.

"What are you doing?"

"Screening your calls like I told you I would. He doesn't seem important enough to warrant the interruption."

She crossed her arms and stood silently until a garbage truck rumbled and clattered past. When the traffic noise returned to normal, she said, "I think I should decide who's important."

"You did. If he was important, he wouldn't be your ex."

She pressed her lips together.

The southbound bus squealed as it stopped and the doors thunked open. Quinn stepped up and fumbled with her wallet. Ryan reached around and slid money in for both their fares.

"Thanks." She took a seat near the back and he followed.

They rode in silence for a while. Ryan wondered how to lighten her mood again. He didn't want to have their dinner date ruined.

She didn't turn to look at him, but said, "I'm sorry. You're right. Nick's not important. It's not that it was Nick. I would've been pissed over any call. It should be my choice whether to take a call."

Ryan didn't respond immediately. The thought of her wanting to talk to her ex while with him gnawed at his gut, though. "No, I'm sorry. Do you want your phone?"

Her eyes met his. "No, if I have it, I'll call him."

The uneasy silence poked at Ryan. He thought of the one thing she was most at ease with. "Why did you become a teacher?"

Her stance immediately relaxed. "I needed a career and I love books. When I started college, I wasn't sure what I wanted to do. I spent a semester tutoring and I knew. How about you? Why own a bar?"

"Family business. It was my dad's dream long before it became mine. I grew up in the bar. It was a natural progression for me to take over." He paused and squashed the urge to tell her about Colin and how the bar was supposed to be his. He stood. "Let's get off here and walk. It'll be faster than catching a crowded bus during rush hour."

Quinn threw open the door to her loft. "I am so done with walking today. I hope you parked close, or you'll have to carry me to your car." She dropped her keys on the side table and bent to untie her sneakers.

Ryan strolled in behind her and went straight to the couch. "Okay, so I misjudged how far you live from Clark. It was still a nice walk."

"How dressy is this place we're going?"

"Casual is fine. It's a steakhouse. By the time we get there, I'll be ready to eat a side of beef."

"After all the exercise, they better have a great dessert menu too," she commented as she plodded up the stairs. From the top, she called, "Help yourself to anything in the fridge. I'll be ready soon."

She sat on her bed and mentally ran through wardrobe options. Exhaustion dragged her down, but it had been well worth it. She'd had a great time with Ryan. Maybe she'd been too quick to brush aside his offer of friendship. She couldn't recall the last time she had so much fun with anyone but Kate or Indy.

This is what dating is supposed to be. Having fun while getting to know each other. Why doesn't this happen on a real date?

This felt like a date. The notion nagged at her. After a quick shower, she tugged on her favorite black dress and found sandals to match. Expectations. That was the problem. She and Ryan held no expectations for each other or their relationship. They enjoyed their time because it was just today.

She suddenly realized she'd been gone much longer than planned and hurried downstairs. Ryan had sprawled across her couch with his eyes closed. "Are you sleeping?"

"Just dozing." He pushed against his elbows to sit and rubbed his hands over his face. He looked her up and down. "Wow. If that's your idea of casual, I'd love to see dressed up."

Despite how her nerves tingled over his examination, her response was light. "It never hurts to look good. You never know who you might meet."

"Are you trying to find Mr. Right tonight?"

"I won't be actively seeking him, but you're my wingman. You can teach me what to look for."

A thump sounded at her door. She swung it open and Nick almost fell on her. "Nick?"

"Hey, babe," he slurred.

Ryan was at her back as Nick stumbled to lean on the doorjamb. His dark, shaggy hair hung almost to his deep-set brown eyes. Ryan's warmth radiated through her clothes. "How did you get up here?" she asked.

"The old lady downstairs let me in when she left."

"I'll have to remind Mrs. Cannon you don't live here anymore."

Nick pushed away from the wall to stand semistraight and ran a finger along the scalloped neckline of her dress. "I guess this explains why you didn't call me back."

Before she even had the thought to step away from Nick's touch, Ryan had Nick pinned against the wall. He held him with his forearm against Nick's chest. "Did she say you could touch her?"

Nick put his hands up in surrender. "Hey, man, relax. Quinn and me go way back."

The movement startled Quinn. Ryan was always so laid-back, she never would have guessed he had a violent streak.

"Ryan, let him go. It's fine." She laid a hand on Ryan's shoulder.

He released Nick and took a cautious step back, offering no apology. Quinn took a step to stand beside Ryan.

"Who's he?" Nick asked, tilting his chin toward Ryan.

Quinn inhaled deeply. "Ryan, Nick, my ex. Ryan is a friend. Why are you here?"

"I got fired. I wanna talk."

"You're drunk at six in the evening. I don't need this."

Nick stumbled past them. He went to the couch and plopped down. "I texted before I started drinking."

"You have to go, Nick. I'm on my way out."

"Aw, come sit with me, Quinn." He patted the cushion next to him. His eyes were slits, and his sloppy grin told her he would pass out soon.

"Did you drive here?" She struggled to keep her voice from shaking.

" 'Course I did."

"Stupid son of a bitch. Give me the keys." She held out her hand and swallowed tears. Nick knew how she felt about drinking and driving. He'd met her father, hadn't he?

Nick fell over trying to reach into his pocket and laughed.

She shook her head and turned to Ryan. "I'm sorry, but I have to ask for a rain check for dinner. I can't let him drive like this."

"I'll take him home if you want."

Quinn assessed his face. He was serious. Why would he offer to take on this mess? "No, he's not your problem."

"He's not yours either." He reached out and rubbed his hands up and down her bare arms.

Before she could respond, a snore sounded behind her. "Unfortunately, since he passed out on my couch, he is."

"I'll stay and help pour him into a cab."

She shook her head at the offer. "No, you should go. Your evening is still salvageable. Thank you for a great time."

"I don't like this. I don't trust him."

"He's passed out. Even totally sober, he's mostly harmless."

"Mostly," Ryan repeated.

"He spent the majority of our marriage like this. I can handle him. Thanks for the offer, though." She didn't mention that the rest of the time he smelled like other women's perfume.

Ryan pulled out his wallet and handed her a card. "Here are my numbers. If you have any trouble getting rid of him or need anything else, call."

"Thanks." She curled the card in her palm, unsure what to do.

"When will I see you again?"

Her heart thumped. "That sounds like this was a date. I thought we're just friends hanging out."

"I guess you're right."

About which part? The date or the just friends? She wanted to ask but feared the answer. She didn't know which she wanted it to be. "I might stop by after work on Friday. Maybe I'll see you then."

Quinn locked up after Ryan walked out, kicked off her sandals, and walked to the kitchen to make coffee. She needed to sober Nick up and make sure this didn't happen again. She wanted to start fresh this summer and she couldn't afford to have Nick get in her way.

The list glared at her from its post on the fridge. She grabbed a pen and placed a small check next to the first item. Seven more to go. Below her list, a photo caught her eye. It was a postcard of Buckingham Fountain lit up in colors at night. *Where did this come from?* She turned it over. A simple message read, *"One down.—Ryan."*

Quinn sat at her desk reading a note from the substitute. Nothing dramatic had happened in her absence. Her mind wandered back to her free day in the sun. With Ryan. She hadn't thought about school or her students all day. A small pang of guilt blipped in her chest.

It was only one day. Get over it. They were fine without me. And walking through the city on a quiet Monday felt fabulous.

"That's a heck of a smile."

Brian's voice startled her and she clumsily dropped the papers in her hand. "Hey, Brian."

"You received a delivery. I was in the office and offered to bring them up." From around the corner he produced a vase full of daisies, dyed in a rainbow of colors.

"Who sent me flowers?"

He set the vase on her desk and handed her the card stuck to a plastic stem.

She read the card aloud, *"Heard you called in sick yesterday. Hope you're feeling better. Ryan."* She leaned over and sniffed the flowers.

"Ryan. As in O'Leary's?" Brian prodded.

"Yes," she answered, touching the petals of a pink daisy.

"Sounds like a story dying to be told."

"Not so much. He hung out with me yesterday. It was fun."

"Which explains the happy glow. I'm glad you took the day."

"So am I." To her surprise, she meant it. The bell rang, forcing Brian into the chaos of the hall.

Quinn moved the vase to the bookcase by the window. She wondered how Ryan knew she loved daisies. Teens buzzed into the room and questioned her absence. Thoughts of Ryan and her list were pushed aside.

It wasn't until on her way home after school that Quinn realized she didn't have her phone. Ryan hadn't given it back to her yesterday. Her brain was clouded from a long night of futilely trying to wake Nick.

She should head to O'Leary's to get her phone, but she was tired. If Ryan wasn't there, it would be a wasted trip. She had his card at home. She'd call and make arrangements to pick it up later.

As she rounded the corner of her building, she saw Nick leaning near the door.

God, I don't need more of this.

He straightened as she neared. He didn't look as bad as she felt, and he'd been drunk. Life wasn't fair.

"Hi, Quinn."

"What do you want?"

He stepped closer. "I want to apologize for last night."

"Fine. Accepted. Good-bye." She tried to move around him and caught the scent of his cologne clashing with the stench of stale whiskey. The all-too-familiar mix assaulted her.

He grabbed her arm. "I am sorry. I was pissed about being fired and I didn't want to be alone."

"You've never lacked company." She wished she'd kept her mouth shut, but old hurts still burned.

"I wanted to hang out with you. I've missed that. But you didn't answer my text."

"I was busy." She forced a calming breath into her lungs.

"Yeah, I saw. Sorry I ruined your date."

"Ryan is a friend, which is none of your business. You did, however, ruin our dinner plans." She tugged her arm free from his grasp.

He leaned back against the building with a smirk. "You may not think it was a date, but it was to him."

Her eyes rolled as a sigh escaped. "You don't know anything about us."

"No, babe, you're the one who doesn't know. A man doesn't step up to fight unless he's protecting his territory."

"You would think so. Good-bye, Nick."

"See ya later."

She put her key in the door and mulled over Nick's words. Sure, Ryan was attracted to her, but it had been his idea to be friends. Did she misread his signals? It's not like it would be a first. Getting involved with Ryan would be like setting up a train wreck. She was supposed to be looking for a summer romance. Someone who would be gone at the end of the summer, before she had a chance to ruin it. Ryan didn't fit the bill. At least she didn't want him to. She liked whatever they had going on and didn't want to see it end.

Outside Quinn's loft, Ryan waited. She was home. Her car was parked in its usual spot behind the building. As he raised his finger to ring again, Quinn's irritated voice crackled out of the speaker.

"What do you want now?"

He glanced quickly around looking for a camera he hadn't noticed. None. She didn't know it was him. "To return your phone."

"Oh." The slight syllable was followed by a buzz releasing the lock.

Ryan grinned as he imagined Quinn covering her face when she realized she snapped at him instead of whoever she thought he was. She left the door open for him, but he didn't see her. "Quinn?"

"Up here. I'll be down in a minute."

He sat on the couch. *Ferris Bueller's Day Off* played on the TV. True to her word, Quinn bounded down the steps and turned into the kitchen.

"Hey. Thanks for the flowers. They're beautiful."

He looked around but didn't see the flowers.

"I left them in my classroom. They brighten the institutional atmosphere. What made you pick daisies? They're my favorite."

He quickly debated if he should reveal his source and decided against lying. "I asked Indy."

"Oh." She paused as she rattled around the kitchen, putting something on the stove. "And here I thought you were an incredibly good guesser."

"Sorry to disappoint."

She entered the living room and plopped on the couch near him. She was definitely warming up to him. The worn-thin T-shirt and shorts were far from her teacher clothes. Stretching her legs out, she rested her bare feet on the coffee table.

"Unexpected flowers are never a disappointment." Her smile was warm and genuine.

"Who did you think I was?"

"Huh?" Her eyes squinted and crinkled at the corners with the question.

"At the door. You sounded pissed."

"Sorry. I thought you were Nick. He was outside when I got home." She leaned back and a frown tugged the corners of her mouth.

"What did he want?" He didn't like that her ex found it acceptable to show up unannounced.

"To apologize for last night." She crossed her arms and stared at the TV.

"When did you finally get him out of here?"

She shrugged. "I didn't."

"What do you mean?" He leaned forward and rested his elbows on his knees.

"I tried for hours. Every time I thought I roused him enough, he'd flop back down. I gave up by midnight."

She still wouldn't look at him. She was hiding something.

"Why didn't you call me? I would've come back." He scooted closer to get her attention.

"It wasn't your problem."

Ryan touched her shoulder, drawing her eyes up. "Did he do something to you?"

"No." She followed her answer with a shake of her head.

He felt the familiar niggle of fear clawing below his anger. Before he pressed the issue, a kettle whistled in the kitchen.

"I'm getting tea. Do you want some?"

"No, thanks." He followed her and leaned against the counter while she made her tea. "He did something to upset you."

"He irritated me by crawling into my bed." Her back was to him while she dunked her tea bag.

Ryan moved without thinking. He grabbed her shoulders and spun her around. "What happened?" His fingers tightened involuntarily and her eyebrows drew together.

"None of your damn business."

"Oh." He released her and stepped back. "It's like that."

"No, you don't," she fired at him. "Don't you dare toss a judgmental look my way. Every time I'm at the bar, I see women sliding all over you. I don't judge you."

"I don't fuck every woman I meet."

"And I didn't screw Nick. He slept in my bed. I didn't even realize he was there until I woke up for work." She turned toward the living room and added, "Not that you have any right to question what happens in my bedroom."

She had him there. He'd agreed to be friends. She didn't know he planned on having more. Would he have had the same reaction if it had been another woman? He thought of his sister, and decided, yes, he would. He followed her back to the couch.

"Look, I thought maybe it wasn't consensual. You have the right to sleep with whomever you want." His stomach burned saying it. He wasn't all right with the idea.

She sipped her tea. "I know I do, but thanks for your permission."

"You don't need to get bitchy. I came here to drop off your phone. Here." He pulled it from his pocket and tossed it at the couch.

"Thank you." She curled both hands around her mug and sighed. "I don't want to fight with you. I'm sorry. It was nice of you to send me flowers today. Have a seat. Things with Nick are complicated."

"How? You're divorced, right?"

"We've always been friendly. He shows up now and again to check on me. He came by a few weeks ago because he got some woman pregnant. He needed a friend to talk to."

She looked sad when she talked about Nick. Was she still hung up on him?

He settled beside her on the couch and they fell into a comfortable silence watching the movie. Cameron was complaining about how everything always worked out for Ferris.

Ryan chuckled. "You're Cameron."

Quinn raised an eyebrow as she sipped her tea. "And what, you're Ferris?"

"Without a doubt. I'm the fun one."

"Without a doubt. I'm the responsible one." She sighed and then smiled. "I should've guessed Indy would've put playing hooky on my list. This is one of her all-time favorite movies."

"What's one of yours?"

"Favorite movie?"

"Yeah."

"Hmmm . . . It's toss-up. Either *Benny & Joon* or *Never Been Kissed*. I remember Indy took me to see *Benny & Joon* and when Mary Stuart Masterson looked at Johnny Depp and said, 'Having a Boo Radley moment?' I was the only one in the theater to laugh out loud. I don't think anyone else got it."

It figured. *He* didn't get it.

"Boo Radley? From *To Kill a Mockingbird*? It's a classic."

This woman was more intelligent than he was used to. Maybe she was out of his league.

"What's yours?"

Her question startled him back into the conversation. "That's easy. *Die Hard*."

She shook her head. "Guys. Never happy unless things are blown up."

"Yeah, well, we like excitement." Ryan thought of the relaxed, laughing woman he'd spent yesterday with. "How's your list coming?"

She grunted. "There are eight items on the list. Only one is done, which happened because you dragged me out of here yesterday."

"What's your plan?"

"School is over in less than a week. Then I can focus on nothing but my list."

Ryan looked at her and remembered Indy's advice—help with the list. "What's the next thing on the list?"

"What's your sudden interest in my list?" She leaned forward and put her cup on the table.

"I'm offering my help. What any friend would do." Besides, he planned to be her summer romance. He scooted closer to her.

"I need a karaoke bar and a motorcycle." She crossed her arms and waited.

"At the same time?"

"Ha-ha. No. They're the next two things I want to accomplish."

He'd seen the list. She was still playing pedestrian. She didn't want his help with stripping naked and having a wild orgasm. "What about the second half of the list?"

Her cheeks grew pink. "What about it?"

He wagged his eyebrows at her. "I can help with all of it."

Her laugh was a nervous flutter. "No, you can't."

"I'm sure I can."

She shifted in her seat. "You can't be my summer romance, and the other stuff goes along with it."

"Why can't I be your summer romance? We're off to a good start."

She bit her lower lip, her habit as she considered options. She wouldn't agree that easily.

"You can't be my summer romance. A summer romance ends in the fall. I don't want to not see you anymore." She shoved up from the couch and flicked off the TV in the middle of Ferris singing "Twist and Shout."

"When you start a relationship, you don't give it a deadline. You let it play out."

"I don't want to lose this." She fidgeted and bit her lip before continuing. "I don't have many people I consider real friends. You snuck into a spot and it'll be ruined if we get involved romantically."

Was this Quinn letting him down easy, or did she really believe this? He grasped her hand. The simple gesture brought a smile to her face. So he was back to helping her finish her list, including finding her a date who wasn't a loser, but who couldn't compete with him. "A motorcycle, huh?"

"And a karaoke bar."

He stood, leaned over, and kissed her cheek. "I'll figure it out and call you tomorrow."

After he left, Ryan mulled over the entire problem. He didn't see an easy fix for the mess he'd gotten himself into. He wanted Quinn. She had a valid point about their friendship. Unlike her, he was more of a gambler.

"Hey, Griff, it's me. I need a favor," Ryan said into his cell phone as he drove.

"Since you're calling from your cell, I assume you don't need bail money."

"I haven't needed that since my misspent youth. I need your motorcycle."

"I'm not giving you my bike. You've never driven one."

"I mean, I need you to give someone a ride."

"If this someone is a she, I could probably arrange it."

Ryan kept his sigh from being audible. "Yes, she is a woman. All I need you to do is give her a ride on your motorcycle. Fully clothed."

Griffin's laugh burst over the earpiece. "Are you sure you're not a lawyer? You're always looking to close the loopholes. How hot is she?"

"Don't worry about how hot she is." Quinn wasn't Griffin's type, if he had one. Ryan was pretty sure anyway. "I'm trying to help a friend."

"A friend. Sure. I'm booked for the next day or so, but I think I can squeeze in a motorcycle ride."

"Call me later so we can set up the ride. Thanks, Griff."

"Anything to impress a lady, huh?"

"Yeah." Ryan hung up. He wanted to do more than simply impress Quinn. Ryan needed time to think and plan a list of his own.

Quinn would have her adventures. He'd even help her look for a summer romance. If he could draw out the completion of the list through the end of the summer without Quinn falling for some asshole, she'd have to give him a chance. Summer vacation was less than three months. Quinn hadn't had any luck with her dates so far.

Odds were in his favor.

CHAPTER 6

As the last bell rang ending the last regularly scheduled class of the year, Quinn slid the remaining essays she had to grade into her bag. She'd have to come back for the rest of the week for meetings and in-services and to input her grades, but for all practical purposes, the school year was over. She sighed, hooked her bag on her shoulder, and lifted her vase of daisies. The flowers still brought a smile to her face. They sat in the passenger seat on her ride home.

As she pulled into her parking lot, her phone rang. The caller ID read, "Ryan's Cell." *When did his number make it into my Contacts?* She answered while easing into her usual spot. "Hello."

"Hey, Quinn. It's Ryan. Are you home yet?"

"I just pulled in." She turned off the ignition.

"Good. Your motorcycle is waiting out front."

"Huh?" she asked, mid-reach, trying to grab the vase.

"You said you needed a motorcycle, so I got you one."

"I don't know how to drive a motorcycle."

"This one comes with a driver. Griffin's out front."

"Uh . . ." Her thoughts blurred.

"Hurry up and take your ride. I'll call you later."

He clicked off before she could question or thank him. She fumbled for her keys, forgetting her bagful of essays and her daisies.

She turned the corner of her building and stopped. A leather-clad man leaned against a huge motorcycle. If she had to guess, it was a Harley Davidson. The man's eyes hid behind amber wraparound shades, but she felt his assessing gaze. His black hair ruffled in the breeze, and his five-o'clock shadow looked permanent.

A smile cracked across his chiseled face and lines bracketed his mouth. *Figures Ryan would know a gorgeous, motorcycle-riding bad boy. Too bad Indy's not here. She'd be drooling.*

He stepped forward. "Quinn?"

"Yes."

"I'm Ryan's friend. He asked me to give you a ride." He handed her a leather jacket. "Put this on. When you're riding behind me, either hold on to my waist or these handles next to your seat."

She slid into the jacket. It fit perfectly. What kind of guy carried a woman's leather jacket with him? Did he have a variety of sizes at home?

"Any questions?"

She squinted as she looked up at him. "How safe is this?"

His chuckle didn't make her feel any better, but he pushed a helmet on her head. He climbed on the motorcycle and extended his hand to help her board.

I can do this. She stepped forward and took his hand. The leather surrounding her creaked. She straddled the black seat and gripped the handles beside it, grateful she wore jeans. Her back stiffened as she tried to stop her toes from tapping in her sensible shoes.

The driver called over his shoulder, "You need to relax a little. This won't hurt." He started the engine and the vibration of her entire body caused her eyes to widen.

Her knuckles whitened on the handles, and she clenched her jaw to keep her teeth from rattling. Motorcycle man reached behind him and patted her thigh. The simple, friendly gesture had her rethinking. She didn't know this man. What if he was some nut job taking her somewhere to kill her? What if he was a maniac who planned on scaring her spitless by weaving in between cars on the highway? She hadn't given him any parameters. She didn't even know how long this ride was supposed to last. She had essays to grade.

The motorcycle eased forward a few inches. He was Ryan's friend, so he should be safe. Quinn released the handles and closed the gap between her body and the driver's. Her arms circled his waist and she felt another chuckle rumble his diaphragm.

They sailed out into traffic with her eyes closed. The vibration of the motor under her proved to be calming. She slowly opened her eyes and the city whizzed by. Everyday sights became smudges of watercolor. They zoomed up the onramp to the Kennedy expressway. Her heart sped and her stomach rose to her throat.

It was too early for rush hour traffic, so the lanes were pretty clear. The sun warmed her arms as the black leather absorbed the heat, but the wind cooled her interlocked fingers. She wiggled her fingers to restore circulation.

The abdomen she held was solid. She imagined it naked. The thought made her realize his hips were nestled between her thighs. She took a slow, even breath. *No wonder so many people think motorcycles are sexy.*

At the next exit, they rolled down the ramp and back onto the streets of Chicago. The crowded avenues slowed the motorcycle's pace.

A bead of sweat trickled down her back and her head itched. She wished she were brave enough to ride without a helmet. It must be a fabulous feeling with the sun on your face and wind whipping your hair. *That* would be freedom. Or total stupidity, her sensible side answered.

The motorcycle turned the corner in front of her building and her heart sank. It was like watching a roller coaster edge up the last hill. Like a five-year-old, she wanted to scream, "Again! Again!" Instead, she waited for him to cut the engine.

When the motor stilled, Quinn inched her butt back, pulling her body away from motorcycle man. Twisting his torso, he extended a hand to help her dismount. She tugged the helmet from her head. Her hair stuck to her scalp, and running fingers through it only coated them in sweat.

She handed the driver the helmet. "Thank you for a great ride."

"No problem." He started the engine.

"Wait. Your jacket," she called as she unzipped the leather.

"It's yours. Ryan sent it." He revved the engine and sped away with the helmet strapped to the rear seat.

Quinn stood for a moment and watched as he turned into a speck far down the street. Nerves hummed throughout her body. Her leg muscles tingled. Like spasms after an orgasm. She took an unsure step toward her building. Her weak but excited legs held her up, so she continued.

In her loft, she slid the leather jacket off and folded it over her arm. The scent enveloped her and she inhaled. *Way better than new-car smell.* She laid the jacket on the arm of the couch and picked up the phone.

She needed to share her excitement with someone. Although Ryan deserved a thank you for the ride and the jacket, Quinn dialed Kate's number. She knew it had been Kate who added the motorcycle to the list.

"Hello?" The yelling and banging in the background nearly drowned Kate's voice.

"Hi, Kate. It's Quinn. What's going on?"

"Hey. Nothing. Hold on." Shuffling ensued and Quinn knew Kate took the phone into hiding. "Sorry. The kids decided to do a last day of school parade with every noisemaker they could find."

"Sounds like fun." *Not.*

"Just wait. You'll get your turn eventually. What's going on with you? I haven't heard from you in a while."

"Oh my gosh. You should've told me how great motorcycles are."

Kate laughed. "Who did you find to give you a ride?"

"One of Ryan's friends. Now I know why you were so eager to cut class in college to ride around with what's-his-name."

"His name was Derek. He introduced me to many, many wonderful things." Her voice floated away for a moment. "But your first motor-cycle ride . . . You never forget it."

Quinn stretched out on the couch. "God, it was almost as good as sex."

"Now that's something you should try."

Quinn rolled her eyes. "I think I have. Maybe not often enough, but—"

"I mean sex on the motorcycle, engine running. *So* hot."

"Listen to you. You're a mother of three small kids. You're not supposed to talk like that," Quinn teased.

"They can't hear me and I'm not dead. Like I said, Derek intro-duced me to wonderful things."

Quinn sighed. "Before you get lost in reminiscing about Derek, I need to let you go. I have to get my bag and stuff from my car. I think it's safe since the feeling in my legs has returned to normal."

"I need to check on the kids anyway."

"Thanks for putting it on the list."

"No problem. Thanks for the quick trip down memory lane."

Quinn disconnected and went to her car to grab her bag and rescue her daisies from suffocating in the heat.

She settled back on her couch and took note of the many ways Ryan had insinuated himself into her life—daisies on her table, leather jacket on her couch, postcard stuck to her fridge. He was suddenly everywhere. Her cell phone rang. Ryan. As if she needed to punctuate her previous thought.

"Hi, Ryan."

"How was the ride?"

"Fabulous. Exciting and scary and . . . I don't know, hard to explain." She suddenly felt fifteen babbling to her first boyfriend. "Thank you for arranging it. The jacket, however, is too much."

"Does it fit?"

"Perfectly, but that's not the point."

"Sure it is. It's a memento. Are you free for dinner?"

"Yeah. Where do you want to go?"

"That was easy."

"I have a huge stack of papers to grade, but I'm too pumped to even think about them. I need to wind down first. Plus, I owe you for ditching last week."

"Excellent. I'll be there in thirty minutes."

"I'll be ready."

I'll be ready? What was she thinking? She needed to shower and dress. Her legs muscles may have stopped tingling, but her whole system hummed.

Ryan had a hard time waiting the entire half hour. Quinn sounded so excited; he wanted to see her face.

She buzzed him up without answering the intercom. Her door stood wide open. He'd have to talk to her about the unsafe nature of doing that. He went in and closed the door behind him.

"I'll be down in a minute," her voice floated down to him.

He surveyed the living room. His daisies sat on the table and the leather jacket lay on the couch.

"Are shorts okay?"

"What?" he asked.

"Can I wear shorts, or do I need something less casual?"

"Shorts are fine." He enjoyed seeing her bare legs and hoped sandals would accompany them.

Moments later, she flew down the stairs wearing black shorts and a tank. She wore no makeup, but the smile brightened and colored her face.

"So tell me about your ride."

"I don't know if I can describe it." She paused and closed her eyes. A hand went to her heart. "I was scared. Borderline terrified."

Ryan moved forward and touched her arm. "I told Griffin to take it easy. What did he do?"

"Nothing. Really nothing. He didn't even speak much. It was . . . I don't know." She spread her arms in front of her and stared at the empty space. "This big hulk of a machine I had no control over and I had to trust a guy I'd never met."

Her eyes rose to meet his. "It was fabulous. The noise, the vibration, everything blurring by. It—" She stopped and closed the gap between them.

Her hands reached his shoulders and she brought her face to meet his. Her lips grew hot on his mouth. Her fingers curled into his shirt to pull him closer as her tongue darted into his mouth.

His right hand splayed on her lower back, pressing her close, as their tongues danced. His left hand tugged at the hem of her shirt. He needed to feel her hot skin. As his fingers brushed the bare skin above her hip, she nibbled on his lower lip. Blood pounded and his brain shorted out.

Then she stepped away.

He stared at her. "Wow."

"Yeah, that sums up my ride. Thanks for arranging it." She turned to the front closet. "What are you in the mood for?" As she asked, she bent over to reach for something in the closet.

His dick twitched to answer what he was in the mood for. He was ready to take her right there on the floor. Instead, he answered, "Pizza?"

"Sounds good." She straightened and slid her feet into a pair of strappy sandals. Her toes poked out in vibrant pink, screaming for attention.

He rushed past her and held the door open, hoping she wouldn't notice his hard-on. He'd been friends with plenty of women, some of whom he'd even slept with. He'd never walked around sporting wood as often as he did with Quinn. It wasn't natural. He needed to get laid. In the meantime, he'd have a nice dinner out and enjoy Quinn's company. Unless, of course, he could convince her they could enjoy more of each other's company naked.

Quinn sat in the car and fidgeted like a nervous ball of energy, so unlike the quiet, always-composed Quinn he usually saw. When he pulled up to Sorrentino's Italian restaurant, she popped the door open and jumped out before he even had his keys out of the ignition.

"Something wrong?" he asked as he closed his door.

She turned and clutched the strap of her purse. "I'm sorry. I shouldn't have kissed you. We agreed we'd be better as friends, and I don't want to screw it up by sending mixed signals."

So much for convincing her to get naked.

"I don't know what came over me. I needed to explain the physical high of the motorcycle ride and it just . . ." She grew more flustered with each word. "And you were so nice to arrange the ride and . . ."

"No problem. You caught me a little off guard, but there are worse things to have happen than a kiss." He put his arm over her shoulder and pulled her close. The fruity smell of her hair swirled around him. "Don't let it happen again."

She held up three fingers. "Scout's honor."

Her earnestness disappointed him.

The host showed them to a table immediately. Ryan pulled out a chair for Quinn and sat across from her. The room was dimly lit. Candlelight flickered against her face, making her look sexier.

"Tell me about motorcycle man."

"Who?"

"Griffin. Is this the same guy you gave Indy's card to?"

"Yeah, he's an old friend."

She shrugged. "He didn't seem too friendly. He said all of ten words to me."

Ryan laughed. "I told him to do nothing but give you a ride on the motorcycle."

"Why?"

"Because he's not your type."

She tilted her head and wrinkled her brow. "How do you know what type I want?"

"You're the one who said you wanted me to be your wingman. Griffin's not looking for a romance, summer or otherwise. He's a great guy, but he likes to spread the love."

"You're right. He's probably not my type. I definitely don't need a charming bad boy." She spread her napkin on her lap as the waiter arrived with a bottle of wine. "Have you known him long?"

"Since we were kids." Ryan nodded at the wine selection and the waiter poured two glasses.

"How'd you meet?" She took a slug of wine.

"We went to school together."

"You did?" Her eyes crinkled in confusion.

"Where else would two kids meet?"

"I don't know. I thought . . . he's rich, and rich people usually hang out with other rich people."

He feigned offense. "You think I'm not good enough to hang out with the rich?"

"It's not that. You're not rich. Are you?"

He laughed. "Not by a long shot. But Griffin wasn't born rich. He's worked his ass off for every penny."

She drank more wine, draining the glass. "Sounds like a fascinating story."

The waiter returned and Ryan ordered a garbage pizza. He refilled Quinn's glass.

She leaned forward eagerly. "Tell me."

Ryan felt the nick of jealousy and reminded himself again that Quinn was only a friend. At least for now. Besides, Griffin wasn't her type. "He grew up poor. Poorer than me. His dad took off when he was little, and his mom had to work two jobs to keep them living in a decent neighborhood.

"We met in first grade. The class clown made fun of Griffin's name and he punched the kid. Gave him a bloody nose."

Quinn tucked her hair behind her ear. "Good for him. You were the clown?"

"Yeah, we've been friends ever since."

"Boys bond over the strangest things. How did he become a millionaire?" She sipped her wine now. The nervous energy seeped from her.

"Computers. He discovered everything he could about computers. Hardware, software, all the technical mumbo jumbo. He learned to take the machines apart and rebuild them. Then he learned how to write software. Before he hit twenty-five, he'd created three top-selling video games."

"He's a computer geek." The awe in her voice returned to interest. "He can be my type. Sexy, smart, independent, hardworking."

"Playboy, controlling, demanding."

"No one's perfect. I bet he'd be fun for the summer." She winked at him.

His blood pumped hot. It was one thing for her not to sleep with him, but another to go after his best friend.

The waiter arrived and placed their pizza on a pedestal between them.

Quinn reached up and placed two outer-edged pieces on her plate. "Relax. I'm joking. I'm not going to try to sleep with your friend. That would be tacky. And awkward. It would be like you going out with Indy."

They spent the remainder of the meal chatting about inconsequential things. They finished the bottle of wine and Quinn looked at her watch. She blinked and tapped the face. "Oh my God. We've been here for hours."

"So?" The uptight clock-watcher had returned. He'd wondered how long it would take.

"I have papers to grade."

He signaled to the waiter for the check. "I have to ask. Do you read every single one of them?"

She was genuinely surprised. "Of course. How am I supposed to assign a grade if I don't read it?"

"At the beginning of the year, sure, but you've had these same kids since September. Don't you know who's going to get an A and who'll be lucky to get a D?"

"Yes, mostly."

"So give them the grade."

"I can't do that."

He pulled money from his wallet to cover the bill and tip. "Why not? It would save you hours of work. I bet the kids wouldn't even know."

She sighed heavily. "You're probably right. But the first time I do something like that, it would be my luck to have a kid question the grade. How can I explain the grade when I assign it arbitrarily? Plus, it would feel like cheating."

"Like Indy said, pedestrian."

She shoved away from the table, clearly irritated. "No, *responsible.* I take my job seriously. It's not a game. It's everything to me. I read those papers because they did the work. They deserve for me to hold up my end and read them. I also enjoy seeing their growth. Most of them are different than they were nine months ago."

"I stand corrected. It seemed like an easy solution for you to save time. I didn't mean to offend you. At least not much." He stood and followed her out to the car. Her passion for her job surprised him. He knew she would be good at what she did, but he didn't expect her to get fired up.

In the car, she rummaged in her purse. "What do I owe you for dinner?"

"Nothing. We were celebrating your first ride and another item checked off your list."

She smiled warmly. "Thank you."

When they pulled up to her building, she didn't invite him in. She opened the door and he asked, "Since school is over, will you still be coming to the bar?"

"Sure, sometimes. You're my wingman. I'll have to have you check out my prospects for romance." She closed the door and walked to the apartment.

He waited to make sure she was in safely before pulling away from the curb. He needed to check out her romantic prospects to make sure he had no real competition. Plans formulated in his head that would allow him to simultaneously support and sabotage Quinn's plans.

Girls' night in was an early evening days later. Quinn asked Kate and Indy to come to her house. She needed help developing a plan to conquer the rest of the list. She had turned in her grades and was officially free for the summer. She also wanted to discuss her plans for getting pregnant.

The buzzer rang as she set bowls of chips and dip on the table. She pressed the buzzer. Minutes later, Kate stood in the doorway with all three kids in tow.

"Hi, guys." Quinn hoped the shock in her voice wasn't too apparent.

"I am so sorry. Mark's not home. I should've called and canceled, but I needed to get out of the house. Never underestimate the power of adult conversation."

"No problem. We're kid-friendly." She lowered herself to child-height. "Hi, Kyra."

"Hi, Aunt Quinn." Kyra moved forward and wrapped her arms around Quinn's neck. Her younger siblings attempted to join, but only succeeded in knocking the group to the floor.

"Kyra, get off Auntie and take the bag of toys to the living room." Kate tried to smooth the hair that had escaped her ponytail. She asked Quinn, "Are you sure this is okay?"

Quinn got off the floor. "Why wouldn't it be? It's just us. I'll move the chips to the counter, and the kids can spread out over the couch and table. We can always pop in a Disney DVD for a while."

"Thanks." She picked up four-year-old Thomas and two-and-a-half-year-old Nicole and carried them to the couch. Kyra had already opened a ziplock bag of Little People toys and dumped them in a pile on the area rug in front of the couch.

Quinn set the TV to a kids' show. Kyra looked up at her, "Can I change this?"

Kate answered, "No."

"What's that about?" Quinn asked, nodding her head toward Kyra.

"She asked for your permission, not mine. She's figured out she can ask Daddy for things after I've said no. He usually says yes. God forbid, he think ahead and actually be a parent." Kate sighed heavily. "Sorry, I don't mean to unload on you."

"Unload away. I do it to you. What's going on?" Quinn eased onto a bar stool at the counter. The spot afforded them privacy for a conversation and the ability to keep an eye on the kids.

"I don't know where to start. I'm miserable. Mark is never around. When he is, he plays with the kids and disappears. He's busy. He's tired. What, like I'm not?" She pulled a chip from the bowl and ate it. "This is lunch for me."

"I'll make you a sandwich for now and we'll order dinner in a while."

"I'd rather have a margarita."

"I can do that too." Quinn moved into the kitchen and pulled out a blender and margarita mix. "Go on."

"I think Mark might be overwhelmed by everything, but I don't know because he's not talking to me. He works more and more hours every week. I talk to his voice mail more than I do him." She munched on another chip.

"I can take the kids for a night, or even a weekend if it would help. Maybe you guys need some alone time. I can't imagine trying to have a serious heart-to-heart with the kids around." Quinn poured drink mix and dumped ice cubes into the blender and pulsed the concoction.

"I might take you up on that. I'll have to check with Mark and his forever-growing schedule."

"Let me know when. I'm a free woman for the entire summer. I don't remember the last time I had a summer off. I don't know what to do with myself. The kids will be a nice distraction."

Kate took the glass Quinn handed her. "You have things to do. You have a list to accomplish and romance to find."

The buzzer rang again. Kyra jumped off the couch. "Can I get it?"

"Sure. Press the intercom button and ask who it is."

Kyra stood on tiptoe in front of the intercom and pressed the button. "Who is it?"

"You have to let go of the button for them to answer," Kate said.

She let go of the button.

"It's Indy. Let me up."

Kyra needed no further direction. She pressed the other button and danced in place. "Auntie Indy's here." She pulled the door open and peered out. When the elevator dinged, she ran out in the hall. "Auntie Indeeee!"

"Why don't I get that kind of welcome?" Quinn asked as Indy came through the door carrying Kyra.

"Because I'm the fun aunt." She deposited Kyra on the couch and tossed her purse over the back of one of the stools.

"I'm fun."

Indy rolled her eyes. "Sure you are. In the conventional, safe kind of way. I break the rules."

"Whatever." Quinn knew she was right. It irked her to hear it out loud, though. Kyra loved her too. She didn't need her name screamed in the hallway to prove it.

"Early for drinks, isn't it?"

"Rough day," Kate answered.

Indy took a swig from Kate's glass and looked over at the couch. "With the three of them, I'd think every day would be rough."

Kate took her glass back. "Most are good. And they're not the problem."

"Mix one up for me," Indy said to Quinn, who was already back at the blender. "What's wrong in *Leave It to Beaver*-land?"

"I wish my life were a TV sitcom. I don't want to think about it anymore. Quinn needs help."

Quinn knew this would be difficult. Announcing life-altering decisions over margaritas would cause a stir, but she needed Indy's and Kate's support. She decided to rip off the bandage, get it over with, so she blurted, "I'm going to get artificially inseminated."

Indy stared at her. "You're crazy. I know you want to be a mom, but have you considered how hard it will be to do it all alone? There will be so much you won't be able to do."

Kate interjected, "Indy has a point. I'm in the thick of it. I can't go to a movie whenever I want. The thought of a vacation brings chills. I can't remember the last time I went shopping for myself where I got to try things on before purchasing them."

Quinn turned toward Kate. "But would you change anything?"

Kate smiled. "No, I wouldn't."

"See?" Quinn turned back to Indy. "That look on Kate's face? I want that." She took a deep breath before continuing. "This is not the life I planned. I'm supposed to be married with a couple of kids and a house in the suburbs by now. Nothing I've been doing has worked, so I've developed an alternate plan."

"But you're alone," Kate said. "Regardless of how rocky my marriage is, I have Mark to fall back on. His paycheck allows me to stay at home with the kids. If I need to run out in the middle of the night for Tylenol because a kid is sick, he's there. I have support."

"You said yourself Mark doesn't do a whole lot when it comes to the kids. He loves them and plays with them, but you're the one who takes them to school and the doctor. You're the one who takes care of them when they're sick. What is his involvement?"

Kate's eyelids lowered and she shrugged.

Indy moved forward. "She at least has a sense of help. If it was really important, Mark would step up."

"Millions of women are single moms and they manage. They manage with little or no education, a low-paying job, and no benefits. I'm already so far ahead of so many people. I can handle this. I'm not naïve. I joined an online loop for single moms a few weeks ago. It's opened up their world to me."

Quinn went to her desk and pulled out her master schedule and plan. "Look. I've thought it all through."

"What the hell is that?" Indy asked.

"It's my plan. I started with conception dates because really, everything hinges on that." She pointed to the calendars coded in yellow, purple, and green. "These show the dates I can conceive and have a summer baby. If I give birth over the summer, I don't have to take any time off work. If I come too close to the start of the school year, I have sick days saved that I can use, but with any luck, I'll get pregnant earlier and have the whole summer with my baby."

"What about the cost? Most families are struggling with two incomes."

Indy obviously thought she was an idiot. "I have enough money saved that I can try to get pregnant three times. The odds aren't in my favor. It takes an average of six times, but I'm hoping I won't need that. Insurance covers the actual pregnancy."

She flipped the page to show her income and expenditures. "The only thing that I'm iffy on is whether I should sell the loft and get a small house or stay here for a couple of years. Sooner or later, I'm going to want a house and a yard for my kid."

Kate moved closer to inspect the charts, graphs, and lists. "You definitely did your homework."

Indy shook her head. "I think you're nuts. You need to make sure you've lived all the life you want before you trap yourself. Even if it is a trap of your own making."

"Nothing's definite yet. I haven't talked to a specialist. I've been doing research. Did you know for five hundred dollars I can order sperm online? Not only that, but I can choose a guy's height, weight, eye and hair color, education, race, and nationality? It's insane. Click-click and I choose a father who looks like me."

"No way," Kate said.

"Seriously. I spent a good hour the other night playing around with it."

Indy shook her head. "I think you need to spend more time with kids and less playing who's the baby's daddy."

"I have plenty of experience with kids. I babysat all through high school and college. But just to prove to the two of you that it's no big deal, I'm offering to take Kate's kids for a while. No big deal."

Kate's eyes lit. "Name the time and they'll be here."

Quinn continued to lay out her plan. "I've planned out the timing for this. If I take my vacation in early August, I can come home, choose my donor, and inseminate by the beginning of the school year." She sipped on her drink and waited for Indy's next blast.

"What's your hurry? You have plenty of time."

"I told you before. I'm tired of waiting for life to happen. I'm going after what I want, but I'm still researching to figure out what the best course of action is for me."

One side of Indy's mouth lifted. "I know you. If you're bringing it up to us, you've already made up your mind."

Quinn bit her lip. "The more I look into it, the more people I talk to, the more excited I get. The prospect of having a baby and being a mom makes me feel like I've found the missing component in my life."

Kate reached out and covered Quinn's hand. "We're here for you."

"Good, because I need help with a couple of things on the list," Quinn answered.

"What's next?"

"I need a karaoke bar, somewhere to pose nude, and a summer romance. And I need to figure out where to take my vacation."

"Sure, let me whip out my phone book," Indy responded.

"You don't need to be sarcastic. I'm looking for ideas. Obviously my usual way of doing things isn't working. I should get bonus points for asking for help instead of finding the easy way."

"Go to the Art Institute and some other local colleges. They might have a bulletin board advertising for models for the art classes." Kate put her drink down and swiveled off her chair. "I'll be right back. The kids are too quiet. They must've gotten into something."

"Let's talk vacations. What kind of atmosphere are you looking for?" Indy asked.

"I have no idea. I suppose it would depend on whether or not I find my summer romance before I go on my trip."

"You're supposed to go alone. That's the deal."

"I know. But if I don't have a summer romance, I'll be depressed, so I'll need someplace to cheer me up. A place with a high male-to-female ratio so I can find someone there, so I can have a quickie romance."

Kate came back to the counter.

"Kids okay?" Quinn asked.

"Yeah, they were smelling the beautiful daisies on the table and pretending their Little People were getting married. It was kind of cute." She took a drink. "I say regardless of whether or not you find a man, you go somewhere fun."

"Like?"

"The Bahamas," Indy offered.

"I don't think I want beach. I don't know if I'll have to start taking hormones. What if they make me feel bloated and fat? No swimsuits."

The buzzer sounded and Kyra shot up again. "I'll get it."

Indy looked at Quinn. "Expecting someone?"

Quinn shook her head. "You guys."

"Who is it?" Kyra asked into the intercom.

"This is Ryan. Is Quinn home?"

"Yeah," Kyra answered, but didn't move to buzz him up.

"Can I come up?"

"I don't know." Kyra looked over at Quinn.

"Let him in, Kyra. He's a friend."

"Spending a lot of time with your *friend*, aren't you?" Indy leaned forward, expecting juicy gossip.

Quinn turned back to the blender. "I spend a lot of time with you, too, and you're nothing special."

"Hey, Auntie. He's not on the elevator," Kyra called from the hall.

"He always takes the stairs. Give him a few minutes." Right after she said it, she heard the stairwell door clunk.

"Hi," Ryan's voice echoed in the hall. "I'm Ryan. Who are you?"

"I'm Kyra."

"Nice to meet you, Kyra. Can I go in to see Quinn?"

"Sure." Kyra reentered the loft, tugging Ryan behind her.

He looked around the open space. Quinn tried to imagine how he would view it. In the short time they'd been there, Kate's kids had managed to make a huge mess in her living room. Toys and crayons were scattered across the floor.

Kyra released his hand and closed the door. Ryan carefully stepped over toys and around toddlers. Nicole looked up and smiled at him. He wiggled his fingers at her and she waved back.

"Hi, Ryan." Indy got off her stool and kissed his cheek. "It's been a while."

"Hi." He nodded to Kate. "I'm guessing the kids are yours?"

"You guess right. You met Kyra in the hall. That's Thomas and Nicole," she said, pointing to each child.

"Hi." Quinn finally turned away from the blender. The last time she'd seen Ryan, she practically threw herself at him. It didn't matter that they'd shared a friendly dinner afterward, the embarrassment still hung around her. So did the flurry of heat in remembering the kiss. "What brings you by?"

"I wanted to give you this." He slid a flyer on the counter next to the chips.

She picked up the glossy paper with writing in deep blue and purple: THE TWILIGHT CLUB. "What's this?"

"It's a good blues bar, but once a month, it's karaoke night. Next Thursday is the next night."

"Thanks."

"Well, aren't you a knight in shining armor," Indy purred.

"Huh?" He took a chip, slathered it in dip, and popped it in his mouth.

"We were discussing this list and Quinn's plan of attack. By my count, you've helped her with roughly half the list."

He popped another chip in. "I'm doing what any friend would. I've offered to help with the second half of the list, but she declined."

Indy laughed.

Quinn's face warmed.

"So what's next on the list?" he asked.

Indy answered, "We were telling Quinn where she should go—"

Quinn saw the glint in Indy's eyes and cut her off. "On vacation." She did not want Ryan's help figuring out where to pose nude.

"She needs to go somewhere alone," Kate said.

"And it can't be job-related," Indy tossed in.

"A job-related vacation?" Ryan asked.

"Whenever she goes on vacation, she explores things she can go back and teach. She'll visit the graves of dead authors and stuff. This needs to be about her." Indy's smile held something devious. Quinn was afraid to wonder what.

"How about Vegas?"

"No," all the women said in unison.

"Whoa." Ryan put his hands up. "Just a suggestion. Nothing academic in Vegas."

"I don't do Vegas," Quinn said grimly.

Ryan eased his hip against the last free stool. "Why not?"

"Nick and I were married in Vegas."

Ryan choked on a chip. "*You* got married in Vegas?"

"Yes." Quinn turned her back on them and wiped off the counter. "You want a margarita?"

"No, thanks."

Quinn gulped her margarita. She hated talking about Nick and her pathetic wedding and marriage. It seemed so romantic at the time. A whirlwind romance, a cross-country drive. They landed in Vegas and got married in a little white chapel.

She hadn't done anything spontaneous since.

"Let's think of some other places to go. Florida?" Kate nudged them forward in conversation.

With her composure regained, Quinn turned back to her guests. "I am not going to Disney World alone."

"There's more to Florida than Disney World," Kate said.

"Yeah, beaches. No, I want something different."

"New York." Indy's eyes lit. "There's shopping, night life, shopping, restaurants, shopping . . ."

"Crowds, rude people, and I don't like to shop that much."

Kate rested her chin in her hand. "How about Niagara Falls?"

Quinn crossed her arms over her midsection. "I want to go there, but I'm saving it."

"For what?"

"It's where my mom and dad had their honeymoon." She sighed. "I always hoped I could go there on mine too."

Indy pushed away from the counter. "I think it's time to have intelligent conversation. I'm going to talk to the kids."

Quinn's eyes closed and she shook her head. She hated not being able to mention her parents in front of Indy.

Kate's voice was full of sympathy. "Don't worry. She'll be fine. You know how she gets when it comes to your parents."

"New Orleans," Ryan blurted.

Quinn and Kate both looked at him.

"Don't tell me there's another ex-husband who married you in Louisiana."

Quinn smiled and shook her head. He'd done it again. She wouldn't have thought of New Orleans.

"New Orleans is full of culture. It won't be as exciting this time of year as it would be during Mardi Gras, but since you don't like crowds, you'll enjoy it."

Indy didn't get up from her spot on the floor with the kids, but she called out, "That makes it exactly half the list you've helped with. What's his reward, Quinn?"

"No reward necessary," Ryan said, much to Quinn's relief. "I have to get back to the bar. I'll call you tomorrow. Enjoy your night."

On his way to the door, Thomas stepped in front of Ryan and handed him a truck with its wheel popped off. "It's broke."

Ryan knelt down and held out his hands. "Let me see." He fiddled with it for a few minutes and reattached the wheel. He handed the truck back to Thomas and ruffled his hair on his way past. "Absorb all you can, little guy. This might be last time they let you hang out in a roomful of girls."

"Real funny, O'Leary. We didn't throw you out," Quinn called.

"Only because I'm charming. And I'm your problem solver."

He slipped out the door before Quinn could respond. She couldn't argue. He'd been charming from day one, which is why she refused to go out with him. Since then, he had proved to be quite the problem solver. He'd become a better friend than she imagined.

She clapped her hands. "Okay, looks like I'm going to New Orleans."

Indy leaned her arms on the counter. "Now that the vacation is settled, you guys didn't notice the present Richard gave me. I wore my hair up to show them off, but I guess vacations and baby talk trump jewelry." Indy shifted her head so the lighting caught and sparkled on the sapphires dangling from her ears. "What do you think?"

"They're beautiful," Quinn responded. She personally preferred jewelry less flashy, but they looked perfect on Indy.

Indy inclined her head toward Kate.

"It's not a diamond ring," Kate pointed out.

Indy's face turned cold. "Why do you always try to ruin my happiness? What kind of friend are you?"

Kate stiffened. "I'm the friend who's been telling you what a mistake Richard is from the moment you told us the whole story. He is *married*. All you're going to get is hurt."

Indy's eyes flashed with anger. "He's getting a divorce. You need to accept we all don't want the perfect marriage you have. Richard offers me a good time. It's all I'm looking for."

Quinn would never understand Indy's affinity for unattainable men. Indy never searched for any permanency in her life. Quinn, on the other hand, couldn't wait to be tied down with a family.

CHAPTER 7

Ryan and Griffin sat on the black leather couch in Ryan's living room. They each held a bottle of beer. The White Sox game played on the TV for lack of anything more interesting to watch. Ryan shifted in his seat. He hadn't been able to get Quinn out of his head for the past week. The more time he spent with her, the more he wanted her, and the more he realized he needed to distance himself from her. Nothing was working, though.

"If you don't sit still, I'm going to hit you. What's wrong?" Griffin threw one arm over the back of the couch and leaned back into the corner.

"It's Quinn."

"How can you be so hung up on her? You just met."

"I'm not hung up. I told her I'd help her with her list. What do you know about speed dating?"

"Not much. I've never done it. All I know is a bunch of people move from table to table and try to hook up in a couple of minutes."

"I'm thinking of setting up a speed dating night at O'Leary's. What do you think?"

"Isn't your bar already a place where people go to pick up strangers?"

"The format takes the awkwardness out of it. I think it'd be easier for shy people."

"Like Quinn. I can't believe you're trying to . . . woo her."

"Woo? Who the fuck says that?"

"I can't think of another word to fit. You're going out of your way to do a bunch of crap to make her like you. What's next, a love poem? Why don't you ask her out?"

Ryan puffed out his cheeks with a breath of frustration. "I have. She won't date me because I can't be her summer romance."

"Why not?"

"Because her romance ends with summer. If we get involved, we'd lose our friendship."

"That makes no fucking sense." He stood to get another beer.

Ryan shrugged. "It's her list, her plan."

From the kitchen, Griffin called, "When the hell are you going to unpack all of these boxes? I'm tired of stepping around them at every turn. How important could the crap be if it's been in boxes for two years?"

"It's probably not important. This was a temporary move, remember?" An easy place to go and lick his wounds after Cassie dumped him.

"What do you tell women when you bring them here?"

"I don't bring them here."

Griffin returned carrying two fresh bottles of beer. He popped the cap off one beer and took a drink. He set the other on the table in front of Ryan. "So you're going to help her find some other guy?"

Ryan settled back in the couch. "No. Yes." At Griffin's raised eyebrow, he continued, "I'm going to help her complete her list, making sure she doesn't find a guy better than me."

"And you say you're not hung up on her."

The following afternoon before the crowds picked up at the bar, Ryan called Mary into his office. The petite blonde entered and closed the door behind her.

"What's up?" she asked, still holding the towel she'd been using to wipe down the bar.

"Remember when you asked about setting up a speed dating night?"

"Yeah, I remember. You shot me down."

Ryan smiled at the spunk of his manager. "I didn't shoot you down. I had other, more pressing projects. Like running another bar. Do you still have the information?"

Mary hopped a little with excitement. "I can do it?" She straightened. "I mean, we can do it?"

"Put together the information. How long will it take to plan it, what would the bar be responsible for, how many people we'd need on staff, how much business we'd lose to close for the event. You get the picture."

"Can I ask why the sudden change of heart?"

"Someone I know told me how difficult it is to meet someone. I'm trying to help her out." He settled back in his chair and thought of Quinn. She was enough of a reason for the headache Mary caused.

"Her?"

Ryan nodded. "A friend."

"If you say so. I'll be out front if you need me."

The last thing he'd do was ask any more questions. Mary pontificated enough on the merits of planned singles events to last him a long time. He wanted to kick back and relax. Without thinking, he dialed Quinn's number.

"Hello?"

"Hi. It's Ryan."

"Hi. How's it going?" Her voice melted across the line like warm butter.

Yes, she was well worth the headache. "My manager talked me into hosting a speed dating night here at the bar. I assume you'll be up for it. Your Romeo might be there."

"You need to stop trying to fulfill everything on my list. These are supposed to be things I accomplish."

"You will accomplish them. I'm providing extra opportunities. Besides, there are things on your list that require a partner." He imagined her stripping naked for him. He'd like to see her lose total control—during orgasm.

"I appreciate the opportunities, but it feels like cheating."

"How's the rest of the list coming?"

"I want to kill Indy for making me pose nude. I've scoured so many art classes this week. I hoped to find a senior citizen group to pose for. I figured it would be less embarrassing."

"Now, *that* would be cheating."

"I know. I didn't have any luck anyway. One class I answered an ad for was horrible. I walked in thinking I'd ask questions, get some information; instead, I found myself staring into a roomful of naked people. It was like being part of a nudist colony. I was mortified."

"Hold on. Let me grab a pen. Now where was this?" He pretended to fumble for a pen on his desk.

She laughed. "You're funny. They all weren't naked, but the group in the middle of the room was. In retrospect, it might not be as terrifying if I wasn't the only one in the room naked, but it caught me off guard. I couldn't even speak. I turned thirty shades of red and bolted."

"I can come by with my camera if you want. You can pose for me." He toyed with the idea of where it could lead.

"No, thanks. I'm talking to photographers tomorrow. Hopefully it will go better. What have you been up to?"

He heard her shift her position and pictured her curling her legs under her on the couch, settling in comfortably. Like she planned to hang on and talk for a while. "I've been working. Nothing exciting. What are you doing with all your free time?"

"Looking for a place to get naked. Sounds crazy. I also looked into planning my vacation to New Orleans at the end of the summer."

"So you liked my idea. You'll have a great time. Next time we get together, I can give you some ideas of places to go. Actually, Griffin would know. I've only gone once, during Mardi Gras, so there are some blanks for me. He's been there a few times. He could tell you the best of everything so you don't waste your time."

"Thanks, I appreciate it."

"What else have you been up to?"

Her quiet told him she had something going on but wasn't sure if she wanted to tell him. When had he become so adept at understanding her moods? "Come on, spill it."

"I've been thinking about getting pregnant."

The air left his lungs as silence swallowed the room. She planned to have some guy get her pregnant? It didn't make sense. It didn't even fit who Quinn was. He didn't even know what an appropriate reaction was. "Why?"

"Because I really want to be a mom." Her deep breath sounded in his ear. "The thing is, I always thought I'd find the right guy, get married, and have babies. That was always my plan. I want a family more than I've ever wanted anything. I've decided that after I complete my list this summer, I'm going it alone. I want a baby."

Indy should've told him, at least warned him off. Instead, she pushed Ryan in the direction he wanted, which was straight into Quinn. He remembered Quinn telling him she didn't want to be alone. He couldn't understand her fear. He'd always had family. Even when they drove him crazy, they were his and he would never be alone.

Ryan swallowed the pity stuck in his throat. "You won't ever really be happy. You have to know that. You're the kind of girl who wants the whole deal."

"I can't find the whole deal. You've seen the dates I find. The men I attract. You're a guy. You don't get it. You have years to decide to have kids. Women have an expiration date."

"So you'll settle for half of what you really want."

"Half is better than nothing."

He wished they were face-to-face. He wanted to touch her, shake her until she saw what a mistake she was making. They mumbled good-bye with plans to talk later.

This at least explained why she kept pushing him away. Her plan didn't make any sense to him. It wasn't like she couldn't still find someone. She was just so closed off, most people found it hard to see past her defenses. But he had and he wanted more.

Raucous laughter reached him from the bar, pulling him from his thoughts about Quinn. Not the normal lunch crowd noise.

Sure enough, Colin sat on a stool, telling stories to the crowd around him. Everyone loved Colin.

Some things never change.

Ryan didn't interrupt but turned back to his office. He wasn't quick enough.

"Ryan. Wait."

He looked over his shoulder and saw Colin make parting gestures to his new friends. Ryan continued to his office.

Moments later, Colin entered and closed the door behind him. "Do you have time to talk? I've been trying to catch up with you for days. I figured I'd get you here."

Ryan settled behind the huge solid oak desk that had been their father's. All of the fixtures in the room had been standing in the same spot for more than a decade. Except the chair. Ryan had replaced his father's broken chair with a high-end black leather desk chair. "What do you want? I have work to do."

Colin rubbed his hands together. A sure sign of another scheme. "That's what I want to talk to you about. Work."

Ryan leaned back and waited for the pitch. He wouldn't be as easily sucked in as their father had.

"Look. I know I left on bad terms after Dad died." He took a seat in front of Ryan, making them eye level. "But you have to admit I had reason to be pissed off. This bar was supposed to be mine."

Ryan leaned forward, putting his elbows on the desk. "You had the bar and you fucked it up, so Dad brought me back in."

Colin raised his hands in surrender. "I know. It took a lot of time, but I get it. Dad spent his life building this place and I almost totally screwed it up."

He hadn't expected that. An admission of guilt from Colin? Ryan didn't respond and waited for the lead-in.

Colin stood and walked the room, touching various pieces of furniture. "I'm not making excuses, but I was young. The bar was already established. I didn't think about the work Dad did daily."

"Sounds like excuses to me. I was no older than you when I started Twilight. From the bottom."

"But you had Dad's support. And money."

Ryan stood. "Is that what this is about? Dad gave me the seed money for Twilight, sure, because he knew I loved this place and I wanted to run it. But because you're first-born, he felt he had to pass it on to you. I worked my ass off to make Twilight a success. Three years after I opened, I was in the black and I bought Dad out."

Colin's eyebrows shot up on his forehead. The information was news to him.

"Dad was a partner in Twilight only for three years. I've been sole owner since. There is no money for you there."

Colin hung his head. "I wasn't looking to get a cut of Twilight. I know it's yours. I'm proud of what you built there." He met Ryan's gaze. "I want to build my own bar."

Ryan crossed his arms on his chest. Here it comes. "What do you want from me?"

"Help." He moved back to the chair in front of the desk. "I want to move back here permanently and buy a bar."

Ryan didn't move. "I'm not giving you money to throw out the window on a whim."

Colin stiffened. "It's not a whim. I've been thinking for a long time. I miss the family."

"So visit more often. It'll give you more chances to break Mom's heart."

"Shit. You're not going to make this easy." Colin ran his fingers through his hair.

Ryan offered a slight shrug. "Why would I? Dad always made it too easy for you."

"He did. No argument there. He should've kicked my ass a long time ago. But he didn't and he's gone. You're not him." Colin paced the windowless room again.

"Are you done? I have work to do," Ryan reminded his brother.

"When did we stop being able to talk to each other?"

"When you decided Dad's money was more important than family. You walked away and I've had to step up for everyone." Recalling the nights of juggling two bars to keep them afloat and his mother's weeping and depression made him weary. "We needed you."

Colin leaned against the small table along the wall and tucked his hands into his pockets. "I'm sorry. I was too busy being selfish to understand. I've changed."

Ryan returned to his seat and picked up mail he needed to sort. "I should take your say-so."

"No, I'll prove it. I went to bartending school a couple of years ago. I want a job."

Ryan's head shot up, expecting a joke from Colin. His brother was full of surprises today. "You want to work for me?"

"How better for me to prove I'm serious? The more time I spend here, the more I'll learn how to run a bar the right way."

Damn. The sincerity in Colin's face hit him hard. He was cornered and they both knew it. As much as he wanted to turn Colin away, he couldn't. *Mom would kill me if she found out I wouldn't at least give him a job.* "I'll check the schedule. My regular people get the best shifts. I won't give you preferential treatment."

Colin straightened with an eager smile. "I'll take whatever you got. Here or at Twilight. But I'd prefer here."

"Jeans and a bar shirt are fine for here, but you need black dress pants for Twilight. I'll provide the shirt there too."

"Thanks. You won't regret this."

"I hope not. I'll call you later after I check the schedule."

"Okay."

"Now leave. I have work to do."

"I can help."

Ryan pointed to the door. Colin left, closing the door behind him. Ryan rocked back in his chair and drummed his fingers on the armrests. He hoped Colin was back for good. Their mother couldn't handle much more heartache.

He wanted to believe Colin had changed, but he'd watched their father's hopes get trampled by Colin too many times. Patrick O'Leary had wanted his two eldest sons to work side by side and run the bar. Maybe add a couple of bars and create an O'Leary empire.

Colin's irresponsibility washed the dream away.

Ryan straightened and focused on his clipboard. He couldn't change the past, just guard his family in the future. His life had gotten even more complicated since Colin's return. How could he start a relationship with Quinn when he had to protect everyone from Colin? Maybe it was a good thing they were only friends.

As he picked up the phone to call a supplier, the raucous laughter erupted from the bar again.

Yep, some things never change.

Quinn was tired of talking to artists and wannabes. She hadn't thought it would be so difficult to find a class to pose nude for. She'd spent the morning looking for photographers. She could always pay someone to take her picture. In her mind, though, she justified being painted naked by strangers as art.

Paying a photographer would feel like porn.

She walked to the address she'd gotten during her search. Finding a photographer with her own studio was a priority. She couldn't bare all in a storefront studio where any stranger walking past could see.

She'd been surprised to find one not only in her neighborhood, but only a few blocks away. The building looked almost identical to hers.

She rang the bell. The intercom buzzed her in. No one asked for her name or the reason for her visit. The bell for Hill Studio was marked 2B, so she walked up a flight of metal stairs and said a silent prayer she wasn't walking into the den of a serial killer.

The door to 2B looked much like her own metal door. She knocked and questioned her sanity. Someone called out from inside, but the heavy door muffled the actual words.

The locks clunked and the door swung open. A man stood before her and the only word that came to mind was *hot*. She rolled her gaze over an athletically muscled torso covered by a thin, taut T-shirt. Her journey stopped at wide warm brown eyes. *If this is the model the photographer is used to, I'm in trouble.*

"Hi. Can I help you?"

I wouldn't mind seeing you pose. "Uh, yeah. My name is Quinn Adams. I called earlier."

"That's right. Cindy told me. Come on in."

Quinn stepped into the loft. Shades, umbrellas, sheets, tripods, and cameras were stationed across the huge space. *This is either a real studio or the serial killer is putting up a great front.*

"Can I get you a bottle of water?"

Quinn hadn't paid any attention to where the sexy man went until his voice jarred her. He stood next to a mini-fridge in the corner. "No, thanks."

"Okay." He grabbed a bottle for himself and gestured to two chairs near the wall where he stood. "Have a seat."

She settled in one of the chairs and gripped her purse in her lap. He sat on the edge of the chair opposite her and leaned forward with his elbows on his knees.

"What can I do for you, Ms. Adams?"

"Not to be rude, but I'd prefer to speak directly with the photographer."

He smiled crookedly. "Shoot."

"You're the photographer? I thought the woman I spoke with this morning was the photographer." The grip on her purse tightened.

"Sorry about the confusion. Cindy is my assistant. I'm Xander Hill." He extended his hand with the introduction.

Quinn stared at this man who only minutes prior was nothing more than eye candy. She tried to realign her thoughts. When she'd called in the morning, she didn't ask any questions, just asked for a time to stop by for information. This is what happened when she didn't do enough research.

She abruptly stood. "I'm sorry. This won't work. I apologize for any inconvenience."

He stood, looking alarmed. "Did I say something to offend you?"

"No. No, I expected—assumed—you were a woman." She fumbled to get the purse strap on her shoulder.

He reached out and slid the strap in place for her. "He's one lucky guy."

Why is he touching me? Quinn stepped to the side. "Who's lucky?"

"Whoever you plan to have photos taken for. A nude photo says a lot about the trust and strength in a relationship." Xander walked to the desk on the opposite wall and flipped through a Rolodex.

Quinn stood, stunned. She hadn't said what kind of photos she wanted taken. "What makes you think I want nude photos?"

He looked up from the note he scribbled. "You blushed when you realized I'm the photographer. The only people who blush are those who think about getting naked in front of a stranger."

"Oh."

"Here." He handed her a slip of paper. "She's a photographer. Not as good as me, but she's female."

"You're sending me to your competition?"

"Honestly, I'd prefer for you to have a seat, look through my portfolio, and give me a chance. But if you can't get comfortable around me, Cathy is a safe bet. I'd rather see her get the work than some hack you find on the Internet."

Quinn swallowed the giggle in her throat. "I found you on the Internet."

"Not everyone on the Web is a hack, but you can't tell from the computer. Take one of my cards in case you change your mind." He held out a glossy black business card with silver lettering.

In a matter of minutes, Xander had put her at ease. He seemed legitimate. Maybe he warranted another look. "Have you done these kinds of pictures before?"

His smile was slow and easy. "Quite a few. Would you like to see my portfolio?"

"I think so. Yeah." She returned to the chair and put her purse on the floor.

Xander joined her and held out a three-inch-thick black book.

Quinn flipped open the cover. A woman lay on her stomach, resting her head on her hand. From the angle, Quinn knew the woman was naked, but she couldn't "see" anything. She turned the page, fascinated. Women of all sizes and colors, in every pose imaginable, from playful and flirty to serious and thoughtful. Some photos were in black and white, and others in full color.

She lingered over each page. Part of her felt like she was looking at a girlie magazine, but the rational, critical part of her realized she was looking at art.

Quinn closed the book and found she was alone. Xander was nowhere in sight. Odd, she hadn't heard him go anywhere. She looked at her watch. She'd been studying his portfolio for nearly an hour.

"Hello? Mr. Hill?"

"I'll be right there."

Quinn walked across the room and saw a back room she hadn't noticed before.

Xander came from the room eating a sandwich. "Finished?"

"Yes, I'm sorry I took so long. I totally lost track of time. You're good."

He put the sandwich down on a nearby table and wiped his hands on his jeans. She handed him the portfolio. He took it and asked, "Do you have any questions?"

"No, I don't think so. I wouldn't even know what to ask."

"Are the photos for an anniversary or birthday gift or what?"

The question shattered through Quinn's good mood. "Nothing. They're not a present."

His eyes narrowed a fraction. "So what's the purpose, if you don't mind my asking?"

Quinn blew a breath, puffing the bangs away from her face. "It's a pretty long story. Basically, my sister and my friend created a list of adventures for me to accomplish with my summer off, to break me out of my comfort zone. Posing nude is on the list. So I guess they're for me." Her ears burned and she stared at her feet.

"That is one of the best reasons I've ever heard for doing nudes."

Her eyes shot up. She expected to see him on the verge of laughter, but he was serious.

"If you're interested, I'd like very much to take your portraits."

The heat spread to her neck. She felt naked with his eyes on her. "I don't know. Would I end up in your portfolio?"

He laughed. "Not unless you want to. I have permission to use all of those photos. If at any point a client asks me to pull theirs, I will."

If he were half as honest as he appeared, she'd be in good hands. "So what happens? I come to the studio one day and get naked?"

"Pretty much."

She shivered at the thought. "I'll have to think about it. I thought I could do this, but I'm not sure."

"You have my card and Cathy's number. It won't be as painful as you imagine." His gaze wandered the length of her. "Would you like to go to the deli down the street? It could be a working lunch. I'll give you my professional background and you can tell me what you're looking for. If we're not a good fit, we go our separate ways and you call Cathy."

Quinn's mind screamed, "Bad idea," but her gut whispered, "He looks like fun." Before she responded to his offer, the loft door swung open.

"Cindy, this is Quinn Adams, prospective client."

Cindy crossed the room in a halter-top and short-shorts. Her blond hair stood up in short spikes revealing brown roots. Her sandals flapped against the concrete floor as she approached.

"Hi." She extended her hand. "We spoke this morning." The smooth, professional voice didn't match the incredibly young exterior.

"Yes, we did."

"You won't regret hiring Xander. He's the best." The statement came from an adoring fan, much more package-appropriate.

"I haven't hired him yet." Quinn felt old. "I better get going."

"It was nice to meet you," Cindy said. Xander simply nodded as Quinn turned to leave.

I'm such a chicken. Indy was right.

CHAPTER 8

Quinn and Indy pushed through the smoky glass doors of Twilight. Quinn stood still while her eyes adjusted to the atmosphere. The room immediately gave off the same feeling as the glossy flyer Ryan had given her. Sleek and mellow. The tables were black and shiny, as was the bar itself. A purplish glow illuminated the edge of the bar.

It was like stepping into a vintage movie. She could almost smell the clouds of cigarette smoke that would've hung in the air if Chicagoland hadn't gone smoke-free. Even as a nonsmoker, she could appreciate a smoke-filled blues bar. She scanned the area to find Indy. The woman walked like she owned the place. She flicked her wrist for Quinn to follow. She'd already nabbed a table.

Quinn wove through the crowd carefully, afraid her short dress would ride up if she walked too quickly. As it was, she had to remind herself not to tug at it. She cursed Indy's taste in clothes. In payment for being the designated driver, Indy chose Quinn's outfit. Being totally sober and embarrassed in front of a crowd was sounding better than having even one stranger get a peek at her bare ass.

Indy sat at the outer edge of the seating area at a booth with high-backed seats. They only had a view of the stage and dance floor. The bar and front door were behind them. Quinn slid into the curved booth next to Indy. With the exception of color, the arrangement felt much like O'Leary's.

"Are you sure Kate will find us here? Maybe we should sit at the bar."

Indy whipped out her phone. "I'll text her. She'll find us. Besides, these are excellent seats for the performance."

Quinn's eyes went back to the stage where a guy fumbled with the words to Bon Jovi's "Wanted Dead or Alive." He shook his fist and his head with the beat of the music. This promised to be a long night.

The waitress appeared at the table carrying a small, round tray. She stood to the side so she wouldn't block the view of the stage. She wore tailored black pants and a crisp white blouse. "Hi. My name is Rachel. Tonight is karaoke night at Twilight. Here is a playlist of the songs available. If you want to sing, go up to Dan the DJ, and give him your name and song title. What can I get for you ladies tonight?"

"Vodka and cranberry."

Quinn's head snapped around to face Indy. "We had a deal."

"It's one drink. I promise to switch to Sprite after this." She turned back to Rachel. "Okay, Rachel? I'm designated driver, so no matter what I say, after this, no alcohol."

Rachel smiled brightly. "No problem. Nonalcoholic drinks for the DD are on the house. How about you?"

"Margarita," Quinn answered automatically.

Indy sighed.

"What?"

"Try something new. Be adventurous."

"How am I supposed to know what to ask for or if I'll like it if I've never had it?"

"Your boyfriend owns a bar. I'm sure he can arrange a sampling."

"First, he's not my boyfriend. Second, that won't help me right now."

"Can I offer a suggestion?" Rachel interrupted. She squatted to Quinn and Indy's eye level.

"Please do," Indy answered.

"One of our most popular drinks is Blue Smoke. I've never had a customer try it who didn't like it."

Indy perked up. "Sounds great. Make it two and scratch the vodka cran. Thanks, Rachel."

Rachel turned the corner out of their sight.

"I'm capable of making my own decisions. Isn't it enough you dressed me tonight?"

Indy shook her head. "Obviously not. The point of this summer is to try new things. If the drink sucks, you never order it again. Chalk it up as a mistake. As far as the dress goes, based on the number of guys checking you out as we walked through, that is no mistake."

Quinn tugged at the hem on her thigh and glanced around as if she was being watched. "At least if they're ogling my body, they won't pay any attention to my singing." She picked up the play list and scanned the titles.

Rachel returned with their drinks. She placed small, square, purple napkins on the table and topped them with their glasses. She spun away to deliver the rest of the drinks on her tray. The drinks were a completely unnatural smoky blue color. Quinn turned the glass in a circle.

"Wasn't it George Carlin who made jokes about there not being any blue foods?"

"Yeah, and I'd bet he'd chug this down. Come on. Cheers." Indy held up her tall slim glass.

Quinn picked up hers and clinked. She took a tentative sip. Sweet. Smooth. When it slid down her throat she felt the slight burn of alcohol. The drink had kick. It was *good.* She took a full drink. Still smooth. Hardly any aftertaste.

Rachel returned. "Well?"

Quinn smiled. "You were right. Excellent choice. Thank you."

"What's in this?" Indy asked.

"I don't know. The owner came up with it. The bartenders are sworn to secrecy. Let me know if you need anything else."

"I bet I could get the recipe out of the bartender," Indy commented, almost to herself.

"Hey, guys," Kate said as she sat next to Indy. "What are you drinking?"

"We're trying a really good new drink." Quinn slid her glass toward Kate.

She sipped. "Wow. That *is* good. What's in it?"

"No one will tell. Some hush-hush recipe created by the owner." Indy sounded irritated by the secret.

Kate looked around. "I like this place. It's so much closer for me to get here. I put the kids to bed and haven't missed any of the fun."

Rachel returned to the table for Kate's order.

"I'll have one of those," Kate said, pointing to Quinn's glass.

Rachel nodded and left.

"What did I miss?"

"Nothing. We've only been here a little while. This is our first drink." Quinn drank from her glass.

"How have the singers been?"

"We've only seen one. They must be taking a break."

They all looked at the empty stage. Sure enough, DJ Dan picked up the microphone. "Next up . . . Kelly," he read from a small card.

The girl who stood wore a halter dress in a bright flowered print barely skimming her butt. *And I thought my dress was short.* The bright lights made Kelly squint as she took the stage.

The music started. Quinn didn't know the song, but it was something Britney Spears-ish. Kelly's eyes fixed on some point in the middle of the dance floor. The poor girl was obviously nervous, which didn't help her carry a tune. Every note was off. Quinn's stomach clenched nervously, but Kelly finished. She didn't run away screaming.

No one heckled her.

Quinn glanced around at the other tables. Although many people carried on their quiet conversations, no one laughed at poor Kelly. It was a good sign. When Kelly bowed at the end of her performance, people actually clapped. *Maybe I can do this.*

Indy nudged Quinn from her musing. "Let's pick a song."

"Let me have another drink first. I think I'll be ready by then."

Indy caught Rachel's attention and pointed at Quinn. Moments later, her fresh drink arrived, along with a Sprite for Indy, and a new singer took the stage.

After her introduction, Sadie stood onstage in a loose, glittery black tank top and skintight black pants. Her orange-red hair rolled in waves past her shoulders. Her makeup was heavy, and it took Quinn a minute to recognize Sadie's attempt to hide her age. She must've been at least fifty.

When she took the microphone, Sadie reintroduced herself. Her voice was smoky and a bit raspy. She chose to sing Stevie Nicks's "Stand Back." A perfect choice.

By the end of the song, the crowd had hushed. Instead of the polite claps the previous singer received, they applauded Sadie.

"Oh, please. She's good, but I can do better," Indy commented.

Quinn raised her eyebrows. She had no doubt Indy could do better, but she was rarely a snot about it. The comment confirmed Quinn's suspicion that something happened to trouble Indy. "What's wrong?"

"Nothing." She took a drink of her pop. "Are we singing or what?"

"I'm not ready. Besides, I don't want to follow her. I want to follow someone who sucks." With another gulp of Blue Smoke, the glass was half empty.

"Scoot over and let me out. I'm singing."

Indy walked toward the DJ, who shuffled cards at his table. Before he rose to announce the next singer, Indy leaned over and offered a wink and a flash of cleavage. The next minute, she took the stage.

There was no introduction. She didn't offer her name. Within the first thirty seconds, most people in the room stared at Indy. She'd chosen "Stay" by Sugarland. The country ballad told the story of being the other woman. The accompaniment was so soft, Indy might as well have been singing a cappella. And she had the voice to do it.

Quinn leaned forward with her chin propped in her hand. Her sister's voice always sucked her in.

"She's really good."

"She always is when she sings from the heart." After the words left her lips, Quinn's mind registered that the comment had come from a man.

She looked over her shoulder and looked up at the tall man behind her. He looked vaguely familiar.

"Hi." The broad smile clicked in place and recognition dawned.

"You're motorcycle man."

He chuckled so deep and rumbly, her fingers remembered feeling his diaphragm vibrate. "I usually go by Griffin."

"We weren't introduced last time we met."

"I think Ryan planned to introduce us tonight, but it looks like he got distracted."

She turned back to the stage. The song ended and tears waved down Indy's cheeks. Before the last beat, the crowd stood, cheering.

Quinn saw movement to the left of the stage from the corner of her eye. She stood and turned her attention to see Ryan parting the crowd to get to the stage. With a spotlight on his back, he handed something to Indy. A handkerchief? She blotted her eyes.

He held his hand for her to take. Ryan put his arm around Indy's shoulder and hustled her through the mass of people.

Griffin leaned close to Quinn's ear. "Now that the entire room thinks my best friend is a married lech, maybe you'll tell me why you weren't the one onstage."

Quinn shrugged in response. She only halfway paid attention to the question. She focused on Ryan and Indy. Ryan didn't look like Ryan tonight. He was dressed in all black—pants and a collarless button-down shirt, the top two buttons undone. She was used to seeing him in jeans and a T-shirt. It didn't occur to her to imagine him wearing anything else. She became aware of the crowd, nudging each other and pointing in Ryan and Indy's direction. The way they were huddled together, they did appear to be a couple. The same irritation pricked her. Rationally, she knew it was stupid, but she couldn't control her emotions.

What was Ryan doing here anyway? How could he have known she planned on singing tonight instead of one of the other Thursdays? Unless someone told him. Her irritation grew, this time not because she felt like Ryan was making a play for Indy, but because Indy seemed intent on getting him to make a play for Quinn. She felt the muscle in her jaw twitch. The crowd swallowed up the path Ryan and Indy walked, and Quinn lost sight of them.

She eased back into her seat and gulped the remainder of her drink. The noise of the crowd leveled off once they figured out Indy wouldn't sing again.

"Would you like another one of those?" Griffin asked, still standing next to her seat.

Quinn straightened her shoulders. "Yes, I would. Thank you."

Griffin returned quickly, carrying two glasses of Blue Smoke and a bottle of beer. Quinn inched over to make room for him to sit. It would've been rude to accept the drink and not offer a seat. When he was settled with his long black denim-clad legs stretched out under the table, Quinn made introductions.

"Griffin, this is my friend, Kate. Kate, this is Ryan's friend, Griffin. He's the one who took me on a motorcycle ride."

Kate extended her hand. Griffin shook it politely and slid a glass in front of her. "I figured you could use another one too. How do you like it?"

"The drink? It's fabulous."

If Kate gushed any more, it would become a swoon. Quinn bit her lip to stop the smile and a smart-ass remark. Kate had always been a sucker for a man with a motorcycle.

"I'm glad you like it. I helped Ryan create it. That was one long night of drinking." He took a pull on his longneck.

Quinn sucked in a sharp breath. Kate simply sipped her drink. "You helped Ryan create it? Our waitress said the owner came up with it."

Griffin nodded. The smiled eased across his face again. "You didn't know, did you?"

"Know what?" Kate asked.

"This is Ryan's bar." He enjoyed telling her, like a gossip releasing a well-kept secret.

Kate focused on Quinn. "I thought he owned O'Leary's. You never mentioned him having another bar."

"He didn't tell me. You were there when he handed me the flyer for karaoke night. He said nothing about this being his bar." Another big gulp of alcohol. The buzz felt good, but it didn't ease her anger.

"Why are you pissed? He probably didn't think it was important." Griffin's logic made sense, even to her increasingly fuddled brain.

"I wouldn't have come here if I knew he owned it."

"Why not?"

She waved her hands in an attempt to gather her words. "Because he's all over my . . . stuff."

Griffin leaned close. "How many drinks have you had?"

"Three?"

"You don't drink often, do you?"

"Often enough." The alcohol was hitting her system hard, but she didn't care.

Griffin took a drink from his bottle of beer. "I thought you wanted his help with your list."

Quinn shrank back into a slouch. "He told you about my list?"

"Was it supposed to be a secret?" He drained the bottle of beer and set it down.

"No, not a secret. But it's personal. I don't go around blabbing to everyone I meet."

"He doesn't either. I'm his friend. And he asked me to take you on a ride."

The anger sizzled in the air between them. What right did Griffin have to be mad at her? He had nothing to do with what was going on between her and Ryan. Kate sat on the opposite side of the table, not commenting. She watched, like a shark spying its prey. Quinn felt Kate's visual dissection. "What?"

Kate raised her eyebrows. "I didn't say a word."

"You want to. Since when do you hold your tongue?"

"Since I was trying not to piss you off. I'm having a good evening and I don't want it to end on a bad note. Griffin is right. You shouldn't be pissed. Ryan has gone out of his way to help you with your list. In fact, he's done more to help you accomplish things than I have. Instead of brewing up an argument, you should be giving him a huge kiss. Or more, if you're so inclined." Kate took another small sip of the drink Griffin brought her and offered a smug smile over the rim of her glass.

"Please tell me you're single," Griffin smoothly said.

Kate held up her left hand and wiggled her fingers. "Married."

Griffin shook his head and his mouth formed an exaggerated frown. "All of the beautiful, intelligent ones are these days." He stood. "Another round?"

Her anger gone, Quinn reached for her purse. "Yes, but I'll get this one."

"No way. I got it. The entertainment is worth the price of a few drinks."

Quinn watched him as far as she could without leaving her seat. What did he mean by that? She fished a five-dollar bill out of her purse and waved Rachel over.

"Need another drink?"

"No, I wanted to give you a tip before I forgot. Do you guys have a food menu here?"

"Sure. I'll go grab a couple and bring them by."

"Thanks." Quinn hoped having some food would absorb the alcohol streaming through her system. Blue Smoke was certainly more potent than it appeared to be.

"Are you okay?" Kate wrapped her cool fingers around Quinn's wrist.

"I'm feeling a little light-headed. I drank the last one too fast. I don't think when I get irritated."

Rachel breezed by and deposited menus on the table. "Let me know when you're ready."

"Where's Indy? She's been gone a long time. She never stays upset this long."

"I'll go look for her. You don't look steady enough to walk. Ryan might've taken her outside for air. She looked pretty rattled." Kate exited the side of the booth and disappeared into the crowd.

Quinn felt odd sitting by herself in the large booth. She hoped no one would notice. She wasn't sure she could string together a coherent sentence at the moment. Griffin slid in next to her. She must have dazed out because she didn't notice him until he was in the booth.

"Where's Kate?" he asked, placing her drink and a glass of water in front of her.

"To look for Indy." Quinn took a deep breath and attempted to steady her gaze. "Can I ask you a favor?"

"I guess."

"Will you order something for me off the menu? The alcohol is hitting me pretty hard, and I don't think I can focus enough to read." She felt the rumble of his laughter. She recalled the feel of her hands wrapped around him on the motorcycle. The memories of the excitement flooded her. She slid closer to Griffin until his denim rubbed her thigh.

"Anything specific you're looking for?"

"Mmm. Whatever you think." She propped her elbow on the table for stability.

Rachel returned and Quinn heard Griffin say something. She didn't care what he ordered. The sound of his deep voice cascaded over her.

"Drink this." He pushed the glass of water in front of her. "You're not gonna puke, are you?"

"No. Why do you go to the bar to get drinks?"

"Because that's where they come from." He spoke like she was a dim-witted three-year-old.

She inhaled deeply and tried again. "I mean, why go to the bar instead of asking Rachel to get the drinks?"

"Because Rachel knows I'm Ryan's friend and he told her not to take my money. I can blend in at the busy bar."

"Oh." She couldn't think of anything else to say. She turned her attention to the stage. The singer was a blur and her blood thundered in her head, preventing the music from penetrating. She had no idea whether or not he was any good.

CHAPTER 9

Ryan pulled up short on his way to Quinn's table. Griffin faced his direction, legs stretched out, a beer in his right hand, and Quinn nestled against his left side, with her head on his chest. He finished his journey to the table with his jaw clenched, but then he saw Quinn wasn't nuzzling Griffin. She was sleeping on him.

"What the hell did you do to her?"

"She got herself drunk on Blue Smoke. Someone should've warned her." He took a drink of his beer. "I ordered food. She talked for a few minutes. The next thing I know, she scooted closer and put her head down." He shrugged, at least as much as he could with only one free shoulder.

Kate came around the other side of the table from behind Griffin. She looked at Ryan. "Where's Indy? I've looked all over."

"She left. She was really upset. I took her outside for a few minutes. We came back in, but when she saw Griffin, she mumbled something about work and asked me to bring Quinn home."

Kate came around the table and saw Quinn. Griffin smiled at her. "Your friend doesn't drink much."

"No, she doesn't." Kate shook her head. "If it wouldn't be too much of an imposition, could I ask you guys to dump her into my car so I can get her home? It's a long drive for me to get her to her place and come back home."

Griffin shifted, and Quinn wrapped an arm around his waist.

"I'll take her home, Kate," Ryan offered, trying not to be annoyed by Quinn's hands on Griffin.

She considered it, but answered, "No, thanks. I can't expect you to do that."

"I live a lot closer to her than you do. I'll take her to the office and let her sleep a bit. She'll feel better and I'll take her home."

Kate's hand went to her hip and she cocked her head to the side. "No funny business?"

He couldn't decide if she was serious. He'd only met her a few times. "Quinn is my friend too. I won't let anything happen to her."

Just then, Quinn stirred and Griffin looked a bit uncomfortable. Ryan tilted his head to tell Griff to get out of the booth. Griffin eased Quinn upright, and while her eyes opened, Ryan took Griffin's place. Kate resumed her position on the opposite side.

"Hey, Quinn."

Her head swung toward him. "Hey. I ordered food, I think." Her eyes narrowed. "I'm mad at you."

He waved to Rachel to check on the food. "Why are you mad at me?"

Griff remained standing beside the table. "I'll go check on the food."

"You didn't tell me you owned this bar." She paused and pointed to her empty glass. "With these fabulous drinks."

He slid her glass of water closer, hoping she'd take the hint. "That made you mad?"

"Yeah, but I can't remember why. You're such a good kisser. Your mouth is the best I've had since . . . ever."

Ryan looked at the unfocused glaze in her eyes and tried to ignore her words. If he didn't, he'd be hard again in a minute. He couldn't forget the kisses they shared and felt better knowing she couldn't get past it either.

Her eyes widened. "Did I say that out loud?"

He leaned closer and whispered, "Yeah, I'll make sure to remind you later."

She turned and looked at Kate, who continued to nurse her own drink. "Where's Indy?"

Ryan answered, "She left. She asked me to bring you home."

"Figures." She looked back at Kate. "She was really upset, wasn't she?"

Kate patted Quinn's arm. "Indy will be fine. She's a big girl."

"Why was she upset? She's a really good singer." Ryan wondered if he'd ever understand women's emotions.

Quinn turned back to him and closed her eyes for a moment. The back-and-forth motion probably made the room spin.

She took a breath. "She doesn't mix her personal life with business. Griffin is definitely business for her."

He knew Griffin didn't see it exactly the same, but withheld his comment. "So? Does she think he'll fire her for having a great voice?"

"Given the song she chose, it probably has something to do with her boyfriend." She finally picked up the glass of water and drained it.

Griffin returned to the table carrying Quinn's food. He placed the plate in front of her and sat next to Kate. Quinn giggled.

"Something funny?" Griffin asked.

Quinn chose a French fry and bit it. "You're a computer geek by day, waiter by night?" She chuckled alone.

Ryan watched her bite into the cheeseburger with her eyes closed. Had she thought to eat before going out tonight? As she swallowed the first bite, Rachel returned with another glass of water. She shot Ryan an apologetic look. He shook his head.

"Why would he think less of Indy?"

Quinn took another bite of her burger and rolled her eyes. Like he was stupid for not understanding. "It's not that he heard her sing. She wouldn't want him to read too much into the song."

Ryan absorbed the information and recalled the song. *She's involved with a married man.* Quinn continued to attack her cheeseburger. Kate focused intently on the stage. Griffin stared at him, his look revealing he, too, understood.

Griffin shrugged and asked Kate, "Would you like to dance?"

She looked startled. "Seriously?"

Griffin stood and extended his hand to help her up. She beamed at Quinn. "I'll be back. Don't disappear."

Ryan studied Quinn's face. "Feeling better?"

"Much. What the hell is in that drink? It was a total sneak attack." She finished her water and checked the dance floor.

Dan had chosen two singers with ballads to keep couples on the dance floor. Ryan's eyes found Griffin. He appeared to be having a good time with Kate. They were in deep conversation.

Ryan leaned closer to Quinn. "Sorry. I can't tell you the recipe. It's a highly guarded secret."

"I need to know so I can avoid whatever's in it. I went from feeling pleasantly buzzed to having numb lips in a snap."

He watched her form the words. "Numb?"

"That's how I know I'm drunk. My lips go numb."

"So you can't feel this." He touched his lips to hers gently. He found her soft and unguarded.

She pulled back. "I feel that just fine. The food adequately absorbed alcohol and feeling has been restored." She touched his cheek. "Thanks for testing, though."

Griffin and Kate came back.

"Have a nice dance?"

Kate laughed. "It was interesting."

"I'm ready to go whenever you are," Quinn told Kate.

Kate looked startled again. "Oh, okay. Let's go."

Ryan touched her arm. "I'll take you home, Quinn. It doesn't make sense for Kate to drive all the way into the city and back again when I live so close to you."

Griffin stood with his hands in his pockets, grinning. "Kate, can I get you another drink?"

She smiled. "A Diet Coke. I have to drive home, and I don't want to end up like Quinn."

Griff went back to the bar after nodding good-bye to Ryan.

Quinn inched out of the booth. "Don't do anything I wouldn't do."

Kate laughed. "I'm a married woman. I'm having a pop and great adult conversation."

Quinn winked. "But this conversation comes in a pretty hot package. And with a motorcycle. Control yourself." She stood next to the table.

Ryan had stepped back to make room for Quinn. He'd intended to make a comment, but he suddenly got an eyeful of leg and a curvy body in a tight dress. He was beginning to regret not having a chance to take Quinn to the dance floor.

He looked up to find Kate watching him checking out Quinn.

"You too," Kate replied. The self-control comment seemed aimed at both of them.

Quinn picked up her purse, opened it, and fumbled with its contents. "I think I owe Griffin money. I know he bought me a drink and I'm sure I didn't pay for my food."

Ryan put his hand on Quinn's. "Don't worry about it."

"Are you sure? I don't want him to think I'm some sponge who can't pay." She closed her purse.

An image of Colin flashed in his head. "It's fine." He nodded good-bye to Kate and put his hand on Quinn's back to guide her through the crowd. It took great restraint to keep his hand from drifting downward.

Quinn lifted her head and her eyes swept the crowd.

"Looking for someone?" Ryan said near her ear. Her perfume wafted up and he leaned in closer.

"I wanted to thank Griffin for the drink, and food, and letting me lay on him."

Ryan straightened at the reminder of seeing Quinn snuggled into Griffin. "Trust me, it was no hardship for him."

They pushed their way out into the quiet suburban street. Quinn looked up at the sky briefly and closed her eyes. Ryan stepped closer, waiting for her to fall over.

Her eyes flicked open and she nudged him with her purse. Pointing up, she said, "Make a wish."

Ryan couldn't stop the smile. Steadfast, practical Quinn wished on stars? Instead of looking up, he took her hand. "I don't need to wish for anything." Being alone with her was enough for his night.

He led her to his car. The night was warm and still. No wind, only the low hum of cars sporadically interrupted the music of the night.

Ryan opened the door and turned back in time to catch her tugging at the hem of her dress. She eyed the SUV, obviously distraught with having to climb up in her short dress.

"Here." He maneuvered Quinn so her back was to the front seat. "Duck your head a little." He boosted her up so her butt slid into the passenger seat.

She swiveled and brought her legs in front of her. "Thank you." Her relief was as plain as the distress had been moments earlier.

Ryan started the car and the radio turned on. He lowered the volume of the country station before leaving the parking lot. He enjoyed all types of music, but on the way to the bar, he'd listened to country, which fed his melancholy mood. Seeing Indy belt out the song on-stage with tears sliding down her cheeks amplified his feeling. He'd missed seeing Quinn.

He hadn't realized how much until they were together. He'd been so busy dealing with Colin and his family, he hadn't had time to focus on Quinn.

He'd hoped lowering the volume would encourage conversation. Quinn rested an elbow on the door frame and stared at the buildings flying by. They hadn't spoken in days. Had her interest faded already?

"You can change the station if you want."

Quinn turned to him, looking blank. "This is fine."

"What's wrong?"

"Nothing. Just tired and still buzzing."

He didn't believe her, but she obviously didn't want to talk. They sat in brooding silence as they hit the express lanes on the Kennedy expressway leading them back into the city.

It took less than thirty minutes. Ryan pulled down Quinn's street and into her lot.

She had the door open before he came around. She slid off the seat with her left hand stretching her dress down.

"I'm okay. You can go home. I'm sorry I pulled you away from bar business to drive my drunk ass home. Again."

"I'd be happy to drive your ass wherever, whenever. I came to see you tonight, not to work."

Quinn's mouth dropped open.

He grabbed her hand, pulled her away from the car, and shut the door. "I'll walk you up."

She linked her fingers through his, but said nothing. Inside, Ryan immediately walked toward the stairwell.

Quinn tugged him back to the elevator. "I'm still buzzed. Unless you have a cape and plan to fly me up those stairs, it's the elevator."

He leaned forward and pressed the button. "What have you been up to? We haven't talked in days."

She shrugged. "Failing at completing my list. I gave up on posing nude for an art class and settled on hiring a photographer."

"And?" he prompted. The elevator doors swooshed open and they stepped in.

"I found one. I met him and he has an amazing portfolio of portraits."

"I hope he's gay," Ryan mumbled.

"What?" The elevator lurched to a stop at the third floor.

"Nothing."

"Uh-oh." Quinn pressed the button for her floor again. She pressed the Door Open button.

"Don't tell me we're stuck."

She laughed. "Okay, I won't say it."

Ryan moved to the panel of buttons. "I knew this thing was a death trap."

He pressed every button. The emergency bell rang, but after thirty seconds, Quinn turned it off.

"Relax. I told you this happens sometimes. It'll fix itself in a few minutes." She moved away from the doors and leaned against the back wall.

He turned and joined her. "Finish telling me about the photographer."

"Xander? He's hot. Like Abercrombie-and-Fitch-model hot."

Great.

"Okay. I know that's not what you were asking. But it's what I noticed first. I assumed he was a model and the woman I'd spoken to on the phone was the photographer. It turns out she's the young, enthusiastic assistant and he's the photographer." She took a moment to kick off her sandals. Purple toenails today.

"Did you check his references?"

"Not yet. He gave me the name of another photographer, a woman, since I was uncomfortable with getting naked in front of him. But he's good."

Ryan clenched his jaw and forced it to relax. "What's the problem?"

"I'm a chicken."

Ryan moved over to stand next to her. "I have a camera. In fact, my phone can take pictures."

"Thanks, but no thanks. You should've asked while I was really drunk."

"I had to offer. So what are you going to do?"

She shrugged. The movement of her slouched shoulders widened the deep V-neck of her dress. The tops of her breasts were visible from his position.

He took a deep breath and stepped back.

She didn't notice.

"This isn't right. The elevator's never been stuck for this long." She went back to pressing buttons. No response.

Ryan pulled out his phone to check for a signal. None.

"Shit. I can't believe how wrong this night went." She ran her fingers through her hair.

"That was your own fault."

"What?" She spun to face him but held the side rail for balance.

"You let Indy take the spotlight. You had to know she's a great singer, but you let her steal your night of adventure."

"It wasn't like that."

Ryan crossed his arms on his chest. "Really?"

"Yes. There was some woman who sang Stevie Nicks. She was good. I'm an okay singer, but I didn't want to follow her. Indy was in a mood. So she sang."

"You chickened out."

"I planned to sing."

"Then you should've been on the stage instead of Indy."

"You can't stop Indy. When she's down, she doesn't stay that way for long. She does something to feel better. Tonight, singing was it." As she spoke, she moved closer to Ryan. Her perfume, the sultry one, grabbed him again.

"She didn't look too happy at the end of the song."

"But she was the star. The center of attention. Everyone in the room, even you, looked at her and said, 'Wow.'" Her eyes flashed in anger.

She's upset Indy got my attention again. Ryan wrapped an arm around Quinn's waist and pulled her body to his. "I said 'Wow' when I saw you in this dress."

He lowered his mouth and covered hers. The kiss was slow and deep. She needed no coaxing to participate. As soon as his tongue sought entrance, her lips parted.

She took a half step closer and slid her leg in between his. Ryan's hand cradled her ass and pressed her into him. He wanted her to know how much he wanted this.

The leg that slid in between his inched up and down, her bare foot caressing his calf. Ryan felt the hem of the short dress hike up. His mouth left hers. He trailed kisses down to the pulse at her neck while her perfume enveloped his senses.

His hand moved from her ass to her thigh and under her dress. He was dying to touch her. His mouth returned to hers as his hand brushed the small triangle of panties. Moist heat radiated through the scrap of lace.

Her low, deep moan vibrated against his lips. He swallowed it. The throbbing in his pants drove him crazy. He pressed his pelvis against her, his erection bumping her. The barrier of clothing was too much.

He reached and tugged at the panties.

"Wait," she said, breathless. "What's the date?"

"Huh?" He tugged some more and nibbled her ear.

"The date."

From his foggy brain, he offered, "The twentieth."

"God. I'm ovulating. Please tell me you have a condom."

Ryan pulled his body inches from her and braced an elbow near her head. "No, I don't. I'm clean, Quinn. I wouldn't lie to you."

He leaned in and kissed her neck.

"I know you wouldn't, but I'm ovulating. Chances are good I'd get pregnant. We have to stop."

He licked her pulse. "I'm willing to take my chances." He nipped her earlobe.

Her hands pressed against his chest. "I'm not."

Ryan stepped away from her. They were both panting. She tugged the hem of her dress back in place, but not before he caught a glimpse of the black lace. He shifted and adjusted in hope of finding comfort for his hard dick. The only relief he wanted was inside Quinn.

Before they could say anything else, the elevator dinged.

CHAPTER 10

The following morning, Quinn awoke with a pounding headache. Her eyes were barely slits as she sat up. Cottony didn't begin to describe the horrendous condition of her mouth—a sweaty gym sock would smell better than her breath. She staggered to the bathroom, splashed water on her face, and brushed her teeth twice.

She felt chilled and realized she was naked. She wrapped a robe around herself and closed her eyes, but she couldn't remember how she got to bed. So much of the evening blurred incoherently.

How did anyone find this enjoyable? Her father had spent years waking up like this. How could he function? She couldn't imagine waking up in this condition next to a man. A hangover looked good on no one.

She stumbled downstairs and made a pot of coffee. While it brewed, she checked her messages.

"Hey, babe. I wanted to see if you were free tonight. Give me a call if you want to get together." *Nick must be broke and looking to drink for free.*

"Hey, it's me." *Indy.* "Sorry about last night. I had a fight with Richard, but I didn't want to ruin your night." *Yeah, that worked real well.* "Call me later."

"Hi, Quinn. It's Kate. Just checking on you. Give me a call." *Kate certainly sounded perky.*

Quinn decided she'd have to call Kate if she wanted to find out what happened last night. She poured a cup of coffee and inhaled the scent before drinking. She swallowed two ibuprofen with the next drink. Sitting at her counter, she tried to piece together her evening.

The damn blue drink. Indy singing onstage was clear in her mind. Griffin sitting next to her. She had the sudden recollection she'd wanted to kiss him. She'd been mad at Ryan and Griffin was there.

Ryan.

Hearing his name ring clearly in her mind caused a flood of images. They'd kissed and then some. In the elevator? Yeah, they got stuck and he kissed her. She'd wanted so much more, but they stopped.

She couldn't remember going to bed. Her face flushed at the thought of Ryan's lips on her. The warmth spread through her body.

Had they continued in the loft? Was that why she was naked?
Oh, God.

She picked up the phone to call Ryan and ask, but she didn't know how. What an idiot. *Hi, Ryan, I know I should remember, but did we have sex?*

No, this was not a conversation to have over the phone. She'd have to go see him. The embarrassment of the situation made her shiver.

The clock on her stove said eleven o'clock. O'Leary's would be open for lunch. Hopefully she'd catch Ryan there, since she realized she didn't know where he lived.

She poured more coffee into her mug and carried it back upstairs to the bathroom. The hot shower relaxed her muscles and eased the headache. She felt a little more human, at least until she looked in the mirror. Her eyes were still bleary and shadows ringed them.

Oh well. No beauty contests today. Adding makeup helped, as did putting on fresh clothes. The denim shorts and black tank top wouldn't win any fashion contests either, but at least she was comfortable.

The sunglasses perched on her nose didn't cut down the glare from the sun nearly enough, and the pulse behind her eyes let her know her hangover was far from over. She drove to the bar, practicing what to say. She'd never had this kind of conversation. Everything she thought of sounded lame. Ryan would probably find this humorous. He enjoyed seeing her ruffled.

She parked in the bar's lot and noted there were only a handful of cars. She spotted Ryan's SUV in the back. Running her fingers through her still-damp hair, she inhaled deeply. *This is no big deal. Ryan's a friend. You can handle this.* What a load of shit for a pep talk. She should've called Indy for advice.

She strode into the bar and peered around. The dark, quiet interior was a blessing after the blazing sun. She removed her sunglasses and looked for Ryan. A small blonde whisked through the bar, attending to customers as she went.

Quinn approached her. "Excuse me. Sorry to interrupt, but can you tell me if Ryan is here?"

"Yeah, he's in the basement doing inventory."

Quinn waited a painful moment.

"I'll call down and ask him to come up. What's your name?"

"Quinn." She breathed a sigh of relief.

"Quinn, I'm Mary, bar manager."

"Ryan's told me a lot about how good you are." She followed Mary to the bar.

"Can I ask you a personal question?"

Quinn shrugged.

"Are you single?"

"Yep."

"Oh. In that case, we're having a speed dating night here next Tuesday." Mary whipped out a flyer with attached registration form. "You'd be doing me a great favor if you'd sign up. I'm already full of guys. I need to add to my roster of women."

"Ryan mentioned this. I've never done speed dating."

"I have to make this a success. I told Ryan it would be."

Quinn read the flyer. How bad could it be? "Okay."

While she filled out the registration, Mary used the phone. Quinn couldn't hear the conversation, but Mary didn't look happy.

She turned to Quinn, still holding the phone. "He says now is not a good time. He's busy with inventory."

"Please. This is important."

Mary spoke the message into the phone. She hung up and told Quinn, "He said you can come down if you want to talk."

"Thanks. I appreciate it. Here." She thrust the completed form and twenty dollars back at Mary.

Mary paused, tilting her head in appraisal of Quinn. "There's something familiar about you."

"I come here with the other teachers from Jones High School on Friday afternoons."

"That's probably it. Thanks for signing up. We'll be sending out e-mail reminders the day before." She walked Quinn down the hall past Ryan's office and the bathrooms to a door adjacent to the rear exit. "Right down those stairs. You can't miss him. He's the moody guy counting bottles."

"Thanks again." Quinn opened the door and took a brief moment to relax her fluttering stomach. She descended the stairs and faced rows of boxes. Ryan stood with a clipboard in hand.

"Hi."

He barely looked up from the paper. "What do you want, Quinn? I'm busy."

Okay, so he was pissed. "First, I wanted to thank you for bringing me home last night."

"I told you it wasn't a big deal."

"The thing is . . . I don't remember everything."

"Tends to happen when you get drunk."

"I know. I didn't plan on getting drunk, but I did." She huffed out a breath. "Look, I need to know if we slept together last night."

He placed his clipboard on top of the nearest box. "You don't re-member?"

She stared at her feet and shook her head.

"We almost did in the elevator, but you called it off."

She raised her head to find him standing with his arms crossed. Is that why he was mad? "I remember that part, but I woke up naked and I don't remember how I got to bed."

He stepped closer and lowered his voice. "So you think after you told me to stop, I forced myself on you? I told you a long time ago, I don't go where I'm not invited."

Her hand flew to her heart. "No. God no. I never thought that for even a second. I thought maybe we continued what we started in the elevator."

"We didn't. You said no. I respected you."

"I wanted to, it was just . . ."

"I know. You didn't want to risk getting pregnant by me."

"Why are you so angry?"

His eyes shone with anger and the muscle in his jaw twitched. "Because you'd rather have some tool knock you up than take your chances with me."

She pointed between the two of them. "This is exactly why I didn't want to take my chances. I value your friendship." Her voice grew louder as she spoke, but she couldn't prevent it. The volume increased the throbbing of her brain.

"I care about you and respect you. Somehow that's a bad thing." He was inches from her and she felt his anger vibrating in the air around him. It spurred her own anger.

The words flew uncensored and her arms circled in gesture as she spoke. "If you were backed into a corner, it would all change. You're not the kind of guy who could father a child and forget it. You can't even walk away from your family, and they're grown. Even if we never saw each other again, you would want to be a part of the child's life. You'd feel trapped. So I'd lose a good friend and you'd be saddled with a kid you didn't want. Another burden in your life. I'd say I saved us both a bunch of heartache."

She'd hit the mark. They stared at each other for a minute, breathing heavily. "My intention is not to go and have sex with a random guy to get pregnant. I know I tend to attract assholes. I plan to do artificial insemination so I can pick a good genetic donor. I'm not picking a father. I'm picking sperm."

"Pretty pessimistic." His fight left. He reached for her arm.

She pulled farther away. "It's realistic. I don't have high hopes for a husband." She felt tears welling in her eyes. She turned to head back up the stairs. She'd gotten the information she wanted and then some. He didn't try to stop her from leaving.

At the top of the stairs, she gathered herself and blinked a few times to push back the tears. She opened the door and walked through with her back straight. As she entered the bar, a few patrons looked at her. She had the sinking feeling they heard her yelling at Ryan. She continued on, trying not to draw more attention to herself by running out. Mary looked at her, eyes wide. Quinn simply nodded and pushed the door open to the heat and glaring summer sun.

On her way to the car, Quinn berated herself for the entire episode. Hadn't Indy always told her men and women couldn't be friends? One or the other always wanted something more. Such a load of crap. Why couldn't she find a guy who wanted what she wanted in life? Was there something wrong with marriage and family?

Or maybe it was her.

She unlocked the car door and sat behind the wheel. *They don't know what they're missing. I'm going to finish this damn list, and I'm going to have a baby.*

Who needed Ryan's help anyway? On her drive home, she created her plan of attack. She had use of the dating Web site, so she'd utilize it. She'd start making dates immediately and see what clicked.

She'd also call Xander Hill and make an appointment. She still had to sing karaoke. Next time she wouldn't make the mistake of going with Indy or drinking. She needed to find a different bar, though.

Her cell phone rang as she entered her building. She eyed the elevator and remembered making out with Ryan. She opted for the stairs and allowed the phone to go to voice mail.

The blast of cool air from her loft washed over her. Her anger simmered into determination. She sat at her laptop and navigated to the dating site. While the site loaded her profile, she checked her voice mail.

Brian's voice said, "Don't answer your house phone. Call me."

Weird. She dialed his number. "Hey, Brian. What's up?"

"Before I tell you anything, promise me you won't answer your phone for school because you're on vacation."

"That doesn't sound too good."

"Promise or I won't tell you."

"You sound like a kid. Fine." She leaned back in her chair and waited.

"Ackerman is making noise about quitting summer school."

"What?" Quinn shot out of her chair. "She can't do that."

"She claims she's never taught such a difficult group of kids. They don't want to learn."

Quinn's eyes rolled. "Who the hell did she think she was getting? These kids *failed* English during the year. Most of them weren't interested the first time around and they're even less so now. It's summer, for Pete's sake. No one wants to be in a hot building instead of at the lake."

Brian's laugh broke her rant.

"What is so funny?"

"Nothing. I'm glad you're pissed off. Maybe you won't rush in to rescue her."

"Rescue her?"

"We both know if she calls you for help, you'll do it. Before you know it, you'll be in the class teaching it for her."

"I would not." It was a lie. Brian was nice enough not to call her on it. "Thanks for the heads-up. I'll avoid my phone."

"No problem. Talk to you soon."

"Bye." She hung up and went back to her computer profile. She'd ramp it up and find new guys to date. She could plan dates for every night of the week. Her phone rang as she typed. She paused and listened for the machine to pick up.

"Hi, Quinn. It's Mr. Carlson. I hoped you could stop in one day this week and talk with Shari Ackerman about summer school. She's having some difficulties, and since you've always taught the class, I thought you might be able to talk her through it. Thanks."

Brian was good. He always knew the gossip before anyone else. Quinn had no urge to talk about work. Instead, she focused on finding someone to love for the summer.

CHAPTER 11

Hours later, Ryan's neck was cramped and his eyes bleary. He stretched at his desk and rolled his head from side to side. The bar had quieted, as it did every day after lunch and before dinner. He headed to the bar to check with Mary before going to Twilight. He had another few hours of inventory there. Twilight wasn't open until evening, though, so he'd have no interruptions.

To his surprise, Colin was there, but he stood behind the bar, drying glasses. Ryan didn't comment. If his brother wanted to dry glasses, why should he care?

The tables were clean and empty. A few regulars sat at the bar, nursing an afternoon beer while they watched sports on TV. The old guys often reminded him of his father. Even though he'd handed the daily operation of the bar over to Ryan, Dad still sat at the bar every day, like he didn't know what to do with himself.

Mary walked by. "Hey, boss. We're looking good for Tuesday."

"Tuesday?"

She shook her head at him. "Speed dating."

"Oh, yeah. Good. I'm going to Twilight. I don't know if I'll be back."

"Okay." She turned to walk away.

Ryan touched her arm and lowered his voice. "Colin can occupy himself doing whatever you need him for, but I don't want him at the register."

Her eyebrows raised a fraction at the request, but she nodded. He felt a little crappy for saying it out loud, but if he learned anything from his father's mistakes, it was to never underestimate Colin.

He turned back to the bar. On his way out, he stopped between the old timers. "How are you guys doing?" he asked, patting them each on the back.

"Hiding from our wives, like we do every day."

"It's not hiding if they know where to find you."

The men chuckled and returned their attention to the TV. Ryan's gaze followed theirs. The Cubs were playing.

The Cubs reminded him of Quinn and the fight they'd had earlier. He didn't even know why he was so mad. She was right. He didn't want to be a father. At least not right now. He was stupid for saying he'd take his chances. Thinking with his dick usually led to stupidity.

He'd been mean and even a little cruel, but she needed to hear it. Ryan turned from the TV and walked out the door. He'd stay away from Quinn. Give her time to cool off. Then he'd try talking to her again.

Space might do them both some good.

Quinn stomped into her loft and threw her purse at the couch. A scream of frustration clawed at her throat, but she refused its escape.

She'd thought it was serendipitous that within an hour of posting her improved profile, a man contacted her. His profile said he was a lawyer, never married, and liked outdoor summer sports. Nowhere did it mention liking kink.

The memories made the burn of embarrassment return to her skin.

If she were Indy, she would've had a smart-ass comment to throw at him, but she'd had nothing. She was so flustered, she barely remembered to grab her purse before storming out.

She sank down on the couch, her rolling emotions taking their toll. *Two minutes of self-pity. I'm allowed that.*

When the two minutes were up, Quinn changed into a pair of shorts and an old T-shirt. She went to the kitchen to bake.

The smell of chocolate would comfort her. The mixing of ingredients gave her time to think and reevaluate.

The first pans went into the oven and the doorbell called Quinn's attention. She went to the intercom. "Yes."

"It's me," Indy said.

Quinn pressed the buzzer and turned the knob on the door. She went back to the kitchen to prep the next pan of cookies.

Indy closed the door with a slight thud. "Mmm. I smell chocolate. Someone's having a bad day."

Quinn peered at her sister from the kitchen counter. "You don't know the half of it."

Indy moved through the living room, pausing only to take off her navy pumps. She wore a matching business suit with a deep-cut white blouse. Indy looked sexy in everything. She slid onto a stool on the opposite side of the counter. "Ooo . . . you just started," she said, eying the bowl of dough. "Let me go change."

Quinn waited while Indy went upstairs to borrow clothes. If Indy wanted to join her in baking cookies, she was having a crappy day too.

Indy returned wearing clothes similar to what Quinn wore. The T-shirt was a little too tight and the shorts a little too short, but Indy seemed to be comfortable. She walked barefoot into the kitchen and stood beside Quinn. "I haven't had Comfort Cookies in ages."

"That's because you don't like to bake."

Indy nudged her with her elbow. "Not true. I'm not as good as you. Yours are better than Mom's."

Quinn blushed at the compliment. Mom's cookies were what saved every childhood disaster. "I looked everywhere for the recipe after she died. I couldn't find it. I re-created what I could from memory. These aren't necessarily better. They're different. I can't figure out what these are missing."

Indy laughed. "There isn't a recipe. Don't you remember? Mom made it up as she went along. No two batches were ever the same." She dipped her finger into the bowl and licked it.

"She had a recipe. I remember a few times she tried to mix in other stuff. But I don't remember them being different every time. They were always good."

"Not always." Indy scooped up more dough. "There's something to be said for consistency. Yours are better."

"Thanks." A smile tugged at Quinn's lips and she was glad Indy came by.

The timer dinged for the first batch of cookies. While they cooled, Indy made a pot of tea. She'd turned on the radio for quiet background music as she worked in the kitchen. Quinn briefly wondered if Indy knew she was channeling their mother. In Mom's world, Comfort Cookies were only served with tea and music to soothe their souls.

"What's wrong?" Quinn asked. Indy never moved into the comfort of home mode unless something troubled her. Her own free spirit tended to fix itself.

"Richard wants to take a break. He still wants to keep our relationship a secret from his wife. Every time they have a deal on the table for the divorce, she comes up with something else to add. He thinks if she knows about me, she'll drag her feet even more."

Quinn eased onto a stool and patted the one next to her. Indy took it and exchanged a cup of tea for a handful of warm, gooey cookies.

"I know you don't agree with our whole relationship. I have a good time with him. Until last night. I didn't want to bring it up and ruin your evening, but I guess I did anyway. I told him if he thought I would sit around and wait on him, he'd better think again."

"Good for you."

Indy shook her head. "We both know I lied. I like the simplicity of our relationship. No strings, no worries. Even my chances with Griffin were ruined after last night. You didn't see the way he looked at me. With the same disgust I get from Dad."

"That's not true. You should forget Richard. You can have any man you set your sights on. I can show you the finer points of Internet dating," Quinn said sarcastically. "We can share stories of misery. I had my worst one so far earlier today."

Quinn walked around the counter and pulled cookie sheets from the oven. She checked the raw dough remaining in the bowl and decided Indy would probably finish it.

"You had a date tonight? It's only eight now. How early did you go out?"

Quinn returned to her sister's side. "I was pissed because Ryan and I had a fight, so I came home and redid my online profile. Within an hour I got a message. This guy Ken and I chatted for a while online and agreed to meet for coffee."

"What did you fight with Ryan about?" Indy stuck her finger in the dough for another bite.

"I don't want to talk about it."

"Please tell me you didn't go on a date looking like that." Indy eyed the shorts and T-shirt.

"No, I changed into this when I got home. Anyway, I met him at a coffee shop. We kind of hit it off. I mean, it wasn't love at first sight or anything, but there was chemistry."

"So how did he end up at the top of the list ahead of the lizard kisser?"

"Because while we were talking, this woman showed up and sat next to Ken. He introduced her as his girlfriend, Candy. They were hoping I would join them for a night in a hotel room."

Indy rolled her upper lip in and bit it.

"Go ahead and laugh. I'm over it."

Indy let the laugh out. "Where do you meet these guys? Sleaze.com?"

"No, it's a reputable dating site. I don't know where he came from. The whole thing definitely whittled away my resolve for finding romance soon. This afternoon I was willing to set up dates every night for the next two weeks. Now I'm rethinking."

"Don't let one date—one more bad date—ruin your summer. There are millions of guys looking for a great woman like you."

Quinn pulled another cookie off the cooling rack and broke it into pieces.

"Why don't you go out with Ryan? He seems like a good guy."

"He is. We're friends. I don't want to risk the friendship. I can't imagine starting something with him and ending it in August. He's not looking to be a dad. I really want to be a mom. We fought about it today."

Indy picked up her cup of tea. "Let's go find a chick flick on TV and wallow in tears for the rest of the night. Tomorrow has to look better."

* * *

Ryan entered his bar looking for escape. He'd spent the weekend mostly alone, except for a brief visit with his mom where she spoke of nothing but Colin. After that, he was more than happy to seek solitude.

Until he found it.

Then he thought of Quinn working her way down her list. The thought adequately ruined the rest of his weekend.

New week. New perspective. No Quinn.

Mary sat at the bar with a cup of coffee at her elbow and papers in her hand. She swiveled the stool to face him. "Good. You're here. I need to talk about setup for tomorrow night. Speed dating."

"I remember," he grumbled. He also remembered the reason he'd had Mary plan the event.

"Grab a seat." She spread a couple of sheets out on the bar where he sat. "I think everyone will fit comfortably if we take over the dance area. It will shut that section down for a few hours, but it's the best area for traffic flow."

Ryan inspected the sketches. "Whatever you think. You're the expert." He stood to go to his office and noticed the clipboard with blue and pink sheets. He pointed. "Participant list?"

"Yeah, I asked Nate to type it up. He thought it would be cute to use blue for the men and pink for the ladies."

Ryan picked up the clipboard and read down the pink sheet. It was alphabetized, but he still read it twice. No Quinn.

"Looking for someone?"

"Yeah, I thought my friend Quinn would've signed up. She was here on Friday."

"She did. I took her registration myself." She took the clipboard back and went down the list.

"I know how to read, Mary. There's no Quinn Adams on the list." Part of him was relieved he wouldn't have to worry about her finding someone. Despite the fact that she'd turned him down, he wasn't done with her. Another part of him was irritated because he'd spent hours lining up men who were totally wrong for Quinn. He let Mary do some of the advertising; he'd feel bad if the whole event was a flop because of his sabotage.

Mary flipped the page up. "Oh, Christ. I'm going to kill him."

Ryan peered over her shoulder and saw Quinn's name typed in at the top of the blue sheet. He chuckled. "To be fair, Quinn can be a man's name. It's no big deal. Just move her over to the right list."

"It is a big deal. I thought I had exactly fifteen men and fifteen women. Now I have sixteen women, but only fourteen men. I need to come up with two more available men before tomorrow, and I need to figure out where to squeeze in an extra table."

Ryan touched her shoulder. "Breathe. It's not a big deal. Shit happens. Maybe someone won't show and it'll even out."

Her shoulders relaxed a bit. "You're right. I'll send out e-mail confirmations to the list and see where I am. I want this to be a success." She reclaimed her seat and opened her laptop.

"I'm sure it'll be fine." He moved toward the back.

"Hey, can I use you as a fill-in if I need to?"

"Hell no."

She laughed. "Why not? You're unattached. If you're a participant, Quinn would be forced to talk to you for a full three minutes." She turned back to the computer with a knowing smile.

He hated she saw right through him. Mary was like the big sister he never had. Or wanted. He had enough sibling issues.

The thought barely left his head when the back door swung open, flooding the dark hallway with sunlight. Colin strode in whistling an obnoxiously happy tune.

"Hi, boss. How are you this fine morning?" he asked with a fake brogue.

"Can the leprechaun shit. What are you doing here?" Ryan opened his office door and walked in, expecting Colin to follow.

"Mary called me in for some extra hours. She needs tables pulled from storage and cleaned."

Ryan tossed his keys on the desk. "Fine. Get to work. Mary's at the bar."

"Someone got up on the wrong side of the bed this morning. What's her name?"

Ryan turned back. Colin leaned against the door frame, relaxed and waiting for gossip. "Who?"

"Whoever has you so twisted up you're snapping at me."

"No one. There's no one."

Colin straightened. "Maybe that's the problem." He walked away and his whistled tune echoed in the empty hall.

Colin was right. He had to work out the funk he was in.

He didn't know where to start. He wasn't ready for the whole family thing Quinn wanted. They hadn't even had sex. How was he supposed to think about the future? But he wanted her.

He remembered her leg curling around his. Her tongue tangling with his. Her scent. His dick twitched at the memory.

Indy had told him to make Quinn choose him. He'd done the opposite. He had to fix that.

He went to his Rolodex and looked for the florist's number. Daisies made her happy before. He'd try his luck again.

Quinn checked her e-mail, searching for the next horrible date. One caught her eye. The sender was O'Leary's. Her heart jumped.

She clicked the message.

Hi. This is a friendly reminder you are registered to participate in our first ever Speed Dating event tomorrow, Tuesday, June 25. Please respond to this e-mail to confirm you will attend and whether you will bring a friend.

Quinn's cursor hovered over the Reply button. She'd forgotten she signed up. It was right before she fought with Ryan. Her eyes wandered over the text again. "First ever" jumped out at her. He'd done it again. Ryan maneuvered himself into a position to help her complete her list. She didn't know if she should be pissed or grateful.

She clicked Reply and typed, "I'll be there with a friend." Indy would have to go with her. Knowing Indy, she'd have a date lined up before anyone else. It would do her good.

Quinn finished her cup of coffee and dressed in a simple yellow sundress. She packed makeup in her purse and brushed her hair one more time. Her stomach flipped every time she thought about the appointment.

She hadn't thought Xander would have an opening so soon. It made sense, since Mondays are not big for weddings. Luckily, Indy was free and would meet her at the studio.

Sliding her feet into white canvas sneakers, she checked her reflection in the mirror. *What does it matter what I look like now? All of this is coming off.* She shook her head and left, hoping it wasn't too humid out. She didn't want to drive such a short distance, but she didn't want sweaty, glistening skin either.

The air outside was warm, but not stifling. The sun on her face was hot. Her sunglasses shaded her eyes, and a slight breeze tossed her bangs. A gorgeous day to walk.

Her shoes slapped the cracked concrete, and Quinn thought of anything except where she was going. She thought of Indy and Richard. She'd only met the man once. He was stuffy and rigid. *Even more than me.* He wasn't right for Indy. He'd never accept all parts of her. She needed stability, someone she could count on, but also someone who could enjoy and appreciate the spontaneity that kept her going.

Quinn didn't see Richard fulfilling the role. Their father would have a stroke if he found out Indy was dating a married man. Disloyalty and betrayal were unforgivable in his eyes. Almost divorced was still married. Maybe that's why she chose Richard.

She turned the corner and stood in front of Hill Studio. She saw no sign of Indy or her car. She checked her cell phone. No messages, but she was five minutes early.

The minutes ticked by with her feet tapping the pavement. She dialed Indy's number. No answer. She bit her lower lip. She didn't want to be late and have Xander think she was blowing him off. She texted Indy that she should come right up. Hopefully, she hadn't forgotten about this.

Taking a deep breath, she pressed the doorbell and waited for admittance. No intercom crackled. The door buzzed and she walked in. A blast of cool air skimmed over her. She walked up the flight of stairs. Before she could prepare herself, the door opened.

"Hi," Cindy said. "Come on in. We're almost ready for you."

Quinn followed the bouncy girl. The spiky tips of her hair were purple today, and Quinn saw a few piercings she hadn't noticed on their last meeting.

The loft had been reconfigured. Tall bamboo screens broke up the airy, open space. Privacy in case someone else came in?

"Would you like something to drink?"

Quinn returned her gaze to Cindy. "No, thanks. But my sister is supposed to meet me here. She's running late." *As usual.*

"No problem. I'll be around to let her in so you won't be interrupted."

"Hello, Ms. Adams," Xander said behind her.

She turned around. He stood in a small space between two screens. He wore low-slung jeans and a painted-on white tank. He held a camera at chest height and fondled the buttons.

"Hi." She froze in place, not knowing what to do or say.

He shifted his body and tilted his head. "Ready to get started?"

She nodded and followed him. Her toes curled tightly inside her canvas shoes and she clutched her purse. Behind the screens, a platform stood, looking like a bed covered with a blue sheet and scattered with colorful pillows. Only the pointed corners revealed it wasn't a mattress.

"Do you have a specific pose or look you want?" he asked as he busied himself setting up lights and umbrellas.

Quinn shook her head and realized he wasn't looking at her. "No, I figured you would tell me what to do."

"That's fine. Have a seat while I finish this." He gestured to the platform.

She stepped on a stool and sat on the hard box. She sat still, afraid the sheet would slide and ruin his setup. Her stomach threatened to heave and she toyed with the strap of her purse in an attempt to calm herself.

Xander suddenly looked up as if feeling her tension. "Relax. This won't hurt." He held her gaze for an extra moment. The automatic smile from his lips eased its way up to his eyes.

Her fingers fidgeted with her purse. "I brought makeup because I didn't know how much to apply with the lights and stuff."

He continued to watch her as he adjusted the height of a tripod. "A client who thinks ahead. Always good. In general, a little heavier than normal shows up best. Unless you want a more dramatic look." He paused, studying her face. "You strike me as more natural."

She nodded. "Do you have someplace I can put my makeup on?"

"If you want, Cindy can do it for you."

Her eyebrows shot up in question.

"She's good. Her mom's a cosmetologist. Cindy changes her look weekly, but she knows what suits people."

Quinn shrugged. "Why not?" Cindy's hands were bound to be steadier than her own.

Cindy came around the edge of the screen. "Let's see what you've got."

Quinn dumped her purse out beside her.

Cindy picked through and turned to Quinn. She held Quinn's chin between her thumb and forefinger and tilted it up. "You have great skin. He won't need to airbrush you, that's for sure."

Quinn blinked. "Airbrush?"

"You know, digitally erase. He can make anyone look darn near perfect."

"I thought airbrushing was for celebrities in magazines."

"Uh-uh. Anyone can have it. Cellulite? No more. Stretch marks? Not in our photos."

"Huh." She hadn't thought of that. Maybe Xander's portfolio was so good because it was fake.

Cindy dusted Quinn's face with a light coating of powder foundation. Quinn closed her eyes and said a mental prayer she wouldn't end up looking like a clown.

"Open your eyes," Cindy said. She stood, poised with eyeliner. "Are you going to freak when I come at your eyes with this? It'll totally ruin it if your eyes flutter and tear up. If that's gonna happen, you should do it yourself."

"I'm fine. Go ahead." Anything was better than thinking about getting naked. She didn't know where Xander went. He hadn't spoken since he'd invited Cindy in. She heard movement and assumed he was still rearranging equipment.

The doorbell hadn't rung yet. Indy must've forgotten the appointment. At least she wasn't alone. Cindy had said she'd be there.

"All done." Cindy scooped up the makeup and dumped it back into Quinn's purse.

"Do you have a mirror?"

Cindy pointed next to Quinn's thigh. A large, square, purple-handled mirror stared up at her. She lifted it and studied her face.

"Wow. You're good." The makeup gave her a natural, polished look.

Cindy blushed at the compliment. "Thanks. I'm going to move

your purse over to the chair. You can go to the bathroom to undress and put on one of the robes there. Unless you're cool with walking through the studio in your birthday suit."

It was Quinn's turn to blush.

She pointed to the corner of the room. "The robes are washed after every client."

Quinn stood stiffly and forced her legs to carry her to the bathroom. Her antiperspirant was suddenly failing her. Her armpits felt moist even in the air-conditioning.

She shucked the dress and toed off her shoes. She took some toilet paper and dabbed her underarms. Taking a pink robe from a hook, she hung her dress in its place. The robe was lightweight cotton and landed mid-thigh. Modest enough. She shimmied out of her panties and hung them on the hook underneath her dress.

Tightening the belt on the robe, she stared into her own eyes in the mirror. *You can do this.*

She opened the bathroom door and padded quietly across the room with her head down. Her silent pep talk did nothing for her nerves. She stood next to the platform and waited for direction from Xander.

He looked up from the camera. "Ready?"

"As I'm gonna get," she whispered. She undid the sash from the robe and exhaled.

"Stop right there."

She snapped her head up at the immediate command. The robe parted only four inches. Four inches of bare, exposed Quinn.

"Sorry. I tend to snap when I see a good shot. Open the robe slowly and let it slide down your shoulders and drop to the floor."

She stared at him and followed his direction, hearing the whir of the shutter on his camera.

"Lie down on the platform. Sorry it's not a real bed. A mattress sags and contours and ruins things."

She lay down on her side and felt her boobs hang sloppily. They weren't huge or anything, but they weren't meant to hang sideways. She shifted and tried to make them stand up and look better—perkier. She spoke silently to her stomach, begging it not to hurl as Xander continued with his barrage of directions: tilt your chin up, look this way, look down, smile, show me teeth. She painfully followed every instruction.

Every inch of her was exposed. She'd never been naked in front of a man she wasn't intimate with. And this was so . . . *intimate*.

After what seemed like hours, Xander blew out a heavy breath. "I think we need a break."

Quinn glanced at her watch. It had only been twenty minutes. "Is there a problem?"

"You're not comfortable, and it's coming across in the shots."

"It's that bad?"

"I'll let you be the judge. If you relax a little, we can try again."

She shook her head. She didn't know how to relax that much. "I'll go change."

She draped the robe over the toilet tank, so they would remember which one she wore. She slid into her dress and panties. She carried her shoes back into the studio with her to put on while Xander talked to her.

She took the seat near his desk as he worked on the computer. She tugged her shoes back in place. "Can you show them to me?"

"I'll have your photos up in a minute. Before we look at them, though, I want you to be prepared. I don't have a real good feeling about these. You were stiff and uncomfortable. I'd say you even looked scared. We might need to try again when you're more comfortable with the idea."

She nodded. How bad could they be? The list didn't say she had to have good pictures. She just had to pose. She posed. Xander clicked the mouse a couple of times and turned the monitor to face Quinn.

The slideshow flipped by on screen in slow motion. They were horrible. Worse than horrible. Her eyes filled. She didn't look uncomfortable. She looked *constipated*. This couldn't be worse. She stood abruptly and grabbed her purse. "Thank you for trying. I appreciate the effort. Send me the bill for your time."

She turned and ran for the door. As she bounded down the stairs, she heard Xander call her name. Her embarrassment wouldn't allow her to turn back. By the time she hit the street, tears spilled down her cheeks. Her stride ate up the sidewalk on the way back to her loft. Her phone rang. Indy. She was glad she hadn't shown. She didn't need another human being to witness this. She worked to steady her voice. "Hi."

"Hey. I tried calling after I got your text, but it went straight to voice mail. I was running late. Where are you?"

"It didn't work out. You can go home. Thanks."

"Are you okay? You want me to come over?"

Another deep, steadying breath. "No, I want to be alone."

"You sure?"

"Yeah." She closed her phone and turned the corner to face her building. She lost her wish to be alone as well as her battle for control over her tears.

Ryan stood at her front door clutching a bouquet of daisies.

CHAPTER 12

Ryan felt the moment she saw him. She paused and her body language screamed, "Run the other way." He couldn't see her eyes to read her expression, but given her pace, she wasn't happy. She only moved like that when she was trying to get away from something unpleasant. The body language contradicted the easygoing appearance of her dress. She looked ready for a picnic in the park.

As she neared, he realized she wasn't pissed off or irritated. Tears streaked through makeup on her cheeks, leaving odd striations on her skin. "What's wrong?"

"Nothing. I don't want to talk right now." Her voice shook and her breath hitched as she inhaled.

He closed the distance between them and slid her sunglasses from her eyes. Her eyes were puffy and red. She sniffed. "I brought you flowers to apologize." He handed the bouquet to her.

She cradled them in her arms. "Thank you." She stepped around him to get to her door.

"What happened?"

"I said I don't want to talk." Her hand trembled as she tried to shove her key into the door.

Ryan reached over and placed his hand on top of hers. "Let me help you."

"I'm beyond help."

He unlocked the door and held it open for her. She didn't tell him to leave again, so he took it as an invitation to follow. He braced himself for another elevator ride, but she surprised him by entering the stairwell. They walked up in silence, giving her time to compose herself. He was afraid to say anything that might start the tears again.

In her apartment, he put her keys on the side table and folded her sunglasses next to them. She walked straight to the kitchen, put the flowers in a vase, and disappeared into the bathroom. He sat on the couch and waited for her to return. Manners wouldn't allow her to hide from him for long.

She entered the room, put the flowers on the table in front of him, and sat at the end of the couch. She had washed her face. The makeup and teary streaks were gone, but her cheeks were still blotchy. "Thank you for the flowers. They're beautiful. If they're from the same place you got them last time, they'll last a long time."

"So, where were you coming from?"

She shot him a look letting him know she still wasn't ready to talk. Pulling a pillow onto her lap, she plucked at its edges. "What have you been up to? Besides organizing a speed dating event?"

"Mary's been bugging me for a long time to do singles events. This is her project."

Quinn tilted her head and narrowed her eyes. "So this happening right now has nothing to do with my list?"

He couldn't lie. Her voice already told him she knew. "Your list was the push I needed to give Mary the green light. Not *everything's* about you."

She smiled. "Thanks. It seems like the only way I can be successful with that damn list is with your help."

"What else have you tried to accomplish?" Part of him feared the answer, but he needed to know.

One hand tightened on the pillow. Her eyes focused intently on the seam. He waited. She needed time, but she would tell him.

"After we fought on Friday, I was determined to complete the list without you. I went online and re-created my profile for a dating site. I also called the photographer and made an appointment to pose and have pictures taken."

Another long pause. Fingers pulling at threads of the pillow. "I made a date with a guy for coffee. Turns out, he and his girlfriend were looking for a threesome. Mega-false advertising there."

Ryan tensed. He wondered what was on her profile to attract maggots. "What about the photographer?"

She didn't look up. A fat tear dropped onto her hand. He moved closer to her and lifted her face to meet his. Anger gripped his stomach. "What happened? Is that where you were coming from?"

She nodded. "It was horrible. Humiliating."

His left hand held her chin and his right closed into a fist. "What did this creep do?"

"Nothing. His job. He took my picture." She swiped at the fresh tears. At least she wasn't sobbing.

He relaxed his hands. "You're upset because the pictures didn't turn out well?"

She shoved him away and stood with her back to him. "Go ahead and make fun of me."

"I'm not laughing. Everyone takes bad pictures." He stood behind her and touched her shoulder. "Even supermodels aren't perfect."

"You weren't there. You didn't see. Pictures don't lie. Airbrushing couldn't fix that."

With his hands on her shoulders, he turned her to face him. "I can't believe they were as bad as you think."

"They were so bad the whole photo shoot lasted only twenty minutes. Then he felt the need to warn me they were bad."

"Maybe he sucks as a photographer." He brushed a tear away with his thumb.

She shook her head. "I've seen his portfolio. Of nudes. Lots of different women. They were all beautiful."

The women or the photographs? "You're beautiful, Quinn."

She snorted in disbelief.

He wished she could see herself through his eyes. "You were nervous, right?"

She nodded.

"What did he do to put you at ease?"

She shrugged. "He's not a babysitter. I hired him to do a job."

"Part of his job is to get the best picture possible. If he let you go through the whole shoot with your guard up and your stomach in knots, how could he get a good shot of you? I've seen you smile and burst out laughing and so pissed off you could bite someone. I bet he didn't get any emotion from you." He leaned over and kissed her cheek. "You are beautiful through and through."

Her tears dried and her eyes reflected something other than sadness.

She turned her head and captured his mouth with hers. Her glassy eyes locked on his. She sucked his lower lip. This was no friendly kiss. She was definitely picking up where they'd left off last week. All coherent thought left his head as blood rushed south. His fingers threaded into her smooth hair and he changed the angle of the kiss.

His tongue grazed her teeth and touched hers. Her eyes fluttered closed as their tongues mated. He inched his body to close the slight gap between them, wanting to feel the heat from her body. Her arms circled his waist. Fingers crawled up his back, causing a shiver. He pressed his pelvis into her. His hard-on sought her softness.

She broke the kiss to whisper, "Upstairs."

He looked into her eyes, red from crying, and wondered, why now? She was feeling low and he didn't want her to regret this later. "Are you sure?"

She nodded and laced her fingers through his.

As she led the way up the stairs to her bedroom, he watched the sway of her hips. *Does she always walk with the invitation, or is this for me?* At the top, he grabbed her body and pulled it back into him, pressing his erection into the curve of her backside. He kissed the side of her neck and she rocked into him. She brought her hand back and caressed his thigh. He propelled their bodies toward the bedroom.

Unlike the brightly sunlit first floor, her bedroom was dark. She had the two east-facing windows covered with blinds and drapes. He left her standing at the side of the bed, and pulled the drapes open and twisted the wand of the blinds.

"What are you doing?"

He walked back to her and wrapped an arm around her waist. "I want to see you. I won't let you hide in the dark." He reclaimed her mouth while tugging her dress up. When it was to her chest, he stepped back to pull it over her head. She hadn't worn a bra and his eyes widened. "Absolutely beautiful."

She took a deep breath. Her hands touched his chest. "What happens tomorrow?"

"I'll still respect you in the morning," he said with a smile. He stepped closer to those wonderful, firm breasts.

"But will you still be my friend?" The question was tentative and fearful. It tore into his chest.

"I'll be whatever you want." He hoped it was more than a friend.

He lowered his head and pulled on her nipple with his teeth. The sharp intake of her breath ended the questions. He moved to the other breast. A whimper escaped her lips. He went back to her mouth and walked their bodies to the bed.

Quinn lay back. "Get naked."

He kicked off his shoes while whipping his shirt over his head. His hard-on strained against the zipper of his jeans. He slid his underwear off with his pants in one motion. Before joining her on the bed, he pulled her panties off, leaving her naked.

She scooted back near the pillow, covering her body in shadows. He wanted to watch her lose control, lose herself in his arms.

"Uh-uh." He grabbed her ankles and dragged her body into the sunlight. He covered her body with his and kissed her. He trailed kisses down her neck. "I want to see you."

"I like the dark," she whispered.

He lifted himself to see her face. Her eyes were closed and her head turned. Still hiding.

Ryan turned her face to him. "Open your eyes, Quinn." She complied. "You are beautiful and sexy. I want to be inside you more than you can imagine, but if you're not comfortable, say so now."

"I want this. I'd prefer the curtains closed."

He leaned close and pulled her earlobe between his teeth and released it. "We'll do it your way next time."

The little voice in his head pointed out that she didn't argue about there being a next time. Hope surged through him.

She reached for his erection, but he pulled away and continued to kiss the soft flesh of her torso. He wouldn't last long once she touched him, so he had to satisfy her first. Goose bumps rose on her skin under his touch.

With one nipple in his mouth, his fingers spread her folds. She was already wet and hot. He slid one finger in, then another as his thumb massaged her. Her hips rose instinctively seeking rhythm and release.

He felt the moan start deep in her chest and he knew she fought to swallow it. Her hands clutched the sheets in her fists. She was near peak. He stroked gently, suckling her breasts, licking her throat. He worked his way back up to her face.

"Condom?" he asked quietly, hating to disturb the pace.

She blinked and focused. "Drawer," she answered, and flopped her arm toward the nightstand.

He reached across her body and grabbed a condom. Her body continued to wiggle beneath his. He rubbed himself against her center.

Quinn pulled his face close for a kiss and lifted her hips to meet his.

Ryan guided himself into her, burying himself in the warmth and wetness. He thrust again and her legs locked around him. She rocked her body.

"Let go," he whispered in her ear. "I want to watch." One hand tugged at a nipple while he trailed his tongue on her neck.

Her thighs pulled him all the way into her and she created the rhythm of thrusts.

He knew the minute she lost all sense of self-consciousness. Her nails dug into his back and she leaned up to bite his shoulder. "Faster," she commanded breathlessly.

Ryan obeyed. Their hearts pounded against each other. Their bodies became slick with sweat. She tightened around him. Her body went rigid and her thighs trembled. One more deep thrust and he exploded inside her. He collapsed on top of her, mingling his sweat with hers. They both huffed breath, chests heaving.

Quinn trailed a finger down his back. "God, that was good. It's been so long, I forgot how much fun it is with a partner."

He laughed. "Good to know I'm better than a vibrator."

She laughed loudly in his ear and her walls closed tightly around him again. He hardened from his semi-soft state and rocked against her.

"Mmm. More?" Her breath tickled his ear.

"Yeah" was all he could muster. It had been far too long.

She rolled him over, obviously pleased with the prospect. Up on her knees, she came down on top of him and leaned back. He didn't think it possible to sink deeper into her, but he did.

He reached up and massaged her breasts as she bounced on his dick to her own rhythm, seeking her own pleasure. She leaned forward and pressed her breast to his mouth. She ground down into him and came again.

Her body throbbed around him as she lay fully on top of him. As their breathing returned to normal, she slid off his body and shivered.

Ryan pulled her close and covered them both with the blanket. She curled into him and fell asleep. His hand rested on the curve of her back near her hip.

How could she doubt her beauty? Every time she walked into the bar, heads turned. Could she be that unaware? He closed his eyes and pictured Quinn entering the bar. If alone, she walked with her head down, purposefully cautious. But she was rarely alone. She came in with a crowd, or she was with Indy. Although uninterested, Ryan couldn't ignore Indy's sexy confidence. She was actress-beautiful, where Quinn was everyday pretty. Quinn didn't know her own beauty because she made sure she was shielded.

Quinn shifted next to him and stretched. He must've dozed off. Shadows bathed the room, though not yet night. She rolled away from him onto her back, gripping the sheet at her chest, and sighed.

It didn't sound like a contented, happy sigh either. "What?" he asked, propping on an elbow.

Her arm lay across her face, concealing her eyes. "It was real. I didn't dream it."

Ryan ran a hand over her stomach and inched her closer. "So you dream about me. This was completely real." He paused and pushed her arm away. "Regretting it?"

"I don't know. I told you I'm not good at the friends with benefits thing."

"Trust me. You're plenty good."

She sat up, still clutching the sheet. "I'm going to get water. Want some?"

"Sure." He slid toward the headboard and propped pillows behind him. He watched as she cautiously slid off the bed and grabbed a T-shirt to wear.

What was he doing? Did he think he'd convince her to abandon her mission to get pregnant so she could start a relationship with him? Griff would smack him if he heard what was going on in Ryan's head.

Quinn returned, holding two bottles of water. Her short hair was mussed and her skin glowed. Regardless of her mental turmoil, physically, she looked happy.

He cracked open the bottle she offered and let the icy liquid run down his throat. "So what's your plan?"

"For what?" she asked, covering herself with the sheet.

He lay uncovered and relaxed. "For the photographer."

Her face darkened with sadness. Shit. She lifted one shoulder in response and gulped some water.

Ryan leaned closer and kissed her shoulder. "Want me to beat him up? Then we can destroy the pictures."

She chuckled. "He didn't do anything wrong. The pictures aren't real. It's all digital."

"What do you mean?" Suspicion crept into his mind.

"He didn't print the pictures. I viewed them on his computer."

She didn't see it. Not even the possibility yet. But some guy had naked pictures of her on his computer. He could do whatever he wanted with them. It would destroy her completely.

Quinn looked fully in his eyes. "What's wrong?"

He forced a smile. "Nothing. I'm starving. I was preoccupied at lunchtime. Let's order food. Chinese work for you?"

"Sure."

"You have a phonebook?"

"In the drawer to the right of the fridge I have menus for different places."

"What do you want?" he asked, getting off the bed.

"Whatever you order is fine. I'm going to take a shower. Make yourself at home."

Ryan didn't bother with clothes and walked downstairs to the kitchen. She didn't move from the bed until he left the room. Her reservation and modesty must have returned.

He pulled a menu from the drawer and used her phone to place an order. When he returned the flyer, his eyes landed on her list. Number eight—"Have a night of mind-blowing sex with multiple orgasms."—

had the precise X over the number and a smiley face after it. He'd earned the descriptor of mind-blowing and a smiley face and he hadn't even been trying.

Quinn started the water, allowing it to warm up. What was she thinking? She looked at her reflection in the mirror above the sink. She couldn't deny the sex had been fabulous. Her skin tingled at re-membering Ryan's touch.

This was wrong. He didn't fit her plan. He couldn't be her sum-mer romance, and he certainly didn't want to get her pregnant. They'd had great sex.

And he's still here.

That was the crux of her problem. She didn't know what to do with the friend who continued to be a friend after sex. There had been guys who were so-so in bed and she couldn't wait for them to leave so she could curl up with a good book. Then there was Nick, who had skills, but would practically hit the door running as soon as they were finished.

Ryan had offered to order food. He planned to stay. To hang out like they usually did.

She stepped under the hot spray and closed her eyes. The warmth spread over her and she realized she was creating problems for her-self. What was she worried about? Ryan only wanted this: friendship and great sex. He knew exactly what her plans were.

Then a new thought entered her head. What if she asked Ryan to be her sperm donor? Sure, he wasn't ready to be a dad, but he was the perfect candidate. He was a good man. That's exactly what she wanted for her baby. It didn't hurt that he was gorgeous too. If they were friends, he could see the kid, but he wouldn't have to be a dad. Since she wouldn't be getting pregnant in the conventional way, he wouldn't feel like a dad.

But what if he didn't want any part of it? She might lose him as a friend.

She considered how to broach the subject.

When Quinn came down the stairs, Ryan had already opened the white containers of Chinese food and arranged them on the coffee table in front of the couch. The tantalizing smell of sweet-and-sour something reached her nose. She closed her eyes and inhaled, the scent making her mouth water. Ryan had even gotten plates and silverware. She had him pegged for an eat-out-of-the-carton man.

He came from the kitchen carrying two cans of pop. He wore only his jeans, and they hung low on his hips. Delicious. His hair was unruly and she imagined that was as styled as it got any day. She felt frumpy in her T-shirt and shorts.

She sat on the couch and picked up a plate. Her stomach growled so loud Ryan looked up. She felt her cheeks blush.

"I'm not the only one starving." His easy smile relaxed her.

They loaded their plates with generous helpings of sweet-and-sour pork and Moo Goo Gai Pan, and settled in on the couch. Quinn pulled her feet up and crossed them, balancing her plate on her knee. Ryan held his plate at his chest and extended his legs to rest on the table.

"Where does your name come from? Is it a family name or something?"

Quinn groaned with a mouthful of rice. After she swallowed, she answered, "It's kind of a long story. I don't particularly like to tell it. It's not cute or amusing. It's not even interesting."

"Now you have to tell me. You and your sister have unusual names. I don't even know what Indy is short for." He paused to take a drink. "I assume she's not named after Indiana Jones."

"No, though she might prefer it." Quinn ate another big bite of chicken before beginning her explanation. She washed it down with a swig of Diet Coke.

She blew out a slow breath, tired of the story. "First, you need to understand our father is very, uh, patriotic. He planned on having two sons. He really counted on it. The first would be named John, the second Quincy." She paused, waiting for it to sink in.

Ryan eyed her and the smile broke across his face. "John and Quincy Adams. You said it wasn't funny. That's pretty funny."

She resisted sticking her tongue out at him. "When Indy was born, he realized he couldn't name her John. So he named her Independence."

Ryan's mouth dropped open. "Where was your mother in this?"

"Stopping him from naming her Freedom. Mom figured Independence would give her more choices for nicknames."

He nodded understanding. "Your name isn't Quincy, is it?"

She chuckled. "No, I was his next disappointment. Had I been a boy, I would've been John Quincy. Instead, he shortened it to Quinn. Even with the occasional gender mix-up, I think I got the better name." She picked up her plate and continued eating.

"Kind of crappy to know you were a disappointment just by being born."

She shook her head. "It wasn't like that. I mean, my dad loves us. He always wanted a son." She lifted a shoulder. "Don't all men?"

Ryan slid his back against the arm of the couch to face her. His long legs extended under her crossed legs and touched the other end. "I guess so. Every guy has an image of fishing or playing catch or wrestling in the yard with his son."

Quinn had a quick mental flash of shirtless Ryan tussling on the living room floor with a young boy. He would be a fun dad. "Your turn."

"For what?"

"Tell me about your siblings. You have a boatload, but you haven't told me much."

"You thought your story was long? It was nothing." He put his empty plate on the table. "Colin is the oldest. We're Irish twins."

"Huh?"

"We're only a year apart. Basically, Mom got pregnant with me right after having Colin. Because we're so close in age, people would see us together and think we were twins."

"Oh." There was another one of him?

"Colin dropped out of the picture for the last few years, but he just blew back in. You'll see him around. He's working at the bar."

"Which one?"

"Both. Wherever I schedule him. Michael is next in line behind me. He's the fireman. You've seen him at O'Leary's. Liam comes next. He's a chef at Porter's downtown. He's making a name for himself and wants to open his own restaurant."

"Are all of you single? You haven't mentioned any wives or kids."

He smiled crookedly. "Much to my mother's dismay, we're all single. Michael has been with the same girl for three years now. I think they might be the first."

"Four boys in a row. You're all close in age?"

Ryan nodded. "The biggest span is four years between Michael and Liam."

"I can't believe your parents kept going. Your house must've been insane. Did your mom want a girl?"

"Actually, it was Dad who wanted a girl. But we're also Irish Catholic. No birth control. Moira came after Liam. She's a reporter for the *Herald* in the 'burbs. Maggie is the baby. She's still in school working on some creative writing degree. No one knows what she'll do with it."

"Quite a household. Are you all close?"

"Pretty much. We don't talk all the time. We have our own lives, but we get together for Sunday dinner with Mom after church at least once a month. They all pitch in if I need extra help at the bar. Everyone works Saint Patty's Day. It's tradition."

"I think I'm jealous. It must be cool to have a big family."

"It has its moments, but there are pitfalls too."

"Like what? I can see the fighting and stuff as kids, but as adults, it must be like having your own crew of friends."

"Sometimes."

He got quiet and Quinn knew something was bothering him about his family. "Why did your brother drop out of the picture?"

His eyes darkened a fraction and she knew she hit the right nerve. "When my father died, he left O'Leary's to me. Well, my mom is still part owner, but it's mine."

"Colin wanted it?"

"It should've been his. He's oldest and Dad counted on him to take over. But Colin's a fuck-up. Always has been. Lucky for us, my dad saw it before he died, or O'Leary's would be history."

She stood and began closing containers. Ryan followed her lead and took their plates to the kitchen. "Are you mad he's back? Didn't you miss him?"

"I missed my brother, not the trouble he brings."

There was more to it than some trouble. A deep, simmering anger rose beneath the surface, but he tried to conceal it. The sun had begun its descent, so Quinn turned on the light over the counter. Ryan eyed the clock on the microwave.

"Need to go?" she asked.

He leaned against the counter. "Not yet. But Mary has a lot to set up for tomorrow. I didn't plan on being gone this long."

Her eyes widened. "You mean you didn't plan on coming over here to seduce me and screw my brains out?"

"It wasn't on my agenda for today. I thought maybe we'd have lunch."

She leaned into the refrigerator and placed cartons on the shelf. "We certainly had more than that."

When she stood and closed the door, Ryan pressed against her and kissed her full on the mouth. He pulled away and they were both slightly breathless. Quinn knew it was now or never. She wouldn't find the guts again to ask him. "I have a serious proposition for you."

His hands roamed her body. She knew she didn't have his attention, so she grasped the sides of his face and brought it close to hers. "Will you consider being my sperm donor?"

In an instant, his face went from aroused to confused. "Huh?"

"I've told you that I plan to get pregnant in the fall. I've looked at a bunch of options. It's important for me to know the sperm donor is a good person. Like you said, anyone can lie on a piece of paper."

"You want me to get you pregnant?"

"Not conventionally. You'd just give me sperm in a cup and the doctor will do the rest. You wouldn't have any other involvement." Her stomach churned as she questioned her sanity. Hadn't she been afraid of losing him as a friend? Judging by the look on his face, this was like a shove out the door.

"I don't know what to say."

She shrugged as if this was no big deal. "Don't say anything. I know it's a huge decision. Will you give it some thought?"

"Okay." His phone rang and echoed from the bedroom upstairs. He groaned.

"Shouldn't you answer that?"

"It's probably my family." He trailed more kisses down her neck.

The phone rang again. He lifted his head. "I guess I better get it. It might be Mary. You can come to the bar and keep me company."

He doesn't want to go. "Thanks, but I have stuff to do here."

He pulled away, his fingers lingering at the base of her skull. "Okay. You know where to find me if you change your mind."

She nodded, helpless to answer. He jogged upstairs to get the rest of his clothes and she filled the sink with water. She was suddenly lost again in a field of sex and friendship, not knowing which path to take. She feared she might've made a huge mistake—maybe more than one.

Quinn wiped her hands quickly on her shirt and picked up her cell phone. She sent a brief text message to Indy.

Had sex with Ryan. Help.

She turned on the radio and sunk her hands into the water. The song playing was familiar, so she sang along and didn't hear Ryan come back into the room.

"You're a good singer. You should've taken the stage."

Her hands froze in the sudsy water. She'd never sung for anyone. Not since she was a kid. Having Ryan walk in was like being caught dancing naked in her living room. Her muscles filled with tension.

Ryan came up behind her and rested his hands on her hips. He kissed the side of her neck. The warmth of his hands spread across her hips to her center. She inhaled his masculine scent and she relaxed. His kiss ended with a nip on her earlobe.

She almost leaned back into him, wanting more, but she stopped short. He needed to leave. Their romp was fun, but over. They needed to get back to the real world.

"I'll call you later."

"Okay." She didn't turn around. If she did, she might ask him to take her back upstairs. That would be a mistake.

Right after the door closed, her cell phone chirped. A text from Indy.

R U Kidding?

She responded with a no.

B there soon.

Good. Indy to the rescue. She would know what to do and how to handle this. She knew what to do with most men.

* * *

The enormity of Quinn's request for his sperm weighed in Ryan's chest. He had no idea how to respond to her. He supposed if he had a really good friend who couldn't get pregnant, he might think about donating sperm, but this was weird. What would they be? She didn't want him to be the father; she'd said she only wanted sperm.

He looked at his phone. For a change it hadn't been his family who had interrupted his day, but Mary, at the bar. Ryan called to find out what emergency needed his attention. Couldn't he even get one afternoon away?

"O'Leary's."

"Hey, Mary, what's up?"

"Oh, thank God it's you. I've got a bar full of people talking about getting free drinks. I have no idea where they came from. They say they're participating in a pub crawl and they were promised a free drink with the flyer."

"What pub crawl?" he asked as he got into his car.

"Your guess is as good as mine, but the natives are getting restless. What do you want me to do?"

"Shit. Offer them all a free beer. Nothing else. Tell them there was a mistake on the flyer. I'll be there as soon as I can." He stepped on the gas. This had Colin's name all over it. He said he wanted to learn the business. What bullshit.

Pushing through the front door, he couldn't believe the crowd. He got behind the bar and asked Mary, "How's it going?"

"Most are pissed that I'm only pouring beer, but they're taking it. What the heck's going on with this? How am I supposed to set up for tomorrow with this crowd? I was counting on the usual business tonight."

He patted her arm. "Don't worry. We'll get you set up. This won't last long."

She moved away to continue to gather flyers and pour beer. They worked side by side for an hour before the crowd dwindled. Grabbing one of the flyers, he leaned against the register.

NEW ADDITION TO THE PUB CRAWL.
FINISH YOUR NIGHT AT O'LEARY'S.
FLYER ENTITLES HOLDER TO ONE FREE DRINK.

He eyed Mary. She looked beat. Her shift had ended a while ago, but as usual, she stayed because he needed her. "Have you seen Colin?"

She stopped wiping down the bar. "I think he's in the back room. He was here earlier, but I haven't seen him in a while."

"Okay. Go home. Tomorrow's a big day. Jenna can handle the bar."

"See you tomorrow."

Ryan walked around the bar and headed toward the back. If Colin wasn't still there, he'd track him down. Luckily, he didn't have to look far. Sitting at a table, surrounded by drunks, his brother waved to him.

"Hey, Ry. Great crowd tonight, huh?"

"Yeah, great." He nodded to the other guys at the table. "Can I see you in the office for a minute?"

"Sure." Colin slid from his seat and loped toward him. It seemed the man had only one speed—snail.

Once in the office, Ryan began to pace, trying to rein in his temper. "What's up?"

Ryan held out the crumpled flyer. "What do you know about this?"

"Last night I heard about this pub crawl that was starting at McGuff's. It's a tour of Irish pubs in the area. People were going from bar to bar. I asked around and thought it would be a good way to drum up business for a slow Monday night. I met the crawlers at McGuff's and handed out the flyers to bring them here."

Ryan inhaled deeply. His brother had been trying to do something good. He couldn't help that he was selfish and didn't think before he acted. "You should've checked with me first."

"I get that this is *your* bar. But it's a family business. I took some initiative. What's the big freakin' deal?"

"The big deal is that you brought a ton of people into the bar without warning, offering them free drinks. At the *end* of a pub crawl. These people only showed for the free drink. It's a Monday night. They have to work tomorrow. They're not staying and spending their money. They took their free drink and left. By my estimation, you just cost me money."

Colin's face dropped.

"This is exactly what got you into trouble with Dad. You don't think. You just do whatever the fuck sounds good. You said you wanted to learn the business. Here's your first lesson—in order to make money, you can't give away the product." He turned and sat on the edge of his desk.

"I was trying to help. Mondays are slow. I thought bringing in more customers would be a good thing."

"If they were spending money, it would've been good. Now in addition to losing money and pissing people off because they got a free beer instead of whatever top-shelf liquor they thought they were going to get, Mary's exhausted and she's got to set up for her speed dating tomorrow night."

Colin shoved his hands in his pockets, not making a move toward the door.

"Go home. I have a bar to run."

"I'll help. What do you need me to do?"

"You've done enough." Ryan was suddenly exhausted. He scrubbed a hand over his face as he watched Colin leave. He couldn't keep cleaning up after Colin. Part of him wished Colin had stayed wherever he'd been. At the rate things were going, he'd never be able to have his own life; he'd be too busy fixing Colin's screw-ups.

CHAPTER 13

Quinn finished washing dishes and went to check her e-mail while she waited for Indy. Three notices from her online profile. She could potentially set up three more dates. The thought of the last one soured the idea.

One e-mail from Mr. Carlson asking her to stop by Tuesday, if at all possible. She'd have to think about it. How bad could it be? Summer school hadn't even been in session for two weeks.

Another e-mail from O'Leary's confirming her attendance plus one for speed dating on Tuesday.

Her phone rang. The machine picked up. No message. Cell phone rang. Nick. She pushed the phone to the side and resisted the urge to answer it.

The doorbell rang less than a minute later. She debated answering it. She dialed Indy's number instead.

"Why are you calling me? Buzz me in."

Thank God. Quinn hit the buzzer and unlocked her front door. The landline rang again.

"Hey, babe. It's me. We haven't seen each other in a while. Thought maybe we could get together. I miss you."

Indy entered at the last sentence. "Please tell me that wasn't Nick."

Quinn nodded.

"At least you didn't pick up. You're improving." She shut the door behind her and kicked off her heels. She fell onto the couch. "Now tell me what happened."

Quinn curled up on the opposite end of the couch and told the story, beginning with her photo shoot. Had it really been less than twelve hours ago? It seemed like weeks.

She offered only the briefest highlights of the phenomenal sex, but Indy understood.

"That good, huh? Number eight crossed off the list?"

"And then some. If I had to sum it up, all I could say is Hoo-doggie."

Indy burst into an outrageous laugh. "I haven't heard that since we were kids. He must be something to pull the hillbilly out of you."

Quinn let her smile say it all.

"So what do you want help with? Sounds like things are going great."

Quinn blew out a deep breath. "Yes, the sex was great, but I need to find balance or boundaries for the friendship."

One of Indy's eyebrows rose. "You think after today you're still just friends?"

"Yeah. It was weird in a good way. We ate together, talked about our families, and cleaned up. We hung out, but it wasn't uncomfortable at all."

"Honey, that's called a date."

"No, a date ends in sex. It doesn't start with it." Quinn curled her legs under herself.

"Are you sure he's on the same page?"

"He didn't say otherwise."

"Yeah, he did. If it was just sex, he would've left. He wouldn't have stuck around to chat."

"That would make sense if it was a one-night stand. We're friends. He promised he'd still be my friend."

Indy snorted.

"Besides, a relationship with him doesn't fit into my plans." She paused, not sure how to continue. "I asked him to be my sperm donor."

"You what?" Indy's eyes widened and the fear in Quinn's mind exploded.

"I asked him to consider being my sperm donor. I don't know

what I was thinking. It was just that he was so nice to me, and we were talking and all I could think was 'what a great guy.' That's what I'm looking for in a donor."

"That's what you should be looking for in a *boyfriend.* What did he say?"

"Not much. I think I freaked him out."

"Ya think?"

"Sarcasm is not helping."

"You're not giving anything a chance because of your stupid plans. You're going to throw away a potentially great thing because it follows a different path. Don't fear detours. They can lead to exciting places."

Quinn shook her head. "I don't need a lecture on my choices. I need help."

"Let the relationship develop its own course. If it's meant to be, it will find a way."

"You sound very Zen. What about having sex?"

"Do it. It's fun," she answered with a wink.

"Again, not helpful." Quinn knew the conversation was going nowhere. Indy kept pushing her in Ryan's direction to try to waylay her pregnancy plans. She switched gears to her other pressing problem. "I need you to go with me to a speed dating thing tomorrow night."

"No."

"I don't need you to do the rounds. You'd be there for emotional support and to be my wingman." Even with Ryan claiming to be her friend, she knew he wouldn't want to be her wingman to find another date.

Indy flipped her long blond locks over her shoulder. "Fine. But I won't promise to be nice. Where and when?"

"O'Leary's at seven-thirty."

"Are you fucking nuts?" Indy's hands flailed, matching her irate tone.

"What?"

"You're seriously going to Ryan's bar to find a date. You're going to flaunt yourself in front of him and flirt with other guys. After you had the nerve to ask him for his sperm."

"Ryan set this up to help me meet someone for my summer romance."

"For someone so smart, you can be totally clueless. He's a man. Everything changed when you had sex with him." Her arms continued to punctuate her statements.

"You make Ryan sound like a teenage girl. You're right. He's a man. By definition, he should be okay with no strings sex."

Indy blew out an exasperated breath. "He won't be okay with seeing you with other men. Even if he knows it happens, he doesn't want it in his face."

"Can we forget Ryan for a minute? I'm doing speed dating tomorrow. I need help selling myself in three minutes or less."

Indy crossed her arms.

Quinn waited for the irritation to pass. Indy never stayed angry long.

"You're making a huge mistake. You'll regret screwing this up."

Quinn looked at her sister. Indy was rarely this serious. "I appreciate your concern. But Ryan knew from the get-go I wasn't interested in dating him. If he walks out of my life because we had sex and I want to date other people, then he's not much of a friend." The thought sickened her a little, but she wanted to believe it.

"You're wrong."

"It's my life. My choices." She hoped to God Indy was wrong.

Indy uncrossed her arms and leaned forward. "You're starting to sound like me. That should be a red flag announcing you're messing up." She stood and stretched. "I'm hungry. What do you have to eat?"

"Leftover Chinese food." Quinn led the way to the kitchen, mulling over Indy's words. Roles had been reversed for so many years, she didn't know what to do. She'd always been the responsible one, pointing out Indy's mistakes.

They spent time devising questions and answers for speed dating. Indy agreed to come and help weed out the assholes. Then Richard called and Indy scurried out to meet him, ending their sister time.

So much for taking a break. Why couldn't Indy see what a waste of time he was? Indy's words echoes back at her. Was she as bad as Indy?

No, I plan things. I set goals and do what I need to do to reach them. Indy flies around and takes things in stride without trying to adjust them to suit her.

I'm right about Ryan and my plans to get pregnant.

She grabbed a book to read in bed when her phone rang. She answered without thinking. "Hello."

"Hey, babe."

"What do you want, Nick?" She leaned against the arm of the couch, regretting answering the phone.

"I'm outside. Can I come up?"

"I was getting ready for bed."

"I could join you."

Surprisingly, he sounded sober. "Not a good idea."

"Can we talk?"

"Why?" Her impatience grew.

"I can't do this over the phone. Please let me up."

Quinn pinched the bridge of her nose. How many turns could one day take? "You have five minutes." She disconnected and buzzed him up.

Moments later, Nick stood in the doorway looking ragged as hell. He hadn't shaved. His eyes were shadowed, and he looked drained. He stared at her. "You look great."

She reached up, smoothed her hair, and looked down at her clothes. "I look the same as always."

He stepped into the room. "No, you look different. You have a glow."

She snorted a laugh. "Give it up."

Nick shook his head. "I'm serious. You look happy."

Her lips barely curved. "I guess I am."

"Good. I'm glad." He walked through the room stiffly, his hands fidgeting.

"What's up?"

"I'm not."

She waited, arms crossed.

"Not happy. I haven't been in a long time." He turned and stepped closer to her. "I've been doing a lot of thinking. I haven't been happy since we split up."

"I'm sorry to hear that. What happened with your . . . girlfriend?"

"False alarm." He shoved his hands in his pockets. "You always did like to make things difficult for me." He inhaled deeply. "I miss you. I miss us. Things were good when we were together."

Quinn's hands dropped and anger balled in her stomach. "Things were good for *you* when we were together. You were responsible for nothing, except having fun, which meant sleeping with every woman in sight."

"We had fun together."

"Yeah, but I live in the real world where bills have to be paid. People count on me. Life is more than a good time." She realized her arms were waving every bit as much as Indy's had been. She crossed her arms again.

He inched closer. "I don't have a shot?"

She shook her head softly. He kissed her forehead and walked toward the door.

Without turning around, he said, "I hope you don't mind, but I'll check in with you every now and then."

She didn't answer. She knew he would show up periodically, but she also knew she was really over him. After locking up, she snuggled in the sheets and inhaled Ryan's scent that still clung to the pillow.

CHAPTER 14

Early the next morning, Ryan slogged through the bar. He had spent a lot of time the previous night getting the dance floor ready and blocked off for speed dating. Mary was truly excited. He was surprised to see her behind the bar.

"Hey, what are you doing here?"

Mary looked up from the cup of coffee in her hand. "I'm doing one more run-through for tonight. I want to make sure everything goes as smoothly as possible. You are going to be here, right?"

"Yes, I said I'd be here." He paused, not wanting to ruin her optimistic mood. "My friend Quinn might be a no-show, though."

She slumped forward. "What? She confirmed. Not once, but twice. She's bringing a friend."

She plans on coming? The news startled him more than seeing Mary after her long night. Quinn must've responded before they spent the afternoon having sex. She would show, since she'd committed. "I could be wrong."

Mary put her cup down. "Could you call her?"

"You have her number."

"She might agree to still show if you asked her."

I don't want to ask her. "I'll try."

"Thanks." She drank from her cup again.

"Go home. I'll see you tonight. Who's coming in now?"

"Jenna called. She's running a little behind."

"Okay." He headed for his office. A few minutes later, he heard Colin's happy whistle in the hall.

Colin stuck his head in. "Hi. What's Mary doing here? I thought she was running the dating thing tonight."

"She's nervous and wanted to check on things again. What are you doing here?"

"I figured I owed Mary some help." Colin was as calm and laid-back as ever. No anger or tension rolled off him after last night.

Ryan looked at his brother quietly for a moment and decided he could confide in him. Regardless of their issues, they were still brothers. "What do you know about photography?"

Colin crossed his arms and leaned on the doorjamb. "Is this a trick question?"

"No."

"Not much. What are you looking for?"

"What if someone had pictures taken they don't want anyone to see?"

"You got a Playboy Bunny I haven't met?"

"I'm serious." He ran a hand through his hair and reconsidered telling Colin.

"It was a joke. What's the problem?"

"I have a friend who had some unflattering pictures taken. What's the likelihood they'd be destroyed?"

"I don't know. If the guy's less than professional, it's a couple of clicks of the mouse and her image is all over the Internet."

"That's what I thought." He picked up his keys again. "Keep an eye on things. Jenna will be here soon. Tell her I'll be back before we hit lunch."

"Need any help?"

Ryan shook his head. "I can handle this."

He drove to Hill Studio. On the way there, Ryan told himself he would speak calmly and rationally. There was a possibility this guy was legit and Quinn's pictures would be safe. Given her track record, though, he was scum looking for a quick buck. Ryan would pay whatever price to save her the embarrassment. He figured the possibility would occur to her soon, once the embarrassment left, and she could focus clearly.

Ryan parked in front of the building and strode quickly to the door. He rang and was buzzed up without question.

At the door, a young girl met him with a smile. "Hi, can I help you?"

"I hope so. I wanted to speak with the photographer."

She opened the door wider. "Xander's not here, but he should be back in a minute."

He followed her in and scanned the loft. It was mostly empty space, except for the photography paraphernalia. "So what happens after pictures are taken? Do you give me the only copies?"

"No, we save it on our computer in case something happens to the client's file."

Ryan narrowed his eyes at the girl. "So my photos could be spread anywhere?"

Her eyes widened in shock. "No. Xander would never do that. He's a professional."

The door behind her swung open. A man entered. Based on Quinn's description, this was the photographer. He did look like a model. He was younger than Ryan. His eyes registered the girl's distress. "Hello. Can I help you?"

"Hi. My name is Ryan. I need to speak to you about some pictures." He turned pointedly to the girl. "Will you excuse us?"

She hesitated. "Xander?"

Xander looked at her. "Go around the corner for a coffee break. We'll be fine."

She exited quickly. When she was gone, Ryan focused on Xander. "Quinn Adams."

Xander's head snapped up and his gaze locked on Ryan's. "What about her?"

"Her pictures. Where are they?"

"None of your business."

Ryan stepped closer, his nerves thrumming.

Xander put his hand up. "I don't know who you are, and I can't release a client's information." If he had any inkling he was about to get beaten, he showed no sign.

"She's embarrassed. You managed to destroy her self-confidence with your inability to take a good picture. I don't need to see them. I want them destroyed."

Xander straightened, puffing his chest out. "I'm good. She wouldn't relax. It's not my fault she's got hang-ups and her photographs didn't turn out."

"I don't give a fuck how good you are. She's a teacher. If those pictures get out, her entire life will be ruined." Reining in the need to punch this pretty boy was getting more difficult by the minute.

Xander stepped forward. "I'm not a hack or a porn peddler. I don't send around my work for a few laughs, and I don't release a client's project to a lunatic who comes in here threatening me."

"The threats haven't even started. Call her. Get her permission." Ryan stepped back and pointed to the phone.

Xander opened a drawer and pulled out a sheet of paper from a file. He dialed and waited a few seconds before saying, "Hi, Ms. Adams, this is Xander Hill. I need to speak to you. Please call me back." He turned to Ryan. "No answer."

Ryan pulled out his cell phone and called Quinn's cell.

"Hello?" Her voice was heavy with sleep.

"Hi. Tell this asshole you want those pictures deleted."

"What?"

Ryan passed the phone to Xander at his desk.

"Hello, Ms. Adams?"

Ryan couldn't hear Quinn's voice, but he knew she'd panic.

"I can't remove anything without your permission. Okay. I'll be here." He closed the phone and tossed it back to Ryan. "She's on her way."

"Fine." Ryan crossed his arms and stood stiffly.

"Sit down. I think you woke her up, so she'll be a while." His tone had changed and he was no longer confrontational.

Ryan sat and propped his right ankle on his left knee.

"This is my business. My livelihood. I wouldn't risk my reputation to ruin hers."

Ryan didn't respond. He didn't trust this guy.

Xander leaned back in his chair. "She told me she was taking pictures for herself, not a man. Who are you?"

"A friend."

"Uh-huh." He smirked as he straightened. "You should probably leave. She doesn't want you to see them."

Ryan's shoulder rose and fell. "I don't need to see them. I've seen the real thing."

Xander's eyes shot back to his. One eyebrow rose. "A friend, huh?"

Ryan's knee bounced. He hadn't yet thought of how to categorize his relationship with Quinn. His only thought was to protect her.

They sat in silence. Xander shuffled papers on his desk and Ryan watched the clock. The young girl came back and set a cup of coffee in front of Xander. She looked from Xander to Ryan and back, then escaped to another room.

Twenty minutes later, the bell rang and both men rose. Xander pressed the buzzer. Ryan waited for Quinn to come in, expecting to see her panicked.

She came barreling through the door, head up, eyes blazing. The panic was there, buried under the anger. She wore no makeup, a loose T-shirt, and shorts. His gaze wandered to her feet. Her purple toenails peeked out from the sandals.

"Hi," Xander said. "Thanks for coming."

Quinn nodded to him but walked past. She stopped within a foot of Ryan. Her subtle scent gripped him. Looking up, she spoke through clenched teeth. "Can I speak to you?"

Xander took the hint and disappeared.

"Why are you here?" she demanded.

"Take a breath and relax."

"Don't tell me to relax. Just because we had sex doesn't mean you can run all over my life."

"You're not thinking clearly. Listen to me. The photos are digital. They're on his computer. He can do whatever he wants with them." He saw the moment the possibilities registered in her brain. "Or he could get hacked."

Her face paled and she covered her mouth with a trembling hand. "Oh, God."

He pulled her close and kissed the top of her head. "It'll be okay. We'll have him delete everything."

"How am I going to know that's it? How can I be sure?"

"I'll be sure."

She stepped back and looked up at him. "What the hell was I thinking?"

"You were taking a chance. Completing your adventures. Don't let this stop you." He leaned down and kissed her. She tasted like mint. She must've brushed her teeth and flew out the door.

Her muscles relaxed as she melted into the kiss. He pulled back.

"Thank you." She tucked her hair behind her ears. "You can go now. If you had said something, I would've handled it myself."

"I'll wait."

Her look bore into him. "I don't want you to see them." She crossed her arms to let him know it was non-negotiable.

He leaned close and whispered in her ear, "Like I told the artist over there, I don't need pictures. I've seen the real thing."

Color rose to her cheeks. "I still don't want you to see them."

"Fine." He reclaimed the chair.

"Xander, we're done," Quinn called.

Xander walked to his desk and clicked the mouse. "Regardless of what your boyfriend thinks, I would never send these out on the Internet."

"I believe you and I apologize for him busting in here. I'd just feel better if they didn't exist."

He clicked the mouse a couple more times. Quinn's body shielded the screen, so Ryan saw nothing, but Quinn's posture stiffened again.

She shook her head. "They're not any better the second time."

Click-click. "There. All deleted."

"Please empty the trash and secure it."

Click-click.

"Thank you." Quinn turned and headed for the door. She nodded at Ryan. "We're done."

Ryan stood but waited for Quinn to reach the hall before he moved. He spoke quietly to Xander. "If those photos ever resurface, I will make sure she sues you for every penny you have and I'll beat the shit out of you."

He strode out without looking back.

Quinn was waiting in the hall. When he closed the door behind him, she asked, "Do I want to know what you said to him?"

"Probably not." He grabbed her hand and interlocked his fingers with hers. "What are you up to today? Want to grab breakfast?"

They walked side by side, holding hands down the stairs. "Breakfast sounds great, but I can't. My principal asked me to come in today."

Outside in the late-morning sun, he assessed her face. Her color was back and she was more relaxed. "It's summer. Why would he call you?"

"I usually teach summer school. This is my first summer off and the teacher who took my place is having problems."

"How is it your problem?"

She blew a breath that puffed her bangs. "You sound like Brian. It's not my problem, but I'm a team player, and I do care about the kids."

"Okay. Will I see you later?"

She shifted and stared at the ground. "Yeah, I'm doing speed dating tonight."

Mary had been right. Quinn signed up to legitimately find a date. Now she was nervous. If he said the wrong thing, she'd run away again. "Okay, see you then."

"See you." Although she raised her eyes, they didn't meet his. She turned and walked quickly down the street.

Indy was wrong. Ryan confirmed it. He was okay with her participating in speed dating. Furthermore, he'd told her not to give up on her adventures. He's a guy. Guys do casual.

Her speed walk back to her loft left her breathless. The sun beat on her head, and beads of sweat made her scalp itch. It was almost eleven. The morning summer-school session would be over soon. If she wanted to catch Ackerman and Carlson, she'd have to move fast.

She looked down at her clothes. The clothes she'd slept in. *God, I let Ryan and Xander see me like this.* She needed something more appropriate for school. Although, Carlson would definitely get the impression she was on vacation if she walked in like this.

No, she couldn't do that. Vacation or not, she was a teacher when she entered the building. She took a quick shower and dressed in a pair of cropped khakis and a loose blouse. She had to make some concessions to the heat.

Within thirty minutes, she parked in front of the school. She didn't bother pulling into the lot. She didn't plan on staying long. The bell rang as she yanked the heavy door open.

Halfway down the hall, she pushed open the door to the main office. Two standing fans whirred and clicked as they oscillated. When the door thunked closed, Louise looked up.

"Quinn, what the heck are you doing here? I thought you were disappearing for the summer." Louise was mother hen to everyone and was one of the most lovable women Quinn knew.

Quinn leaned on the counter separating the two of them. She spoke quietly. "I've been summoned."

Louise's mouth made an "O" and she added, "I didn't think it was that bad." She picked up her phone. "I'll let him know you're here."

While Louise buzzed Carlson, Quinn checked and cleared her mailbox. Catalogs and junk mail cluttered the box. Mixed in the middle of the mess was a plain white envelope with *"Ms. Adams"* scrawled on the front. She hadn't brought her purse, so she folded the envelope and tucked it into her pocket. The rest went into the recycle bin.

"You can go in now," Louise called.

"Thanks, Louise. How's it going this summer?"

"Same old."

The corner of Quinn's mouth lifted. She eased around the counter to the back office. She tapped on Carlson's closed door to announce herself and pushed it open.

Mr. Carlson sat behind his desk. Quinn's first thought was always what an imposing man he was. His body completely filled the leather desk chair, and she knew he stood a foot taller than her. His head was bald, the dark brown skin smooth and shiny. When she entered, his thick lips parted and white teeth gleamed.

"Quinn, I'm glad you could make it. Have a seat." He pointed to the chair directly in front of him.

"Hi, Mr. Carlson. What's going on?" She pulled her keys from her pocket so they wouldn't jab her thigh when she sat.

"Did you get my message about Shari?"

Quinn crossed her legs and clasped her hands in her lap. "Yes, but I'm not sure I understood it."

He took a deep breath and leaned back in his chair, locking his hands behind his head. "She's struggling. Discipline is an issue, and she feels swamped."

"I gave her all of my daily lesson plans. All she had to do was follow them. They easily fill the three hours." She tamped down the irritation that rose.

"It's more than the material. It's the caliber of students working against her inexperience."

Quinn looked into his wide brown eyes. *I was inexperienced once too. No one handed me anything. I had to figure it out.* The nasty thought fought its way to her lips. Instead, she asked, "What do you want from me?"

He leaned forward and put his elbows back on his desk. "Talk to her. Give her words of encouragement. Maybe observe her and offer some tips."

Quinn raised her eyebrows at the last statement. She was all for being a team player, but she wouldn't work for free.

"Spend a day or two with her and I'll give you comp time."

Quinn smiled. "I thought comp time was a big no-no these days with the board."

"We'll figure it out. I think Shari's still here. Do you have time to talk to her now?"

She nodded. Shari Ackerman wasn't her favorite person. She didn't dislike her. They were different, especially in the way they taught. Quinn wasn't surprised Shari struggled with her lesson plans. They were designed to suit Quinn's teaching style. Shari wasn't adept enough to know how to pick and choose and adapt what would work for her.

Quinn grabbed her keys and headed to the classroom to make the rescue she swore she wouldn't.

CHAPTER 15

Quinn tossed her keys on her side table inside her door and took a moment to absorb the silence. She couldn't believe she'd spent five hours talking to Shari Ackerman.

She'd been able to scrounge enough change together to get a Snickers bar from the vending machine in the lounge. She'd eaten nothing else all day and was paying for it now. A headache throbbed behind her eyes. Food became her priority as she dragged herself through her apartment.

Peanut butter and jelly sounded perfect. Too bad she didn't have any squishy white bread. That would be the ultimate. Instead, she sat down with PB&J on whole wheat. Her body sighed as the comfort settled in her stomach.

Her phone rang. Was there anyone she wanted to talk to right now? Not really.

"Hey, Quinn. It's Brian. I hear you caved."

Quinn snatched up the receiver. "How did you know? I just walked in the door."

"I have my ways. I thought we agreed you weren't going to answer your phone."

She picked at the crust of the bread. "I didn't. Carlson called and e-mailed. I figured if I didn't make an appearance, he'd never leave me alone."

"So what happened?"

"I went to talk to Shari, see where she needed help, and ended up spending five hours poring over lesson plans to show her how to make them work for her."

"You're crazy."

"Carlson offered comp time. When you're slaving away on a hot September day, I'll be able to take the day and lounge without losing a sick day." *Maybe take in a Cubs game.*

"Like that'll happen."

"I think it might. My hooky day proved to be pretty successful." She tossed the remaining piece of sandwich in the trash and took a swig of water.

"How is everything else going? Find Mr. Romance yet?"

She sighed and debated telling him about Ryan. No real need to. "I'm going speed dating tonight. Maybe I'll have luck. Nothing else has worked quite the way I've wanted it to."

"Sounds like fun."

"I hope it is. I need to go get ready. I'll call and let you know what happens." She disconnected and went to find something to wear.

She settled on a sundress similar to the one she'd worn to her photo shoot, except this one was deep blue. Kind of matched Ryan's eyes.

Before tossing her clothes in the hamper, she emptied her pockets and discovered the envelope from her mailbox. She sat on her bed in her underwear and opened it.

The writing was round and bubbly. She glanced at the signature— Tamika. Quinn had an immediate image of a girl with pitch-black, chemically straightened hair with hot-pink tips. She'd just completed sophomore English with Quinn last year. The girl talked too much in class on a daily basis, but she was engaging and wrote some heart-wrenching poetry.

> *Dear Ms. Adams,*
> *I'm in summer school to make up my freshman English class. I have Ms. Ackerman now. I wanted to tell you that your class was the best one I had. I didn't know it then, but you made it easy and fun to learn. This summer I'm not sure if I'll finish. I wish all teachers were like you.*
> *Tamika Holmes*

She didn't need a guilt trip. Why should she feel guilty? She did her job and did it well. Everyone deserves time off and a personal life.

The facts didn't remove the sting.

Quinn dressed quickly, applied her makeup, and fished through her closet for a light sweater. Indy wanted to meet at O'Leary's so she'd have her car if she got bored. They agreed to arrive early to check everyone out.

Butterflies bounced in her stomach. She should've eaten more. Maybe she and Indy could go out for a late dinner.

Quinn entered the bar and was surprised to see it looked no different. Tuesday nights were not big for bar hopping, so the crowd was light. She started to wend her way around tables when she was tapped on her shoulder.

She spun around to see Indy. "Hey, you just get here?"

"Yeah," Indy responded. "Let's get a seat and do reconnaissance."

"You seem suddenly excited."

Indy looped her arm through Quinn's. "I'm trying to be supportive."

"And?"

"And nothing. I plan to help you find the best guy here." Indy led her to the dance floor.

The space had been transformed. Small, square, linen-covered tables fanned out to form two circles. Taller bar tables with stools lined the perimeter of the room.

Indy chose a table with a good view of the center of the room.

Quinn scanned the room and found Mary bustling around with a clipboard. "I need to check in."

Mary looked up from her list. "Hi. You're Quinn, right?"

Quinn nodded, hating that her fight with Ryan had left a lasting impression.

Mary handed her a sticker name tag, which she stuck to her dress. "We'll start in twenty minutes. You can get a drink while you wait."

Quinn returned to Indy's table. Indy had ordered a beer for herself and a Diet Coke for Quinn.

"Thanks. I can't drink tonight. I've hardly eaten today." She slid up onto the stool. "These past two days have been the longest in my memory. I don't know if I can even focus on this."

"What happened today?"

Quinn told her about Ryan and Xander, and spending the afternoon with Shari Ackerman.

"Are you sure you want to do this?" Indy asked.

"Do what?"

"This," she said, pointing to the smaller tables.

"I guess. I can't back out now."

"I think you can. Walk straight back to Ryan's office and plant a big sloppy kiss on him." Indy turned her bottle in her hands. "I'll take your place in the datefest."

"What?" Indy either really wanted her to be with Ryan or she really wanted to find someone new.

Indy's eyes met hers. "He took care of you today. If it was just sex between you, he wouldn't have gone to the photographer."

"He did it because he cares about me as a friend. I'm not discussing this anymore. I thought you were being supportive." Quinn twirled her seat around. "Who looks interesting?"

People milled around, drinks in hand. Participants and their guests clustered together in hushed conversations, conducting recon like Indy.

"Look at the one at two o'clock. He's tall and good-looking. He's smiling but doesn't look cocky."

Quinn's gaze moved to the man in question. "He's wearing a suit and he's got to be pushing fifty."

"So? Maybe he came from work. Having a job is a bonus."

"He's too old." She twirled her straw in her drink.

"What about him? Straight behind you. Don't turn too fast. He's too short for me, but height doesn't matter to you."

Quinn slowly spun her seat with her glass in hand. She saw the man Indy indicated. He was less than six feet, which was short in Indy's eyes. He wore Dockers and a navy button-down shirt with the sleeves rolled up. "He's not wearing a name tag."

"So?"

"He's a friend, not a speed dater." Quinn tapped her own name tag as she turned back to Indy.

Indy continued to scan the room. Quinn's eyes watched a small group of men enter. Two went to see Mary; two found a table behind

Indy. When the two received their name tags, they turned to find their friends. Quinn followed one with her eyes.

"Find someone interesting?"

"No, this guy looks familiar."

Indy shifted her position. "He's kind of young for you, isn't he?"

"Yes. He's cute, I guess, but I swear I know him from somewhere."

Mary tapped the microphone on the stage. "Hello, everyone. Can I please have your attention? Welcome to O'Leary's Speed Dating. I need all of our female participants to come forward and take a seat in one of our two inner circles."

Quinn stood, as did a bunch of other women.

Indy touched her shoulder. "Get a seat on this side, so I can see."

As the women took their seats, Mary gathered the men at the other side of the room. They were at her back, so Quinn couldn't see anyone. She focused on the friends of the guy she thought she knew. None of them looked familiar. She refocused on the table in front of her. A small pad of paper and a pen sat on each side of the table. Mary had thought ahead, giving participants paper to exchange numbers. A long metal stem sat in the middle of the table with a plastic card sticking out of the top. She sat at table five.

Mary entered Quinn's line of sight with the men following her. Each man had a number below his name. Before she led the line all the way around the table, Mary brought the microphone back to her face. "Ladies and gentlemen, we are ready to start. I will lead the men to the table corresponding to the number on their tags. The numbers are arbitrary, a way for us to have a starting point. I will lead the line around to show the men the path they will take as they maneuver around the tables. Please wait for my signal before you take your seat to begin."

She moved around Quinn's table and the men followed like a line of preschoolers on a field trip. In a moment, Quinn had the tall man with a suit in front of her table.

Mary's voice echoed around them. "Men, take your seats. When you hear the bell, you will move one space to the right." *Ding.*

The man pulled the chair out in front of him, but extended his hand before sitting. "Hi, I'm John."

"Hi, I'm Quinn."

He sat in the chair and immediately began firing questions at Quinn. "What do you do for a living?"

"I'm a teacher. How about you?"

"Lawyer. Where do you live?"

"Here in the city."

"How long did your last relationship last?"

The question shook her. Nothing like diving right in to the nitty-gritty. "I was married for three years."

His brows crinkled. "Kids?"

Quinn shook her head.

"How long have you been divorced?"

"Five years." All of her preparation the day before with Indy went out the window. This guy talked fast and plowed ahead without giving her a chance. She began to pray for the bell. Three minutes was longer than she thought. Luckily, she didn't have to think anymore. John began telling her about his life. He droned on for a full minute.

Ding.

He stood. "It was nice to meet you."

"You too." Her eyes wandered briefly to Indy. Indy shrugged.

The next man slid comfortably into the seat. Quinn's eyes moved back to find Griffin sitting across from her. She couldn't stop the smile. "Hi, Griffin. It's nice to see you again."

"Yeah, you too. How are you feeling? Last time I saw you, you weren't doing too well."

"About that . . . thank you for everything."

"Everything? Something happen I don't remember?"

"You bought me drinks and food and let me lean on you."

"I figured it was the least I could do since I bought the drinks that got you drunk."

She shrugged.

"Why are you here tonight? I didn't expect you."

"Mary asked me to step in. She was short a couple of guys."

Quinn leaned forward. "So you're not really on the hunt? Many, many women will be disappointed."

He leaned farther back in his chair. "I hear you're going to New Orleans this summer."

She nodded. "That's the plan. Ryan said I should tap you for good places to go."

"Give me a call. I love New Orleans."

"Actually, I have another question for you. What's a great, expensive restaurant?"

"Why ask me?"

She cocked her head to the side and whispered, "Because you're rich."

"How expensive?"

"The best." She quickly added, "Without making me mortgage my house."

"Foreign cuisine?"

She shook her head. "I'm simple."

He leaned forward on the table so they were nearly nose-to-nose. "There's nothing simple about you."

What had Ryan told him? Her entire life was simple, but she didn't think arguing would be a good use of time. He inched away and began naming restaurants.

Quinn scribbled notes frantically even as the bell rang. Griffin stood.

"See ya later, Quinn."

"Uh-huh." She didn't look up from the pad of paper.

As the men shifted, the brunette sitting to Quinn's right leaned over and tapped her shoulder. Quinn looked at her.

"That guy is so hot and you didn't give him the time of day."

Quinn shrugged. "I know him. There's no love connection for us. He's a friend."

She thought about how quickly she tossed the comment out, but then she realized that she did consider Griffin a friend. They didn't know each other all that well, but he was someone she never felt the need to duck away from. She enjoyed his company. Odd. For someone so used to having few friends, her circle was suddenly growing.

The woman shook her head in disbelief and refocused her attention on the man in front of her. Quinn did the same.

A little more than half an hour and eight men later, Mary called for a quick break. They had ten minutes to run to the bathroom and get a fresh drink. Quinn chose to take her break with Indy. She stood beside Indy's table to stretch her legs.

"So how's it going?"

"Long." Quinn slapped business cards on the table and stretched her arms over her head. "The cards are in the order I met the guys. The first guy didn't give me a card or his number. Not that I asked. The second guy was Griffin. The rest were all too old. Would it be too much to ask to have guys in their thirties? Some of them look near retirement. I took their cards to be polite. I can call them if I'm interested."

Indy stacked the cards neatly again. "But you're not, are you?"

"Not what?"

"Interested. I don't think any of those guys earned a smile from you. Except Griffin."

"I'm so overwhelmed. How am I supposed to make a judgment about someone in less than three minutes? I need to digest the information. It's like bam-bam-bam. I can't catch a breath."

Indy stood and threw an arm around Quinn's shoulder. "It's *speed* dating. You're not supposed to think and digest. Feel and enjoy." She squeezed Quinn's shoulder and gave her a little shove back to her table.

"Feel and enjoy. Feel and enjoy," Quinn mumbled on her way back to her seat. "Some of us need to think and digest. We can't just feel and enjoy."

She took her seat and realized she was mumbling loud enough to earn glances from other women who had already returned. She inhaled deeply and closed her eyes. *A great guy might be here. I'll miss him if I don't relax. I could actually find someone for the rest of the summer if I give this a chance.*

She reopened her eyes and felt at ease. The worst that would happen was she'd have a pile of phone numbers to toss out. The best would be a date with someone decent.

Mary rang the bell and men shuffled to find their spots.

The man standing in front of Quinn was the familiar-looking one. At least he was young. "Hi."

"Hi," Quinn answered, still desperate to place him.

He took his seat, his eyes never leaving hers. "You don't remember me, do you?"

Quinn narrowed her eyes, searching her memory. "I've been trying to figure out where I know you from since you walked in."

He extended his hand. "Joe Cardena, Ms. Adams."

Her hand had barely touched his when it hit her and she dropped her hand. Her face flashed hot. "What are you doing here?"

"Same thing as everyone else. Looking for a date."

"Are you even old enough to be in a bar?"

"I'm twenty-four. Want to card me?" His smile was boyish and playful.

Quinn shook her head. She remembered Joe. He'd been in her English class seven years ago. Her mortification must've been plain on her face.

"Hey, we're all adults here. Tell me about yourself. Are you still teaching at Jones?"

She nodded. "I can't do this. You know we can't do this."

Joe leaned back in his chair and crossed his arms. "Why not?"

"You were my student."

"Was. I'm all grown up now. I'm out of college. I'm an ad man working at Burnet and Smith. I don't live at home with Mom. I even have a car."

"It's weird." Her stomach churned.

"I'm not feeling weird. If we never met before today, you'd talk to me, right? Maybe even give me your number." His head tilted in question and his smile was disarming.

In her mind, he was still a kid. "I doubt it, Joe. I'm still a lot older than you."

"Age shouldn't be a factor."

Ding.

Joe stood. He leaned close and slid a business card in front of her. "It was good to see you, Quinn. Maybe we can have a drink later."

Another man took Joe's place. She could hardly focus. Only Indy would detect her plastered-on smile as fake. It was the same one she used at parent–teacher conferences.

Her brain buzzed. She had a student hit on her. Correction, former student. And he was serious, unlike a student who had a crush. He was grown and old enough to drink legally. The thought had never crossed her mind that she'd ever run into a student in a social situation.

Ding.

She'd see a student occasionally at the grocery store or the mall.

They usually smiled awkwardly and mumbled a hello. Sometimes one of the more gregarious girls might run up to her, squealing in excitement to see her as a real person.

None had ever tried to strike up a personal conversation with her. *Never* had she been hit on by one.

Ding.

Three more men had appeared in front of her and she couldn't recall a single detail about any of them. Quinn looked over at Indy, whose eyes were wide with concern.

Quinn gave herself a mental shake. She offered a genuine smile and a wink to Indy. A man entered her vision. She turned her eyes from Indy.

He extended his hand. "Hi, I'm—"

"Colin." The name slipped from her lips as truth even though she had never laid eyes on the man.

He sat. One eyebrow rose. "Have we met?"

"No, I've heard about you."

"That can't be good."

Ryan was tired of hiding in his office. He'd told Mary he'd stay, but he had no desire to watch Quinn flirt with other men.

They should be almost finished. He left his office and walked the perimeter of the dance floor, looking for Quinn. Sudden, loud laughter drew his attention. He immediately recognized the sound. He rounded the tables to confirm his suspicion.

Colin was sitting with Quinn, making her laugh. Ryan's fingers tightened into a fist. It was one thing for her to flirt with other men, but *not* his brother. He took two more steps before his path was blocked.

Indy touched his arm. "Hi, Ryan. I didn't know you were here." She kissed his cheek. She didn't need to reach up far because her heels added a good three inches to her height.

"Hi." His fingers loosened.

She tugged his arm. "Come sit with me. We can make fun of all these people."

He looked at her from the corner of his eye.

"Come on. How successful will any of this really be? Sure, you might get a few dates out of it, but the whole thing reeks of desperation."

They were already moving toward her table. She'd effectively maneuvered him away from Quinn. She was slick.

"I'm Quinn's scout. You can help me weed out the bad ones."

Ding.

Ryan turned in time to watch Colin kiss Quinn's cheek before moving to the next table. "Bad one," Ryan said quietly, his eyes locked on the back of Colin's head.

"He made her laugh. He was the first guy to get more than a phony smile out of her since Griffin left her table."

"Griffin's here too?"

"Yeah." She kept her eyes trained on Quinn's table. "That's Colin, right? Wow. A lot of competition."

"It's no competition." Indy quieted, sensing his mood. He scanned the rest of the crowd and shook off some of his irritation. He should've guessed Colin would be a fill-in for Mary. He'd always take a chance to meet more women.

Ryan let another moment of silence tick by. "Is she having any luck?"

Indy fanned out business cards on the table. "She got these before the break. The first half was rough. She felt overwhelmed. It didn't help that most of the men are too old for her."

Ryan smiled.

"There was a guy she thought she recognized. He came to her after the break and upset her. She blushed, paled, and then plastered on the phony smile. Until your brother, that is."

Ryan turned back to study Quinn. She wore her cool, polite exterior as always. He leaned to the side but couldn't see under the table. If she was upset, he'd see her tapping, almost imperceptibly.

Ding.

The man sitting with her stood and in the brief moment before another took his place, their eyes met. Hers pleaded for escape. He forced a smile and she returned it stiffly.

Another "date" blocked his view. This was like watching a disaster movie. You kept watching to see how bad it would get. Part of him felt bad for putting her through this.

Indy touched his arm, drawing his attention. "I tried to talk her out of this."

"Hmmm?"

"I tried to get Quinn to blow this off. I don't know what she thinks she's looking for."

"A romance that will end by the fall."

Indy grunted. "She needs to learn how to walk away from a plan when something better comes along."

Ryan shook his head. "She wants a baby."

"It's crazy, right?"

"Yeah, but what are we supposed to do? Walk away from her?"

"I'm her sister. I can't."

"Neither can I." The words slipped passed without thought. It wasn't an admission he planned to make. Certainly not to Indy.

"Oh my God." Indy hopped off her seat and stood in front of him. "You love her."

Her words startled him. "What? I didn't say that." He tried to look around Indy, but she shifted to block his evasion.

"You said you can't walk away."

His brain flipped, searching for a reason for the slip. "I care about her. She's a good friend."

Indy's eyes burned on his face. "That's it? You're friends?"

"Yes." He hoped he sounded convincing.

Indy returned to her seat. "You both need a huge dose of reality."

Jenna stopped by and cleared Indy's empty beer bottles. Indy ordered another, and Ryan asked for a glass of water.

"We're both grounded in reality. Quinn more so than anyone else I know."

"She told me she asked you to be her sperm donor."

He swallowed hard, grateful to see Jenna return with their drinks. He took a gulp of the ice water. "Yeah, she did."

"And?"

He didn't have an answer. He'd barely had a chance to digest the question. "I don't know. I want her to be happy. Last week she didn't want to take a chance on me getting her pregnant because I wouldn't be able to walk away. The thing is, she's right. I can't walk away from my family. How would I walk away from a baby?"

Indy's eyes widened and her mouth opened in exasperation. "So tell her no."

"But then who knows what she'll end up with. I wish she wouldn't be in such a hurry for a baby."

"Convince her to wait. Make your move."

He scrambled to find the words to explain to her. "A relationship would . . . our friendship . . . It would get messy. Quinn's afraid of messy."

She contemplated as she drank her beer. He'd never have pegged her as a beer drinker.

"I hate to admit it, but you have a point. She needs to get used to messy, though. Life is messy. She misses out on so much." She took a small drink and added, "She always has."

Indy tugged at the label of the beer bottle. She peeled carefully as Ryan absorbed her words. Maybe Indy wasn't as flighty as she seemed. She removed the label in one piece and smoothed it onto the table.

Ryan just watched.

"What?"

He pointed to the label. "Looking to get laid?"

Suddenly Quinn stood between them. She lightly slapped his arm. "Stop flirting with my sister. You're not her type."

"Done already?"

"Yeah."

Indy slid the label over to Quinn. "Maybe you can use this."

"For what?"

Indy shook her head pityingly. She looked at him. "She never was much of a drinker. Not even in college." She turned back to Quinn. "If you can peel the label off in one piece, it's good for a free lay."

Quinn's forehead crinkled. "That's ridiculous. First, I'm not going to sleep with any of these guys tonight. Second, peeling off the label is no big deal for you. You've had lots of practice." Quinn stomped her feet as if she'd lost circulation.

Ryan barked out a laugh. "Did you just call your sister a slut?"

Quinn's cheeks reddened. "No, I meant she had practice because she's worked at a lot of bars."

"You okay?" he asked.

"Yeah, I'm tired of sitting. Ready to go?" she asked Indy.

Indy held up her bottle, showing it was more than half full. "Tell me about the second half."

"Worse than the first. I don't remember much."

"What was with the guy you recognized?"

Quinn shifted again.

Indy took a drink, waiting for Quinn to elaborate.

Quinn leaned forward between Indy and Ryan, and whispered, "He's a former student."

Indy began to sputter and pressed her hand to her mouth to stop from spewing beer. Ryan handed her a napkin.

Once she finished choking, Indy began a full-on laugh.

Quinn stiffened. "This is *not* funny."

Unfortunately, Indy's laughter was contagious and Ryan chuckled.

Quinn turned to him. *"Et tu, Brute?"*

Laughter burst from his chest. He couldn't prevent it even if he tried. Right now, she looked so offended, he didn't attempt to stop laughing.

As Indy dabbed the tears from the corners of her eyes, his laughter abated. Quinn stood with her arms crossed. "How can you think this is funny?"

He took a deep breath. "It's not, but as soon as you said it, all I could think of was 'Hot for Teacher.' " His comment caused another round of laughs.

Griffin walked up to the table. "This looks like a fun table. What's the joke?"

"There is no joke." Quinn glared at Ryan.

Griffin waited while Ryan and Indy regained their composure. Ryan couldn't remove the smile, but he touched Quinn's arm. "I'm sorry. I couldn't help it."

Indy looked up at Griffin. "One of the speed daters is Quinn's former student."

"Oh shit."

Quinn's head tilted. "See? *That* is an appropriate response. Not laughing at the situation like a couple of kids sharing bodily function jokes."

Ryan clamped his mouth shut and Indy bit her lip. They glanced at each other briefly but realized it would quickly result in more laughter. They looked away, allowing Quinn to think her reprimand worked.

Griffin pulled two stools around the edge of the table, gestured for Quinn to sit, and waved Jenna over.

They quietly placed their order and Ryan drained the rest of his water.

Mary tapped the microphone at the front of the room. "Excuse me. I wanted to thank everyone for coming out tonight to make O'Leary's first singles event a success. Please drop me a line if you've met a love match tonight."

Quinn snorted.

Mary continued, "And keep an eye out for information on our next event." Her eyes locked on Ryan's as the crowd applauded. She swept her arm out to draw his attention to her success.

The smaller groups began to mingle and talk with drinks in hand. No one seemed to be in a hurry to leave, so it seemed like it would be profitable night after all. Unlike Colin's debacle last night.

With a straight face, Indy asked again, "What about the rest of the guys?"

Quinn shrugged. "I was so upset after Joe appeared, I couldn't focus. I think a couple gave me their cards out of pity."

Colin strode up behind Quinn. "I thought you were fine." He placed a hand on her shoulder and she jumped.

Ryan's hand tightened on his empty glass.

Colin nodded to Griffin, placed his beer on the table, and reached across him to Indy. "Hi. I'm Colin, Ryan's brother."

She shook his hand coolly and evaluated him as she spoke. "We met years ago when I worked here. I'm Quinn's sister, Indy."

Colin leaned his arms on the table and focused on Indy. "I think I remember you. You used to sing during closing while cleaning the tables."

"Good memory." She took a drink from her bottle.

"We should catch up."

Indy ignored Colin's offer to catch up. "What about you, Griffin? Any sparks?"

Jenna returned with drinks for everyone, including Colin, who hadn't been there when they ordered.

"The women were nice enough. I might make a call or two." He took a drink from his bottle of beer, the same brand Indy was drinking. Intense gazes flashed between Indy and Griffin.

"Only a couple?" Ryan asked. "Are you slowing down in your old age?"

Colin had inched his way closer to Quinn, effectively blocking her from Ryan's reach.

He whispered something only Quinn could hear, and she laughed.

Ryan quickly stood. "I need to go check in with Mary. See you guys later." He left his glass on the table and glanced over his shoulder to see Colin shake his head and shrug.

Colin knew. He had to know Quinn was off limits. Yet there he was moving in. What if she fell for him? Shit. Could he be her summer romance? Colin would walk away. It was something he was good at.

He suddenly had a thirst for something much stronger than water. He waved to Mary and pointed to the bar to let her know where he was headed. His hand ran along the cool, smooth mahogany before he signaled for Michael to pour him a bourbon. His fingers continued to stroke the wood as he pushed images of Colin groping Quinn from his mind.

A group of young guys stood at the bar. Something in their conversation snagged his attention. He picked up his glass and shifted over to eavesdrop.

"She's hot. Especially for an older woman."

"Tell me about it. I've been wanting to tap that since I was a teenager."

Uh-oh. Quinn would keel over if she heard this conversation. Ryan leaned back to get a view of the one speaking. Sure enough, he still wore his name tag. Joe actually thought he had a shot with Quinn.

He saw Mary coming from the dance floor. She spied the men he stood near and stopped to chat first. "Hey, guys. How did it go tonight? Everyone have a good time?"

They nodded at Mary and elbowed each other. She swung her attention back to Ryan. "I told you this was a good idea. The event is over and we still have a full bar on a Tuesday night."

He tilted his glass in her direction. "You were right. It seems like most people had fun. These guys are a little young."

Mary blushed. "I actually had a couple of women request I invite younger men. You know, the whole cougar craze."

He'd have to share that one with Quinn. She wouldn't appreciate being lumped with cougars. He bit the inside of his cheek. She'd probably hit him if he told her. Joe and his friends were on the move. They walked as a group back to the dance area. Joe shifted, obviously looking for Quinn. Ryan slammed the rest of his drink. He followed the young guys, not wanting to miss Joe being shut down.

Ryan reached the archway that led to the dance floor. Mary already had tables moved and music playing from the jukebox. He leaned against the wall.

Quinn looked safely insulated, sandwiched between Colin and Griffin, with Indy across from her. Ryan doubted Joe would approach. His group sat at a table, two down from Quinn's. She hadn't noticed them.

Her smile was only slightly warmer than the one she offered the speed daters. Colin must've been wearing on her. She nodded politely and slid from her seat. Purse in hand, she headed for the bathroom. Joe saw his opening.

Ryan straightened from the wall. Joe quickly caught up with Quinn and touched her arm. She turned, saw who it was, and her face went blank. Whatever he said, she wasn't buying. She shook her head and stepped back. He stepped forward and reached for her hand.

Ryan left his spot but pulled up short. Quinn didn't need his help. She squared her shoulders and stared Joe down. Her words had minimal effect on the cocky look Joe had, but he stepped away from Quinn. He shrugged and nodded. She tilted her head and lifted an eyebrow. Her parting words were final. He retreated to his friends and she turned into the hall.

Ryan followed. By the time he reached the spot where Joe had approached her, she had already disappeared into the bathroom.

CHAPTER 16

In the dimly lit hall, Quinn eyed the door to Ryan's office. She'd find refuge there. Her body urged her to knock, but her mind pushed her toward the bathroom.

She entered a stall and sat on the lidded toilet. She needed solitude. The night's events replayed in her mind. What should've been a fun outing turned out pretty disastrous.

Meeting Colin was worth it, though. He and Ryan had the same charm that made a woman want to hang around. He was bigger than Ryan and his hair longer, but their faces were so similar, they could still pass for twins. Colin gave her insight into Ryan she'd ignored. Colin was the playboy. Even as he hit on her, one eye roved to find something better.

When Ryan spoke to her, all his attention focused on her.

She'd told Colin that Ryan was a friend. Something lit in his eyes. It was like he was determined to win her over somehow. She pondered the impact of that while she took in her surroundings. She'd never paid much attention to the décor in the bathroom. She was usually a get in and out quickly person.

The bathroom looked like any other with its deep green industrial stall partitions and black-and-white mosaic tile floor. But she noticed a sign on the stall door. She stood to read it. It was full of statistics about rape. Creepy.

She exited the stall and washed her hands. While refreshing her makeup, she actually read the sign above the sink. She'd always assumed it was a DRINK RESPONSIBLY sign or EMPLOYEES MUST WASH THEIR HANDS BEFORE RETURNING TO WORK. The kinds of signs every bar patron ignores.

This one read, IF ANY MALE CUSTOMER IS HARASSING YOU OR MAK-ING YOU FEEL UNCOMFORTABLE, LET A STAFF MEMBER KNOW. IF YOU NEED A RIDE HOME, WE'LL CALL A CAB AND ESCORT YOU TO THE VEHI-CLE. YOUR SAFETY IS OUR PRIORITY.

Hmm. It gave pause for thought. Quinn considered the neighborhood. She'd never felt uneasy going to and from her car. She'd never had any problems. How many women did in order to warrant these warnings and an invitation for help?

The door swung open and Indy entered. "Are you all right? You've been gone a long time."

"I'm fine. I needed a break."

Indy reapplied lipstick and touched up the rest of her makeup. Quinn watched with the same fascination she had when they were teenagers. Indy was an artist with makeup.

Quinn picked up her purse. "I think I'm going home. Will you be okay?"

"I'm fine. I'll finish my beer and head out."

"Will you tell Griffin and Colin I said good-bye?"

Indy turned, her eyebrows drawn together. "That's not like you. What's wrong?"

"I don't want to run into Joe again. He caught me on the way in here and wanted to buy me a drink. He didn't want to hear no. I had to go into bitch mode for him to get it."

"I'll ask Griffin or Colin to walk you out."

"No, there's a back door right out here."

"You sure?"

"Yeah, I've used it before. I'll talk to you tomorrow."

Indy gave her a quick hug and swung back out the door. Quinn followed.

In the hall, she looked at Ryan's office door again. She plowed forward and knocked quickly. If he didn't answer, she'd slip out the back door.

"Come in."

She opened the door and took a hesitant step in. Ryan was lying on the couch with his eyes closed. As soon as she took a small step, his eyes popped open.

"Hey, sorry to interrupt."

He sat quickly. "You can see I was hard at work."

Her hand still gripped the doorknob. She didn't know what she was doing here, hadn't thought about it. She wanted to see him before she left. "I'm going home. I wanted to say good night."

One eyebrow lifted. "Colin not entertaining enough?"

She chuckled. "He's plenty entertaining. I'm going into work again tomorrow, so I need some sleep."

His gaze swept across her body and she remembered his hands touching her everywhere. She barely withheld a shiver. She spoke quietly. "If you don't mind, I'm going to use the back door to leave."

He shot off the couch, concern etched on his face. "What happened?"

She blinked. "Nothing. I don't want to run into Joe again. I don't know how else to turn him down."

"So you're going to sneak out the back?"

"Yeah, I'm tired. I'm done."

"I won't let some pissant make you sneak out of my bar. Again. Come on." He slung his arm over her shoulder and switched off the light.

"It's not just Joe. Colin will want to talk, and although I told Indy I was leaving, if I go out front, someone will stop me." She tried not to pull closer to him to enjoy his warmth. She patted his chest. "Thanks for the offer."

She meant to step away and head down the hall to the exit, but she looked into his eyes. Her feet forgot how to move.

"I'll walk you to your car."

"Why don't you follow me in your car?" She whispered so quietly she wasn't sure if he'd heard. It was the closest thing to an invitation she knew how to offer.

"You sure?"

She nodded and walked to the door. She immediately missed the warmth of his body, but she felt his eyes on her as she walked. Excitement stirred her blood. It took a lot of restraint not to bolt out the door and run to her car. The sudden urgency to be alone and naked with Ryan overwhelmed her. She didn't care. It had been a crappy day.

On the short drive home, she tried to come up with reasons why this was a bad idea. Everything she thought paled in comparison to going out with Joe or calling Nick. She and Ryan had already had sex. Really, really good sex. What harm could this do?

She shoved the gear lever into Park and stood outside her car while Ryan parked. He joined her but didn't say anything. He took her hand as she led the way into the building.

They took the stairs up, with Quinn carrying her sandals. Ryan was fascinated by the fuchsia on her toenails. She often opted for vibrant or deep-colored polish. Her fingernails rarely sported color, but having sexy feet was her thing. It was akin to women who wore silk and lace under everything.

Ryan seemed to appreciate it.

In the loft she felt a little lost. They hadn't spoken or shared any touch other than holding hands since they left the bar. Ryan slid the bolt home on her lock.

When he turned, she pressed him against the door with the length of her body. Without even the small heels of her sandals, she felt diminutive, her eyes level with his chest. She poised on tiptoe and kissed his lips.

She had to be sure last time hadn't been a fluke. Closing her eyes, she parted her lips. His arms wrapped around her back. His hard-on rubbed her abdomen, and the pull of desire tugged at her center. She melted with a kiss. This didn't happen to her. It was insane. Her brain fogged.

Ryan moved and she walked backward, not caring where he was leading her.

The room was dark except for the table lamp she'd left on. She hated coming home to a dark house. She was especially grateful for the glow as Ryan maneuvered them through the living room.

He broke the kiss, but not their bodily contact, to ask, "Upstairs?"

"Yes." The husky whisper sounded foreign. *Was that me? What the hell happened to my voice?*

She reached up to kiss him again but felt his lips curve into a smile. "We can't go up like this. We'll fall."

Leave it to him to suddenly become practical. He stepped back and spun her by her shoulders. She jogged up the stairs only to reach the top and find Ryan hadn't followed. "Where did you go?"

"I'm getting some water." His voice floated up the stairs.

Quinn went to the bathroom to freshen up. When she came out, Ryan was standing shirtless and barefoot beside the bed. She had debated whether or not to strip down in the bathroom. Now she was glad she didn't. It would be awkward to stroll past a mostly clothed man.

She ran her hands up his torso and back down to his jeans. She tugged at the buttons. Whoever invented button-fly had not been thinking. "We won't be needing these."

His hard cock strained against his boxer briefs. She stepped back and began to gather her dress when Ryan's hands closed over hers.

He stepped closer and whispered, "Let me."

She released the flimsy rayon blend of her skirt.

He kissed her neck, then her shoulder. He nibbled at her collarbone. This time she didn't even try to suppress the shiver.

"Are you wearing anything under this?"

"Why don't you check?"

His hands slid up her outer thighs. When he found no underwear, he groaned and kneaded her ass. She felt herself getting wet and his hands couldn't move fast enough. They traveled up and the pads of his thumbs rasped across her nipples. Her dress was bunched around his forearms. She lifted her arms above her head for him to remove the garment.

He inched it up, following with kisses and licks. The dress was at her neck and she attempted to pull her arms loose to touch him, but he tightened his grasp on the material, holding her in place. He nibbled her collarbone some more and sucked her nipples to hard points. She clenched her thighs together, sure she would come any minute.

Ryan slipped the dress off, flinging it across the room, and pushed her on the bed. The room was dark except for the night-light glow coming from the bathroom. He was a shadow hovering above her. She reached past the waistband of his underwear and stroked him.

His tip was moist and he was rigid with want. He slid from her grasp, bit her earlobe, and said, "I want to taste you."

He moved lower, trailing his warm, wet lips. Nudging her thighs wide, he lowered his head. His tongue swirled and lapped, sucked and nibbled, until her legs wrapped around his shoulders, pinning him in place. Her hips bucked as he slid fingers into her while he licked.

"Oh, God. Yes!" she screamed. She moaned. Even as the sounds echoed, she didn't recognize her own voice.

Her entire body tingled and vibrated. She tried loosening her thigh muscles, afraid Ryan would suffocate, but he kept at her until her legs spasmed and trembled.

He knelt above her spent body and wiped his chin. His underwear was gone and he reached across her for a condom. She was still panting, her muscles lax, but as soon as he rubbed against her, her senses jumped. He eased into her torturously slowly.

She pulled his face to hers and kissed him hard, tasting herself and his sweat. Her tongue battled with his as her hips thrust upward. She wanted him deep and hard. Her body collided with his and she began building again.

Her hands reached lower and clawed at his ass, pulling him deeper, while he sucked at the pulse on her neck.

No words passed between them. Their bodies spoke and responded until they were a crumpled heap of relaxation.

Quinn lay on top of Ryan. His heart pounded beneath her palm. Their bodies were slick with sweat and sticky from sex. She wanted to shower but couldn't move. Her muscles refused to cooperate.

"Are you trying to kill me?"

"Huh?" She tried to look up at him, but it required too much effort.

"I think my heart rate is in heart attack range."

She laughed. This was *not* the effect she had on men. She turned her head and bit his nipple. "Maybe we should refrain from doing this. I don't want to be responsible for your untimely death."

"Like hell. I'll take my chances."

The words hung over her like a heavy curtain. Those were the same words he'd used in the elevator. She had said she wouldn't take a chance on him. Yet here she was drawn to him over and over. And not only for the great sex.

His hand skimmed over her hair. "Something wrong?"

"I was trying to convince my body to go to the shower."

"Hmm. How's that working for you?"

"It's not." She sighed and closed her eyes to enjoy the moment.

When Ryan's heart was a steady and calm thump, she sat. She thought he fell asleep, but his hand snaked out to her hips to pull her close again. She grabbed the water he'd had the foresight to bring up and chugged half a bottle. When she pulled it from her lips, a few drops fell onto Ryan's chest, the cold startling him.

"Sorry." She wiped his chest. "I'm going to the shower."

She turned the corner and quietly closed the door. In the mirror above the sink, her reflection showed a well-satisfied woman, albeit an exhausted one. It was getting late, she still hadn't eaten a proper meal, and she had to get up early for school.

Steam billowed from the shower, letting her know the water was ready. As she stood under the spray, she catalogued the food she had in the fridge.

Ryan lay in the bed, every bit as sweaty as Quinn, and debated following her. She was struggling with something. Maybe the same thing he was—the donor issue. Listening to his gut, he went to the bathroom and opened the door without knocking. He left the door ajar to allow the clouds of steam to escape. "Can I come in?"

She froze. Her silhouette behind the frosted glass paused with a shampoo bottle in hand.

"I don't think that's a good idea." Her voice hesitated, but she stuck her head out the door with a smile. "I can't carry you out of here if you drop dead."

He slid the door all the way open and stepped in. "I promise not to keel over."

He actually wasn't looking for a second round. He wanted to be with her. Taking the shampoo from her hand, he filled his palm and lathered her hair.

Her eyes narrowed at his movements. He massaged her head and allowed the scent to swirl around him.

"What are you doing?"

"I'm helping you wash." He tilted her head toward the spray and she closed her eyes. "I love the feel of your hair."

The hot water turned her pale skin bright pink. Her body responded to his nearness, his touch. The water sluiced over her head and down her back. Her lips parted and she arched forward.

Although he hadn't joined her with the intention of having sex, his dick had its own idea about what was happening. She turned slightly and her side flicked against his bobbing cock. Her eyes sprung open and she grasped him hard.

"You have a death wish, don't you? I don't know if your feeble heart can handle more."

He pushed her against the wall and stroked her. "I'll make sure I add cardio to my workout regimen."

"I'm cold. You're pushing me out of the water."

"Here." He stepped back and spun her around. The water cascaded down the front of her while he massaged her breasts and tweaked her nipples. The warmth of her body seeped into his. She cradled his dick against her back.

He stroked her until he felt her warm juices flowing over his hand. She reached up and around to hold on to his neck. He began to fold her forward, but she resisted. Moving his hand, he grasped both her hips and brought them to him.

His left hand slid over her back and prodded her shoulders forward. Her hands slapped the wet tile as she spread her legs, understanding what he wanted. He leaned close and entered her from behind, his fingers holding her hips firmly. She ground her ass against him, so close to release.

He folded himself around her. The water beat on his back. His fingers found her hard clit and flicked it as he pulled out and thrust back in. She reared up, clenching her walls around him. The sudden movement shocked him. He couldn't hold out and he began spurting.

He withdrew from her quickly, not removing his hand from bringing her to another climax. They both leaned against the cool tile.

"We have to stop meeting like this," she said.

He backed off and grabbed the bar of soap. They washed each other slowly and enjoyably. He needed to tell her he started to come inside her. But right now she looked . . . happy.

Happy was not a word he'd normally use to describe Quinn. Content suited her. At this moment, hair slicked back, soap running down her body, she smiled openly and warmly. This was beyond contentment.

She rinsed and stepped out of the shower. She wrapped a towel around herself and plopped on the closed lid of the toilet. Water rinsed suds from his body and he noticed a lack of movement in the bath-room.

"You okay?" he asked, sticking his head out.

"I'll be fine. Just a little light-headed."

He was going to spout off a joke but stopped when he saw she was pale. He twisted the water off and squatted in front of her on the fuzzy purple bath mat.

"What's wrong?"

She smiled weakly. "Too much great sex. Hot water. No food." She closed her eyes and leaned back.

"When was the last time you ate?" He knew she ate nothing at the bar tonight.

"I ate a sandwich before going out. And I had a candy bar at school."

"What the hell is wrong with you? Don't move."

She lifted her arm and gave him a thumbs-up. "I'll be fine in a minute."

He went to the kitchen and poured a glass of orange juice. He brought it to her and put it to her lips. Her color had already started to return. She drank greedily.

"This happen often?"

"Only when I don't eat and have wild monkey sex."

"I'll be sure to take note. No monkey sex without food." She stood and he grabbed her elbow, wanting to make sure she was steady.

"I'm fine." She jerked her arm back. "Let's go find something to eat."

She pulled an oversized T-shirt from her dresser and put it on. Her hair dripped on the gray cotton covering her shoulders. He looked around and realized he didn't have anything comfortable to wear. He pulled on his underwear and followed Quinn.

In the kitchen, she was pouring two bowls of Lucky Charms cereal. "That looks nutritious."

She glared at him. "It's my favorite childhood cereal. It's not like I eat it every day. Besides, I can't eat anything heavy. I have to go to sleep since I'm working tomorrow."

He accepted the bowl she placed in front of him. "Why are you going into work?"

"I told that teacher who's having trouble that I'd help her." She used the back of her spoon to push the cereal into the milk.

"That's nice of you."

She shrugged. "I feel guilty for not teaching this summer."

"Why?" He took a bite of the cereal and the crispy marshmallows melted on his tongue.

"I got a letter from a student who was in my class this year. She's in summer school and not doing well, at least not as well as she did with me."

"How is it your fault?"

Quinn chewed and shook her head. "It's actually a nice letter. She doesn't blame me. She passed my class but had failed the previous year. She wanted to tell me she enjoyed my class and she wishes more teachers were like me."

"You have a regular fan club going on."

"Not usually."

They finished their cereal in silence, rinsed their bowls, and left them in the sink.

Quinn stilled and looked at him. "I'm ready for sleep."

It was neither an invitation nor expectation.

"Tossing me out?"

A slight blush pinked her cheeks. "No, I just . . . I didn't want you to think . . ." She inhaled deeply and closed her eyes.

"I'm teasing, Quinn."

She released the breath. "I told you I'm no good at this."

He stepped closer and touched her warm cheek. "I want to stay."

"I'd like that."

He interlaced his fingers with hers and pulled her toward the stairs. When they entered the bedroom, the smell of sweat and sex accosted them. Her nose crinkled.

"Would you be offended if I changed the sheets before we went to bed?"

"No."

"Good. Do me a favor and yank those off. I'll get fresh ones."

He stripped the bed wondering what she would've done if he had been offended. The yellow cotton was pretty ripe. She must not have changed them after their Monday afternoon romp. He balled them up but couldn't find a laundry basket.

Quinn returned carrying a pile of light purple sheets. "Sorry. It's been kind of a crazy day and I didn't get around to changing the sheets. I normally don't have guests make the bed."

"Have guests often?"

"No," she said sharply, eyebrows drawn together. She shook out the fitted sheet. "I—"

Her eyes met his. She was so much fun to rattle. He didn't know how she survived teenagers all day.

"Why do you keep doing that to me?"

"It's fun." He grabbed the corner of the sheet and tucked it around the mattress. "You're funny when you're flustered."

"I'm not flustered."

He raised an eyebrow to call her a liar.

"Okay, maybe a little nervous."

They stuffed pillows into cases and arranged the bed. Quinn switched off the light and crawled in.

He waited to see where she would lay and took the spot next to her. He laid on his right side and wrapped his left arm over her waist.

"No reason to be nervous. It's sleep. Good night, Quinn." He kissed her cheek and her eyes closed.

It was early for him to turn in, but it wasn't a bad feeling. He tucked Quinn into his body. She had come to him tonight after having her pick of men, including Colin.

CHAPTER 17

The alarm buzzed. Quinn swung her arm at it. *Ten minutes. I need ten more minutes.* She turned over to doze and felt the empty bed beside her.

He left? The pain stabbed her chest. It shouldn't have been a big deal, but it felt like Nick all over again. Sleep was lost.

She got to the top of the stairs and smelled coffee. Huh? She tried not to trip as she hurried down. Her heart thumped against her ribs when she reached the floor.

Ryan stood at the stove with his bare back to her, wearing only the underwear he'd slept in. He looked over his shoulder and smiled.

Trying to cover the shock of finding him in her kitchen, she returned the smile.

"Something wrong?"

"No." Her puzzlement took over. "What are you doing?"

"Making breakfast. Coffee's ready." With a black spatula, he pointed at the nearly full pot.

"Thanks. I usually just grab a cup of coffee." She took down her favorite mug and filled it, generously adding milk and sugar.

"But you hardly ate yesterday and almost passed out. You need real food."

He had a point. "In my defense, I don't do that often. I'm not typically woozy."

She pulled two plates from the cabinet and set them next to the stove. She peered into the pan, expecting scrambled eggs. He was making omelets and they smelled delicious.

She sat on a stool and sipped her coffee. He unceremoniously plopped the omelets onto the plates and brought them to the counter. The first bite reminded her how truly hungry she was. The smell and explosion of flavors made her mouth water. "Who taught you to cook?"

"My mom refused to let any of us grow up like Dad. He couldn't cook anything."

She broke off another piece. "This is great."

"Did you think I lived on McDonald's?"

"Not McDonald's, but a lot of takeout, yeah. The only guy I know who cooks is Brian."

"The gay guy?"

She choked on her coffee. "Why do guys do that?"

"What?" His plate was nearly empty, showing he was at least as hungry as she had been.

"Being gay doesn't make it part of his name."

"I wanted to make sure I knew who you were talking about."

"Uh-huh." She glanced at the clock. She'd have barely enough time to shower and get to school.

As if he'd read her mind, Ryan said, "Go get ready. I'll do the dishes."

"That's not fair. You cooked. Leave them in the sink and I'll do them later."

"I got 'em. You can owe me." He stood, grabbed both plates, and kissed the top of her head.

Quinn took her coffee with her into the bathroom. After taking care of business, she saw her period had started. *It shouldn't be here yet. Did I miscount?*

During her quick shower, she replayed her evening. Ryan had definitely made up for the disastrous speed dating.

When she went back to the bedroom to dress, Ryan was there, sitting on the edge of the bed. He'd pulled on his jeans, but not his shirt. His hair was messier than usual.

She wore only the towel she'd wrapped around herself in the bathroom. Modesty claimed her again and she held the edges tightly closed.

"You got a minute?" His voice sounded different, uneven.

"Sure." She sat next to him on the bed, hoping the towel would stay closed.

He took a deep breath and blew it out. God, he was going to try to let her down easy.

"About last night," he started.

She swallowed hard and tugged the towel closer. What had she been thinking?

"In the shower," he continued.

Huh? This isn't how the speech goes. She lifted her eyes to meet his. Worry clouded the blue irises. She touched her palm to his cheek. "What?"

The words rushed without pause. "I started to come inside you. I didn't mean to and I pulled out. Hell, I didn't think we'd have sex in the shower. I'm sorry."

She laughed with relief. He was a babbling idiot and she loved it. She leaned over and hugged him. "It's okay. Neither one of us was thinking straight. I got my period this morning, so I think it's safe to say you're not a father."

He pulled her into a kiss and made her forget her towel. It slipped from her hands.

Ryan pulled back and gathered the towel around her again. "You better leave that on or you won't make it to work."

She held the towel at her breasts and felt herself blush under the look he gave her. He still wanted her. There wasn't an "I like you, but . . ." speech coming.

He picked up his shirt and shoes from the floor. She stood to get dressed. Before he left, he turned and said quietly, "I wanted you to know I'm disease-free. I wasn't worried about you getting pregnant."

She stood stunned for a moment. What the hell did that mean?

Running behind schedule now, she hurriedly dressed. She didn't hear the door clunk with Ryan's departure, so she thought he might still be downstairs. She dumped the remnants of her coffee in the sink, where he stood rinsing the last dish. He put it in the rack to dry.

"How late are you?"

She looked at the clock. "Not very. Thanks for breakfast and doing the dishes."

"Don't worry, I'll expect payback." He leaned down and kissed her briefly. "I'll walk you out."

He made things easy. She wasn't in the habit of leaving her door unlocked, but she didn't want to offer him a key and scare him off. Not much rattled him, though. He kissed her again at her car before heading to his own.

The sun was bright and the air heavy with humidity. It was the kind of day that made her want to do a rain dance. Sitting in the driver's seat, her shirt already clung to her back. This was one thing she didn't miss about teaching summer school.

Quinn arrived at school after the first bell had rung. Although she wasn't officially on the clock, the familiar burn of fear bubbled in her stomach. She hated being late. She took a deep breath to ease her anxiety. This wasn't a big deal. She was doing a favor. She could show up whenever she wanted as long as she documented her time for Mr. Carlson.

Feeling better, she strode into the building and stopped in the teacher's lounge to grab a bottle of water. She tapped on the office window and waved to Louise to let them know she was there.

The heat inside the building was as miserable as outside. No sun beat down, but the air was stagnant. Inside the classroom, she took a seat at a table in the back of the room. A few kids took notice of her entrance and waved fingers in polite greeting. Most remained focused on Shari in the front of the room.

They were reading *Romeo and Juliet*, predictable ninth-grade fare. Quinn studied the students in the room. Since she was staring at the backs of their heads, it was difficult to pick out anyone she knew. Except Tamika. She easily spotted the girl's magenta hair.

Shari reviewed the previous day's material with little involvement from the kids. Quinn had come prepared to take notes and offer advice after class, but she didn't even know where to start. Thirty minutes in, she was as bored and sleepy as the students, and they hadn't even cracked open the book.

Quinn struggled to both stay awake and in her seat. She wanted to stand and take over, but it wouldn't help Shari. They'd only read the first act of the play and the kids didn't get it. Quinn edged closer to the front of the room to see the students' faces. Many played with bottles of water dripping condensation onto the scarred desks.

Did Shari think they would read Shakespeare for homework and understand it?

Shari tried to extract a summary from them. She got nothing but blank stares. She turned pleading eyes to Quinn.

Quinn stood and walked to the front of the room. Her sudden movement caught the attention of the class.

"Class, this is Ms. Adams. Some of you might already know her. She's also a teacher here at Jones and she's here to help out." Shari gave her introduction and hurried back to her desk.

"Okay. First, forget anything you read last night. We're going to start over. I want everyone to close your eyes for a minute." She waited through the snickers and muffled comments.

When most had followed the direction, she continued, "Girls only. Imagine this. Your neighborhood school closed. Jones becomes your new school. In your first week, you see a guy in the hall. He's cute. He smiles at you and offers to help you find your class. On the way, you talk. You like him."

At this point the boys were getting restless. "Okay, guys. Your turn. You're standing in the hall when this beautiful girl walks in. You check her out. She smiles at you and you immediately think, 'Hmmm-mmm. I'm gonna get me some of that.' "

Instant reaction. The boys burst into laughter. From the back, a girl commented, "Oh no, she didn't."

Quinn waited. They were awake and engaged. "I've been teaching high school for a long time. I know the first thing on a teenage boy's mind."

She began to walk down the aisles between the desks. "So you have this new and fabulous thing going on. You really like each other. This boy, this girl, they're different. But then . . ."

The room dropped into silence. "Imagine this girl is with the Latin Kings and the boy . . . you guessed it. He's from a long line of Disciples."

"Ah, hell no."

"No way."

"Couldn't happen."

Quinn stopped, turned in a circle. "We all know what happens beyond these walls. But in here, without flashing your signs, without your colors, you're just a boy and a girl. You love each other, but your families will never accept this."

"Well, I'd be done with that ho."

"If it's easy, then you didn't really love her." She had them. They were thinking. This was the moment she loved. "The question is, what are you going to do to save this relationship?"

Eyes narrowed at her and arms crossed chests. She continued, "This is the real thing. No one has ever loved you like this. No one has ever accepted you for who you are until now."

Some shifted uncomfortably. Quinn knew a fantasy was as close to love as some would feel. "Everyone take out a sheet of paper. Write a letter to the one person in your family—blood or otherwise—you trust. Try to convince that person you should be able to keep this newfound love. You have thirty minutes to write."

Some kids grumbled. Most didn't like to write, but they did it.

The late-afternoon sun glared through the windows when they finally called it a day. Shari had plenty to work on. Quinn drew the line at taking papers or lesson plans home. She sat in the stifling heat trapped in the car and started the engine. It had been a great day and she felt fabulous. She hadn't felt this energized in forever. Days like this made her love her job.

She drove without a plan. She wanted to see Ryan, but she didn't want to seem clingy.

She wanted to ride the high of her good mood. The list needed attention. She had research to do on the expensive restaurants Griffin had told her about, and she needed to find a karaoke night.

Only a month remained before she was supposed to go to New Orleans. She needed to plan that as well. All of a sudden her summer off had shrunk. How did it blip by so quickly?

CHAPTER 18

Ryan fumed and kicked at boxes in his path while talking to his mother on the phone. "How could you tell her it was a good idea, Mom?"

"Because it is."

"No, it's not. Anything could happen to her. And she'll be too far away."

"We need to trust she'll take care of herself."

"But—"

"Maggie's not a child anymore. She needs to live her life. She needs to move past the bad memories."

He sank onto the edge of the couch and pinched the bridge of his nose. "Running away won't help."

His mother's sigh sounded the same as Maggie's had an hour earlier. "She's not running away."

"Traveling all over Europe, thousands of miles from home, is running away."

"No, it's not. She's traveling, expanding her horizons. Think of it as an adventure."

Damn women and their adventures.

"She feels stifled here, Ryan. She needs to get away."

"Because of me, right? That's what you're saying."

"It's everything from the last three years. She needs to live her life. And it's about time you started living yours again."

He shook his head at the phone. How did she manage to turn every conversation in this direction? "I'm living my life, Mom."

"Work is not life. I know you love the pub, but you need more. When was the last time you had a date?"

Did sleeping with Quinn count? He couldn't mention Quinn to his family.

"I'll take your silence to mean it's been too long. Has there been anyone since Cassie?"

"I'm fine, Mom." The last thing he needed was for her to pressure him so she could meet Quinn. She'd love her.

"Will you be at Sunday dinner this week?"

"Of course."

"You missed last month with your brothers and sisters."

"But I came to see you the next two weekends."

"I like for the family to be together."

"I'll be there. I have to go now."

"Stop worrying, Ryan. Things have a way of working out."

"Uh-huh. Love you." He disconnected, irritated his mother had encouraged Maggie.

He felt grungy still wearing yesterday's clothes, so he showered and changed. Maggie was smart. He'd give her that. Sneaky, but smart.

She'd called early in the morning, knowing he'd take her call, but hoping he'd be too tired to focus on her words. She hadn't counted on him being awake because he'd just gotten home. There was still half a week before family dinner. Enough time for him to get pissed and cool off. She definitely approached this with a plan.

He went down to the bar, brooding over Maggie's decision. Mary startled him two steps in the door.

"Look at this," she said, beaming. She thrust a handful of pages at him.

"What are you doing here? You should be at home asleep." He took the papers without giving them a glance and moved to the bar.

"I left by midnight last night. I was too excited to sleep late. Sit and read. I'll get you coffee." She moved around the bar and poured him coffee.

He read the papers she'd handed him. They were all e-mails from last night's speed daters. From the glowing compliments, it looked like Mary had been successful. There was even one from a friend of a dater.

"Congratulations. You did good."

She blushed. "I'm sure I'll get more feedback that won't be so positive, but it felt good to wake up to this."

Not as good as it felt to wake up next to Quinn.

"Your friend Quinn left early. I hope she had fun."

"It turned out fine." *In more ways than one.* He sipped his coffee.

Mary wiped down the already clean counter. She was building up to something.

"Good job last night. You impressed me."

"Good. Can I ask a favor?"

"As long as it's not asking for a raise."

Her smile broadened. The thought hadn't occurred to her. "I want to plan another event."

"That's not a favor. And you don't need permission. Do whatever you think will work."

He walked back to his office feeling battered. First Maggie informed him she was taking off halfway around the world. Then his mother brought memories of Cassie back to the surface.

He'd loved Cassie. Their split made sense, though. He knew it. It still stung because she was the one to call it off. She'd been too needy.

Cassie had put up with a lot. When they started dating, he only had Twilight. His father called him in to help straighten out O'Leary's. It had been a huge task. Colin fucked it up good.

And Dad died.

Cassie stuck with him through everything. When they started drifting, he'd thought he owed it to her to keep trying. He cared for her.

When Maggie had been raped, his life boiled over. It had been too much for Cassie. She needed more of him than he could give. His family had to come first. She didn't want a big family of her own. He couldn't imagine marrying and not having a brood. That thought made him think of Quinn. She was still waiting for an answer about him being her sperm donor.

Too bad he didn't have one for her.

At his desk, he began logging in the previous night's receipts. The night hadn't just been a success for Mary's singles; it had also been hugely profitable. If every event she hosted brought a draw like this, he'd owe Mary a raise.

After the lunch crowd slimmed, a childhood friend and local beat cop pushed through the doors. Charlie Boyle had always been tall and gangly. Even weighed down by police paraphernalia, he looked too skinny.

Ryan was chatting with the old timers in the corner when Charlie sat at the bar. Mary took his order, so Ryan topped off the old men's coffees before going by Charlie.

"Officer Boyle. How's it going?" Ryan extended his hand across the bar.

"Good. How about with you?"

"Same. Colin's back in town. He'd probably like to see you."

"Shit. It's been a long time. What's he been up to?"

"Whatever floats his boat."

"So he hasn't changed, huh?"

Ryan left the question unanswered. He didn't believe Colin had changed, but Charlie should form his own opinion.

"You don't stop in for lunch often. Is there a reason for the visit?"

"Actually, yeah." He waved his hand to bring Ryan closer and lowered his voice. "We're alerting local bar owners. There's been an increase in rapes in the area."

"Shit. Why haven't I seen this on the news?"

"It hasn't been on. I'm not talking drag-a-woman-in-the-alley rape. These guys are picking up women in bars and drugging them with roofies."

Ryan stilled. Ice pierced through his body. "Who? Where?"

"Shooter's on Ashland. Take a Cue on Belmont. And twice at Duffy's." No location was needed for Duffy's. They were Ryan's biggest and closest competitor.

"Four women?"

Charlie nodded. "That we know of. You know what that shit does to women."

Ryan thought of Maggie and his stomach clenched. "Any leads?"

"All four women are in their thirties. All of the attacks happened on weeknights when they were having drinks after work at neighborhood bars. They definitely have a type."

Mary placed a Reuben sandwich and fries in front of Charlie. She turned to refill his Coke. The men waited silently.

"You said 'guys.' You have suspects?"

Charlie took a huge bite of the sandwich and chewed. "Yes and no. The women said some younger guys were hitting on them. Not much to go on."

"Descriptions?"

Charlie shook his head. "We've got nothing solid. Younger than thirty, good-looking. They travel in a pack."

"What can I do?"

"You already do more than most bars, given your history. Talk with your people. Tell them what to look for. Remind women not to leave their drinks unattended and not to accept one unless it's delivered by an employee."

Ryan nodded. "The bar staff doesn't remember these guys?"

Charlie shrugged with another mouthful of food. "Nothing rang a bell. No credit slips matching. These guys probably use cash."

Ryan rapped knuckles on the bar. "Thanks for stopping by. I appreciate it. Enjoy your lunch."

As he passed Mary, he told her not to charge Charlie for lunch. He went to his office. He needed to forward this information to his staff without causing panic. He made notes and told Mary Charlie's news. He'd call everyone in for an emergency meeting before dinner. Mary would deliver the information. He was too stirred up and knew it.

Quinn searched for a bar hosting karaoke. She figured it would be cheating to reserve a quiet room in a karaoke bar because she wouldn't have much of an audience. Plus, she didn't want to compete with people who took karaoke too seriously. She was revved up and knew she could sing tonight. She thought of calling Ryan. He'd have ideas, but he might want to come with. She didn't know if she could perform with him in the audience.

She called Kate instead. "Hi, Kate. It seems like forever since we talked. Can you go out tonight?"

Kate's voice was tight. "God, I'd love to get away from here. Mark's probably working late, though. I haven't heard from him."

"I have *so* much to tell you."

"Sounds good. Indy coming?"

"You know, I'm trying to find karaoke for tonight. I don't think I'll call her." She felt a ping of guilt. It wasn't Indy's fault she was the better singer.

"Let me call my mom and see if she can babysit."

"You must want to go out really bad to call your mom."

"You have no idea."

"I'll call you back when I know where I'm heading."

They clicked off. Quinn scanned her brain for a way to find karaoke. Ryan came back to her mind, but when she pushed him back this time, Colin popped up. He'd have the same connections Ryan did. He also seemed to be more of a partier.

She eyed the phone. She could call O'Leary's and hope Ryan didn't answer the phone. Or she could just go in. If Ryan was there, she could say hi. She wouldn't mind seeing him. Even if Colin wasn't around, someone else might have ideas.

On the drive to O'Leary's she had the windows down and the radio up. She sang every song. She belted it out and energy hummed through her nerves.

The bar's parking lot was abnormally full for a Wednesday afternoon. It wasn't even dinnertime yet. The outdoor patio was empty. She entered the bar and found few customers.

Colin stood behind the bar alone. A rope had been pulled across the archway leading to the dance floor. A sign hung from it declaring it was a private party. She sidled up to the bar.

"Hi. Remember me?"

"How could I forget? You snuck out last night." He was drying glasses and sliding them into place on a shelf.

"Sorry. I was tired and needed to get out of here. It had absolutely nothing to do with you." She brought one foot up to rest on the brass pipe running along the bottom of the bar and leaned forward. "I have a favor to ask."

He put down the glass he held and slung the towel over his shoulder. He, too, leaned forward on the bar. "Anything, beautiful."

"Do you know where I could find karaoke?"

"Twilight will have it soon."

She crinkled her nose. "No, I'm looking for something for tonight."

"There's something going on at Duffy's. You need directions?"

She'd been there before. It was another Irish pub, but not nearly as homey and friendly as O'Leary's. "Sending me to the competition?"

"You asked. I provided information. I would beg you to stay with me if I thought it would work. It would make for fun competition." He brought her hand to his lips and kissed it.

She pulled it back smoothly. She didn't want to be rude and jerk away, but the "ick" factor shuffled through her.

"Can I get you a drink?"

"No, thanks. I have to get going." She tilted her head toward the back room. "Another big event tonight?"

"Staff meeting."

She pulled back from the bar. "Shouldn't you be there too?"

"Someone has to tend the bar. Ryan figures I'm the most expendable."

She backed toward the door. "Those are harsh words. Thanks for the information. I owe you one."

"Anytime."

She waved and left.

When she got home, she called Duffy's. They were actually having a karaoke competition and the woman who answered the phone didn't know if Quinn could sing without entering. Worst case, she'd have to pay the ten bucks to be in the competition. She called Kate, who said she'd be at Quinn's in an hour.

They planned to go out to eat first because Duffy's food wasn't good. Quinn dressed down in long denim shorts and a plain purple T-shirt. She knew better than to wear something skimpy to Duffy's. A rougher crowd hung out there. It was one of the reasons she and her colleagues started going to O'Leary's.

Kate arrived at six so they could carpool.

"Are you sure we can't go to Twilight?" Kate asked for what seemed like the hundredth time.

"What is with you? They don't have karaoke tonight. They won't have it again for another couple of weeks." Quinn swiped a brush through her hair one last time and took a long look at Kate.

She'd gotten used to seeing Kate in a baggy sweatshirt and peanut butter–smeared jeans. She'd dressed tonight as she had when they'd gone to Twilight. A short, slim black skirt and a black shell. This was lawyer-Kate out for a drink after work.

"I had a good time at Twilight. I liked the music and the atmosphere."

Quinn turned ideas in her mind. "Or maybe it was the company. What happened with Griffin after Ryan took me home?"

"Nothing." Kate blew out a depressed sigh. "I don't want to talk about the crap in my life. My mom has the kids and she's keeping them overnight. So I'm a free woman. Let's go have fun. You said you had lots to tell me. How's the list?"

"Nearly finished."

"Number eight?"

"You memorized the list?"

Kate nodded. "I said I'd live vicariously through you this summer."

"Number eight is not only marked off, but it has a huge smiley face next to it."

"Who?"

Quinn stood. "Come on, I'll tell you everything over dinner."

Ryan made another round through the bar. They weren't extremely busy, but they had a crowd. He scanned the tables of customers.

Did they always have so many women drinking in groups?

The night was starting to pick up. The jukebox blared. Not too many people were dancing. The numbers on the floor would increase as more alcohol was consumed. He'd already told the staff to swoop down and remove any unattended drinks. If a woman complained, they brought her a fresh one.

He didn't want to scare his customers off. It was worth losing a few bucks if it meant saving one woman from being raped. He thought of Maggie and their argument. She didn't often go to bars anymore, but he'd called her and left a message of warning anyway.

It didn't matter that she was younger than the other victims. If something happened to her again, he didn't think either of them would come out the other side.

Ryan stood at the bar, his back leaning against it so he could watch the crowd. He was exhausted, drained. He didn't think he'd be able to keep up this hypervigilance. Maybe he'd hire a couple more bouncers to work the crowd.

Colin tapped him on the shoulder.

Ryan turned his head, but not his body. "What?"

"You're strung pretty tight there, bro. Why don't you take a break?"

"I'm fine."

"Uh-huh. Here." He slid a draft next to Ryan's elbow. "It'll help you relax."

Ryan absently sipped the beer. He couldn't relax. He didn't know how Colin could expect him to. But then Colin hadn't been here for Maggie. Hadn't seen what it had done to her.

"You didn't tell me Quinn was a singer."

Broken from concentration, Ryan turned. "What?"

"You didn't tell me Quinn sang. Is she any good? Seems like she would have a sultry voice."

"What are you talking about?" Colin had his full attention now.

"Quinn came by earlier looking for a place to sing karaoke."

"Why didn't you call me?"

"She stopped in during the staff meeting and didn't ask for you. I think she wanted to see me again."

Ryan snorted. "Not likely."

"What do you know? We had a good time last night. She's a bit tame for my taste, but I wouldn't kick her out of bed."

Ryan's blood ran hot. "Stay away from her."

Colin tilted his head. "Why? She's single and apparently looking for dates."

"This isn't a joke. Quinn is off limits."

Colin stepped closer. "Says who?"

"Me."

"I think Quinn is capable of making her own decisions. She can decide who she'll go home with."

"She already has."

Colin stopped, mouth half open, probably with his next barb on its way. "Interesting. Come to think of it, you did disappear about the same time she did last night."

Ryan cooled his throat with a long drink of beer. Colin braced his elbows on the bar like a neighbor leaning on a fence waiting for gossip.

"So?"

"What?"

"Details, man. How hot is she?"

"Drop it."

Colin snickered. "You got it bad."

"I said stay out of it."

Colin eased off the bar as two new customers walked in. "If you're so hot for her, why are you here watching other women instead of singing with Quinn at Duffy's?"

"I told you why. Wait a minute. You sent her to Duffy's?"

"She didn't want to wait to sing at your swanky Twilight."

"You dumb fuck."

Anger flashed in Colin's eyes. He held up a finger to the waiting customers. "Don't go there. Your lady asked for information. I provided it. It's not my problem you can't keep her satisfied."

"Two of the rapes happened to women at Duffy's." Ryan's voice was low and anger fled Colin's face, replaced by concern.

"I didn't know. You didn't give me those details either. Look, I'm sure she's fine. Give her a call and warn her." He walked away, apologizing to the couple waiting patiently at the end of the bar.

Without thinking, without offering explanations to anyone, Ryan bolted from the bar. Calling would be the sensible thing. Make sure she was at Duffy's. But he had no sense when it came to Quinn.

He drove like a maniac to get to Duffy's. The lot was packed. He didn't see Quinn's car, but if she planned to drink, she'd have taken a cab. He circled the block, beating a rhythm on the steering wheel. When he saw a car pulling out, he jumped two lanes of traffic and whipped a U-turn to take the spot.

Entering the bar, he was immediately reminded why he disliked Duffy's. It wasn't that they were competition. They wanted to be an Irish pub, but they thought the name was all they needed. Cheesy leprechaun pictures hung on the wall, leftover from a long-ago St. Patrick's Day celebration. College kids came here for the cheap beer.

O'Leary's had won the patronage of the Irish community. His parents had strong ties, being immigrants themselves. The bar did such a brisk after-work business because of the immigrants. Irishmen liked to drink, but they rarely did it at home.

Ryan focused on faces at every table. He didn't see Quinn. No one took notice of him as he wound through the crowd. The guy on the platform (it wasn't big enough to count as a stage) was a good singer, making it easier to tune him out.

He turned the corner and entered the second half of the bar. From behind him, he heard the singer leave the stage and the next one start. The voice stopped him.

Quinn.

He spun around and edged to the side of the crowd. She engaged the audience as she sang.

Worry seeped out as her voice washed over him. It held the same smooth quality as when she sang with the radio in her kitchen, and he'd imagined her singing lullabies to a baby. Now, she was putting on a show. Her feet tapped in rhythm and her hips swayed.

From the shadows behind him, someone tapped his shoulder. He couldn't take his eyes off Quinn.

"She's better than you thought, right?"

The question drew his attention. Kate stood beside him. "No, I already knew. I caught her singing the other day."

He looked back as Quinn finished and took a bow. The crowd applauded. Some stood and cheered. She rushed off the stage.

She was moving so fast she couldn't have seen much. It was like watching a cartoon character as she skidded to a halt. The flush of pleasure from singing slipped for a moment when she saw him. Then it returned even brighter as she jumped past Kate and wrapped her arms around his neck.

"I did it. Did you see? By myself. I was good."

"Yeah, I heard." He took a minute and held her pressed against him, inhaling her soft scent. The relief he felt in holding her smacked him so hard he had to take a steadying breath. Anger replaced the worry. Anything could've happened to her in this dive. He stepped back, but held her elbow. "Let's go."

She jerked her arm and shook her head. "I'm not going anywhere. I'm having fun. I might even sing again."

"You sang. You can mark it off your goddamn list. Let's go."

She took a step back and walked away. Kate was no longer at his side. He hadn't noticed her leave.

He followed Quinn and barely caught her elbow before she sat.

"You're not staying at this dive. You want to drink and have fun, go to O'Leary's."

She yanked her arm back. "Why? So you can spy on me some more? Watch my every move and make sure you approve?"

"No—"

"You don't own me, Ryan. So we slept together. Big deal. That doesn't give you the right to tell me what to do."

"It's not—"

She held up her hand to stop him. She turned to Kate. "Let's go somewhere else."

Kate stood, eyes wide in shock, and grabbed both their purses.

Quinn turned back and poked him in the chest. "Don't follow me."

She stormed out. Kate looked back and gave a slight shrug. He'd feel better if he knew where they were going, but at least they left Duffy's.

He looked around at the staff bustling by. Not one of them stopped the slight altercation between him and Quinn. It was no wonder the sleazebags used Duffy's as a hunting ground.

No one paid attention.

"What the hell happened? I leave you alone because you look ready to make out with Ryan, the next minute, you're fighting." Kate started the car but waited for Quinn's response.

"He was being an ass." Quinn turned in her seat. Out the back window, she saw Ryan leave the bar and scan the street.

"How?"

"I didn't tell him I was coming here. He just showed up and said, 'Let's go.'"

Kate glanced out of the corner of her eye.

"Like I don't have the right to go wherever I want."

"Hmm. Why?"

"Why what?"

"Why did he want you to leave?"

"I don't know." Her phone rang. Ryan. She pushed it to voice mail.

"This is what I know. I watched him while you sang. He's really into you."

"Funny way of showing it. You know, screw this. Let's go back in. I want to sing again. I'm not going to let him ruin my night." She stepped from the car and left her phone on the console. She was being petty by not answering it, but he had no right to tell her where she could hang out.

Even more proof that friends with benefits didn't work.

She thought of how good it initially felt to find Ryan standing in Duffy's. How natural it had been to throw her arms around him to share her triumph.

You can't have it all. Either he's a friend or a lover.

The voice in her head nagged her. As good as the sex was, she wanted the friendship. She wanted to be able to call him to chat, or hang out, without being the needy, demanding girlfriend. She felt comfortable around him and didn't want that to change.

Back in Duffy's, she scanned the room. They'd lost their table, so they found a couple of stools at the bar. They hadn't sat for more than two minutes before a hairy, burly guy squeezed between them and faced Kate.

"Hi. Can I buy you a drink?"

Kate tapped her glass. "I'm good, thanks."

"I'll buy the next one."

"That won't be necessary. I'm married."

He shuffled and faced Quinn. "How about you?"

Second choice again, and Indy wasn't even here. She wished she had a ring on her finger that she could flash at him to make him go away. "I'm good. Maybe later."

He shrugged and left. Kate smirked. "Not your type?"

"Not quite. I'm going to go sing again. Want to join me?" She slid off her stool.

"You know I can't sing."

"Neither can most of the people here. It'll be fun." She tugged Kate's elbow. "We'll sing 'Girls Just Want to Have Fun.' It'll be a blast. Trust me."

They moved to the stage and added their names to the wait list. Standing in the crowd waiting for their turn, Quinn studied the people around her. So many of them were young. She didn't fit in here. She wasn't looking for a one-night stand. Sure, a summer romance would be great, but she still believed she wouldn't find him in a bar.

The DJ called her and Kate to the stage. They set their drinks on the table near the DJ and grabbed microphones. The music started and they sang. And laughed. The crowd joined in. For a few brief minutes, Quinn understood why Indy enjoyed being the center of attention.

When the song ended, burly guy met them near the stage. "I'll show you some fun."

He'd obviously had too much to drink. He swayed as he spoke. Quinn didn't respond, hoping he would move on.

He stepped into her path. "Come on. I owe you a drink." He tried to put his arm around her shoulder, but she ducked the contact.

"Actually, we're done for the night." She wanted to end her night on a high note, but this guy was making it plummet fast.

"Uh-uh. You said I could buy you a drink later. It's later. Let's go."

Kate stepped closer. "She said she wasn't interested. Now excuse us."

"No one's talking to you." He shoved past Kate to get close to Quinn.

She smelled the beer and sweat on him and her stomach curdled. What had Ryan called this place? A dive? She was beginning to agree with him. This guy was being obnoxious and no one seemed to notice.

"I'm not interested. Thanks anyway. Now, please move." She took a step, but he mirrored her movement until she was boxed against the wall. Her thoughts immediately turned to Ryan. Why hadn't she left with him? Her heart thumped in panic. If she screamed, would anyone even hear her over the guy singing?

Suddenly, a deep male voice asked, "Is there a problem here?"

Burly turned to face an equally big guy. "No, I'm just talking to a woman. Get your own."

The new guy looked at Quinn.

Kate stood beside the new guy. She reached for Quinn's hand. "We're on our way out. Thanks."

She pulled Quinn through the crowd. "Sorry I left you. I just had a feeling things were going to get bad with that guy, so I went to find a bouncer."

"Thanks. He was drunk and more than a little creepy."

Kate dropped Quinn off and went home. Before plugging in her cell phone to charge for the night, Quinn turned it on. Only one voice mail to go with four missed calls. Not as obnoxious as Ryan could've been. She accessed her voice mail and listened.

"Quinn, damn it. I wish you'd answer. I wasn't trying to tell you what to do. There have been a string of rapes. Some guys are picking up women at neighborhood bars and slipping roofies in their drinks. I was worried."

The message went on for a few more seconds, but Quinn tuned it out. She felt like an ass. *He was worried.* She smiled. The thought brought back the feeling of comfort she had when she hugged him at Duffy's.

Then guilt stabbed at her. She treated him horribly and because of her stubbornness, she had to deal with some creep hitting on her. Ryan had been right again.

Her phone was still cradled in her palm. She itched to call Ryan. Or go see him. She thought of Kate and the problems she was having in her marriage. Quinn didn't want to be there again. One failed marriage was enough. She could find someone to sleep with anytime if she really tried. It might even be pretty good sex.

But real friendship like she shared with Ryan didn't come every day.

CHAPTER 19

It was almost midnight. The crowd had thinned and Ryan finally took a moment to sit. He scrubbed his hands over his face. Worry gnawed at his gut. He still hadn't heard from Quinn.

Jenna laid her serving tray on the bar. She pulled a slip of paper from her apron. "Hey, boss. I forgot to give this to you. She called an hour ago."

Ryan unfolded the paper as Jenna filled her tray again. It read, *"Quinn called. At home. Talk tomorrow."*

The weight he'd carried in his chest for hours loosened. She must've finally listened to his message. She was smart enough not to go bar hopping. By tomorrow she wouldn't even be pissed off anymore.

He looked back at the customers who remained so late on a Wednesday night. Mostly men. Mostly regulars. Mostly trustworthy.

Colin stood behind the bar wiping glasses.

"I'm leaving. You can handle closing, right?"

Colin grunted.

"Make sure Jenna gets to her car safely. Walk her out."

"Got it."

"I'm trusting you to not fuck this up."

Colin put down the glass. "I got it. I'm not the fucking idiot you try to make me out to be."

"We'll see. Good night."

"Yeah."

Ryan felt heavier with every step he took to his apartment above the bar. He dropped his clothes as he walked to the bedroom. He should've taken a nap after making Quinn breakfast. He wasn't twenty-two anymore.

He crawled into bed. The cool cotton sheets rubbed against him, and he thought back to the warmth of Quinn's body as they'd slept. He was beginning to think she had a point. Having sex had changed their relationship. He couldn't decide if the difference was a positive or negative, but he was sure he didn't want to go back.

When he dragged himself from bed at nine-thirty the following morning, his first thought was coffee. His next was Quinn. He'd wanted to call her before she went to work, but he realized he already missed her.

Back to coffee.

He showered and dressed as quickly as humanly possible, knowing Mary would have good coffee made downstairs. He grabbed his keys and cell phone. He'd forgotten to charge it and he'd missed a call from Quinn.

Dialing voice mail, he hoped the battery would hold out.

"Hey, Ryan. Thanks for the warning last night. If you had told me, I might not have been such a bitch. Anyway, I was hoping you had some free time this afternoon. I need to talk—" The phone went dead. It was enough. She'd thought of calling him before she went to work.

In the bar, Mary had music playing, the local country station. She hummed while she set up the kitchen. She came around the corner and stopped. "You look like crap. What happened?"

"Nothing. Just tired and in need of coffee." He moved directly to the pot. The first sip scalded the roof of his mouth, but the pain was worth it. There was no reason for him to be tired after eight hours of sleep.

"I got the information all set for our next singles event, if you want to go over it."

He hid the cringe, afraid to hurt Mary's feelings, but he remembered the amount of information she'd had for speed dating. "I told you to go ahead and schedule whatever you want. It's your baby."

She looked at him over the rim of her coffee cup. "Do my ideas bore you?"

He smiled. "No, but your graphs, charts, and piles of paper do. I trust you."

"Can I schedule it at Twilight?"

"Sure, I guess."

"I think the lock-and-key event would fit better at Twilight. We might not even need to block part of the floor."

He closed his eyes and shook his head. "You're doing it again. Plan it. Put it on my calendar. I'll be in my office."

Behind the closed door of his office, he heard the quiet movements of Mary's setup routine. He stretched out on the couch. He felt sleep pulling at him and searched his brain for a reason to explain the fatigue.

Maggie leaving was a definite stressor.

Rapists prowling his neighborhood.

Wild monkey sex with Quinn. He laughed again at her description.

The long night and early morning with Quinn did him in. They lived opposite schedules. He couldn't remember what it was like. An occasional date didn't matter. Long term, they'd have to make adjustments. His fuzzy brain clouded with sleep. A nap couldn't hurt.

Long term? Where had that come from?

Quinn went to school with the plan of staying only a couple of hours. Part of her regretted taking on Shari's problems.

It added another complication to her life. She was juggling too many things. Too many balls in the air at once. Her normal locked-tight control had slipped.

Other people wheeled in, tossing extra balls at her. She intended to drop some of those balls today.

After working with Shari, Quinn planned to meet with Carlson. He'd given the job she wanted to Shari Ackerman and now she wanted him to know how upset it made her. Diplomatically, of course. She wouldn't risk her job.

Three hours later, frustration still sang through her blood. Shari wasn't good at thinking on her feet with these kids. Dumping an ill-suited lesson plan terrified her. It took Quinn thirty minutes to convince her winging it was less frightening than having kids zone out and not learn. Funny, since she didn't know how to wing anything other than teaching.

Quinn counted on her frustration to get her through her meeting with Carlson. Carlson had to know she'd been bothered when passed over for the position. She swallowed that anger months ago, when she saw Shari working with the Honors kids. The job wasn't a cakewalk and Quinn knew it. But to be pulled back this summer to mentor Shari irritated her. Schedules weren't set for the upcoming year yet, and she wanted another shot at Shari's position.

This time she wouldn't back down. She deserved the chance to not only prove she would be a good fit for the position, but she also deserved the position for doing everything that had ever been asked of her. There had to be some perk for being a team player.

Carlson sat behind his desk with his usual friendly smile. "Hi, Quinn. How's everything going?"

"All right, I suppose. Shari is a little rigid in her lesson planning, but I think it's because she's still new. She'll be okay."

"I'm glad to hear it. I knew you'd be able to help her."

"About that. I wanted to talk about next year."

He leaned forward, his chair creaking with the repositioning of bulk. "Yes?"

"I want the Honors position next year. I've worked my butt off, and I've handled any project or task you've tossed at me over the years. I want this."

"I can appreciate that, Quinn. It's one of the reasons I always feel comfortable passing extra projects your way. I know they'll be handled. But I already assured Shari that she would have the same classes next year."

"But I have seniority. I've proved myself time and again." The anger and frustration threatened to bubble out and she'd look like a fool. She inhaled slowly to calm herself.

"I always place teachers where they're most needed. We need you with the kids who struggle."

What a line of bullshit.

"I really appreciate you helping Shari this summer and my offer for comp time stands. But when the school year starts, I need you exactly where you've been. We've seen annual growth on our state test scores, and I don't want to upset a well-oiled machine."

Translation: *I hired Ackerman to teach Honors and she gets to keep it. I don't trust her with the other kids.*

Quinn now realized why he gave Shari the summer-school class. It was a test, and Shari failed.

The determined set to Carlson's face told her she wouldn't win this battle. So much for standing up for herself and breaking out of her rut. If this rut got any deeper, it would start to feel like a grave.

For the first time since she took this job eight years ago, she considered quitting. She briefly imagined standing up and saying, "I quit," and storming out. But she couldn't afford to quit at this moment, no matter how much she'd like to. If she was going to spend this year pregnant, staying at Jones would make her life easier. She could teach her lesson plans without effort. After this year, though, she'd need a change.

She stood and offered Carlson a tight smile. "I understand. I'll see you later."

With one confrontation behind her, she drove to O'Leary's, determined not to lose her resolve. When she walked in, she waited to get Mary's attention at the bar.

The woman was typing madly on a laptop, checking notes on a legal pad, and frowning. Ryan's car was parked in back, but she didn't see him. The bar was quiet, except for two old men watching a Sox game at the corner of the bar.

Mary looked up. "I'm sorry to keep you waiting. What can I get for you?"

"I'm looking for Ryan."

"Quinn, right?"

She nodded.

"He'll be down in a few minutes. He ran upstairs to change before going to Twilight."

Upstairs? Mary went back to the computer with a frown.

"Is it as bad as you look?"

Mary sighed. "I'm trying to design a flyer for our next singles event. We're doing it at Twilight, so I need something nicer, more elegant."

"Can I take a look?"

Mary shrugged and turned the computer.

Quinn read. "What's a lock-and-key party?"

"All the women get a lock when they arrive. Men get keys. Everyone wanders around, getting to know the other participants, and tries to find a match."

"Sounds kind of sexist. Reminiscent of chastity belts."

A frown creased Mary's face again. "I hadn't thought of that. I thought it would be a fun way to network and meet people. There are multiple sets, so one guy could open a few locks."

"I didn't mean to offend you. It sounds like fun. Pressure free, unlike speed dating, where you have such a short time to make an impression and make a judgment."

Quinn fiddled with the layout and design of the flyer. She dragged clip art and changed the font. "How's that?"

Mary pulled the computer back to face her. "Wow. That's what I was looking for. I've been playing with this for an hour."

"Glad to help."

"Do you know anyone who might be interested in coming?"

Quinn nodded. She didn't know why. She supposed it was because she liked Mary. "Add me and my sister, Indy, too. I'll drag her along."

A flicker of surprise crossed Mary's face, like she hadn't expected Quinn to join. "Same last name?"

"Yep."

The back door slammed. The hall was too dark to see anything, but Quinn knew it was Ryan. She knew the feel of his eyes on her.

He walked into the light while tucking his tailored black shirt into his pants. His hair, usually scruffy, looked styled, as if he actually used a comb. This was the sleek Ryan. A smile brightened his face and she saw nothing but her friend, slick or not.

"Hi." He walked around the bar and waved at the men watching TV.

"Looking uppity there, boy. You're not instituting a dress code here, are you?"

"Don't worry, Pete. I'll never expect you to wear anything but what you do every day. I know better than to try to class up this place."

"Good. Your daddy'd be rolling in his grave if you did."

Quinn heard the affection in their voices. She wondered how long the two men had been coming into the bar.

Ryan reached her, slid a hand around her lower back, and kissed the top of her head. Between the genuinely sweet gesture and his scent, her determination began to dissolve.

No, I'm doing this. She stiffened under his touch. "Do you have time to talk? Privately?"

"Sure. Let's go to my office." He tapped the bar. "I'll be in back, Mary."

Quinn led the way, trying to put distance between them. In his office, she chose a stiff-backed chair over the couch, so he'd be limited as to how close he could get.

"I'm glad you stopped by." The door closed with a quiet click. "About last night."

She held up a hand to stop him. "I got your message. I appreciate the warning. I guess I owe you again."

He sat in the chair beside her, their knees almost touching. "I'll add it to your tab."

She forced a tight smile and scooted farther back in the chair. She held her hands on her knees, but she wanted to tangle them in his perfectly styled hair. "I'm not mad about last night, but I have been thinking."

"So have I."

"You have?" She didn't hide the surprise in her voice.

He touched her thigh. "Yeah, let's face it. Casual sex isn't working."

"I told you that the first time we went out."

"I know. Part of me didn't believe you. I tried to listen, but it didn't work."

"Tell me about it." She wanted to be relieved that he understood the complications.

"There's only one thing to do." He sighed and put his elbows on his knees.

"I'm so glad we agree."

"We do?" His forehead furrowed in confusion.

"I can't risk losing our friendship. Isn't that what you were saying?" She crossed her arms and leaned back.

"No, I think we should jump all the way in and be a couple." He straightened in his seat.

"What?" She jumped to her feet and stepped behind her chair.

"I think we should date exclusively. And have lots of monkey sex." He grinned, and she almost melted.

She braced her hands on the back of the chair and shook her head. "I have no intention of being your experiment with monogamy."

"Are you accusing me of being commitment-phobic?"

"If it fits." What the hell was he thinking? She could never be with him and wonder how long it would be until he tired of her. Then she would surely lose him as a friend.

He stood and anger flashed in his eyes. "You're the one who runs at the sight of a relationship."

"Fuck you. I'm not afraid of commitment. I was married."

"You admitted your marriage was a mistake. How long did it last? How many serious relationships since?"

He moved so he was close once again. She backed away from the chair and his touch. She paced near the couch. "I gave it a serious shot. My marriage failed after three years. But at least I tried."

"I did too."

Her head snapped back to his face. He'd never said he'd been married.

"I was with a woman for six years. I wanted to marry her. I planned to, but she decided she couldn't do forever with me. I believe marriage means forever."

She stood gasping at him. The words wouldn't come. She closed her eyes and turned her back. Marriage? Forever? Did he want to marry her? Her heart beat against her ribs and she was sure it would break free.

"I'm not talking marriage here, but I want to continue what we started." He put his hands on her shoulders. "I thought this summer was all about taking chances."

"If you know me so well, you'd know I'm a chicken." She turned in his arms. "I want to keep you as a friend. I don't make friends easily. At least not real ones. You're one of the best friends I've ever had. I'm comfortable and at ease around you. I can be myself."

"I'm not going anywhere."

"What happens when things don't work out? When there's a new flavor you want to try? Then I lose a valuable friend. I don't think I can handle that."

"We're good together, Quinn. You know that. Why can't we just see where it goes?"

"Because if it doesn't last, then I'll be alone again."

"But you'll be no worse off than you are now."

"I won't have you anymore. That would be worse."

He pressed a kiss to her forehead and pulled her into his arms. She rested her cheek on his chest. His sigh ruffled her hair.

"So what happens when you discover you can't keep your hands off me?"

She laughed and felt his laugh rumble beneath her cheek. After inhaling his scent deeply, she stepped back.

"Friends?" She held out her hand.

"This is a mistake. We can have something special."

"We already do," she responded, patting his cheek.

She left the office and the bar. If this was the right move, why was her heart so heavy?

Ryan left O'Leary's and threw himself into work at Twilight. Over the past weeks, he'd spent a lot less time there in order to be at O'Leary's, where Quinn could find him and he could spend time with her. With her declaration that they remain nothing more than friends, he had no reason to split his time as much as he had.

Friends. He'd always been an equal opportunity friend. Over the years he'd had many women as friends. The chemistry he shared with Quinn was something he'd never experienced with any other friend, though.

Frustration eked into every cell. He'd worked hard to help Quinn with her list. He figured that would be his way in. Maybe he'd done too good of a job.

He wanted her to be happy. She *was* happy with him and he knew that, but she continued to fight it.

He saw in her eyes that telling him they couldn't be more than friends left her unhappy, but there was nothing he could do about it. He couldn't fight for something if she wouldn't accept it.

So, he'd accept what he could get and move on.

He had become good at ignoring the empty space in his chest.

He spent the afternoon booking new bands to appear at Twilight.

He'd been looking for something upbeat and found quite a few. Giving new local bands a chance was one thing he really enjoyed about his position.

After hours of phone calls and being alone, Ryan left his office looking for a distraction. Moira walked through the door.

She walked side by side with another woman, one he didn't know. When Moira saw him, her face broke into a huge smile.

"Hey, Ry. I was hoping I'd find you here." She barely brushed a kiss on his cheek. "I wanted to introduce you to my friend, Kathy. Kathy, this is my big brother, Ryan."

"Hi. Nice to meet you." He extended his hand and she shook it, holding a little longer than what was polite.

"I've heard a lot about you."

"That's never good when Moira's behind it."

Moira slugged his arm. "Jerk. I only told her the good stuff."

Uh-oh. That's when it hit him. Moira was blindsiding him with a setup. She'd pulled this before. She'd brought a friend to the bar for dinner, introduced him, then got an "emergency" call that required her quick departure.

"Can I get you a table?"

"Yes, please," Kathy answered.

He led the way and heard Moira's whisper, "I told you he was good-looking." Unfortunately, he couldn't hear Kathy's response.

He stopped at a booth. "Here you go. Let me know if you need anything. Rachel will be here to take your order."

Moira took the seat beside Kathy and pointed at the bench across from them. "Come on, Ry. Join us. Even the boss needs to eat."

"Oh, yes. Please have dinner with us. I'd like to get to know you."

He tried to muster enough irritation at Moira's meddling to turn them down, but he couldn't. He raked his gaze over Kathy. She was tall with long wild hair bouncing on her shoulders. She openly flirted with him. She was everything Quinn wasn't.

Change might do him some good.

He sat across from Kathy, and Moira started the conversation. "You and Kathy have a lot in common. She's the oldest of four kids and she owns her own business."

"Really? What kind of business?"

"A flower shop."

Kathy leaned forward and offered him all of the unmistakable signs of flirting.

She definitely wasn't interested in being his friend.

Three days passed. Quinn hadn't spoken to Ryan. She didn't want him to think she was avoiding him. Sunday morning brunch was an acceptable thing for friends to do.

Not knowing whether he'd worked until closing, she decided a text was a good form of contact. If he was still asleep, it would be easy to ignore a text. She sent one word: **Brunch?**

She waited, her cell phone in her hand. *How crazy is this? I'm like a teenager waiting for the cute boy from school to call.* It didn't matter that she felt silly. The reality was she missed hanging out with Ryan. The past three days had been productive, but much too serious.

Her phone jingled in her hand, startling her. "Hi, Ryan. I guess you're awake."

"It's ten o'clock."

"I thought you might sleep late if you worked last night."

"Do you do anything without thinking it to death first?"

"I try not to. Are you hungry?"

"Starving. I don't remember the last time I went grocery shopping."

"Where do you want to go?" She looked out her window. The sky was clear and bright. It reminded her of the day she played hooky.

"I'll come get you and we'll decide."

"You're always playing chauffeur. I'll come for you." Besides, it'd be less like a date.

"Sure?"

"Yeah, but I don't know where you live."

He let out a low chuckle. "I live above O'Leary's. I thought you knew."

"No, you never mentioned it." She grabbed her purse and keys.

"Come around the back. You'll see the stairs to come up."

"See you in a few."

He must've been waiting for her because the door swung open before she had a chance to knock.

"Hi."

She lifted her leg as if to step in, but he hadn't moved. "Aren't you going to invite me in?"

Something passed over his face, but she couldn't read it.

"Sure, if you want."

He stepped back from the door that opened to a long hallway. The ancient carpet muffled their footsteps, but the air around her ached for an echo. She followed him to the last door on the right.

"This is temporary until I figure out where I want to live."

She entered to find a small hallway lined with boxes. It looked like moving day. Then she stepped into the living room. The space shouted *bachelor pad*. A leather couch and big-screen TV dominated the room.

He leaned against the back of the couch. "I don't usually have guests. Griffin's the only person who's been here."

She looked down another hall also lined with boxes.

"Bedroom's down there. Kitchen's behind you. This is obviously the living room."

Embarrassment. That's what she'd seen on his face when she asked to come in. It didn't sit well on him.

"Why live above the bar? I'd think you'd get sick of the place."

"It's convenient. When Cassie broke up with me, I couldn't find anyplace I liked, so I moved here. I figured it would be a couple of months. It's been two years." He shrugged and straightened. "I'm ready to eat."

"Good. So am I." She turned to walk out and waited for him to join her. "Thanks for letting me see your place."

He locked the door. "There wasn't much to see."

"Are there tenants in the other apartments?" She looked at the three other doors.

"No, there used to be, but when the last round of leases was up, we didn't renew. My dad wanted to fix them up. He got as far as getting new windows in before he died." He jiggled his keys before shoving them into the pocket of well-worn denim shorts. "My sister Maggie moved in for a while."

"That's a lot of wasted space and income." She walked down the stairs ahead of him.

"You sound like Griff. I've been busy juggling a lot of stuff. I've been meaning to get back to it."

"Uh-huh." She unlocked the car and got behind the wheel.

He buckled up. "What's that supposed to mean?"

"If you made it a priority, you'd get it done. You allow other things to get in the way."

"I don't need a motivational speech. I need food."

She laughed. "Where to?"

Brunch had been perfect. It had been the most relaxing Sunday he'd had in a while. They talked about everything and nothing. He'd thought it would be awkward as he and Quinn tried to stay in the friend zone, but they were naturally comfortable with each other. Maybe she'd been right.

The thought of ruining that relaxation with a big O'Leary dinner wasn't appealing. He stretched out on the cool leather sofa and closed his eyes. He needed to go to dinner and talk to Maggie.

His phone rang, jolting him from the couch. "Hello?"

"Hey, Ryan. Are you on your way?"

Moira. Shit. What time was it? "No, I'm still at home."

"Good. Stop at the bakery and pick up something for dessert."

He scrubbed a hand over his face. How had he fallen asleep? "Your turn for dessert."

"I know. Colin and Liam got into my dessert when I left it unguarded."

"Fine. I'll bring something. But they do my share of the dishes."

"Good luck getting them to agree. See you soon."

He got off the couch and stretched. Splashing water on his face helped wake him fully. He checked the time. He'd have just enough time to stop at Blackstone Bakery before they closed.

A box of pastries—Maggie's favorite chocolate éclairs and cream puffs for Mom—should win him enough time to explain why Maggie shouldn't leave. He called the bakery on his way to the car.

He parked on the street down the block from his childhood home. O'Leary cars lined the street. It looked like he was the last to arrive. He jogged up the concrete stairs and swung in the door.

Liam and Colin were sitting on the couch arguing about baseball, but they both shut up when they saw the white bakery box. They shifted to follow, but Ryan shot them a look. "Don't bother. I'll break your fingers if you untie the string on this box."

He walked through to the kitchen. Bending, he kissed his mom on her cheek. Moira swooped in and snatched the box.

"Did you get something good?"

"I went to Blackstone. It's all good. Where's Maggie?"

His mother turned from the stove, wiping her hands on a towel. "She's not here."

"Oooo. That means éclairs. He's trying to bribe Maggie." Moira smacked her lips.

"Why not?" he asked, focused on his mother.

"She doesn't want to fight with you. I told her we'd talk."

He crossed his arms. "You're not going to convince me this is a good idea."

She imitated his stance. "And you won't convince her it's a bad one. Even with éclairs." She pointed a quick finger at him. "And knowing you, there's cream puffs as well, with your thinking you'd get me to side with you."

Of course his mother would know his every ploy. Not much got passed Eileen O'Leary. "She thinks she can take care of herself, but she can't."

"She's stronger than you give her credit for. We all are." She touched his cheek in a gesture she'd done his whole life.

It softened him, but he knew her ploys as well. "I know you're strong, Mom. I worry about Maggie."

"I know you do, but you need to let her go."

Noise erupted from the living room. It wasn't a whooping sports cheer either. His mother pushed him aside.

"It must be Michael," she said halfway through the door.

Michael. His schedule at the firehouse often conflicted with family dinner. Entering the dining room, Ryan saw the reason for the fuss. Moira and their mom were crying and hugging Brianna, Michael's girlfriend.

On Brianna's left hand, a huge, glistening diamond winked. It certainly explained Michael picking up shifts at the bar. Ryan pushed through the crowd to get to Brianna. "My turn."

He scooped her up and swung in a circle, causing Brianna's long blond hair to swing and making her giggle. As he let her down, he whispered into her hair, "You make him happy. There's nothing else I could want for him."

Still teary-eyed, she reached up and gave him a peck on the cheek. "He makes me happier than I thought possible."

Michael tapped him on the shoulder. "Hands off my fiancée. Get your own."

Brianna beamed at Michael. "Say that again. I like the sound of it."

"Get your own," he repeated, earning him an elbow from Brianna. "Oh, my fiancée."

"Yeah." She kissed him and turned to Eileen. "What can I help with for dinner?"

"Dinner is ready. You can help Ryan set the table."

Moira looked at Ryan. "It's about time you got your own."

"Own what?"

"Fiancée."

He shook his head and followed Brianna and his mother into the kitchen. Ryan grabbed a stack of plates while Brianna carried a tray of silverware. As they worked their way around the table, Brianna asked, "Are you seeing anyone?"

"Not really."

She stopped, holding a fork above a place setting. "What does that mean, not really? It's a yes or no."

From the couch, Colin interjected, "He's got one on the hook but can't manage to reel her in."

"Shut up." He glared at Colin, willing him to follow the command.

"What's her name?"

Ryan said nothing. Colin hoisted himself off the couch and leaned against the antique china cabinet across from the table. "Quinn. Her name is Quinn. She's a teacher and she sings, I think. I never did get a clear answer. She's pretty. About your height, Brianna. Dark hair cut to her chin."

Brianna laid the last fork in place. "You seem to know an awful lot."

"He needs to keep his nose out of other people's business." Ryan shoved his hands deep in his pockets.

"Well, I'm glad he doesn't. Otherwise we might never know you had a life outside the bar." Brianna circled the table again, placing a paper napkin opposite the silverware.

Moira breezed in with the first two bowls, asparagus and corn.

"So where'd you meet her?" Brianna continued.

"Meet who?" Moira spun on her heels to pin Colin and Ryan to their places.

"No one," Ryan answered.

"Did you and Kathy hit it off? I think she likes you."

"Sorry to disappoint you. She's a nice girl, but there was no chemistry."

"How could there be no chemistry? She's gorgeous and smart and friendly."

Colin jumped in. "Hey, where's my introduction?"

Moira eyed him. "Kathy's looking to settle down and you're . . . Colin."

Colin answered with a frown.

Moira turned back to Ryan. "So you have a girlfriend?"

"I don't have a girlfriend. Quinn is a friend who happens to be female." He still had a hard time swallowing it, but even if she was more, he wouldn't want to expose her to this.

"Moira, potatoes gettin' cold," Eileen called from the kitchen.

"I'm coming," Moira yelled back. She turned to Ryan. "Don't say anything else until I get back."

Ryan growled and followed Moira into the kitchen. He returned to find Brianna still waiting and Colin wearing a wicked smirk.

Moira came bustling back with the mashed potatoes and Eileen close on her heels with a huge plate of ham.

The smell of hot food called Liam and Michael from the couch. Michael moved straight to Brianna to take the seat beside her. Without Maggie they didn't need to squeeze one of the kitchen chairs at the corner of the table.

Ryan moved to the head of the table, opposite his mother. Colin now occupied his father's chair, where Ryan had been sitting for the last three years.

Colin didn't even spare a look. Ryan bit his tongue to keep the peace. Colin was baiting him, and Ryan wondered how much further he'd push it.

Ryan sat between Liam and Eileen, across from Michael.

"Colin, say grace."

Ryan withheld a snarl and held his mother's hand. None of them was a churchgoer anymore. A childhood of Sundays spent in church was enough. Their mom overlooked their collective lapse of faith as long as they said grace before Sunday dinner.

"Lord, we thank you for fine food, family, and love. Amen." As soon as the sign of the cross was made, arms stretched, forks clinked, and noise ensued.

Moira's voice rose above the clatter. "Tell us about Quinn."

"Drop it, Moira. She's a friend."

"I don't see how it's fair for you to grill us about every minute detail of every date we have, but you give us nothing." The fork she waved while talking finally made its way into her mouth.

"There's nothing to give. She's a teacher at Jones. She started coming in with the other teachers, and we became friends." He scooped a pile of mashed potatoes into his mouth.

Moira leaned over to see him around Liam. "Did you sleep with her?"

Ryan slammed down his fork. "None of your damn business."

"Ryan, your language," Eileen admonished.

He stood, mumbled, "Sorry, Mom," and went into the kitchen. He paced the room twice before pulling a beer from the fridge and popping the top. The cool bottle had barely reached his lips when Michael came in.

"Better not let Mom catch you."

"It'll be gone quick." He took a long drink.

"Let me have a swig."

Ryan passed the bottle.

Michael took a drink and handed it back. "Colin's being an ass. He's pushing your buttons because you let him. You make it easy. And Moira can't help being nosy. It comes with being a reporter."

"I know. I've got a lot on my mind." Mostly Quinn. Flirting with Kathy hadn't taken his mind off anything. He was a mess.

"Come back to the table before Mom comes looking for us."

"I'll be there in a minute." He drained the bottle and shoved it deep in the trash can. He reentered the dining room determined to keep his cool.

His mother moved on easily. "How's Griffin? I haven't seen that boy in ages."

"He's been out of town on and off for weeks. Some production glitch required his attention. He'll be back sometime this week. I'll bring him by soon."

"Good. He staying out of trouble?"

"As far as I know."

The table settled into the comfortable silence of family sharing a meal. Colin's voice broke the silence. He stared at Ryan. "You need to tell them."

"About what?"

"About the rapes." Jaws and forks dropped. "It'll affect business, and you have women sitting at this table——"

"Shut up."

Eileen touched Ryan's arm. "What is it?"

His muscles bunched. He had intended to tell them, but not like this. "Charlie Boyle came to see me the other day. There have been a series of rapes in the area. A group of guys try to pick up a woman at a neighborhood bar on a weeknight. Slip her a roofie."

Her hand trembled on his arm. He covered her slender fingers with his palm. "No one from O'Leary's. The cops don't have much. I'm going to hire extra guys to work the room. A lot of women stop by for a drink after work. They're all targets."

"I'll spread word at the firehouse. The guys are always looking for a way to make more cash," Michael said.

"Thanks. It would save me an extra step." He swirled a piece of ham through a puddle of brown sugar syrup. His appetite faded, but he continued to put on a show for his mother.

"A new critic came into the restaurant last night."

Ryan faced Liam, grateful for the change in topic. "Yeah? How'd it go?" he asked and hoped he sounded cheerful.

"He said it was one of the best meals he's ever had in Chicago. And the chef, me, is a rising star."

"Congrats, man." Ryan clapped him on the shoulder.

Questions flooded after that. Moira wanted to know about the winning dish. Eileen wanted to know where to get a copy of the review.

Ryan stood and excused himself. He scraped the remaining food into the trash and put the plate into the sink. The sun still blazed through the window above the sink.

Eileen came in moments later. "You're staying for dessert, aren't you?"

"No, I've got to get to the bar. I need to close tonight."

"You work too hard. Like your father that way. You have help. Colin's home."

"Enjoy the cream puffs." He bent and kissed her cheek.

On his way to the car, he tried to push the weight of his life off his chest. Time to put on a friendly face to meet the people at Twilight. As he traveled to the bar, his thoughts revolved around a quiet brunch with Quinn.

CHAPTER 20

Quinn slithered into the black dress she swore she'd never wear again. Indy guaranteed the dress had gotten a reaction when they'd gone to Twilight, and she was rarely wrong.

Tonight Quinn would complete the last item on her list before her vacation. Indulge at an expensive restaurant. Her vacation to New Orleans was planned. She'd leave in two weeks. The summer romance obviously wasn't going to happen. She hated to fail. The summer hadn't been a total waste, though. She'd grown and learned a lot about herself in the process.

She was ready to have a baby.

Indy arrived at seven-fifteen, only fifteen minutes late. Quinn hadn't wanted to go to a restaurant alone. She didn't ask Ryan because he probably wouldn't let her pay the bill.

"You look fabulous." Quinn stared at the deep navy-colored dress shimmering over Indy's body.

Indy twirled around. "You think?"

"It's perfect. In fact, it makes me want to wear a trash bag. I never could compete with your style."

Indy ran her eyes up and down. "Trust me. Your dress competes without a problem."

They took a cab to Gibson's, a premier steakhouse. Griffin had given her a few other restaurants to choose from: RL, Ralph Lauren's

Chicago restaurant, The Shanghai Terrace at the Peninsula Hotel, and Porter's, where Ryan's brother Liam worked.

RL was a restaurant for high-profile socialites, and Quinn didn't think she could pull that off regardless of the amount of cash in her wallet. The Shanghai Terrace offered unique Chinese food, and although the terrace looked like a beautiful place to dine, she only enjoyed Chinese food out of white cartons. Porter's, while it would be similar to Gibson's, she avoided because she needed something that wasn't attached to the O'Leary name.

Gibson's was a place every Chicagoan knew. Celebrities often had their photos taken over a steak at Gibson's. Even with its fame, it wasn't pretentious. That's what made Quinn choose it.

They sat at the bar and sipped expensive margaritas while waiting for their table. Quinn turned on her stool and surveyed the part of the restaurant she could see. The customers were equal parts couples on a date and businessmen making deals. In both cases, Quinn felt surrounded by suits.

"These margaritas are delicious," Indy commented. "Good thing we're not driving."

"Do you feel out of place here?"

Indy's eyebrows drew together. "No, why would I? Richard took me to dinner here once."

"Figures."

"What?"

Quinn lifted her shoulders in an attempt to loosen some tension. "Nothing. It's . . . we grew up in the same house, in the same small town. I don't get why a roomful of men doesn't faze you."

"They're just men under the suits. And not all that different from one another."

"Back home most guys didn't even own a suit. These guys exude power."

Indy chuckled with a glint in her eye. "They only have power in the courtroom or the boardroom. In the bedroom, you have the power."

Quinn laughed. "Not likely."

"You need to walk through the room like you own it, and you will. You've never had faith in yourself. That's what I don't get. If you allowed any of these guys near you, they'd be intimidated."

Quinn wondered exactly how much alcohol was in Indy's drink. She intimidated no one.

The hostess arrived to show them to their table. As they walked through the restaurant, she felt eyes turn to them. Some a quick flick at movement in their field of vision, others a lingering leer. Keeping her head up, Quinn pushed a little more sway in her hips. A smile crossed her lips as she thought of having Indy's power.

Their table was along a side wall, not quite tucked into a corner. A couple nestled in the corner booth, their closeness spoke of intimacy. Indy took the seat with her back to the wall. "This way, I have a good view of any guy coming to hit on us."

"Don't you think I should be able to check a guy out before he gets here?"

"No, you'd shoot down the whole idea."

Quinn rolled her eyes. "Chances are, no man's going to hit on me here. That's why I chose this restaurant. I'm here to enjoy a meal. And maybe catch a glimpse of Johnny Depp."

"We'll see. Men have already noticed us. The single ones did a quick assessment as soon as we popped on their radar."

"Let's just eat, okay? Order anything you want."

"Anything? You might have to hock your car to pay your Visa bill."

"I'm not worried."

Their waiter appeared and rattled through the specials and recommended a bottle of wine. Quinn opted to trust his judgment and ordered it.

A big, fat, juicy steak and a huge baked potato slathered in butter was all she wanted. She stared at the menu to find that even with such a simple request, she had decisions to make.

"The prime rib will melt in your mouth," Indy told her.

"I'm not a big fan of prime rib. I like a regular old steak."

"You've never had it here. I'll order it and you can try some." She closed her menu and set it on the corner of the table.

Quinn decided to let the waiter suggest something for her when he returned.

Indy's face suddenly darkened. "Uh-oh. Vulture at ten o'clock."

"Where?" Quinn began to turn, but Indy caught her wrist.

"Don't. Too obvious. Rock, paper, scissors?"

"God, no. I'll handle this one." *Act like you own it and you do.* She felt the temperature of her cheeks rise as the tall man towered over their table, but she held her resolve.

"Ladies."

I know that voice. Her head shot up to see Griffin's smiling face. She kicked Indy's shin under the table.

Griffin bent and kissed Quinn's cheek.

"Hi. How are you?" she asked.

"Good," he answered. "Busy."

"Must be really busy. I haven't seen you in forever."

"I've been out of town on business." He hitched his thumb over his shoulder. "It's continuing over there."

"Thanks for the recommendation, by the way. I've never eaten here before."

"If you had called me, I could've gotten you a better table." He stood with his hands slipped neatly into the pockets of his perfectly fitted suit. His shoulders sloped, totally relaxed.

She looked around. "What's wrong with this table?"

He bent to speak quietly in her ear. "Honey, you're twelve feet from the kitchen."

In truth, she hadn't noticed, and if she had, it wouldn't have struck her as odd. "Well, I guess my food will be hot when it arrives."

His smile showed deep, dimpled lines bracketing his mouth. This man exuded sexy the way so many others did power. And he knew it.

"I'm starting to understand Ryan a little better," he murmured.

Quinn's eyes popped wide. "What's that supposed to mean?"

"Nothing. I better get back before the lawyers start looking for me." He focused on Indy for a minute. "I'm glad you're here too. I need to put the house search on hold for a while longer. I've got a mess on my hands at work, so I'll be in and out of town a lot."

"Okay. Give me a call when you're ready to resume."

He nodded. "Enjoy your meal."

"Thanks," they answered in unison.

Indy sighed. "There goes that commission."

"What do you mean?"

"He's looking for another agent. I had a feeling it was too good to be true."

The waiter returned with their bottle of wine. Indy placed her order for prime rib. After listening to descriptions, Quinn settled on a sirloin, medium well, with a baked potato on the side. To combat the cholesterol frenzy she was about to consume, she added a salad to start.

They ate in silence. Quinn mulled over the quiet in her life. She hadn't been on any dates. No one who tagged her profile sounded even remotely interesting. She had accumulated more than a full week of comp time at school. Brian had been right. She would probably never use it.

"Do you ever feel restless with your life?"

Indy's question had Quinn putting down her fork. "How do you mean?"

"Like something's not right, but you can't quite put a finger on it. You know you need a change, though."

Quinn nodded. Indy voiced where her own thoughts had been headed. "That's pretty much my whole life right now. I wish I'd never taken this summer off."

"You've had a great time."

"Yeah, but if I had stuck with my safe, predictable routine, I wouldn't be searching for something better now." She pushed the remaining leaves of lettuce around on the chilled plate.

"Then this summer taught you that you weren't really happy before."

She laid her fork across her plate. "But I thought I was. Maybe not giddy with happiness, but I was content."

Indy's mouth formed a straight line. "Don't we all deserve more?"

Quinn realized Indy was talking about herself as much as Quinn. "I used to think so."

"What would make you happy?"

Quinn heaved a sigh. It came back to the list. "I want to have a baby. I want to be a mom."

Deeper than that, she knew her true vision was one of a whole family. She kept trying to adjust the dream to coincide with reality.

Another week closer to her vacation and Quinn had decisions to make. She dialed Indy's number before she lost her nerve. "Hey, Indy. I need a favor."

"Shoot."

"I want you to find out what my loft is worth and put it on the market." Her right hand tightened into a fist, waiting for Indy's explosion.

She didn't disappoint. "What? Your loft is perfect. Why would you want to sell? Especially in this market. Where are you going to go?"

Here goes nothing. "I want to liquidate to get as much cash as I can. I'm going to try to get pregnant as soon as I get back from vacation."

Indy paused and Quinn knew she was trying to choose her words carefully. "Where will you live?"

"I'll rent something small until I have the baby. Then I think I'll move home." She closed her eyes and let out a slow breath.

"Home? To Hooperville? You're kidding, right? You love it here."

"I haven't been happy with my job, and the loft is not the kind of home I want for my child. I want a backyard with swings and stuff."

"So you plan to go home and do what? Buy a single-wide?"

Quinn swallowed hard. "Do you have to put down everything? Home was never as bad as you make it sound."

"Did you think what it'll be like going back there as an unwed mother?"

The words stung, despite her protest. "The town is not that conservative."

"I wasn't talking about the town. I meant Dad."

She hadn't given that any real thought. She'd gotten used to only speaking with their father long distance, with the rare visit. "He'll be fine."

Indy snorted in her ear. "I dare you to run the idea past him."

"It's my life. I'm not a little girl anymore."

"It's a whole lot easier to dismiss his derisive attitude from two hundred and eighty miles away."

Quinn felt a headache coming on and rubbed her temple. "I have time to develop a solid approach for Dad. I'm not even trying to get pregnant yet. No matter what, the loft has to go. Can you please check into it for me?"

"I will. I'll also look into renting it. Get the right person in there, and you'll make money and keep your equity."

"Thanks. Don't forget we have the singles thing I signed us up for

Sunday night. Bye." She hung up quickly, knowing Indy would argue about attending. Quinn was tired of fighting. It would be good for Indy to get out and meet people. She could pass her cards out to possible clients. Even better, she might step out of the box Richard tried to keep her in.

Quinn settled on her couch to review the information she gathered from the fertility specialist. So much to consider. It was a huge step. A rock settled in her stomach.

How would she handle questions about her pregnancy? She hadn't considered all the closed-minded people who would take issue with her choice to be a single mom.

Her doorbell rang. "Yes," she said into the intercom, expecting it to be a mistake.

"Pizza."

"I didn't order a pizza."

"But you want some, don't you?"

She recognized Ryan's voice and buzzed him up. Leaving the door ajar, she went to check the fridge for drinks. They hadn't had plans, but over the past couple of weeks, Ryan had occasionally shown up unexpectedly and they hung out. She'd come to enjoy his surprise visits.

"You always buzz up anyone who asks?" Ryan said, closing the door behind him.

"Only the ones who bring food. Beer or pop?"

"Pop. I'm working tonight."

She grabbed two cans of pop, a pile of napkins, and paper plates. He stood in the living room holding the cardboard box.

"Here. Put it on the table." She set down the drinks and quickly piled up the brochures she'd been reading.

"What have you been up to?" he asked, flipping the lid on the pizza box.

It was an early dinner, but Quinn was grateful for the distraction. Both the brochures and Indy had given her a lot to think about. "I've been preparing for artificial insemination."

He said nothing as he bit into the first slice of pizza.

"No opinion?"

"Of course I have an opinion. You didn't ask for it." He wiped a napkin across his chin.

"I didn't know you needed a formal invitation. I'm asking." She slid two small slices onto a paper plate and settled in on the couch. She stretched her legs out until her ankles rested on Ryan's lap.

"I think you're selling yourself short."

"How so?" She blew on her pizza, wanting to sink her teeth in but fearing a blistered mouth.

"What happens when you find a guy you want to spend your life with? Is it fair for you to expect him to raise another man's child?"

She swallowed a gob of cheese. "First, I don't think I'm going to meet my soul mate. I don't know he exists. Second, it's pretty common to have blended families these days because of the divorce rate."

Ryan finished off two more pieces of pizza and didn't comment. He cleared his throat. "I've thought a lot about you asking me to be your sperm donor."

Her heart kicked, but she kept her mouth shut.

"I want you to be happy, Quinn. But I don't think I can do it. I want a family someday. A big one. I don't think I could live knowing there was a little O'Leary running around that wasn't really mine."

Her stomach sank. She'd known this would be his answer, of course, but hearing it made it harder to swallow. She forced a smile. "I figured as much. It's not like I was counting on it. Thanks for considering it."

After a few moments of silence, she needed to know they were still on solid ground. She needed to connect with him. "How's the bar? Have there been any more rapes?"

His face clouded with anger and she knew the answer before he spoke. "Three more."

"And the cops still don't have any leads?"

He shook his head. Something else bothered him.

"It didn't happen at O'Leary's, did it?"

"No, we've escaped so far. But I also have two off-duty firemen watching the crowd every night in addition to my usual staff." He tossed his unfinished slice back in the box and wiped his hands clean.

He absently began rubbing her bare feet. She closed her eyes briefly and enjoyed the comforting strokes. When she looked at him through slitted eyelids, the strain seeped from his face, but she felt it. She wondered when exactly they'd gotten to the point of solid friendship.

Sure, their attraction still simmered beneath the surface, but the care they had for each other kept it in check. She began to think she made the right choice in backing away.

"Let's talk about something fun."

"Like what?" she asked.

"How's the list? You haven't mentioned it in weeks."

She wiggled her emerald green toes with a proud smirk. "Because it's done. I had dinner at Gibson's last week and I'm leaving for New Orleans next week."

"Easier than you expected, huh?"

"Not at all. I wouldn't have finished half the list without your help. And they all weren't successful. Posing nude was as horrid as it gets, but at least I made the attempt. The summer romance is a complete failure."

"My offer to use my camera is still open." His hands moved over her calf as he spoke.

She raised her knees to pull her legs in. "No, thanks. One humiliating experience is enough."

"We both know I wouldn't humiliate you."

Her heart beat rapidly. Why had she thought their desire was held in check? His gaze caressed her body.

She swallowed hard and her eyes met his. "What are you doing?"

"Nothing. Tell me about New Orleans."

Her breathing slowed as she thought of her vacation. She said nothing as he took her feet back to his lap. "I have a handful of things I want to do, and more that are maybes. I haven't quite figured out a schedule yet."

He laughed. "Schedule? It's a vacation. You're supposed to go and play it by ear."

"I might not fit everything in."

"Then you have an excuse to take another vacation."

She sighed. "Not likely." She paused. "Are you going to tell me what's been eating at you?"

"That obvious?" He ran his fingers through his hair.

"Not obvious, but right there below the surface. For a while, I thought the rapes were bothering you, but it's more."

He leaned forward, bracing his elbows on his knees. "It's my sister Maggie."

"The youngest."

"She's got it in her head to go to Europe."

She swung her legs over the edge of the couch and sat up. "And?"

"Maggie's . . . a kid. She can't take care of herself."

"I hate to burst your bubble, but she's grown. By her age, I was married and starting my career."

He rolled his head to face her. "Exactly. She should finish school, not be running around Europe."

He didn't even poke at her failed marriage. He was seriously worried.

"I took a trip to Europe one summer in college. I was younger than she is. Why does she want to go?"

"She says to study and experience different cultures. She wants to write." He leaned back.

"Why don't you believe her?"

"I do. She's always been a writer, but she's running away."

"From?"

He scrubbed his hands over his face. "Me. Chicago. Everything."

She inched closer and waited. With every word he spoke, the stress lifted from him. He carried a world of worry with him.

"Maggie used to be one of the tenants above the bar. She stayed while my dad started the remodeling. After he died, the work fell to the wayside. We were all pretty shaken. Maggie continued to live there alone. She worked at the bar while she tried to figure out what she wanted to do with her life.

"She was pretty wild. Guys always chasing after her. That's why I liked her working at the bar, so I could keep an eye on her. She had an ex-boyfriend who kept popping up and bothering her. One night, she drank too much, and he took her upstairs and raped her."

He sat, fists clenched, rage vibrating the air around him.

Quinn wanted to reach out to him, but waited. "I'm so sorry."

She thought of how the current rapes must torment him.

"She fell apart. For more than a year, she could barely leave my mom's house. Now she wants to go to Europe."

Quinn clasped her hands. "Sounds like she's trying to reclaim her life."

"I know. I'm worried about her."

She moved closer and wrapped her arms around him now. She

stroked his head until she felt his tense muscles go limp. At that moment, she realized she'd become his Comfort Cookies. "Can I say something without you getting mad?"

He pulled from her embrace but stayed close enough to toy with her hair. "Go ahead."

"It looks to me like she's not the only one running."

He responded with raised eyebrows.

"For weeks you've been showing up here to hang out. I think I'm your escape. Not that I mind. It's what friends are for."

"Perceptive and beautiful."

She had half a second to smile before his mouth covered hers. His tongue slipped past her lips and hers answered. Her mind fogged.

Her hands remained in her lap, and his fingers touched only her head and face, but her body hummed in response.

When her hands rose to tangle in his hair, she caught herself and jerked away from him. "What are you doing?"

"I'm sorry," he mumbled. He tucked her hair behind her ear and she tossed her head from his touch. "I didn't plan to do that."

She moved her body back on the couch. The kiss had been heady and wonderful, but she grasped her resolve. "Don't let it happen again," she joked.

"I'll try." He rose. "I'm heading to the bar."

She stood and took his hand. "Talk to Maggie. Seriously listen to her. Try to understand. She needs that."

"Thanks. I will." He bent and kissed her cheek.

"Will you be at Twilight Sunday?"

"Yeah."

"Good. Mary got me to sign up for the singles thing again."

"I guess I'll have to be there to help you weed through the jerks."

Closing the door behind him, she knew he'd been trying to keep the conversation light, especially after that kiss, but she couldn't think of him that way anymore. He'd become so much more than a wingman that hearing him say it made her want to tell him so. Tell him what? He was more than a wingman? It sounded stupid even inside her head.

Ryan had spent the next two days gutting the apartment across the hall. He had three contractors coming by to give him bids.

Maggie had made some good points when they'd talked. It was time to move on. His life had become stagnant. He didn't even live in his own apartment. Maggie blamed herself.

Since Cassie left, he'd been hiding as much as Maggie had. His collection of one-night stands didn't amount to a social life. He needed to do something.

The manual labor and the rhythmic thumping of the sledgehammer offered him time and space to gather his thoughts. They all centered on Quinn. He never thought helping her might kill him.

Without some man to sweep her off her feet, he was supposed to get a chance, but she'd locked him in as a friend. Now she was talking clinics and sperm donors. He couldn't compete with the pedigree of any of the donors she was considering. The fact that another man wouldn't touch her offered him some comfort.

The weight of the hammer smashed through the last of the plaster and lathe. The entire apartment had been reduced to the old wood studs and the brick exterior.

His confusion hadn't abated. His feelings for Quinn were still a mess. He wanted her, that hadn't changed. He didn't want to be a dad, though. At least not now. He should cut and run. It was the smart thing to do. There were plenty of other women who didn't have baby on the brain.

Quinn had been right. They were good friends.

Anything more would be a mistake.

As long as he kept his hands off her, they would remain friends. He'd been enjoying their friendship. Maybe it would be enough.

He looked over the destruction of the past two days and felt accomplished. For the first time in a long while, his life was moving forward.

A quiet rap on the door made him growl. "Go away."

The knob turned and his mother walked in. "I most certainly will not."

He turned to the door. "Mom, what are you doing here?"

Her dark red hair was streaked with silver, but she never colored it. Her freckles kept her looking much younger than she was. She was short and thin, but far from frail. The woman was made of iron. "What are you doing here?"

"I told you I'm renovating the apartments."

"But you haven't been home."

He took a swig of water. "Between the apartments and the bars, I've been busy."

"You're doing too much."

"The bar doesn't run itself."

"You're not alone, Ryan."

"I know, Mom. It's still my bar. I need to run it."

"It's time you trusted your brother. You need the help. Even your father had you boys to help him. It's too much for one man."

He leaned the sledgehammer against a stud. "I've been handling everything for years now by myself."

"At what cost, Ryan?" She stood next to him. He towered over her. "You talk to Colin. And bring your lady friend to Sunday dinner. It's not a suggestion."

She walked out of the apartment, leaving the door open. Talk to Colin. He had nothing to say to Colin.

Ryan had to give him credit, though. Colin had been handling the repairs and maintenance at the house. Ryan hadn't received one call since Colin had come back. He'd also been a diligent employee. Colin put in his time at Twilight when needed, but O'Leary's was his home. Ryan couldn't think about Colin anymore. He needed a break. He called Quinn.

"Hi, Ryan."

"Hey. My mother would like you to come to Sunday dinner."

Silence.

"Quinn?"

"I appreciate the offer, but I have a lot of packing to do."

Packing? New Orleans. "My mom is expecting you. It wasn't so much an invitation as a command."

"She's not my mother. I don't have to do what she expects. I have to get ready for my vacation. And there's Twilight that night." Her voice was edgy and squeaky.

"Please. I'm asking nicely. And you owe me."

"I don't owe you enough to warrant you parading me in front of your family."

Ah-hah. "It won't be the whole family. We did that last weekend. It'll be us and my mom. Maybe Colin or Maggie if they're around since they live there."

"Still a lot of people."

"But you know half of us. It'll only be a couple of hours. You'll have plenty of time to pack."

She sighed. He was wearing her down.

"Fine. What time?"

"I'll pick you up at one-thirty."

"I'll drive myself. Give me the address."

CHAPTER 21

Quinn's stomach had been fluttering from the moment of Ryan's invitation. She'd managed to pack up cookies to bring to dinner, but she couldn't decide what to wear. She settled on denim Capri pants and a purple shell. Not too dressy like she was on a date, not so casual she'd offend his mom. She already had her dress laid out for going to Twilight later.

She was overthinking. Again.

The sky was gray and a storm threatened. She hoped it would hold off until she got home. Showing up a sopping mess for dinner would be horrible. At least a good soaking might relieve the humidity. What did it matter? She was headed to steamy New Orleans.

Her stomach fluttered more. Thinking about vacation was not as relaxing as it should be.

It didn't take long to drive to the O'Leary house. She drove slowly down the block, scanning for a parking spot and the right house number. She saw Ryan sitting on the front steps. She used her rusty parallel parking skills a half block down.

A dribble of sweat trickled down the center of her back. The humidity or nerves? She rubbed at it as she grabbed the container of cookies. Ryan walked down the block to meet her.

He took the container. "How are you?"

Nervous. "Fine."

"Good. I want to warn you . . ."

She stopped. "What?

"Most of the family is here. Moira caught wind of you coming and she spread the word." He touched her arm. "It won't be that bad."

"If you say so." Her stomach took a dive.

They continued walking until they arrived in front of a yellow brick bungalow. She didn't know what she expected. Something bigger, maybe? Where the heck did they fit six kids in a house this size?

"Ready?"

She nodded and started up the concrete steps. Ryan set his hand at the small of her back. She pulled strength from it as she walked past the battered oak door and into the fray of a big family.

The front door connected directly into the living room. Done in neutral colors, the room would've been warm and friendly, except for the men sitting on the couch screaming at the TV. Quinn jolted at the screams.

Ryan leaned in. "You should see how loud it gets during football season. That's really our sport."

Quinn knew Colin, and she assumed the other man was Liam. She'd seen Michael bartending at O'Leary's, and he wasn't here. Liam was the only brother she hadn't met. He looked nothing like the others. Liam had dark red hair and freckles, where his brothers were all black-Irish—dark hair and brilliant blue eyes.

Liam's eyes never left the screen, but Colin's met hers and he smiled. She returned the friendly gesture and followed Ryan through the formal dining room. The linen-covered table nearly filled the room, and she was grateful for her choice in clothes. Shorts would've made her feel terribly underdressed.

Ryan waited inside the kitchen. "Mom, Quinn's here."

Quinn stood next to him and wondered what Mrs. O'Leary saw when she turned. Rather than take comfort in Ryan's presence, Quinn stepped forward with an extended arm. "Hello, Mrs. O'Leary. Thank you for the dinner invitation."

"Eileen, please." She stepped closer and placed a small, bony hand in Quinn's. "It's about time Ryan brought you. I've been hearing your name bandied about for weeks."

Quinn stole a glance over her shoulder at Ryan, who was leaning comfortably against the refrigerator.

The woman who had been standing with her hands in the sink now turned and joined them. She extended her hand. "I'm Moira."

"Hi." Moira had the same coloring as Eileen, and matched Liam. Quinn wondered if Ryan looked as much like his father as Moira did their mother.

Noise erupted from the living room and Quinn jumped again.

Moira laughed. "You'll get used to it. It's always noisy around here."

"I don't think I'd ever get used to this many people. I only have one sister." She turned and took the cookies from Ryan. "I brought these for you. Ryan didn't call me until late yesterday or I would've made something a little more special."

Moira snatched the container and popped the lid. She sniffed and licked her lips. "I like this one, Ryan. She brings chocolate."

This one? Ryan must be in the habit of bringing all of his "friends" home for dinner. Quinn stopped herself from looking at him, but she knew he was still standing there, waiting to rescue her.

"You shouldn't have fussed. They all take turns bringing dessert for family dinner."

Moira set the container on the already crowded table and selected one. "But we weren't all supposed to be here today, so there is no dessert."

The back door swooshed open and a tall blonde walked through.

Eileen moved into the woman's brief hug and then said, "Quinn, this is Brianna, my daughter-in-law."

"Well, I will be soon enough. I'm engaged to Michael. He's on at the firehouse today. Nice to meet you." She shook Quinn's hand.

The kitchen suddenly felt overcrowded. Quinn fought the urge to hide, or worse, leave.

"I'm going to say hi to the guys." Brianna looked sympathetically at Quinn but seemed happy for the escape.

"What can I do to help, Mrs. O'Leary?"

"First, call me Eileen. Then go relax. Guests don't need to help."

"My help might not be required, but I'd like to. May I set the table?"

Eileen gave her a slight nod. "Ryan, help with the dishes."

Ryan emptied a cabinet of the dishes and placed the stack on

Quinn's waiting arms. She left without him and began setting dishes on the expansive dining room table.

Conversation in the living room abruptly stopped. She knew she'd been the topic. Ryan followed her, putting silverware down.

Feet pounded on the stairs and Quinn looked up. A cute young woman flew down the steps. She had dark hair like Ryan's, cut short like a pixie.

Her face brightened and she smirked at Ryan. "Hey, Ry. I knew if I waited long enough, someone else would set the table. Who's your *friend?*"

The muscle in his jaw twitched. "Don't be rude. Maggie, Quinn."

Maggie's face immediately softened, but she crossed her arms. "I guess I owe you some thanks."

Quinn set down the last plate. "Me? For what?"

"Ryan said you told him to talk to me. He actually listened. I didn't think anyone could get him to do that."

"Shut up," he said tensely, but without anger.

"You're welcome." Quinn had no idea why Ryan was so uptight. She was the one under a microscope. *Another hour. I can make it an hour.*

Ryan hadn't said much, and he'd barely made eye contact with her. If he didn't want her here, he shouldn't have invited her. He could've told his mother she was unavailable.

But Eileen didn't strike her as a woman easily lied to.

Maggie's eyes remained on Quinn as she neared. Quinn froze, feeling stalked.

Moira came in with a bowl of broccoli.

Hoping her chocolate cookies made her a friend, Quinn said, "Is there something else I can help with?"

"Sure."

Quinn followed and helped carry salad, carrots, and roasted potatoes. Eileen came in with a platter of pot roast that smelled divine.

At the smell of food, the men came from the living room. Quinn stood idly on the outside of the horde.

Ryan touched her back. "Just grab a chair. There are no assigned seats."

She stifled a little laugh. She had, in fact, been waiting to see what chair would be left empty.

They all took their seats and Colin said grace. Food was passed and dishes clanked. Conversation was loud. They all seemed to accept her presence and included her.

I want this.

The thought slammed into Quinn so hard, she almost lost her breath. This family was incredible. In her short time there, she saw the different personalities and could tell they'd clash often. But underneath it all was an uncommon love.

That's what she wanted more than anything.

The sad part was, she couldn't offer this to a baby. How selfish of her to think she was capable of being a single mother. Sure, she could do the daily stuff of diapers and bottles, and she would love her child unconditionally, but she couldn't give a child a family.

Didn't every child deserve that?

Especially hers?

This was the life she wanted. She looked across the table at Ryan. Her heart thudded when his gaze met hers. What had she been thinking months ago when she'd pushed him away?

Ryan smiled at her, his reassuring, easy smile, and she knew her plans had been totally and completely derailed.

She held her own.

Ryan watched Quinn constantly for any sign of distress. For a woman who insisted she didn't like crowds, that she didn't do well with them, she held her own with his family. She fielded questions and commented on any number of conversations taking place around the table.

She fit in like she belonged.

And he wanted her to.

He was grateful for the ongoing conversations because his lungs wouldn't work. Air trickled in and he hoped no one would notice.

Quinn had even managed to win over Maggie. They exchanged e-mail addresses so Maggie could send photos from Europe for Quinn to share with her students.

Brianna hadn't even fared this well at her first O'Leary family dinner.

But Quinn was a friend, not a prospective wife. They might not be so amiable if she were.

"When do you leave for New Orleans?" Colin asked Quinn.

"In a couple of days."

"Where are you staying?"

"I don't know yet. I'm driving and taking my time. I'll decide when I get into town."

Moira jumped in. "You're driving alone? What if you get there and there aren't any rooms?"

"I'll figure it out." She smiled at Ryan. "Someone told me a vacation shouldn't be on a schedule, so I'm winging it."

Maggie looked triumphant. She nudged Ryan with her elbow. "Did you harass her as much as you did me?"

He couldn't think of a response to save himself, so instead he stood and started clearing dishes. He hadn't known about those plans or he would've harassed her. When he said no schedule, he hadn't meant no plan at all.

Quinn pushed back from the table. "Eileen, thank you for one of the most delicious home-cooked meals I've ever had." She stood and followed Ryan into the kitchen.

He filled the sink.

She handed him her plate. "Are you okay? You didn't say much during dinner."

Swallowing hard, he forced out words, "I'm fine. You did well. I don't know why you were so nervous."

Liam and Colin deposited dishes in the sink silently and disappeared.

"I gave up being nervous when I realized I had nothing to lose. If they hated me, I'd survive. I don't have to see them every day, you do."

But he wanted her here with him all the time.

Maggie bounded in carrying a stack of plates. "You're not leaving, are you?"

Quinn nodded. "I am. I still have to finish packing and I have plans tonight."

"You can stay for dessert. I hear there's really good cookies here." She filled the coffee maker with grounds and water.

"You go ahead and enjoy the cookies. I'm going to say my good-byes."

Maggie grabbed the container from the table and took it out of the room.

Quinn stayed for a minute. "Thanks for inviting me. I had a good time. Will I see you later?"

She fidgeted again. Why was she nervous now? Dinner was over.

"I don't know. I have to check in at O'Leary's." He hated lying to her, but he couldn't tell her the real reason. He couldn't stomach watching her flirt with other men anymore.

"It'll be tough without my usual wingman, but I guess Indy can fill in."

It killed him to hear those words again. *Wingman.* If he could go back in time, he'd smack himself for even having the thought. "Ready for the last chance to find your romance before vacation?"

"Ready as I'm gonna get." She smiled, but it looked wistful, like she thought she was missing out on something. He wanted to pull her back into his arms but knew he couldn't risk it in front of his family.

He heard her make her way through the house saying good-bye and thank you. He grabbed a beer from the fridge and started drinking.

Colin strode in, loaded with bowls of food to be wrapped up. Eileen bustled in behind him.

"Who's on dish duty with me?"

"You're not children anymore. I don't keep a list." His mother's shortness had him taking another pull from his beer.

"What are you doing, man?" Colin asked.

"Having a beer before I start washing dishes. What does it look like?"

"It looks like you're avoiding everything and letting the best thing in your life walk out."

Eileen left without finishing wrapping the leftovers.

"You don't know what you're talking about." Another sip of beer cooled his throat.

"You love Quinn. Everyone in this house can see it. You're standing here instead of going after her." He leaned against the table.

"Go after her for what? We're friends. I don't figure into her plan."

"You are a stupid shit."

Ryan set down the beer. He wouldn't mind a brawl with Colin to ease some of the tension in his body.

"If you think hitting me will fix things between us, go ahead and do it. I have at least that much coming." He continued leaning against the table, not looking concerned.

Ryan picked up his beer again.

"I know what my leaving did to you. I know what it cost you. Everything fell on you. The business, the family. I should've been here to shoulder some of it. I know it cost you Cassie."

"No, it didn't. It was a factor, but we'd already slid away from each other. She was smart enough to make a clean break." He finished his beer and chucked the bottle into the trash.

"The point is, I'm not going anywhere. Let me help. I figure between the two of us, we can take care of the family and the bar and still carve out lives for ourselves."

"I have a life."

"Yeah, she just left. If you don't go after her, she'll be gone for good."

"She's only going on vacation. She's coming back."

Colin pushed away from the table. "She might come back to Chicago, but not to you. This is her chance for a clean break unless you stop her."

"You go away for a few years and come back a philosopher?"

"Yeah, that's me. Get out of here." He gave Ryan a shove away from the counter. "Moira, get in here and wash while I dry."

"I did dish duty last week. Maggie's turn," Moira called from the dining room.

Maggie returned and poured cups of coffee. "I'll be back in a minute to do dishes." She stopped, holding steaming mugs, and looked at Ryan. "For what it's worth, I like Quinn. She's good for you."

"And you know this from one family dinner?"

She lifted her shoulder. "I knew before dinner. No one has ever gotten you all twisted up like you have been." She kissed his cheek and brought the coffee to the dining room.

"I've got a houseful of advice columnists now." He followed Maggie and kissed his mother good-bye. Outside, the humidity pressed in on him. A storm was brewing in the air, but it had nothing on the one inside his chest.

Quinn wandered aimlessly through her loft. Nothing felt right. Months ago, Ryan had said he wanted a relationship with her. He'd sent her signals, and she really thought she'd read them correctly. That would've been a first. She'd been so close to telling him she'd been an idiot.

He expected her to go to Twilight to find a date. He didn't want her to miss her *last chance* to find a man. The only guy who'd expressed an interest in a relationship with her over the past months thought she was pitiful.

Sending signals didn't work for her any better than trying to read them. After dinner with his family, she thought for sure he'd ask her not to go tonight. That he wanted to spend her last nights in town with her. He was so good at reading people, especially her, how did he not see she would've preferred that?

Unless he didn't want to see.

They were better off as friends. She knew that. She couldn't trust herself to make the right choice. She'd known Ryan would be good for temporary fun, but seeing him with his family played into her own fantasies. That's all it was, a fantasy.

She'd left the O'Learys because she needed to pack, and she'd only gotten as far as pulling out her suitcase. What had she wanted to accomplish by telling Ryan she'd been wrong? Would she give up this trip to see what would happen between them? That would be stupid.

Wishy-washy wasn't how she lived her life, but Ryan messed with her head. And her heart.

Turning to her dresser, she yanked open a drawer. She chose her garments carefully. A silk nightgown stared at her. She loved the feel of it and immediately imagined Ryan sliding his hands over her silk-clad body.

What am I doing?

She shoved the gown aside and grabbed some cotton shorts. She had a plan, and although some of it hadn't worked out, she'd accomplished a lot this summer. She shouldn't change what she wanted because of a man.

Even a really good man.

That was the sticking point. For all of her reservations about Ryan, thinking he was too much like Nick, that he would walk all over her, she'd been wrong. He was a good man. She'd just been too blind to see it. Now, it was too late.

He'd gone out of his way to make her happy, helping her fulfill her list. The least she could do would be to play her part tonight and make him feel like he'd succeeded in his mission.

No matter how much it might kill her.

Hours later, Ryan paced in his apartment. Nothing he did eased his restlessness. Colin's words echoed in his head. Quinn was leaving and she wouldn't come back. He thought about her navigating another singles event. Why did she even bother going? It wasn't like she was going to find a summer romance this late in the game.

She probably wanted to prove to him that she could handle herself and meet men. After all, at dinner she was comfortable because they were just friends.

Guilt nagged him. He'd convinced her to continue looking for dates, and now he was abandoning her because he didn't want to witness the event. He changed his clothes and headed to Twilight without a plan. He just knew he couldn't let Quinn leave like this.

Inside the door of Twilight, Mary sat at a small, linen-covered table handing out locks and keys. She offered Ryan a key, and he quietly declined.

People were already mingling and trying to fit keys into locks. Mary had another hit on her hands. He grabbed a beer and wandered around.

A roomful of single women surrounded him. He should be able to find at least one interesting, even if he refused to play Mary's lock game. But he didn't really want to.

Indy stood near a table sucking on a Blue Smoke. Ryan's mind drifted to the night Quinn got drunk on Blue Smoke. She'd cuddled into Griffin's arms that night, but made out with Ryan in an elevator. He sought out Quinn but couldn't find her.

A tall, willowy blonde sidled up to him as he turned from Indy's direction. He nearly collided with her. "Excuse me."

"No, excuse me. Would you like to stick your key in?" Her breathy voice drew him closer. "Here's my lock. Where's your key?"

"Sorry, I don't have one. I'm just watching."

"Too bad. I'm Brenda. Buy me a drink?"

He held out a hand. "Ryan, nice to meet you." He eyed her nearly full glass. "You look like you're all set with a drink. I'll get the next one."

He brushed passed her and thought he escaped when he felt a tap on his shoulder. He painted on a friendly smile and turned to see Griffin.

"Are you sick? The blonde wanted a piece of you," he informed Ryan and handed him a beer.

"I know what she wanted. I'm not interested."

"Off the market?"

"Just looking for something different."

"Different, like what? A short brunette named Quinn?"

"You're out of the loop. We're friends. That's it." If he said it enough, maybe everyone would believe it, including himself. He took a long pull on the beer. "How did you know I was here?"

"I didn't. Colin brought me. He's here somewhere. He said you've been working on the apartments. Where'd you finally get the inspiration?"

"Quinn and Maggie. It's time to move on."

"Moving to where?" Griff clasped a hand on Ryan's shoulder.

"I wish I knew." His eyes wandered back to Indy and saw Quinn sitting beside her. They were entertaining a couple of suits. Indy was chatting them up with her flirtatious grin. Quinn was along for the ride.

She caught him staring and mouthed, "Help me."

He drank from his beer and shook his head. "Do me a favor and rescue Quinn. I'm going to grab a key to help with this charade."

Ryan grabbed a key from the fish bowl Mary kept in front of her. She smiled when his hand dipped in, but she didn't comment. He returned to the networking area and saw Quinn standing with Griffin.

She was wearing the breezy sundress. The same one he'd stripped from her body the first time they'd made love. He could admit it was more than sex with them. He wasn't naïve, but they were heading in different directions. Quinn had her route mapped; he was still figuring out his final destination. Long term they might end up in the same place, but she was in the express lane while he was sitting on the shoulder with the map upside down.

When he walked up next to her, Quinn looked at him and said, "What are you doing here? I thought you weren't coming."

"I figured you could use the support. I didn't want you to fly without a wingman."

"Some wingman you turned out to be. I think I need to hire Griffin for the job. He rescued me from two of the most boring men I've ever talked to."

Ryan cleared his throat. "He saved you because I sent him over."

"Well, then, thank you. It's kind of slow. Did Mary say more guys would be coming?" She looked past Ryan to the men standing in small groups.

Griff pointed to Indy. "Your sister doesn't seem to be having any trouble finding men."

"She never has." Quinn sipped from her glass of pop.

"You could always go and introduce yourself," Ryan suggested, knowing she wouldn't.

Her mouth twitched into a half-smile and she straightened her shoulders. "You know what? You're right."

She turned and walked away from him and into a crowd of four or five men. He didn't know what had come over her. This was not the normal Quinn. She had a small entourage testing their keys on her. As she laughed at something one of them said, two more men made their way into the crowd. Ryan played his part well, nudging her on, secretly hoping no one would unlock her.

Griffin had wandered off to find a place to stick his own key. Ryan held the key loosely in his hand. Nothing urged him forward to ask a woman if he could try her lock. The lack of the chase or conquest bored him. He enjoyed a challenge. His eyes found Quinn again and he shook his head.

She backed away from the small crowd of men. The lock was still closed and nestled between her breasts. Her cheeks were pink.

"I can't believe I did that," she said when she reached him. "Indy was right. She said walk the room like you own it and you do."

Indy had created a monster. "You were definitely successful. There were, let's see . . . seven men drooling over you."

She relaxed beside him. "They weren't drooling. And not one opened my lock."

His eyes traveled down to the lock. His fingers itched to reach out and touch the soft skin above it. "You want another drink?"

"Another diet would be great. Thanks."

Ryan was incredibly thirsty. If Quinn felt anything from the way he looked at her, she didn't show it. He couldn't keep his dick in line with the idea that he and Quinn were friends. His heart had almost as much trouble.

He returned and pressed the cool glass into her palm, glad she was still alone.

"Thanks." She took a long drink. Worry crossed her face. "God. Not again."

"What?"

"Joe, my former student, walked in. Why is he here?"

"Mary would've invited everyone from speed dating. Sorry, I didn't think to tell her to dump his name." He looked over his shoulder. "We could leave."

"No, I did that last time." She inhaled deeply. He watched the small, heart-shaped lock rise. "I have to get him to realize I'm not an option."

She stepped out from Ryan's shadow. Ryan shifted his body and angled himself to face both Quinn and the oncoming Joe.

"Hi, Quinn. It's good to see you again. I was hoping you'd be here tonight."

Hearing him use Quinn's name with familiarity had Ryan clenching his fists.

"I can't say the same, Joe. There are a lot of women here, but you walked in and came straight to me. I'm not interested in pursuing anything with you." Color rose in her cheeks as she spoke.

Ryan held the urge to cheer her on. She hated confrontation, but she hid it well. Her stomach was probably a mess, but from the outside, she looked like an ice queen.

Unfortunately, her speech had little or no effect on Joe. His determined smile never wavered. "Can I at least try your lock?"

She sighed. When he stepped closer, as if to pick up the lock, Ryan almost grabbed him by the neck. She pulled the lock away from her body. His key slid in, but it wouldn't turn.

He withdrew the key. "I'll be back when I get a new key."

As Joe walked away, Quinn shook her head. "How can one guy be so arrogant?"

Ryan shrugged and watched Joe speed around the room searching for the lock to fit his key. He was obviously a man on a mission, and it wasn't to find a date. He was after Quinn.

The room began to fill as more participants arrived. Ryan lost sight of Joe and was reluctant to leave Quinn's side.

Indy breezed up and hooked her arm around Quinn's elbow. "How are you supposed to find a man if you're standing here looking like you're married?"

"I've met some guys."

"Let's meet more. You don't mind, do you, Ryan?"

He almost answered yes. He minded. He didn't want her running into Joe again. He didn't want other guys fondling her lock. Jealousy snarled in his chest, but he shook his head. "Have fun."

CHAPTER 22

Quinn let Indy guide her into a crowd of men. She spoke quietly in Quinn's ear as they moved. "This is so much more fun than I thought it would be. I've met a bunch of guys who might be potential clients. Some are blowing smoke, but others might come through. I'm glad I let you talk me into this."

"You're welcome."

She pulled Quinn through to the other side of the crowd until they were alone.

"What's going on? It's kind of hard to meet guys if you walk right past all of them."

"You have no intention of meeting anyone. Plus, one look at you and Ryan, and the other guys know it's useless."

"I'm meeting people. Ryan and I are friends."

Indy huffed and threw her arms up. "Your idea?"

Quinn nodded.

"Any fool can see the way your face lights up every time you see him. No other man is interested in trying to compete. You love each other. Admit it and get it over with."

"Of course I love him. He's a great friend."

"That man is *not* just a friend."

"I'm afraid you're wrong this time. I thought about ditching this, but he reminded me this might be my last chance to find a date before my vacation. Now he's here to play wingman, to help me find someone."

Indy smacked her arm. "How can someone so smart be so utterly clueless? You teach hundreds of kids a year to understand Shakespeare, but you can't read Ryan's body language."

"I don't see what you see." She left Indy shaking her head and turned toward Ryan, who still stood alone.

Man, he was so sexy her heart thumped every time she looked at him. More than that, he was kind in a way that touched her heart. She hadn't lied to Indy; she loved Ryan. When his gaze met hers and he smiled his flirtatious grin, she knew she was in love with him as well. She had been since the beginning of the summer.

Her heart stuttered with the full knowledge of it.

He'd wanted to explore their relationship and he said he wouldn't back off for good. Maybe she still had a chance. If she'd learned nothing else this summer, it was that sometimes winging it worked.

As soon as she stepped next to Ryan, Joe rejoined her. She barely held back the growl.

"I have a new key. Can I try again?"

She held the lock out. His new key didn't work either. The lock flopped back against her chest.

"Damn."

"Go find someone else, Joe. I'm not interested."

"But . . ."

Ryan stepped closer and her eyes met his. The smoldering look made her knees weak. His fingers touched her neck just below her ear and slid down the length of the chain until they reached the lock. Her heart rate jumped a notch and her skin warmed under his touch. Electric jolts buzzed in her head, blocking out all sound, like the first time they'd kissed. He plucked the lock and inserted his key. The lock clicked open and slid from the chain.

Then Ryan broke eye contact and sent Joe a very satisfied grin.

Joe stalked away without a word. Ryan's gaze returned to hers.

Her mouth was dry and she swallowed hard, not sure how to play this. "You planned that."

He smiled. "No, I didn't. I picked a random key from the bowl."

"What would you have done if it didn't work?" She spoke, trying to keep her mind on the conversation instead of how close his fingers were to her skin.

He shrugged. "I figured he'd walk away when he saw me touching you. I know I would."

Her skin tingled. "Thank you. You always seem to be rescuing me."

He still hadn't stepped back. "Nah, you can handle yourself."

Not when it comes to you.

Butterflies danced in her stomach. She felt like a fish, flip-flopping on decisions. Let's be friends. Let's have sex. Let's be friends. What if Indy was wrong? What if he laughed in her face? But she had to know. It was now or never.

"I think I'm done. Can you give me a ride home?"

He looked startled, and her conviction began to fade. "Unless you want to stay. Then I'll call a cab."

"I'm ready to go." He took the lock and key back to Mary.

She waved Indy over. "You're right. This is a waste of my time. Plus, Joe is here. I'm leaving."

"Alone?"

"No, Ryan's going to give me a ride."

"It's about time."

"I hope you're right and I don't end up making a fool out of myself."

"I'm not wrong. It's up to the two of you to be honest. I can't control that." She looked over Quinn's shoulder. "Here comes lover boy now."

"Please don't call him that. Are you going to be okay here by yourself?"

"I'm not by myself. Even if I get bored with all of the strangers, both Colin and Griffin are here. Maybe I'll try to work my magic on Griffin to convince him that he should be looking for a house now. With me as his agent, of course."

"Ready?" Ryan asked.

"Yeah," Quinn answered.

"Stay out of trouble," Indy said, and wiggled her fingers at the two of them before inserting herself back into the crowd.

Ryan laced his fingers through hers.

She loved the feel of his strong hand in hers. It felt natural. She prayed that talking with him wouldn't scare him off.

They waved to Mary on their way out. Quinn thought her butterflies would return, but her stomach was calm. Peace settled on her and it felt good.

She didn't know where to start, so she tried casual conversation. "Mary must be thrilled. Another event she planned looks like it's a success."

"Yeah, pretty soon she'll be asking for a raise."

He seemed stiff behind the wheel, and his usual talkative self was nowhere to be found. She didn't know if she could follow through. "So, did you have any luck unlocking locks tonight? I mean, besides mine."

He glanced at her quickly. "I didn't even try."

Was that because he didn't want to or because he was busy playing wingman? Either way, it was enough encouragement for her to go on.

She blurted, "I've decided not to have a baby."

"What?" His question came out loud.

"Having dinner with your family tonight was an eye-opening experience."

"Having dinner with my family freaked you out so much you don't want to be a mom anymore? It usually takes more than one meal for us to scare people." His easy smile returned.

"No, your family's great. The thing is, I can't give a baby that. I can't be a family by myself. Not like yours."

"Who said you had to be like my crazy family? Family is whatever you want it to be."

"I know that in my head." She paused because sadness crushed her with the thought. Tears pricked the back of her eyes. "But in my heart, I won't really be happy. You were right. I want the whole package. And the odds of that happening look pretty slim."

Saying the words out loud stung as much as the tears she held back.

He didn't respond, but he moved one hand from the steering wheel and took hers again. They lapsed into silence and she took comfort from his hand. She'd given him an opening; put it out there that she couldn't find the right guy. If he was interested, wouldn't he have offered himself again?

Doubt crept back into her head. Maybe he had given up even though he'd said he wouldn't. Maybe he was looking forward to summer being over so he wouldn't have to deal with her stupid list anymore. Maybe he'd moved on.

God, she hated maybes.

Before long, he pulled into her lot and parked. If he planned to drop her off, he would've pulled up in front. Expecting to come in was a good sign, right?

But he didn't move. He just stared out the windshield.

She popped her door open.

Without looking at her, he asked, "What's your plan after you get back from vacation?"

"I'm not sure. Indy's looking into selling my loft. I'm considering moving back home."

"What?" He spun to face her, his eyes wide with shock.

Ryan realized that he'd practically yelled the question at her again, but he couldn't hear himself over the roar in his ears. He swung his door open and jumped out, giving himself time to focus as he rounded the car. She was leaving. Of all people, how could *Colin* have been right?

When he got to the passenger door, Quinn stared at him, probably confused because he kept yelling at her.

"Sorry. That came out louder than I planned, but you took me by surprise. Why would you move?" He pushed her door closed and walked beside her toward the building.

"Things here aren't working out the way I planned. I'm still living in the loft I bought with my ex-husband. I can't find a decent date to save my life, even with your help. I don't have anything to keep me here."

Her words shot through his heart, and he felt light-headed. He never really thought he'd lose her. Suddenly his life was falling apart. Maggie, his family, and now Quinn. He'd become unnecessary.

She wouldn't have failed if I hadn't sabotaged her efforts. But she never would've been looking for a date if I'd told her I loved her.

"What about your job?" he managed to ask.

"That's what's always grounded me here. I love teaching, but even there I feel like I've been stuck and there's no movement. No change, even though I tried."

Inside her building, she pointed to the stairs with raised eyebrows.

"I'm okay with the elevator." They entered the rickety box, and this time he sent up a little prayer that it would get stuck. That he could hold on to her a while longer.

Of course, not even that worked, and they sped directly to her floor.

At her door, he finally asked the question he needed the answer to most: "What about me?"

She pushed her door open but didn't walk through. "What about you?"

"I'm in Chicago. So is Indy. And Kate."

She leaned against the doorjamb. "Kate has her own life and family. Indy's always been fine on her own."

She stared into his eyes and he waited, willing her to be honest. The pulse on her neck throbbed.

"You." The word was little more than a whisper. "You have your family and your bars."

"But I wouldn't have you. It wouldn't be the same." He stepped closer. His fingers angled her jaw up, and he brought his lips to hers.

He let the kiss do what his words couldn't. Tenderly, his lips sought the warmth of her mouth. His tongue sought answers. He found comfort in her taste.

He pulled back slowly, and her eyes fluttered open.

"What the hell was that?"

"I had to check."

"Check what? That my lips still work?"

"I wanted to make sure I hadn't imagined it." In that moment he knew that Quinn loved him every bit as much as he loved her.

She stared into his navy eyes, knowing he felt the same spark she did. She pushed away from him when what she wanted was to wrap herself around him. She'd planned to take a chance and tell him how she felt, but he was taking charge again. Frustration propelled her into her living room.

"Don't go."

She stopped. These were the words she'd hoped for. Don't go on a date. Don't go online to find a man. Don't go to a lock-and-key party. Don't go.

"Why?" She spun to look at him. But she knew why. She was always leaving, running away from anything difficult.

"Because I love you. And I know you love me too."

She closed her eyes and savored the words, hoping she hadn't imagined them. She chuckled. "I wanted to leave the bar so I could tell you I wanted to give us a chance. I thought I would have to convince you since I've pushed you away all summer. You're making this too easy."

"I can't promise to always make things easy, but I'll try." His hand cradled her cheek. "My family is . . ."

Her eyes reopened and locked on his to find them filled with worry. "Great."

"They're demanding. And intrusive. And . . ."

"And you love them. I get it. I'm more than okay with it."

"You might think differently once you're an O'Leary."

Huh? "Was that your idea of a proposal?"

He slid his arms around her waist and led her farther into the living room, kicking the door shut behind him. "No, I'm just stating the inevitable. I figured we'd start with a vacation to New Orleans."

She relished the feel of the length of his body pressed against hers. "What about the bars?"

"It's about time I gave Colin a chance to run things for a while."

She stepped back with a smile. "Hmmm. I don't know. It's the last item on my list, and I'm supposed to go alone."

"I thought there was some flexibility in the list. You won't go alone, but I can promise you a hell of a summer romance." He pulled her body back into his. He feathered kisses over her cheek.

Her hand rested on his chest. His heart thumped as quickly as hers. "I don't think so. Summer's almost over. We've barely started, and the romance is supposed to end."

He bent and brushed his lips against hers. "Then let's work on the item not officially on the list."

Her brain fogged and the outside world disappeared. God, the man could *kiss*. She managed a husky whisper. "What's that?"

"Baby making. Practice makes perfect, you know."

Then she finally said the words she knew he wanted to hear: "I love you."

Comfort Cookies

¼ c. (½ stick) unsalted butter
3 oz. unsweetened chocolate
4 oz. bittersweet chocolate
3 eggs
1½ c. sugar
1 tsp. vanilla
1 c. flour
1½ tsp. baking powder
½ tsp. salt
1 c. semisweet chocolate chips

Preheat oven to 350°F. Melt butter, unsweetened chocolate, and bittersweet chocolate in the top of a double boiler or in a heat-safe bowl (metal or glass) over a pot of simmering water. In a mixing bowl, beat eggs, sugar, and vanilla together until mixture thickens. Add the melted chocolate and mix well. In a separate bowl, combine the flour, baking powder, and salt. Mix the dry ingredients into the chocolate mixture until combined. Stir in chocolate chips. (Batter will be gooey.)

Scoop teaspoon-sized cookies onto cookie sheets. If using aluminum pans, line with parchment paper (no paper needed on stoneware). Bake for approximately 11 minutes, until tops are cracked and edges are set. Let cool on cookie sheet for a minute or two, then transfer to a cooling rack.

Yield: 4 dozen cookies

Blue Smoke

1 oz. Bols Blue Curaçao
2½ oz. lemonade
2 oz. Stolichnaya Blueberi vodka
Wisp of absinthe

Combine all ingredients in a shaker cup. Add ice and shake until cold. Pour over ice in a glass. To make the drink "smoke," add a sliver of dry ice.

I'd like to thank Johnny Bellinger from Blues Bar in Mount Prospect, Illinois (www.blues-bar.com), for giving me permission to use this recipe, and Julie Plovanich for creating it in the first place.

Keep reading for a special preview of
Shannyn Schroeder's next contemporary romance.
Look for it wherever eBooks are sold in July 2013!

CHAPTER 1

Tequila was not her friend. Indy Adams couldn't believe she'd forgotten that one simple rule last night. The drum beat behind her eyeball as a blatant reminder. When the guys at the bar offered her a shot after closing, she hadn't seen the harm.

Too many shots and a crappy night's sleep later, she regretted every sip. She got out of her car and raised a hand to shield her eyes from the sun's glare. If she'd planned better yesterday, she wouldn't have had to get up early to come to the office now.

She pulled open the door, and a waft of expensive perfume smacked her in the face and clogged her throat. Indy swallowed the gag and faced the exiting clients with a perfunctory smile. The woman clicked by on her Jimmy Choos, followed by her husband and Indy's colleague Susan, real-estate superstar.

Indy ducked into the office hoping to avoid a conversation with Susan. The clock on the wall showed an hour until her meeting with Griffin. He was finally ready to start his house hunt. Correction, his mansion hunt. The thought of selling a million-dollar house made her giddy. Her giddiness almost made her forget her hangover.

She knew that Griffin had only hired her because his best friend, Ryan, was marrying her sister, but she'd take any connection she could. She'd met Griffin casually on several occasions, usually at Ryan's bar, but he'd put off the search and seeing houses for months.

"Indy," Susan said from behind her.

Shit, she really wanted to escape without this. Every conversation with Susan bordered on hostile.

"I hear your big client is finally ready to buy. I'd started to think you'd made the whole thing up."

After locating the codes she'd left tucked in her desk, Indy faced Susan and her usual pinched expression. "No, Susan, I don't have to make up clients."

"Well, after you gloated about how much money this one would bring in, you kind of dropped off the map."

"Well, I'm here and now I'm off to show houses." She waved the paper and turned to leave. She wouldn't admit that she'd gone back to waitressing because she needed the money.

"You're not going to show a house to a millionaire looking like that, are you?"

Indy stalled in her tracks and turned cautiously.

"Haven't you ever wondered why you don't attract more affluent clients? You don't play the part. You have to act as though you belong in their world and you"—she paused and pointed at Indy's outfit from shoulder to hem—"clearly don't."

"What's wrong with the way I'm dressed?" Sure, she wasn't as buttoned-up as Susan, but she wasn't dressed for clubbing either.

"You look a little trampy, ready to flirt with whomever comes your way."

Heat crept up Indy's neck and burned her ears. "I don't flirt with clients."

Susan arched an eyebrow.

"I'm friendly. You might want to try it sometime." Indy shoved through the door. Anger gnawed her nerves like fire ants. She didn't need to flirt to get the job done.

Once in her car, she studied her clothes. Would Griffin not take her seriously because of how she dressed? Her stomach gave a little squish. She couldn't honestly answer the question. Griffin had always flirted with her, but he flirted with everyone in social situations.

She checked the time. If she hurried, she could stop at home to change.

*　*　*

288 • *Shannyn Schroeder*

Forty minutes later, racing to get to her appointment, Indy felt a little panicked.

"I hope the man who invented pantyhose died a slow and painful death," she cursed. It must've been a man, she thought as sweat snaked down her back and nylon suffocated her thighs. The damn air-conditioning on the car stopped working, and she hadn't planned to fix it yet since it was supposedly fall. Unfortunately, the Chicago weather didn't agree.

The remnants of her hangover made her regret the decision.

She whipped into the circle drive of the first mansion and saw Griffin's silver Jaguar already parked. Double damn. She parked behind him and got out. Her ten-year-old Taurus sagged sadly behind the Jaguar.

I am so out of my league.

She tugged at the collar of her blouse. Her skirt skimmed the backs of her knees, reminding her of church clothes. At least she was ready if the heat really did kill her.

Griffin still sat in his car. The Winnetka house stood in front of her with a gorgeous wide, pillared front porch. Selling a house in the wealthy Chicago suburb would be her first.

Looking back at the Jag, she couldn't quite reconcile the image of Griffin hanging out, drinking beer at his friend's bar with the millionaire video-game developer. Indy threw back her shoulders and faked confidence as best she knew how.

She paused en route to his car. The door swung open and Griffin unfolded himself from behind the steering wheel. He wasn't just good-looking; he was drool-worthy.

His perfectly styled dark hair slicked back from his face. His jaw was surprisingly smooth. He usually sported a dark five-o'clock shadow, and she'd figured it had been intentional.

He spoke into his Bluetooth headset for another moment, acknowledging her with a slight wave of his hand. His finely tailored suit revealed a fit body: broad shoulders and trim waist. He shed his suit coat and rolled his sleeves in concession to the heat, which should've made him look relaxed, but his face was solemn. She preferred him in jeans and a worn T-shirt, drinking a beer at O'Leary's.

Ending the call, he tossed the Bluetooth in the car before closing the door. Indy approached with her hand extended. "Mr. Walker, nice to see you again. I'm sorry I'm late."

He grasped her hand and tugged playfully. "Call me Griffin. I'm not looking for a dog and pony show, Indy."

She liked the way her name rolled off his tongue. "I'm simply greeting you the same way I'd greet any client."

He removed his sunglasses and made no attempt to hide his appraisal of her. She'd been scrutinized by worse. His expression held a hint of laughter. After raking his gaze over her, top to bottom, he smiled. Small lines fanned from eyes nearly as dark as his hair. The act removed the stiff businessman, and he became a drinking buddy. "I'm not *any* client. We've known each other for months. We're friends."

Her tense muscles relaxed a fraction. Their previous encounters had paved the way for a friendly acquaintance. He followed her to the house. Even in her two-and-a half-inch heels, she had to look up to meet his eyes.

As she opened the door, chilly air brushed over her heated skin and caused a shiver. "Would you like a tour, or just want to wander?"

After she asked, she looked at the décor and cringed. The owners hadn't wanted photos of the interior posted online. Now she knew why. *Everything* was white.

Griffin's phone rang. He checked the screen and ignored it.

"You can take that if you need to," she offered. "I can wait." She was grateful to have a few minutes to cool her body.

He stood in the middle of the foyer and turned in a slow circle. "No, I've seen enough. Where to next?"

Indy's stomach flipped. "You don't want to see other rooms?" she asked carefully.

His eyes locked on hers. "No."

"I realize the color scheme . . . or lack of one might be a turn-off, but that's just paint and carpet."

"What else do you have?"

She fumbled with the clasp on her portfolio and pulled two listings from the pocket. "Here are the other two I told you about. We can go to whichever you like next."

"Let's try this one." He tapped the top page.

"Okay. Follow me." She exited the house. Excitement and optimism seeped from her pores like sweat. She'd hoped for a quick sale.

The next two showings went the same. Griffin walked in, looked briefly, and left. In the driveway of the third house, she said, "Maybe if you tell me a little more about what you do want, I won't waste your time looking at houses that don't work."

His broad, charming smile creased at the sides of his mouth and showed the hint of dimples. "You showed me exactly what I asked for. I'll know it when I see it."

"Okay. I'll keep you posted if I find other listings that might suit you." Disappointment gripped her.

"How about dinner?"

"Excuse me?"

"Can I take you out to dinner?"

She pulled her lips into a firm businesslike smile. So much for friendly acquaintance. "I'm involved with someone, and I don't date clients."

At least not anymore.

He stepped closer, picked up her left hand, and looked pointedly at her ring finger. "We already covered that I'm more than a client; we're friends."

"We might be friends if you'd stop flirting with me."

"Flirting is something we both excel at. Besides, how serious could your involvement with your married boyfriend be?"

Quinn and her big mouth. She'd definitely have a talk with her little sister. She bit her tongue for a second and thought of Richard. "There's enough seriousness in life without me adding to it."

As soon as the words left her mouth, she feared she'd given him ample ammunition.

She tugged her hand from his grasp and twitched at his thumb's caress across her knuckles. Little jolts of pleasure shimmied up her arm. Damn, she hated the effect of charming men. He released her hand and moved to his car without another word. His phone rang as he drove off with his engine purring.

Kind of like her nerves.

Griffin had all the markings of a rich playboy. He was charming and arrogant, and women swooned at the sight of him. But she wanted only one thing from Griffin Walker: a big, fat commission.

A block from the last house, she pulled over. The itchy pantyhose drove her crazy. She opened the door and looked up and down the street. Not a soul in sight. Reaching under her skirt, she tugged the nylon from her body. Once she dragged it to her thighs, she sat on the edge of the driver's seat and rolled the pantyhose down. A slight breeze kissed her skin and she sighed.

Just as she pulled them off and stood barefoot on the street, a revved engine caught her attention. The silver Jaguar pulled up beside her. *Could the day get any worse?*

"Everything okay?" Griffin asked through the open window.

"Yeah." She balled the nylons into her fist and stifled a laugh. She didn't care enough to be embarrassed, but she scrambled for an excuse.

"What are you doing?"

"Nothing. I pulled over to take a call."

"With no phone?" His gaze raked down her body again and stopped at her bare feet. "And no shoes?"

She sighed and held out her pantyhose. "You caught me. I couldn't wait to get out of my pantyhose. The heat was strangling me."

His laugh echoed on the empty street and relief washed over her. Her own smile followed. If Richard had caught her stripping off her pantyhose on the street, he'd be mortified.

"Next time, leave them at home. Your legs are sexier without them."

"Flirting will get you nowhere," she said and leaned against the door. Even to her own ears, her remark sounded hollow. The air-conditioning tickled her arms and she repressed a shiver.

One eyebrow rose above his sunglasses. "When something interests me, I go after it."

"Even if it's unattainable?"

"Nothing is unattainable."

She straightened. "We'll see."

He slid his glasses to the top of his head. Dark brown eyes bore into her and no longer held amusement. "Be warned. I always get my way."

He pulled away. She wanted to be pissed, tried to feel indignant and angry, but failed. She would do whatever was necessary to make Griffin Walker happy.

*   *   *

The office door flew open. Griffin looked up from the file to meet his publicist's eyes. Kendra was one of few people who would enter his office unannounced. Some days she stopped in to say hi. Today she looked pissed.

"What's wrong now?" He settled back in his chair. Every time she had that look, he imagined lightning bolts shooting from her spiky blond hair.

"What's *wrong?* Didn't we spend hours talking about your image and how you appear in the press?"

"Yes." It had been the longest afternoon of his life. Almost as bad as the time Sister Mary Bridget lectured him about how discussing a problem didn't involve fists.

"Then what is this?" She slapped the society page of the newspaper on his desk. "A reporter? Not your smartest move, Walker. Especially with the mom brigade downstairs telling the world you're bad for their kids."

"Huh?" He'd already managed to avoid the rally point for whichever parent group hated him today. Every few months, a group showed up at his office building and picketed. He never thought creating video games would be so controversial.

He focused on the picture and smiled. "That's Moira O'Leary, Ryan's sister. She wasn't a date; she just wanted to get into the benefit."

"But now you're linked to a reporter, someone looking to make a name for herself." She slapped a second paper down. Kendra had a flair for the dramatic. The headline read: THE BOSTWICK CHARITY: AN INSIDER'S VIEW.

Moira had gotten a byline in the *Times*. His chest filled with pride, as if she was his sister. "So? I got her in the door; then I left."

"You were photographed with her, and then she wrote the story. If that's not bad enough, they have another picture of you with a senator's daughter." She tapped a small photo on the bottom of the page.

"This is an old picture. I haven't seen Ashley in over a month." He pushed the paper toward Kendra.

Kendra growled. "You don't get it, do you? This is how people see you—different women at every turn. You can't commit, you're not loyal, you're not trustworthy." She drummed her fingers on the photos.

"That's bullshit." He flicked the paper away and stood to pace.

"We agreed absolutely no politicians."

"Who her father is shouldn't matter. She wanted a good time."

"Which is even worse. We talked about this. Given your history, we don't want anyone to dig. The story is going to come out sooner or later and we need to be prepared for it, but we don't want to offer up fuel. All we need is one person to link you to political families."

Griffin didn't respond. Kendra was right. His past would come back to bite him in the ass. Too bad he hadn't been smart enough to hire someone like Kendra ten years ago. "I never did anything wrong."

She inhaled a slow, deep breath. "Look, I know it's bullshit. It doesn't matter if you were right or wrong. All that matters is how people perceive you. I know you and I know what you want to accomplish. You're a good man, but it's not me you have to convince."

"So I'm supposed to give up my social life?"

Kendra laughed, the sound tinny and hollow. Kendra was so good at her job, he never knew when she was being genuine.

"Like that would happen. Discretion, Griffin. Don't date the flighty socialites who enjoy posing for the society page. Keep your *social life* out of the limelight. When people Google you, this is all they see. We need to change that perception."

He shoved his hands deep in his pockets. "Fine. I get it."

She moved to stand next to him. "That's what you said before. The idea for your foundation is fabulous. The program will make a huge difference in the lives of those kids. If the public doesn't trust you, you might as well just keep throwing money in and leave it as that."

"It needs to be more."

"I understand," she said, her voice soft. "It will be, but you have to believe in me. I know what I'm doing."

He thought of his own childhood and what a program like this could've done. Money alone couldn't make the differences he wanted.

"That's why I hired you." He pointed at the newspaper. "I helped a friend, so I don't regret it, but I am sorry it threw a wrench into your plan."

"And Ashley?"

"Has moved on down the list of Chicago's most eligible bachelors. No hard feelings."

Kendra rolled her eyes. "Are there ever? I have a feeling you con these women into thinking they've left you brokenhearted."

He gave her a half-shrug. "It's a gift." A skill he'd nurtured after the one and only time he'd fallen in love had ended in a spectacular fiasco.

She turned and went back to the desk. "Any luck finding a house so you can get rid of the bachelor pad?"

"No." Thoughts drifted to Indy and her bare legs.

"You know that's an integral part of the plan."

He nodded and returned to his chair. "The house will be a bachelor pad, too, since I won't be getting married."

She shook her head at him.

Waving the papers, she headed to the door. "I'm going to see what I can do about this."

Kendra was one of the best PR people he knew, but she was a pain in the ass. He'd listen to her, though, because she understood his goal.

He'd been working toward the creation of this foundation for years. Helping troubled teens gave him a goal. If he could pass on his knowledge and skills, it could change their lives. He was finally in a position to make it happen.

As long as he didn't let his dick screw it up.

He looked over the notes he'd taken on each of the houses he'd visited with Indy. By pinpointing why they weren't the right ones, he should be able to find what would make it right.

He wanted the O'Leary house on a bigger scale. Ryan O'Leary had been his best friend since first grade when he'd punched Ryan in the nose. He'd spent more time at the O'Leary house than he had at home.

At the O'Learys', loneliness was impossible. Six kids, two parents, and however many friends filled the house to bursting. They ate dinner together. Fought over the TV together. Shared victories and suffered defeats together. Home.

That's what he wanted in a house. He had no idea how to explain that to Indy.

His mind wandering to her bare legs didn't help. His mouth watered at the image.

She'd been stiff but professional throughout their meeting. Unlike the steal-the-spotlight woman he'd seen at Ryan's bar, Indy, the agent, was a different person. At least until he'd caught her stripping off her pantyhose.

When he saw that, he wanted to help her loosen the rest of her outfit, starting with her hair. She'd had it all pinned up and neat. He preferred the wild long hair of Indy the singer. He'd been attracted to her from the first time he laid eyes on her, but she'd kept her distance. Being rejected, even subtly, stuck in his gut. He found himself wanting to press the issue just to see if he could change her mind.

His secretary buzzed, interrupting his less than professional thoughts. "Mr. Walker, there's a Mr. Malcolm on line one. He wouldn't give a reason for his call. He said it was personal."

Malcolm. He knew only one person with that name.

"Mr. Walker?"

"Sorry. I'll take it." His finger hovered over the Hold button. He prayed that for a change, his gut would be wrong. "Hello?"

" 'Bout time. How do you like that Mr. Malcolm business? I know how much it bugs you to share my name." The pride in his cleverness sang across the line.

Griffin's shoulder muscles knotted. *Dad.* As if his life needed more complications. "What do you want?"

"Now, is that any way to talk to your old man when we haven't spoken in three years?"

"With you it's always the appropriate response." Griffin pinched the bridge of his nose, grasping for composure.

"I thought I'd stop by for a visit, but you have some crazy protesters in front of your building . . ."

Malcolm obviously wanted to make it clear that he was already in town. Griffin's mind raced. Everything with Malcolm led to one thing—money. "It would be better if you didn't come to my office. We have a lot going on right now." *And the last thing I need is questions about who the hell you are.* "Do you still have the address for my condo?"

"Of course."

"Meet me there later. Nine o'clock. Don't call me at work again."

After they hung up, Griffin paced his office. He wanted to throw something across the room and smash it, but he didn't want to draw attention. He'd actually thought his father was gone for good. Maybe even dead. No contact for three years. Before his mother had died.

If he knew Mom died, he would know that he doesn't have a hold on me anymore. He wouldn't be back looking for more. Tonight Malcolm would learn. No more handouts. No more contact. No fake father–son bullshit.

Griffin pushed down the innate desire to have a real father. Being a bastard was better than being Malcolm Walker's son. He'd get rid of his father one last time.

No one would know Malcolm Walker existed, just as it always had been.

Griffin leaned hard against the drywall and screwed it into place. He wasn't sure how Ryan had suckered him into helping, but it actually felt good. He hadn't done much manual labor since college. Back then he'd worked any job he could to pay tuition. Today it felt like coming home, a nice escape before having to meet with Malcolm.

Ryan's drill whirred away on the opposite side of the room. The radio blared over the noise of their power tools. Kid Rock sang about being seventeen. Before slapping up the next sheet, he grabbed a beer from the cooler on the floor. Having a friend who owned a bar had its perks.

The room came together. Ryan and his brothers had spent many hours over the last month to get this first apartment above O'Leary's Pub fit for habitation.

After taking a long drink of beer, he hefted the next sheet of drywall into place. "So what's the rush with the wedding?"

Ryan answered over the sound of the drill. "When it's right, you know it. Besides, you know my mom."

Ryan's brother Michael crossed the room to the cooler. "Don't listen to him, Griff. The old man just wanted to beat me to the altar."

"Is the bathroom done?" Ryan asked.

"No, slave driver. It's hotter than a three-alarm fire in there."

"Being the big, bad fireman, you should be able to tough it out." He took the open beer from Michael's hand and drank.

Michael took another beer and disappeared back into the bathroom.

Ryan turned a bucket over and sat on it. "Quinn's pregnant," he said quietly.

Griffin stopped, holding the drill poised for driving in a screw. He finished the sheet and took a seat on the floor.

"You have nothing to say?"

Shit, he didn't know how to respond. "Congratulations?"

"Is that a question?"

"Seriously. I don't even get the marriage thing. Now you're talking about a kid." He didn't think he could be faithful to only one woman for the rest of his life. But being a father. That was a forever thing. "How do you feel about it?"

He looked at Ryan. No one hid stress better.

Ryan took a deep breath. "I'm happy. Mostly I'm scared shitless. What do I know about being a dad?"

"You'll be fine. You had a great role model. If you're half the father your dad was, you'll already be better than most." The conversation brought Malcolm back to the forefront of his mind. And he couldn't tell his best friend.

No one could know about Malcolm and the secrets he brought.

"Thanks, but it doesn't make me feel better. What's been going on with you?"

Work. Always a safe topic. "Same old. Production's flying on the new game to get it out for the holidays. Gamers are already buzzing about it."

"You don't sound too excited about making another million."

"I have some group bitching. It's evil, bad for kids, too violent. Same old crap." But the noise could impact the new phase of the foundation.

Ryan laughed. "Whenever you want to give up the corporate life, I've got plenty of work to do around here. Three more apartments after this one."

"Have you and Quinn decided where you're going to live?"

"We'll stay at the loft for now. She wants to sell it. Indy thinks she should rent it. It's one of those places that'll always retain value. Indy's looking for houses near Twilight."

Thinking about Indy proved to be a better distraction than anything for getting his father out of his head.

"I hear you're finally looking for a house."

"Yeah, but I'm not having any luck. The houses Indy's showing me are . . ." He searched for the right word. Pretentious? "Not right."

He finished his beer and pushed to his feet. Feeling the chalky dust on his hands gave him an idea about house hunting. He made a mental note to call Indy later. "Hey, grab me some more screws, wouldya?"

Ryan kicked a box across the floor.

"Thanks, *Dad.*" He smirked at the thought of Ryan holding a screaming baby.

Ryan chucked a small piece of drywall and it bounced off Griffin's shoulder. "Not so loud. No one else knows. We're not saying anything until after the wedding."

Griffin snorted. "You don't think Quinn's already told Indy and Kate? Get real. I don't get the impression they have too many secrets."

"Just keep your mouth shut."

Griffin scanned his living room to make sure it held nothing of value his dear old dad could pocket on his way in or out. Small things lay around, none important. His dad couldn't take anything from him now.

Ten years ago, he'd thought he'd hit the jackpot. His life was going exactly as planned. He'd fought to be at the top of his field, one of the youngest to reach that kind of success. He had Selena in his life; then his father reappeared.

Even then, he'd held no expectations about some great relationship, but he figured he at least deserved some answers about why his father had left, to get his side. If nothing else, he could rub his success in his father's face. Show Malcolm that he didn't need him.

But he didn't have much of a chance to do any of that. Malcolm had gotten the better of him. He charmed his way into Griffin's life, talking about how he'd wanted to get in touch for years but didn't know how. How he had felt ashamed to come back.

All part of his game.

Griffin swallowed the last of the whiskey in his glass. Having more than one before facing Malcolm and things would get uglier than he could afford. The doorbell buzzed at nine-thirty. Just like Malcolm—keep everyone waiting.

Griffin answered the door, and the shock at seeing his father registered in his brain. It was like looking into a funhouse mirror that instantly aged him.

Malcolm looked good. Thinner than Griffin remembered, and grayer, but the charming smile, so much like his own, was the same.

"Griffin." He entered the room with his arms spread.

Here came the deplorable exaggeration of affection. Griffin stepped back to allow Malcolm plenty of room and to make his feelings clear. "Malcolm."

"I see you're still doing well for yourself."

Griffin closed the door, trying to hold back anger and resentment. He'd done well despite his father's absence. His mother had carried the load for both parents. He'd promised himself he'd stay calm and get rid of Malcolm for good. A business transaction. One last time.

He turned to the man who was the object of his disgust and watched Malcolm appraise the room the same way he had ten years earlier. As far as Griffin knew, Malcolm hadn't come back to town since then. Every transaction since happened via phone and wire.

"I guess business is good, eh? I mean all the kids are playing some kind of game or another, right?"

Griffin tucked his hands in his pockets and waited. Sometimes silence was his most effective tool.

"What, you got nothing to say?" Malcolm crossed his arms.

"I've already asked what you wanted and I never received an answer. That would be a good place to start." They continued to stare across the room at each other.

Malcolm broke first. The man wasn't much of a poker player or businessman. "I haven't seen you in ten years, unless you count what I read and see in the paper. I thought maybe we could get to know each other."

Griffin's chuckle came out more as a growl. "Are you getting so old you can't remember which ploys you've already used? You tried that ten years ago. I guess you're here for your last check."

"It doesn't have to be this way."

"Mom's dead. More than two years ago. Did you know?"

Malcolm shook his head. Griffin couldn't read the expression in the older man's eyes.

"That's why this will be the last time you ever contact me. You have nothing else over me. You can't hurt her anymore. You don't even deserve money now, but since you had the balls to actually show so I could say this to your face, I'll give you that." He crossed the room and opened a drawer to the side table. "How much this time? And remember, it has to last."

Now the wheels turned in his father's head. The realization that he couldn't get to Griffin through loved ones ruined his plans. First Selena, then Mom. Griffin made sure no one would ever get that close again. But Malcolm still knew about Selena, and Griffin would do anything to save her parents any more pain. Add to that the damage to his reputation, and paying his father was worth it.

"You drive a hard bargain. You're a lot more like me than the way you look. Keep it simple so no one can touch you. I tried to tell your mother that so many times. She never understood."

The pen in Griffin's hand began to bend, so he released the grip. "Unless you want to get tossed out on your ass without a check, I suggest you shut up and give me a number."

"Fifty thousand." He smirked as if Griffin should be shocked by the number.

Hell, he'd expected twice that. "I'll cut you a check for ten. I'll wire the rest when you leave town."

Malcolm tilted his head, but then nodded. Griffin scribbled out the check and ripped it from the book. Handing it to Malcolm, he said, "Now get out."

With the check tucked safely into his pocket, Malcolm smiled broadly. "A pleasure doing business with you. We'd make quite a team. If we were together, there wouldn't be a safe heart in all of Chicagoland."

Griffin took one step forward and Malcolm jolted from his spot. He quickly left the condo. Griffin returned to his bottle of whiskey and wondered how much he'd need to make him forget where he came from.

Indy dragged her feet toward her apartment. The bar had been slammed with business. The stack of singles shoved in her pocket made the sore feet and aching back worthwhile. Even though she wanted that money to go straight into her vacation fund, she had a feeling it would be poured into her car instead. The beast had begun making strange noises. Again.

She stopped in front of her neighbor's house, surprised to see Richard leaning against her porch. "Hi. What are you doing here?"

At the sound of her voice, he looked up and his back stiffened. "You said you had to work. I thought you were showing houses, not shaking your tits at a bunch of drunks."

She so did not need this right now. She'd had enough of Richard's jealousy. "I'm tired. It's been a long day."

"We need to talk."

She hated that sentence. Nothing good ever came from it. Already sore muscles clenched.

"About what?" she asked, trying to keep the irritation from her voice. She walked up the steps and unlocked the door.

Without turning around, she knew that Richard scanned the street to check on his car. He routinely made comments about the location of her apartment. She shook her head and went in alone.

She kicked off her shoes and sank onto the couch. The cool leather stuck to her skin. She closed her eyes and relished in the quiet. She heard Richard enter.

The familiar sound of crinkling cellophane had her gaze shooting up to his arms. He carried a huge bouquet of roses. He only brought roses when they'd been fighting. Usually because he tried to change her.

The thought came in a flash, but stuck.

Why was she still with him? Her sister, Quinn, and her best friend, Kate, had been asking her that for months. She'd brushed the question aside, but now, as Richard approached her with a serious expression, the question reverberated in her brain.

He sat beside her and laid the flowers on her lap. "You know I don't like you working at that place. I've offered to help."

"I don't want your money. I can pay my own way."

He slid a small black velvet box onto the table. He flipped the lid and a huge, sparkly diamond winked at her. She wanted to reach out and touch it, but shifted the flowers from her lap to the table beside the ring. Her heart raced and her stomach roiled. This was not going to end well.

Marriage had never entered even the remote recesses of her mind. Especially with Richard. He was a guy with money looking for a break and she knew how to show him a good time. Good times tended to end with commitment.

Someone always had to change.

"Marry me. You can quit that crappy job and leave this place." He handed her a key.

"What's this?"

"The divorce is done. I got the house."

He took the house from his ex-wife and kids? "What about your kids?"

"What about them? They've moved to a new house. We can start our own family together."

The snort burst from her before she thought. "I told you a long time ago. I'm not looking for marriage. I'm not marriage material."

"Everyone is marriage material when it's the right person. You wouldn't have to work anymore. You can stay home and take care of the baby." He leaned back and crossed his legs as if this was a done deal.

"Baby?" She laughed, and he jerked back. Startling him hadn't been her intention, but the man was clueless. "What's next? Dinner on the table every night at six?"

"That would be nice. That's one thing I do miss from my marriage to Marion."

Yeah, that's what every woman wanted during a proposal—to be compared to the ex-wife. "I can't do this, Richard."

"Do what?" He scooted forward on the couch.

"Marry you. I don't want to be with someone who doesn't get me."

"I get you, Indy. I love you." He grabbed her hand and held it to his chest.

She tugged free and tried not to laugh. "You love the idea of me, but not me. Not really. I'm the girl who leaves tawdry messages for you in the middle of the day. The girl who loves the ceramic cows in her kitchen. The girl who strips her pantyhose off in the middle of the street."

"Why would you do that?"

The question said it all. He would never understand her. He didn't know how.

"Because I can. I'm not the right girl for you because you can't imagine doing something ridiculous or silly."

"Don't do this."

"You need to move on, Richard. I was a nice distraction during your divorce, but now that it's over, you need to look for whatever will make you happy." She handed him the key and the ring. That part was hard. The price on the ring would pay her rent for months. She moved away from the couch.

"You make me happy."

"But I won't for long." She crossed her arms. "I can't give you what you're looking for."

Backing away from her, his hands balled into fists. "There's someone else, isn't there?"

"No." Priceless. So much for being nice and letting him down easy. Her phone rang. She pulled it from her pocket. Griffin. "I need to take this."

She turned away from Richard, hoping he'd take the hint and leave. "Hello."

"Hey. Sorry to call so late. I planned to leave a message."

His rough voice massaged her irritated nerves.

"It's fine. I just got home. What did you need?"

"I want to refine my search for a house. Are you free for lunch tomorrow? I have some things I want to talk about."

She paused, immediately thinking he was trying to make another date, but something in his voice convinced her otherwise.

"Sure. Text me the time and place." She paused again. "Are you okay?"

"Yeah, long day. See you tomorrow."

She hung up and turned back to Richard.

"There is someone else. Don't try to lie."

"That was a client."

The disgusted *humph* made her want to slap him.

"What kind of client calls after ten?"

"The kind that is a friend. Someone who wants to make plans. Someone who knows that I don't mind late-night calls." She recrossed her arms. Time to end it. For good.

He stared at her with eyes burning. "I've felt it for months now.

You've been pulling away, and I've been trying to hold on. I guess I'm too late."

His eyes darkened and new wrinkles spread around them. Indy's stomach fluttered and she clutched her phone in her hand. He'd never given her any reason to fear him. He was controlling and manipulative, but never violent.

"No one else can give you what I can. Be careful who you choose to be with." He snatched the bouquet of roses from the table. "And remember. I always take what's mine."

He stormed out the door and she stood silently. What the hell was that? She inhaled deeply and locked the door. Good riddance.

I always take what's mine. What was he talking about? Would he want the gifts he'd given her? He could have the ugly-ass furniture he'd insisted on getting for the living room. She stripped her clothes off in the middle of the room and tossed her T-shirt on the white leather couch.

The move would've driven Richard crazy. *Everything has its place.* She smiled and threw her panties on the coffee table.

She hadn't felt so free in a really long time.

Photo: Nicole Morisco

About the Author

Shannyn Schroeder is a former high-school and middle-school English teacher. She holds a B.A. in English and M.A.'s in Special Education and Gifted Education. After having her third child, she decided to stay at home. She's since worked as an editor for a couple of e-publishers and currently works as an editor for an education company that publishes online current events assignments. She juggles writing around the kids' schedules.

In her spare time, Shannyn loves to bake and watches far too much TV, especially cop shows. She started her first book on a dare from her husband and has never looked back. She came to reading romance later than many, but lives for the happy ending, and writes contemporary romance because she enjoys the adventure of new love.

Readers can visit Shannyn online at www.shannynschroeder.com and can follow her on Twitter @SSchroeder_ and on Pinterest at http://pinterest.com/seschroeder

CPSIA information can be obtained at www.ICGtesting.com
Printed in the USA
LVOW11s1851160616

492904LV00001B/144/P